'The "what-if-this-happened-to-me?" factor at times raised the hair on my arms'
Guardian

'An intelligent, civilised mystery . . . a real pleasure to read'
Sunday Telegraph

'Tingling political thriller . . . highly recommended'
Literary Review

'Wonderfully plotted, fast-paced and refreshingly original'
Nelson DeMille

'A distinctly atmospheric thriller'
Mail on Sunday

'Beguiling mystery'
New York Times

'Adam always handles his massive canvases with real panache. The requisite pulse-racing action is wedded superbly to the serious theme'
Good Book Guide

'Brilliantly researched and informative . . . a turbo-charged, white-knuckled thriller by a brilliant storyteller'
Daily Record

D0242540

Paul Adam is the author of nine previous novels. He lives in Sheffield with his wife and two sons. For more information visit www.pauladam.com

Also by Paul Adam

KNIFE EDGE

Paul Adam

Endeavour Publishing

First published in Great Britain in April 2008
by *Endeavour Publishing*

This paperback edition published in August 2008
by *Endeavour Publishing*

A CIP catalogue record for this book is available from the British
Library.

ISBN 978-0-9557277-1-9

Typeset in Palatino by Falcon Oast Graphic Art Ltd.

n by CPI Antony Rowe

ishing
ve

1

There were fifteen of them in the back of the lorry – fourteen men and one woman. They didn't move when the driver threw open the rear doors: they just stayed huddled in the corners behind the stacks of cardboard boxes, their knees drawn up to their chests to keep warm, their faces so well hidden by scarves and hats that in the dim light they looked like heaps of old rags.

'Out!' the driver called in Turkish.

He waited a moment. When no one responded, he swore under his breath and clambered up into the lorry. He squeezed past the boxes and looked down at his cargo of people, prodding one of the shapeless figures roughly with the toe of his boot.

'Did you hear me? I said, out.'

A man's face peered up at him. A narrow, drawn face, the jaw line dark with stubble. The man's eyes were tired. There was a hollow, haunted look in them.

'Uh?' he murmured indistinctly.

'This is it, London,' the driver said.

'London?'

'You deaf? Yes, London. Get up.'

The driver poked the man harder with his boot. He wanted them all out of the lorry. They were nothing but vermin to him. Dirty peasants who stank out the truck with their unwashed bodies and fetid waste matter. He could smell the sour odour of sweat and urine that always permeated the whole vehicle after one of these trips. He'd given them a bucket that was emptied at every stop, but there was always one who missed and pissed on the floor.

'Move yourselves,' the driver snapped, crossing to the other corner and jabbing his foot into another bundle of clothes. There was a startled grunt of pain, then a limb moved, a hand pulled back a scarf and a shadowy face squinted out.

'London,' the driver repeated.

The face looked at him blankly.

'London?'

These stupid Kurds. How many times did you have to tell them?

'Get up!' the driver barked.

He reached down and hauled the Kurd to his feet. The Kurd swayed a little on unsteady legs. After six days in the back of the lorry his muscles were stiff, unaccustomed to exercise.

'Irena?'

The Kurd looked back down at the figure curled up in the corner.

'Irena,' he said again.

The figure stirred. A woman looked up at him, yawning. She was young, with heavy features, high cheekbones and a wide mouth. A few loose strands of black hair straggled out from beneath her headscarf. She'd been asleep, but her face was still pale with fatigue.

'Ismail?'

'We're here,' Ismail said in Kurdish. 'We've arrived.'

For an instant, a tiny spark of emotion flared in the woman's eyes. A mixture of excitement and relief and perhaps a fleeting glimmer of joy. Then, as quickly as it had come, the light was gone, replaced by an anxious wariness. One part of their journey was complete, but their ordeal was not yet over.

Ismail bent down and helped his wife up, putting his arms around her and holding her close to him. Irena clung on tight. Her body was trembling.

'We've made it,' Ismail whispered in her ear. 'We're in London.'

He drew back and gazed at her, smiling. Irena tried to return the smile, but a brief twitch of the mouth was all she could manage.

'Don't look so worried,' Ismail said. 'It will be all right.'

'Get a move on,' the driver broke in, gesturing impatiently towards the open doors of the lorry. 'Remember your bags. I don't want anything left behind. Hurry up, I've got all these boxes to unload.'

Ismail touched Irena's cheek with his fingertips, then stooped over and picked up their luggage – one tiny bag each, that was all they'd been allowed to bring.

They made their way to the doors. The others were leaving too, shuffling awkwardly down the length of the truck. Their movements were slow and laboured, like old people, though none of them was more than thirty. When they reached the doors, they stopped, blinking as the harsh light outside flooded into their faces. The lorry was parked in the centre of a large garage. It was the middle of the night, but the garage was illuminated by rows of fluorescent tubes suspended on chains from the ceiling. There was an underlying smell of petrol and engine oil, with the reek of strong Turkish tobacco superimposed on top of it.

Three men were waiting on the floor of the garage, a few metres away from the lorry. One was in his fifties, a short, thick-set man, conservatively dressed in an expensive charcoal grey overcoat. He was sucking on a cigar, the smoke curling up around his head and drifting away into the darkness above the steel rafters of the garage. His two companions were younger – mid-twenties – and taller. They were both wearing suits and open-necked silk shirts, gold chains dangling from their necks. One had a thick moustache, the other a close-trimmed beard.

The Kurds stared down at the three men, bewildered, disorientated by the strange surroundings, waiting for someone to tell them what to do. In the course of their journey, cooped up together like animals – and treated little better – they seemed to have lost the ability to think for themselves. The man in the overcoat waved his cigar, saying something to the young men beside him. They stepped forward, gesticulating angrily with their hands, beckoning the people down off the lorry.

'What're you waiting for?' the man with the moustache yelled in Turkish. 'Get down here. Now.'

Falteringly, their bodies still weak from their confinement, the Kurds began to climb down, lowering themselves first to the edge of the truck, their legs dangling in space, then dropping down the last few feet to the garage floor. Their clumsy, lethargic pace irritated the lorry driver who put his boot into one man's back and gave him a violent shove. The man toppled out, his arms flailing. As he hit the ground, he stumbled and fell forwards, sprawling flat on his face on the oily concrete. The young man with the moustache gave a staccato snort of laughter and reached up, pulling another Kurd down from the lorry. Ismail, helping his wife descend, paused to protest at this rough treatment.

'Shut up!' the man with the moustache snarled.

'But there's no need for this,' Ismail said in Turkish.

The Turk turned to look at him. He had the coldest eyes Ismail had ever seen.

'Didn't you hear me? I said, shut up.'

Irena pulled Ismail away.

'Leave it,' she said quietly in their own language.

'But they can't . . .'

'They frighten me,' Irena interrupted. 'Please, Ismail, don't make a scene.'

The Kurds were all off the lorry now, standing in a loose

line across the garage. One man, faint with hunger and thirst, collapsed to the floor, his legs unable to bear his weight. Ismail crouched down beside him, checking he was all right. When he straightened up again, Ismail turned to the man with the cigar.

'He needs water, something to eat. Can you give us food?'

The man with the cigar gazed back expressionlessly. He took another puff on his cigar, his eyes never leaving Ismail's.

'This isn't a restaurant,' he said icily.

'We've eaten almost nothing for a week,' Ismail said. 'Just the small amount of food we brought with us. We've had no water for twelve hours. Please, you must help us.'

'Hasan, check their bags.'

The man with the moustache walked to the end of the line and snatched a canvas travelling bag from the shoulder of one of the Kurds. The Kurd didn't try to stop him. He merely watched with frightened eyes as Hasan rummaged through the contents of the bag, pulling out items and dropping them on the floor. Hasan unwrapped a shirt and found a leather wallet hidden inside it. He took a thin sheaf of banknotes from the wallet and handed them to the man with the cigar.

'That's all, Memet bey.'

Memet wedged his cigar in the corner of his mouth and leafed through the money. His eyes flickered back to the Kurd.

'You have more?'

The Kurd didn't reply. Hasan slapped him hard across the face with the back of his hand.

'You were asked a question. Where's the rest of your money?'

The Kurd clutched his face, blood from his nose seeping between his fingers. Ismail couldn't stand by and watch this happen. He took a pace forward.

'That's enough. Leave him alone.'

Irena caught hold of her husband's sleeve.

'No, Ismail, no . . .' she murmured, but it was too late.

'What is this?' Ismail demanded. 'What are you doing, taking his money?'

Hasan turned and looked at Ismail, frowning as if either he hadn't quite caught his words, or he had but couldn't believe them. The Kurds had gone still. In the back of the lorry, the driver and the bearded Turk who was helping unload the cardboard boxes had stopped what they were doing. They were gazing down into the garage, watching as Hasan walked slowly across to Ismail.

Memet held up a finger. Hasan came to a halt.

'We're only taking what we are owed,' Memet said to Ismail.

'But we paid in full in Turkey,' Ismail replied. 'A lot of money.'

'Unfortunately, our costs have gone up since you left Diyarbakir. There's an "arrivals supplement" to pay now.'

'An "arrivals supplement"? How much?'

'Whatever you have on you.'

'But that's not fair. You can't take our money.'

'Let them have it,' Irena said quickly. 'It doesn't matter.'

'No, it's not right,' Ismail said. 'We need all we have. What are we to live on without it?'

'See how much he has,' Memet said to Hasan.

Hasan stepped in front of Ismail.

'Your bag.'

'No,' Ismail said, hugging his cheap plastic hold-all close to his side.

'Give it to him,' Irena pleaded.

'We will be penniless,' Ismail said. 'They can't do this.'

Hasan stroked his sleek moustache with a fingertip. He seemed very calm – unnaturally calm, as if he were making a concentrated effort to control himself.

'Maybe it's not in your bag,' he said mildly. 'Maybe

you're carrying it on you. Maybe . . .' he paused, his eyes straying across to Irena. 'Maybe it's on this whore you've brought with you.'

He reached out with a hand, flipping aside the shawl that was draped around Irena's shoulders. His fingers moved roughly over her body, probing, squeezing. Ismail went for him, pushing him forcefully back.

'Get your filthy hands off my wife.'

'Ismail, no . . .'

Irena tried to pull him away, but he shrugged off her grasp, his anger too violent to contain. He lashed out with a fist, delivering a glancing blow to the side of Hasan's head. Hasan took a step backwards, recovering his balance. His fingers dipped into his jacket pocket. Ismail didn't notice, or didn't care. He kept coming, his arm swinging back to throw another punch. But the punch never connected. Hasan's hand came swiftly out of his pocket. The knife he was holding swung up, the steel blade ripping through Ismail's ribcage and into his heart.

Ismail gave a choking cough, his fingers clawing at his chest, feeling the knife hilt buried in his flesh, the warm stickiness of the blood on his skin. His eyes bulged, his mouth gaped in a rictus of pain and shock before he slumped heavily to the floor.

Irena screamed.

'*Ismail!*'

The scream echoing around the lofty corners of the garage, the anguish in it lingering in the atmosphere long after the sound itself had died away.

Irena flung herself to the floor next to her husband's body, seeing the blood soaking through his shirt, the stiff, frozen expression on his face.

'Ismail!'

She touched his cheek. It was still warm. Warm, yet lifeless. Irena stared at him, feeling breathless, sick. She put her arms around him, lifting his head, pulling him to her.

'Ismail. No, *no*.'

She held him close, his head pressed tight against her breast. Her hand moved over his face, caressing the skin at first, then rubbing harder as she tried desperately to wake him.

'Ismail, I'm here. Ismail?'

She looked up, her eyes wide with horror, pleading.

'Help me. Someone, please, help me.'

The other Kurds were gathering around her. Hands reached down and lifted her to her feet, pulling her away, trying to avert her gaze from the crumpled shape on the floor.

Hasan stared down at the body, breathing hard but showing no emotion. There was blood on his right hand. Memet looked on impassively, still smoking his cigar as if nothing had happened.

Irena backed away. The other Kurds had formed a circle around her, shielding her, wanting to protect her. Hasan and Memet seemed to have forgotten about her. Their attention was focused on Ismail's corpse. Irena caught a glimpse of her husband through the legs of the people surrounding her. He was gone. Ismail was gone. She was numb with shock, a profound, stupefying shock. She could barely breathe, her legs, her whole body was shaking. They'd killed him. She couldn't think straight. Her brain, her thoughts were in turmoil, swirling and spinning. She gulped in air, sobbing, almost gagging.

She glanced around the garage, her vision blurring. There was a glassed-in office at one side, a door next to it. The door was ajar. Through the gap, Irena could see the faint glow of a light on the street outside. She reacted instinctively, knowing she was in danger. There was no conscious thought, just an impulse, a sudden reflex action. She broke through the circle of people and ran across the garage. Whipping open the door, she fled out into the night.

* * *

The Turks came after her – Hasan and the man with the beard, Farok. Irena saw them as she reached the end of the street and paused for a moment to look back. They were standing in the puddle of light from the open garage door, checking which way she'd gone. They turned in her direction, then started to jog towards her. Not hurrying, seemingly unconcerned by her escape. They were two men, she was a woman. A woman alone in an alien city. They would have no trouble catching her.

Irena turned left up another street, running flat out. The long, arduous lorry journey across Europe had drained her, but from somewhere she found a new reserve of strength. She had to keep going. The Turk had killed Ismail. He would kill her too, Irena had no doubt about that.

She passed a side street, then another. They all looked the same to her – rows of identical terraced houses with cars parked outside, the tall streetlamps casting an eerie orange sheen over everything. She'd never been in a city like London before, never been anywhere so big, so different. Where should she go? It didn't matter so long as she kept ahead of the Turks. She glanced back. They were still behind her. The gap seemed to have widened a little. She had to keep it that way, had to find a way of getting out of sight. They were stronger than she was, they would be able to keep running for longer. She needed to find some-where to hide.

There was a pattern to the neighbourhood, she'd already worked that out. A grid layout of narrow streets running parallel to one another, intersected at intervals by wider roads. It was quiet. The houses were all in darkness. There was no traffic. She was conscious of her own breathing, the pad of her soft-soled shoes on the pavement.

She sprinted across the road and turned down a side street, running past the front doors of the small brick houses. She thought about knocking on one of the doors, asking for help. But she spoke almost no English. What would she say? What would the occupants do? Why should they be concerned about her, a foreign woman who was in their country illegally? Besides, there was no time to stop. The Turks would be on her in an instant if she did.

She looked back over her shoulder again. She could see the two men behind her, maybe seventy or eighty metres away. They were running awkwardly, stumbling every so often as if they were tiring. Irena felt a flicker of hope. Perhaps they weren't as strong as she'd thought.

Ahead of her, she saw car headlights flash past on another road. She reached the junction and paused, looking both ways up a broader avenue that was lined with shops. The area was well-lit – plenty of streetlamps, bright neon signs outside the shops, lights on in some of the windows. Irena felt safer for a moment, then realised how irrational that feeling was. Lights didn't mean security, they meant it was easier for the Turks to see her, to follow her. What she had to seek out was darkness, somewhere black and murky where she could elude her pursuers.

She turned left, heading past the shops, her breath coming in painful gasps. Her energy was flagging, her legs were heavy. She knew she couldn't keep going much longer. She glanced round. The Turks had not yet reached the junction. She had a few seconds' grace, no more. She had to make good use of that time.

There was a break in the line of shop frontages just in front of her – a narrow alley between buildings. Irena ducked into the alley. It was darker here, harder to see. She stretched out her arms, feeling her way along the passage-way. After a few metres it opened out into a yard, with a cobbled lane at the far side allowing vehicle access to the backs of the shops. Irena looked around for somewhere to hide. There were several industrial dustbins around the edges of the yard. She wondered whether she could crouch down behind them, but there was no space, and trying to move the bins would make a noise that the Turks might hear. She flitted across the yard, her eyes probing the shadows, searching for a corner, a cavity, anything that might afford her sanctuary. There was nothing.

A white transit van was parked up against the wall of one of the buildings. Irena slipped behind it and waited, listening hard. Would the two men guess where she'd gone? She put her hand over her mouth, trying to deaden the sound of her breathing. Her pulse was racing, the blood throbbing inside her head.

Then she heard it. Footsteps in the alley from the street. They were coming into the yard. Irena dropped to her knees and slithered underneath the van. The footsteps got louder. She could hear the men panting, the faint rasping sound as they struggled for air. She could see them now – only their feet and the bottoms of their trousers. She lay still. The concrete was cold and damp beneath her body.

'Did she come this way?' one of the men said, speaking in Turkish.

'I don't know. You see anything?'

'No.'

The other man cursed.

'We've lost her.'

'Memet bey will be livid.'

'Let's check the street again.'

'She could be anywhere. You want to spend the night just wandering around, hoping to bump into her? What's the point of that? We'll find her tomorrow. Where's she going to go?'

'We'll put the word out in the morning. Somebody will spot her and let us know.'

They turned away and went back along the alley. Irena listened to their footsteps getting fainter. Then she let out a deep breath and rested her head on her arms. She was exhausted. Her face was moist with perspiration. She closed her eyes and lay there for ten more minutes,

11

recovering, waiting to ensure that the Turks didn't come back. Only when the sweat began to cool on her body and she felt cold did she consider what to do next. She couldn't stay under the van for the rest of the night. It was too cramped, too uncomfortable, but it was also too close to the Turks' garage. By morning she wanted to be further away from the enemy lair.

She crawled cautiously out and listened again for a time. She could hear the occasional car going past on the main road in front of the shops, but nothing else. She shivered and drew her shawl tighter around her shoulders. Her eyes had adjusted to the darkness in the yard. She could see more clearly now. The rear walls of the shops were on one side of the yard. On the other side was a high wire mesh fence enclosing the gardens of a row of houses, the row broken in two by the access lane.

Irena knew she had to keep clear of the main road. She had to stay out of sight, away from places where there might be cars or people. It was late – she had no watch so she didn't know exactly how late – but London was a city where there would always be someone around, someone who might see her and remember.

She walked quickly across the yard and along the access lane, feeling the rough edges of the cobbles through the thin leather of her shoes. Her feet were aching, her leg muscles stiffening up. When she reached the street at the end of the lane, she stopped, holding back to survey the area before she ventured out. There were more two-storey brick houses along the street, more parked cars. But there were no people. She tried to work out a mental plan of the district, recalling the route she'd taken from the garage, the streets she'd run along, the turnings she'd made – calculating the distances, the directions. It was an inexact plan, but she was sure of one thing: the garage was somewhere away to her left. That meant she would go to her right now.

She walked quickly – she was too tired to run any more

– her eyes watchful, darting to and fro across the street, glancing back every few seconds to check that she wasn't being followed. A car came towards her at one point and she dived into the shadows by a wall until the car had gone past.

After twenty minutes, she knew she had to rest or she would collapse. Fear and necessity had fuelled her flight from the garage, given her the strength to keep running, but now the immediate threat of the Turks had passed she had nothing more to give. She was utterly spent.

She came to a T-junction with another main road and saw a wrought-iron gate opposite her, an entrance to what looked like a patch of woodland or a public park. She hurried across the road and through the gate, hoping to find a safe haven. There was a sign by the entrance, but she couldn't read the words on it. It was only when she'd gone a short distance along the path and began to notice the rows of headstones and tombs that she realised it wasn't a park at all, it was a cemetery.

She stopped abruptly. A place of the dead! The thought filled her with a superstitious dread. She stared around uneasily. She had a powerful urge to turn and flee, but she didn't have the energy. What did it matter? The people beneath the crosses and ornate marble memorials couldn't harm her. And perhaps this was the safest place to hole up for a few hours. Who would think to look for her in a grave-yard?

The cemetery was overgrown and neglected. There were trees everywhere – birch, ash, sycamore – their trunks smothered with ivy, their branches blotting out the sky, cloaking the ground in dark, impenetrable shadows. There must once have been neat paths criss-crossing the area, but now those paths, like the graves between them, had been taken over by the spreading undergrowth. Clumps of long grass and nettles and willow herb shrouded the smaller headstones, almost hiding them from view. The bigger, grander tombs were decaying – their corners chipped off, decorative stone urns lurching sideways, about to fall, others already tumbled to the ground lying in pieces in the dense vegetation. Jagged stumps of marble pillars poked up through holly bushes, statues of angels, their features long worn away by the elements, stood sentinel over slabs whose inscriptions, so carefully carved, were now just a blur, the names and dates indecipherable beneath the dirt and moss and straggling brambles.

Irena turned off the path into a secluded spot by a large rectangular tomb and lowered herself wearily to the ground, leaning back on the side of the tomb. She'd never been so physically exhausted in her life.

She rested her head on the damp, lichen-coated marble and closed her eyes. She felt the darkness closing in on her and her thoughts suddenly went back to the black, claustrophobic confines of the lorry, remembering the fear, the hardship of the journey from eastern Turkey. They'd sold everything they owned except a few clothes and personal possessions, borrowed more from one of Ismail's uncles, to raise the £10,000 the smugglers had demanded to get them both to England. They'd had such hopes, such wonderful optimistic dreams. A new beginning, it was all Ismail could think about, all he could talk about. They would get away from the oppression, from the Turks, and start afresh in the West.

It was that hope that had kept them going, helped them bear the discomfort of the days in the back of the lorry. The frontiers had been the worst. Coming up through the Balkans, through Germany and the Low Countries, the driver had stopped a few kilometres short of each border and hidden his passengers away in secret compartments built into the floor of the vehicle. The memory made Irena go cold. Squeezing down into the tiny space, a long narrow aperture the size and shape of a coffin. Feeling the suffocating sense of imprisonment, the panic as the panel was slotted into place above her, then lying in terror in the pitch dark for several hours until the driver came to release her.

All for nothing. That new beginning, all their hopes had been brutally destroyed. She saw Ismail's face as it had been in life, remembered his smile, the way he talked, the touch of his fingers on her skin. Then she saw him in death, the knife in his chest, the blood staining his clothes, his face the same but everything that made it Ismail gone forever.

How was she going to survive without him? How could she endure the loss? Her shoulders heaved and she began to weep, letting out all the emotion she'd repressed since that fatal moment in the garage. Alone in the darkness, she gazed bleakly out over the cemetery, the tears coursing down her cheeks.

2

She didn't think she'd go to sleep that night. A part of her wondered whether she'd ever sleep again. But she did. Even her grief couldn't keep her awake.

It was daylight when she came round, surfacing from an unconsciousness that had been surprisingly peaceful. She'd had no nightmares, had not relived any of the traumas of her last waking hours. For a brief instant it was possible to imagine that none of it had happened, but then reality came flooding back in, submerging her beneath a cascade of horrific images. Ismail, a knife, blood . . . She stood up quickly and stretched her limbs, making herself do something to divert her mind from the harrowing memories.

The cemetery was dappled with pale sunlight. Irena looked around, taking in her first English morning. She was accustomed to clear skies, to bright, vibrant colours, but here everything was subdued, somehow diffused as if the light were filtered through gauze. There was dew on the grass in between the graves, the headstones were wet and glistening. The ground seemed to be perspiring, giving off a dank, musty odour. A figure moved along one of the paths – a man in a dark blue jacket out walking his dog.

Irena shivered. Her body temperature had plummeted. There was a core of ice inside her. An intense ache of hunger too. For six days she'd lived on nothing but a few crusts of bread and a handful of dried apricots. She needed to find food, water. She rubbed her face with her hands, massaging the skin, trying to warm herself up. What she wanted, above all else, was to wash. To soak herself in hot water and scrub away the grime from her body. But first, she had to find out where she was.

Picking her way between the gravestones, she headed back to the cemetery gate. In daylight, the area seemed less threatening than it had in the dark. There was something sad, forlorn about the broken tombs nestling in the undergrowth, the surface disintegration mirroring the bodily decay that was taking place unseen beneath the soil.

Irena walked out on to the street and paused, looking at the tall brick buildings opposite, watching cars speeding past, a red double-decker bus pulling in at a stop close by. She felt overwhelmed by the alien nature of the city. Everything about it exacerbated her sense of isolation. She hadn't expected to be alone in London. It was to have been a new home for both of them. That was how Ismail had planned it. He had taken care of all the travel arrangements, he'd made all the decisions. He'd made it sound so simple. They were to get to England, locate his relatives in the Kurdish community and then apply for political asylum. Now he was gone, that plan didn't sound quite so straightforward. Irena had virtually no English. She could say a few words, could recognise numbers, but couldn't read the language. How would she make herself understood? How would she go about claiming political asylum?

Ismail's relatives, his brother Anwar, that was where she had to begin. Anwar would help her, he would know what to do. But how to find him? Irena knew his address. Ismail had made her learn it by heart, even though she didn't understand what the individual words meant. Just in case anything happens to me, he'd said, a chillingly prophetic remark. Six, Alexandra Court, Murray Road, Stoke Newington, London. Irena could recite it like a mantra. But where was it?

Perhaps it was nearby. She knew there were many Kurds

in London, Turks too. It was the Turks who controlled the people-smuggling trade, Ismail had told her that. If illegal Kurdish immigrants were being brought in, would it not make sense to unload them close to the local Kurdish exile community? That way they could slip away and blend in immediately. There was less chance they might be caught by the British authorities, less chance that the smuggling network might be discovered and broken up.

She turned left and walked fifty metres to a junction with a much bigger road. There was more traffic here, long lines of cars waiting for the lights to change, vans half parked on the pavement, their drivers delivering supplies to the shops that ran down both sides of the road. It was an English street, different in sights and sounds and smells from the streets Irena was used to, but some aspects of it were familiar. She saw a sign in Turkish outside a barber's shop, another in Turkish over a travel agency. Two doors away was a Turkish bakery. Irena walked over to it and looked in the window, gazing longingly at the bread and pastries laid out on glass shelves inside, feeling the pangs of hunger in her stomach intensify.

An elderly Englishwoman with a shopping bag in each hand was also admiring the baker's wares. She glanced up at Irena and said something – 'tempting, aren't they?' – that Irena didn't understand. Irena moved off along the street, covertly studying the other pedestrians, surprised by their racial diversity. Most were white Caucasians, but she also saw Blacks and Asians and Chinese people. A woman in a dark burkha came past, followed in quick succession by a Sikh in a turban, a woman in a sari and a Hassidic Jew wearing a black Homburg and black coat, his son walking along beside him, a miniature version of his father in identical clothes and spectacles, only the beard lacking.

From the shops, Irena knew there must be a sizeable Turkish population in the area. Perhaps Kurds too, though she'd seen no signs in Kurdish, no shops she could enter to find someone who spoke her native language. She needed to ask for directions. But whom should she approach? Someone who looked like a Turk? The men were out of the question, of course. She couldn't go up to a man she didn't know and just start talking to him. What about one of the women she'd seen passing by? Irena was wary even of the women. The Turks who had smuggled her into the country were undoubtedly part of some criminal gang. She knew there'd been drugs on the lorry – heroin that had been brought from Afghanistan, then transferred to a different vehicle for shipment to Europe. The driver hadn't made any secret of the fact. He was a smuggler – people, drugs, the cargo didn't make any difference to him. But Irena didn't know how extensive the gang was, how powerful. She didn't know how far their tentacles reached. What had she overheard the two Turks saying last night? 'We'll put the word out in the morning. Somebody will spot her and let us know.' She studied the people on the street. Could she trust any of them? Or were they all potential informers who would report her whereabouts to the Turkish gang? She chewed one of her knuckles nervously. She just didn't know what to do.

A greengrocer, a Turk by the look of his dark skin and luxuriant moustache, was arranging apples on the fruit display outside his shop. He looked at Irena curiously and she edged away.

'Are you all right, dear? You look lost.'

Irena turned her head. The tiny, elderly Englishwoman she'd encountered outside the baker's was gazing up at her. Irena didn't know what she'd said.

'I'm not prying, mind,' the elderly woman went on. 'Only I saw you back up the road, wandering around in a bit of a daze. Are you all right? You look very pale. And worried.'

Irena gave a bemused shrug. She didn't understand a word.

19

'I know it's none of my business, but, well, you know . . .' The elderly woman gave a brief smile and turned to go. 'Never mind. I just thought I'd ask.'

'Six, Alexandra Court,' Irena blurted out quickly, struggling with the pronunciation. The old lady was English. She had a kind, sympathetic face. She couldn't possibly have any connection with the Turks.

'What was that?'

'Murray Road, Stoke Newington, London.' Irena finished the address.

'Stoke Newington?' the old lady said. 'Yes, this is Stoke Newington.'

'Six, Alexandra Court, Murray Road, Stoke Newington, London,' Irena repeated. She searched her memory for an English word. 'Where?' she added.

The old lady seemed to understand.

'Where? You're looking for Murray Road, is that it?'

The question was an incomprehensible juxtaposition of sounds to Irena, but she nodded her head anyway. She didn't want the old lady to wander off and abandon her. She saw her as a lifeline, someone to cling on to if she could.

'Murray Road?' the old lady said. 'It's down there. First right, then – let me see – second on the left after that.' She saw Irena's blank look. 'You don't understand, do you? Come on, I'll show you.'

The old lady moved off. When Irena didn't follow, the old lady turned and gestured with her arm.

'This way.'

Irena went with her. The old lady walked very slowly, chatting all the time, unconcerned that her companion clearly didn't have a clue what she was saying. They turned off the main road into a residential street, just like the ones Irena had run through the previous night. She glanced around anxiously. She knew the garage was a long way off, but she was worried nevertheless. What if the two Turks were driving around looking for her?

'Here we are,' said the old lady.

She'd stopped in front of a three-storey block of flats. She pointed.

'That's Alexandra Court.'

'Alexandra Court?' Irena said, wanting to make sure she'd understood correctly.

'That's right, dear.'

Irena looked up at the building. It was made of red brick, with a flat roof and small iron-railed balconies perched at intervals along the frontage. It was newer, more modern than the terraced houses that surrounded it, but already it was showing signs of dilapidation – rust on the ironwork, damp patches on the bricks beneath the roof line.

'Number six, was it?' the old lady said. 'You'll have to go inside.' She patted Irena on the arm. 'I'll leave you to it, dear. Bye bye.'

'Thank you,' Irena said, wishing she could express her gratitude more fully.

'My pleasure, dear.'

The old lady shuffled away up the street, her shopping bags dangling down, scraping against the sides of her knees. Irena went into the block of flats. Number six was on the ground floor. Its door was chipped and scuffed, as if innumerable heavy boots had kicked it open. Irena knocked and waited.

It was Anwar's wife, Sara, who answered. Her eyes opened wide with delight when she saw the figure outside in the hall.

Irena!' Sara stepped forward and threw her arms around her. 'Irena, at last! We were worried, we didn't know when you were going to get here. Come in, you must be exhausted.' She paused, only just noticing. 'Ismail? Where's Ismail?'

'He's dead,' Irena said.

'He's . . .' Sara gaped at her. 'Dead? What? What're you talking about? When? How? Come and sit down.'

Sara took Irena by the arm and guided her inside the flat, showing her to a chair in the kitchen and making her sit down. Irena was pale and shivering – with cold, with distress.

'You look awful,' Sara said. 'Are you hungry?'

Irena nodded weakly.

'Water? Do you have any water?'

'Of course. I'll make us tea too.'

Sara poured Irena a glass of water. Irena drank it down in one go. Sara put the kettle on, then refilled the glass with water.

'Sip it slowly. Tell me what happened,' she said.

Irena took a gulp of water. Her hands were shaking so much she could hardly hold the glass.

'The Turk,' she said. 'He stabbed him. In front of me. Killed him. Took out a knife and . . . it was terrible. He was there, on the floor. There was blood, the knife was . . . he was dead. I could do nothing. He killed him. The Turk, he killed him.'

'Slow down,' Sara said. 'You're in shock. You're saying Ismail was stabbed? Murdered?'

Irena nodded.

'The Turk. One of the smugglers. He was there, waiting for us. They said they wanted more money. Ismail refused.' She swallowed. 'So they killed him.'

Tears welled up in Irena's eyes. She started to sob. Sara knelt down beside her and took her hands, squeezing them tight.

'When was this? When did you get here?'

Irena didn't reply. She couldn't get any words out. Her whole body was shuddering, her face streaming with tears.

Sara turned her head, hearing a movement out in the corridor. Her fourteen-year-old son, Khaled, was outside the kitchen door, staring at them, his mother on her knees, this other woman he didn't recognise weeping hysterically.

'Go and phone your father,' Sara said urgently. 'Tell him he has to come home.'

'Come home?' Khaled said. 'You mean . . .'

'Just do it. Now.'

Irena had calmed down a little by the time Anwar arrived. Her eyes were red and swollen, her cheeks puffy and damp, but she'd stopped crying. Sara had made cardamom tea, served in little pear-shaped Kurdish glass *piyala*. She forced Irena to drink some, to eat a couple of biscuits.

Anwar listened in silence while his wife repeated what Irena had told her. Then he pulled out a chair and sat down opposite Irena.

'You saw all this?'

Irena nodded.

'Do you know who the man was, the Turk?'

'They called him Hasan.'

'Just Hasan?'

'There were three of them. There was an older man, who seemed to be in charge. They called him Memet bey.'

Anwar stiffened. He glanced up at his wife. Some of the colour had gone from his face.

'Memet bey?' he repeated.

'That's what the other man called him.'

'What did he look like, this Memet,' Anwar asked.

'Short, about fifty years old. He was well dressed, smoking a cigar. He watched it all. He did nothing to stop it.'

'Memet Dil?' Sara said to her husband.

'I fear so.'

'You know this man?' Irena said.

'Everyone knows him,' Anwar replied grimly. 'Or knows *of* him. He's not someone any sane person would want to be associated with.'

Anwar stood up. He nodded discreetly at his wife and left the kitchen. Sara followed him down the hall to their bedroom. Anwar closed the door behind her.

'This is serious,' he said softly.

'She's terrified they'll kill her too,' Sara said.

'She's right to be scared. She's a witness to a murder. They'll come looking for her.'

'There were other witnesses.'

'Memet will have dealt with them.'

'Killed them, you mean?'

'He doesn't need to kill them. They won't say a word. They're here illegally, Ismail was a stranger to them. Memet will have made it very clear what will happen to them if they open their mouths. But Irena is different – Ismail's wife. They won't trust her to remain silent.'

Sara bit her lip, her gaze fixed on her husband.

'What do we do?'

'I don't know,' Anwar said.

3

Joe Verdi paused for a moment on the east side of Holborn Circus, looking around for a cab to hail. He'd walked only a few hundred metres from the Old Bailey, but he could feel a tightness in his chest, a slight constriction of the airways that made him breathless.

He knew it wasn't the exercise that was causing his discomfort. It was the traffic – the continuous stream of vehicles pumping out their noxious exhaust fumes. And the weather. His asthma was always worse in the summer, especially on warm days like today when there was a dampness in the atmosphere, the threat of rain to come. Heat and humidity and the London smog, they were a particularly toxic combination.

Joe fingered the inhaler in his jacket pocket, trying to decide whether he needed a quick puff of Ventolin. His asthma was relatively mild. He could go for weeks, sometimes months, without using his inhaler, but it was that very infrequency of his attacks that made him so reluctant to use the inhaler now. Taking a puff always made him feel like a junkie, or an invalid. He knew that was stupid and illogical, but he felt it nonetheless. He was a fit man. All right, he was the wrong side of forty – only just the wrong side – but that didn't mean he was over the hill. Did it?

In recent days, he'd begun to wonder. Was there some definable point in a man's life when his body started to fall apart and he began the long slide towards decrepitude and death? Joe had always believed that it was a gradual process, something you weren't really aware of while it was happening, but maybe it wasn't. Maybe there really was one moment, one single identifiable moment when your body went abruptly into decline, never to recover. And it felt to Joe as if that moment were now.

It had been a bad week on the health front. Not the asthma. He'd had that for so many years – since childhood really – that he didn't regard it as a symptom of aging. It was simply there in the background, an annoyance that flared up from time to time. It was other things that had depressed him. Monday, for instance, a visit to the opticians to be told that he now needed reading glasses. *Reading glasses!* He'd known that he was finding it harder to decipher small print like the entries in the phone book or the text on his computer screen at work, but reading glasses? They were for old people, not for men in their prime like him – and on Monday, despite the optician's diagnosis, Joe had still felt himself to be in his prime. The doubts had only really crept in on Tuesday evening: the phone call from Ben Montgomery, the player-manager of the Sunday league football team for which Joe had been playing – although not playing very well, it was true – for the best part of the previous decade. Every word of their conversation was imprinted painfully on Joe's memory.

'I don't know how to say this, Joe, but I'm afraid I'm going to have to drop you for Sunday.'

'That's OK, Ben. I don't mind missing a match.'

An awkward silence.

'Well, really, what I mean is . . . look, I don't know quite how to put this, but, you know, there are one or two younger players coming up. Good players. I think I should give them a regular place in the team.'

'You're kicking me out?'

'No, that's not how I see it. I'm thinking of you, Joe. What if you were to get a serious injury? What if, God forbid, you overdid it one day and, you know, collapsed?'

'Collapsed? Why the hell should I collapse?'

'You're the old man of the squad, Joe.'

'What do you mean, old man? How old do you think I am?'

'Forty-five . . . ish, aren't you?'

'I'm forty-two.'

'The next oldest is 32. I'm sorry, Joe, but I think this might be a good time for you to retire.'

Retire! The mere thought of the word was still enough to send Joe's blood pressure soaring. *The old man of the squad?* What a bloody insult that was to someone who'd turned out loyally every Sunday morning for ten years. OK, he was slowing up, he knew that. He was finding it harder to last the full ninety minutes, and he'd been off form a bit recently. And never scored. Well, he had. He preferred not to dwell overmuch on the two own goals he'd slid past the keeper this season. And the one last season. But who was counting? He was in the back four, for Christ's sake. That kind of unfortunate accident happened to defenders.

He'd given his all for that team, and this was how they repaid him. Ungrateful bastards. How dare they call him old. How dare they put him out to pasture like some clapped-out donkey. Yet . . . yet, beneath his anger, Joe couldn't help but wonder whether they were right. Was he really past it? His eyesight was deteriorating – going blind was how he thought of it in his more morose moments – he'd been dumped by his football team, and now he couldn't walk a quarter of a mile without getting breathless.

Sod it, he thought. Just take the drug. Get your fix and forget about it. He pulled the inhaler out of his pocket, gave it a violent shake and shoved the nozzle defiantly into his mouth, depressing the tiny canister and breathing in deeply so that a spray of Ventolin vapour shot down into his lungs. The effect was immediate. The hoop around his chest relaxed, his breathing became easier. He felt – dammit, he felt *younger*. So he was a drug addict. Who cared? There were a few more years left in him yet. His football career might be over, but he wasn't going to go quietly. Going quietly wasn't what Joe Verdi did.

He slid the inhaler back into his pocket and looked over his shoulder up Holborn Viaduct. A black cab was coming towards him, its For Hire sign illuminated. Joe waved his arm. The cab went straight past him.

'Tosser!' Joe yelled after it, nothing the matter with his lungs now. 'What's your problem? Am I too fucking *old* for you?'

A second cab appeared half a minute later. This one stopped. Joe climbed in and gave the driver the address of his father's restaurant in Soho. Then he slumped back in the corner of the seat, his head lolling against the side of the cab. The driver glanced at him.

'You okay, mate?'

Joe nodded wearily.

'I'm fine. I'm just dying, that's all.'

Joe's father, Alessandro, had run a restaurant off Wardour Street for close on forty years. He'd come to England from Italy in the early 1960s to work in a hotel as a sous-chef, met and married Joe's mother, June, who worked as a receptionist in the same hotel, then set up on his own a couple of years after Joe was born.

The restaurant was called Alessandro's, the only appropriate name for an establishment that bore so strongly the mark of its proprietor. Everything about the place – from the décor and lighting, the crockery and tablecloths, to the cuisine was Alessandro's. It was *his* restaurant, it was *his* food. The people who ate there were *his* customers and Alessandro had always prided himself on looking after them as if they were guests in his family home. There were those who found his personal attentions intrusive and overbearing and never came back. But there were others – many more others – who appreciated his attentiveness, the homely atmosphere in the restaurant, and returned time after time. Alessandro took care of his regulars, made them feel special and it was that warm hospitality that had ensured the restaurant had survived when so many others in the area changed hands every few years or had closed down entirely.

The food helped, of course. No amount of Italian charm would have been enough to build such a loyal clientele if the food had been inferior. But Alessandro's food was good. He came from a village near Bologna, the home of Italian cooking – as Alessandro never tired of telling people – and his cuisine was simple, tasty and unpretentious. Sauces were never drizzled around the edge of the plate at Alessandro's. If you ordered sauce, you got a bucket-load of the stuff and as much freshly-grated Parmesan as you could eat. If you wanted chicken, you got a breast or a quarter portion that looked as if it had come from a real animal, not some photogenic arrangement of 'goujons' and a few trimmings that belonged more on the pages of a glossy style magazine than a restaurant.

In the early days, he'd done all the cooking himself, leaving the dining area to his wife and – when they were old enough – his three children. More recently, he'd moved out of the kitchen, employing a chef so that he could concentrate on the front-of-house management – ministering to his customers, which was what he most enjoyed.

He was behind the bar, rustling up a couple of apéritifs, when Joe walked in.

'Giuseppe!' Alessandro cried in his deep *basso profundo* voice.

His father was the only person who still called Joe by his given name. Even his mother had stopped. Joe himself had anglicised it long ago. At the north London comprehensive he'd been to you didn't last long if you were called Giuseppe.

'Ciao, papa. Come stai?' Joe said phlegmatically, his under-stated monotone a deliberate contrast with his father's booming ebullience. Alessandro's sunny geniality was always genuine, but there were times when Joe found it all too much, too stereotypically Italian.

'Bene. And you?' Alessandro said.

He came out from behind the bar and kissed his son on both cheeks, having to stretch up to reach. Joe was several inches taller than Alessandro. He'd inherited his father's dark hair and Mediterranean skin, but his mother's height.

'I'm fine, papa.'

'Henry's already here. I'll come over in a minute.'

Joe's newspaper colleague, Henry Weaver, was seated at a table by the window. Seeing him lifted Joe's spirits, blew away the gloomy cloud that had been lowering over him for most of the morning. Lunch with friends – that was something that always perked him up.

'You been waiting long?' he said, sitting down opposite Henry.

'A couple of minutes.'

Henry picked out an olive from the bowl in the centre of the table and held it up between a chubby thumb and fore-finger, examining it as though it were a precious gemstone.

'These are bloody tasty olives,' he said. 'Where does your father get them?'

'Apulia,' Joe said. 'He says they're the best in Italy.'

'I can believe it.'

Henry slipped the olive into his mouth and chewed it slowly. He was three years older than Joe, but had one of those plump, boyish faces that never seemed to age. He was a columnist on *The News*, but he also wrote a weekly restaurant review for another paper and a wine column for a monthly magazine, appointments that had done plenty for his bank balance but nothing for his figure. With his mop of blond hair and pale skin, Henry liked to claim a pedigree dating back to the Viking invasions, though anyone taking in his soft fleshy jowls and flabby waistline would probably not have been immediately reminded of a Norse warrior.

'Apulia, eh?' he said.

'The heel of Italy.'

'I know where it is.'

'Yeah?' Joe smiled dryly. 'I didn't think you'd been any further than the terrace of your villa in Tuscany.'

'Not for a few years, that's true,' Henry conceded. 'As I get older, I find it's so much more enjoyable to do all my travelling from a sun-lounger by the pool, a glass of Chianti in my hand.'

He helped himself to another olive and glanced at his watch.

'Ellie's late. Shall we order without her?'

'Give her a few more minutes.'

'What about you? What time are you due back in court?'

'I'm not,' Joe said. 'The case is over.'

'Already? That was quick. The verdict?'

'Guilty.'

There'd never been any doubt about it, in Joe's view. Norman Naylor, a fifty-four-year-old unemployed computer technician with a history of mental illness had killed his wife, chopped her body up and deposited the bits in an old, poorly-sealed freezer they kept in their garage. Then he'd gone off to Cornwall – a B&B in St Ives – for a fortnight's holiday, intending to dispose of his wife's remains when he returned. Unfortunately for him, in his absence, a road repair crew accidentally cut through the power supply to the house, but didn't get round to informing the local electricity company for three days. The electricity company, with the efficiency for which they were renowned, had then taken a further four days to repair the break, by which time Mrs Naylor's body had thawed and the neighbours had begun to notice the strange smell emanating from the garage.

'There wasn't much the defence barrister could really say,' Joe said. 'How do you explain away your wife's dismembered body in the freezer?'

Henry topped up his glass with wine and poured some for Joe.

'You news reporters have such exciting lives. I don't know how you have the energy. I've done nothing more this morning than try to think of a subject for my next column and I feel quite drained.'

'I know,' Joe said sympathetically. 'Drinking coffee and staring out of the window can be exhausting work. And you have to do it two days a week as well.'

'It's not easy, you know,' Henry said. 'Coming up with a couple of columns every week on the issues of the day.'

'Especially as now you're deskbound you don't actually cover any issues of the day.'

'I *decide* the issues of the day, you should know that by now. If I write about something, no matter how inconsequential, it automatically takes on a new importance, becomes an essential topic of conversation for the chattering classes. I have my finger on the pulse of the zeitgeist.'

'Zeitgeist? Isn't that German for bullshit?'

Joe turned his head. Alessandro, was coming across the restaurant with a plate in his hand. He paused for a moment to exchange a few words with some regular customers at another table, then came over to Joe and Henry.

'I thought you might like some *bruschetta* while you're waiting,' he said. All the years in London had done nothing to take the edge off his thick Italian accent.

He put the plate down on the table. The aroma of hot tomato and garlic and chopped basil wafted into the air.

'*Grazie, papa,*' Joe said.

'You got everything you need? The wine OK?'

'It's fine, papa.'

'These olives are magnificent,' Henry said, reinforcing the compliment by eating two more.

'You like them?' Alessandro said.

'I'm something of a connoisseur of olives,' Henry said pompously. He licked his fingers, as if he were analysing the individual ingredients that made up the flavour. 'Garlic, a hint of rosemary, that dark rich oil. I'd say these were from, let me see, Apulia?'

Joe rolled his eyes. His father stared at Henry, impressed by this prodigious feat of deduction.

'You're right. That's amazing. How did you guess?'

Henry waved a hand modestly.

'Just a gift I have.'

'I'll get you a jar of them,' Alessandro said. 'You can take it away with you.'

He stepped back from the table as a slender woman in her mid-thirties hurried into the restaurant. She came over, pulled out a chair and slumped down on to it.

'Sorry I'm late,' Ellie Mason said breathlessly. 'Bloody weddings. *Ciao*, Alessandro. How are you?'

Without waiting for a reply, she dumped her shoulder bag on the table and rummaged through it, taking out a comb which she dragged through her mane of tangled hair. She had thick dark hair that curled over her shoulders and around her face, the fringe flopping down over her eyes. She wasn't a beautiful woman. Her features were too individual, too lacking in the symmetry and bland uniformity that the modern idea of beauty requires. But she was attractive. Her face was intelligent, her hazel eyes warm and alert, sparkling with life.

'I thought it would never end,' she said. 'Is that *bruschetta*? I'm starving.'

She grabbed one of the slices from the plate and took a bite of it, still combing her hair.

'Have you ordered yet?' she said indistinctly through a mouthful of bread and tomato.

'I can recommend the lamb today,' Alessandro said. 'Or the *bracciale di pesce spada* – swordfish steak stuffed with basil, pine kernels, sultanas and provolone cheese.'

'I'll have the chicken,' Ellie said without looking at the menu. 'However it comes.'

'You always have the chicken,' Henry said.

'I like chicken.'

Alessandro turned to go.

'I'll leave you to it. Give me a shout when you're ready.'

Ellie wolfed down the rest of her *bruschetta*, then wiped her mouth on a napkin. She'd finished combing her hair, but it still looked unkempt and messy.

'You've been to a wedding?' Henry said.

Ellie reached out for the bottle of red wine and filled a glass. She took a long, grateful sip.

'At an Asda superstore,' she said, grimacing.

Henry gazed at her incredulously.

'A wedding in a *supermarket*?'

'They've got a licence. Can you imagine it, eh? I mean, what woman in her right mind dreams of walking down the aisle in a sodding Asda?'

'You're not serious?'

'She had the whole lot. Long white dress, veil, these little girl bridesmaids, the wedding march playing over the Tannoy and this line of Asda greeters – you know, those scary, smiley-faced freaks who stand at the entrance saying, "Hi, I'm Tracey, I'm here to help you make the most of your shopping experience" – they were throwing confetti. It was truly surreal.'

Ellie paused to drink some more wine. Then she went on, 'The Registrar had set up a table by the in-store bakery, all these shoppers looking on, gawping. Even the catering for the reception was provided by Asda. The biggest day of your life and you get the food done by Wal-Mart.'

'Did they look insane, the bride and groom?' Joe said.

'They met there, apparently, on some singles night,' Ellie replied. 'How sad is that? They have them twice a month on a Friday night. They give you a choice of badge like a traffic light to wear – red, green, amber. You're supposed to display the colour that indicates your "level of availability". What the hell is that supposed to mean? You display a green, does that give some guy the excuse to shag you over the deli counter?'

Ellie looked at each of them in turn.

'Not a word of this to Preston, mind.' Ed Preston was the paper's news editor. 'Or he'll have me tripping along there one Friday evening in a mini-skirt and high heels, every weirdo in north London chasing after me with their trolleys full of one-person ready meals.'

'A wedding in a supermarket,' Henry said pensively. 'There has to be a column in that.'

'They're muscling in on everything,' Joe said. 'Every part of our lives. There's a supermarket somewhere – I read about it – where you can register a birth. Births, marriages, they'll be doing funerals next.'

'Well, they kill enough people, the shit they sell,' Henry said.

'It could be a loss-leader,' Joe said. 'Interments. Buy one get one free.'

'It's sort of pragmatic, very down-to-earth, don't you think though?' Henry said. 'Meeting, then getting hitched in a supermarket. The marriage will probably last longer than if they'd met in a nightclub.'

'Don't you believe it,' Ellie said. 'You meet a guy in a nightclub, you might get a bit of fun out of it, maybe a holiday in Ibiza. You meet him in a supermarket, you know before long you'll be doing his shopping for him. You meet in a laundrette, in no time at all you'll be washing his boxers for him.' She pulled a face. 'Why do I get this crap? It's because I'm a woman. Preston wouldn't dare give it to a bloke.'

'Women are better at things like weddings,' Henry said provocatively.

'I'm sure there's a suitably pithy response to that,' Ellie said. 'But for the time being I'll make do with "piss off".'

35

'No, I mean it. You'll capture the colour of it all, the sense of occasion.'

'*Sense of occasion?* A wedding in a fucking supermarket? Preston's a dinosaur, that's why he gave it to me. He's living in a different century. If I hear one more of his "-getting pissed with Keith Waterhouse in El Vino's" stories, I'll strangle him.'

'He's got enough to fill a book,' Henry said.

'I find that truly terrifying. Fleet Street memoirs. Christ, they're right up there with Jimmy Tarbuck's Great Book of Golfing Stories.'

Joe put a soothing hand on Ellie's shoulder.

'You're having a bad morning,' he said. 'Have this last *bruschetta*, I think you need it.'

He pushed the plate across the table. Ellie smiled at him apologetically.

'Sorry, it's just got me wound up a bit. I'm all right now, I'll stop ranting.'

'We like it when you rant, don't we, Henry?' Joe said.

'You're so good at it,' Henry replied. 'We could listen to you for hours. Come to think of it, we *do* listen to you for hours.'

'Oh, shut up,' Ellie said.

Joe felt his mobile phone vibrate in his jacket pocket. He pulled the phone out and saw the text message on the screen. He studied the words for a moment, struggling to work out what the obscure sequence of letters meant. Shit! This was something he couldn't ignore. Could it wait until after he'd eaten? he wondered. Maybe an hour? He weighed up the pros and cons. He was hungry, looking forward to a meal with Ellie and Henry. But he was also a news reporter, and news didn't wait. Work or pleasure? It wasn't really a choice, not for him anyway. He pushed back his chair.

'I have to go.'

'What, now?' Ellie said.

'Something's come up.'

'But you've only just got here,' Henry protested. 'You must have your lunch.'

'This is important, Henry.'

'What could be more important than lunch?'

'Can't it wait?' Ellie said. 'We don't do this very often.'

'We'll do it again, soon, OK? Enjoy your meal. I'll tell my dad not to bother with the bill.'

'You'll do nothing of the kind,' Henry said. 'I'll put it on my expenses. That's what I love about being a celebrated columnist. No one queries my expenses any more, I'm expected to make them up.'

'I'll catch you later,' Joe said.

He stood up, slipping the phone back into his pocket, and headed across the restaurant. He paused by the bar to explain his sudden departure to his father. Alessandro gave him a look of such abject disappointment that Joe felt a pang of guilt.

'I'm sorry,' he said.

'I was going to come over,' Alessandro said. 'Have a chat. When did we last have a chat, Giuseppe?'

'I've got to go, papa.'

'Give us a call some time. You know your mother likes to see you.'

'I saw her last week.'

'You did? She never said. Where was I?'

'You were working, papa. You're always working.'

'Oh.'

'*Ci vediamo.*'

Joe kissed his father on the cheeks and went out into the street.

The text message had been brief, and unintelligible at first glance: 'hmcd bdy wlthmstw mrshs', which Joe had translated as, 'homicide, body Walthamstow Marshes.'

That was what he liked about being a crime reporter. You got to meet so many interesting new people.

4

Joe took a cab back to the office to pick up his car, then drove north through Hackney, turning on to Lea Bridge Road and heading for the southern end of Walthamstow Marshes. The text message had given him only a minimum amount of information – a body on the marshes – but it hadn't specified where on the marshes. He pulled into the carpark outside the Lee Valley Ice Centre, got out and walked over to the entrance to the Walthamstow Marsh Nature Reserve. The metal barrier stopping vehicular access to the rough dirt track alongside the river was still padlocked, making him suspect immediately that he was at the wrong end of the marshes. He went through the pedestrian gate and out into the nature reserve just to make sure. If he was in the right place, he knew he should have seen some signs of police activity – cars, vans, a taped-off crime scene. A homicide team at work was about as inconspicuous as a travelling circus, and often drew as big a crowd of spectators. But there was nothing here, the marshes seemed deserted.

Joe gazed out across the green open space. The marshes, despite their name, weren't very wet. Not now, at least. At one time, long ago, they must have been boggier, riven with channels and treacherous pools, but they'd been tamed in recent years, the land drained and made more accessible to the local people. Joe had come here when he was a kid. They'd had picnics on the bank by the river, the four of them – Joe, his mother, and his younger brother and sister. His father had never come with them. He could never leave his beloved restaurant, even for an afternoon, but he'd sent food out in a van, had it delivered to the riverbank by one of his waiters. Joe had found it acutely embarrassing. The other families around them – kids that Joe knew from school – would be eating their cheese and pickle sandwiches and crisps while the Verdis were tucking in to spaghetti Bolognese or wild mushroom risotto with tiramisu to follow.

Further to the north, beyond the railway line that dissected the area in two, the marshes had retained more of their wild character. There were ditches full of green, stagnant water, reeds and cow parsley swaying in the breeze, buntings and sedge warblers flitting in and out of the undergrowth, occasionally a kestrel hovering high in the sky. Joe recalled seeing a kestrel swoop down and pick off a mouse on the ground when he was a boy. He could still picture in brilliant detail the speed and grace of the bird as it dived. He looked for one today. There was a speck in the distance flying towards him, but as it drew nearer he saw that it was only a pigeon.

He waited for a moment, enjoying the sensation of being in the countryside though the grimy urban sprawl of the city was only a few hundred metres away, marvelling that a place like this could somehow have escaped the developer's bulldozers. A train came rattling along the track from the south, a blue and silver Stansted Express heading out from Liverpool Street. It passed over the river and then across the brick arches of the viaduct where a hundred years ago, in the first decade of the twentieth century, an inventor named Alliott Verdon Roe had rented a workshop to build a prototype triplane. He'd tested the plane over the marshes in a series of short hops, the first person to fly over British soil in a British-designed flying machine. He'd gone on to make such famous planes as the Lancaster bomber, but almost no one now had ever heard of him.

Joe turned round and went back to his car. The body must have been found at the other end of the marshes. There was no direct route to the north side of the area. To get there, Joe made a wide detour to the west and then cut in again near Springfield Park. He left his car in the carpark behind the rowing club and walked across the footbridge over the river. A path took him round the side of Springfield Marina, brightly-painted narrowboats moored along the water's edge, to the fringes of the marshes.

That was when he saw the police vehicles – four marked cars, three unmarked and a couple of transit vans – parked at the side of the road that came in from the waterworks to the north-east. Where the track into the marshes left the road was a small wooden footbridge over a drainage ditch. Scene-of-crime officers in white overalls and hoods, their shoes sheathed in white plastic bags were moving back and forth across the bridge – from their transit vans to a patch of scrubby vegetation a few metres off the track. More officers, some in plain clothes, were in the process of unfolding a tent, assembling the telescopic poles that would support the structure.

Joe walked over to the footbridge. A uniformed police officer stepped out to block his path.

'I'm sorry, sir. This area is closed to the public.'

Joe showed his press card. The officer scrutinised it carefully, then gave a nod and moved aside. Joe crossed the bridge. The water in the drainage ditch beneath him was black and smelly, the surface thick with duck weed. A square of land next to the track had been cordoned off with blue and white plastic tape. Along the near side an access channel had been created to allow the Socos to move freely in and out with their equipment. A photographer – a civilian on contract to the police – was lining up his camera on some object on the ground, snapping off shots from different angles. Joe couldn't see the object clearly – the surrounding grass was too long – but he knew it had to be the body.

He took out his mobile phone and called the office. One of the assistant news editors answered. Joe told him where he was, outlined what little he knew about the case, and asked for a staff photographer to be sent out. He was putting the phone away when one of the plainclothes officers standing over by the body turned round and saw him.

She was a striking woman in her mid-thirties, maybe a little older. Tall and slim, with the rangy build of a hill walker, she had short, black hair and a pale complexion, her face almost devoid of make-up. Everything about her – the hair, the lack of cosmetics, her jacket, trousers and sensible low-heeled boots, seemed chosen for practicality and easy maintenance. She was a good-looking woman, but there was a masculine edge to her appearance, as if she were making a conscious attempt to play down her gender.

Joe knew who she was: Detective Chief Inspector Louise Crawford, head of one of the Metropolitan Police's MITs – the Major Investigation Teams – that dealt with homicides in the capital. She knew who he was too. And she didn't seem pleased to see him. Her expression was a complex mixture of irritation, annoyance and long-suffering weariness. She said something to one of her colleagues and walked across the grass towards Joe.

'How the hell did you get here so quickly?' she said with a scowl.

Joe grinned at her insolently.

'Hello, chief inspector. How are you today?'

He was on first name terms with many of the officers in the Met, but was always careful not to be too familiar with Louise Crawford. She wasn't a copper who had much time for public relations, for consorting with the press.

'I was doing fine until you showed up,' she said caustically. 'Why is it that every case I handle you somehow contrive to put in an appearance and get in the way?'

'I'm not in the way, am I?'

'Not yet. But you have form. I don't want you poking around being a pain in the arse.'

'That's my speciality,' Joe said.

'Who tipped you off? Someone on my team?'

Joe pretended he hadn't heard the question. He took out his notebook and pen.

'What've we got here?' he said. 'Who's the deceased, a man, a woman, a child?'

Joe edged forward a little, craning his neck to try to catch a glimpse of the body before they erected the tent over the scene.

'You stay back!' Crawford said sharply. 'This is as close as you get.'

'Is it a man?'

'You'll get a statement from the press office later, like everybody else.'

'Come on, chief inspector. The sooner you give me some information, the sooner I'll be out of your hair.'

She looked at him. In his crumpled jacket and trousers, his hair all over the place, he had an appealingly dishevelled appearance. There was a forlorn air of vulnerability about him that had always stood him in good stead in his job. People didn't like saying no to him, they didn't like being cruel. It would have been too much like kicking a stray dog that was sniffing around your ankles, trying to be friendly.

Crawford gave a sigh.

'Yes, it's a man. Male Caucasian. Mid-twenties, I'd guess, but don't quote me on that.'

'How did he die?'

'We don't know yet. We'll have to wait until after the autopsy.'

'But there are suspicious circumstances?'

'Why else are we here?'

42

'Would you care to elaborate on that?'

'No.'

'The doctor been out yet?'

'He's on his way.'

'You want to speculate on the cause of death.'

'You know better than that.'

'Who found the body?'

'That's all you're getting, Mr Verdi. Don't let me detain you any longer.'

Crawford headed back into the taped-off area. The photographer had finished taking pictures and was packing his camera away. Crawford gave instructions to her team and they manoeuvred the white tent into position over the body, protecting the scene from the weather and prying eyes.

Joe waited on the track, making a few notes on his pad, watching Louise Crawford as she went about her work. He liked the way she handled herself, her team. You had to be good to make chief inspector at her age. He'd heard male officers in the Met griping about reverse discrimination, promoting women just for show, but even the most chauvinistic of them conceded grudgingly that Crawford knew what she was doing.

One of those men was coming away from the tent now. Detective Sergeant Danny Chisholm, twenty-eight years old with bow legs and a gunslinger's swagger, his grey jacket flapping open to expose a cream shirt and emerald green tie.

'Hi, Danny. Thanks for the tip-off.'

Chisholm stopped next to Joe and glanced back at the tent. Crawford was inside, talking to one of the Socos.

'Joe,' he said.

'Crawford's being cagey. Male Caucasian, mid-twenties, that's all I've got,' Joe said.

'I have to be careful. She'll have my balls.'

'Cause of death?'

'Looks as if he was stabbed,' Chisholm said, still gazing warily at the tent.

'Where? Which bit of the body?'

'Chest.'

'Murder weapon?'

'No sign of it, unless it's underneath him. We can't move the body until the doc and the Socos have finished.'

'Who found him?'

'*Sergeant!*'

The chief inspector was outside the tent, glaring across at Chisholm.

'If you've nothing better to do than gossip with a journalist . . .'

'Yes, ma'am.'

Chisholm turned away, his back to the tent now.

'Time of the month,' he murmured softly.

He inclined his head, his eyes jerking sideways, conveying a message. Joe looked round casually. There was a man standing back over the footbridge near the police vehicles. He was partially hidden by the open rear doors of a transit van, which was why Joe hadn't noticed him earlier.

'Thanks, Danny. I owe you a pint.'

'You owe me more than that, mate,' Chisholm said.

'Where are you drinking?'

The Met's MITs moved around London, taking their mobile incident rooms with them – big caravans complete with electric generators, toilets, desks, computers and phone lines. The first thing they did after setting up base camp – sometimes before – was decide which local pub was to be the designated team watering hole.

'The Victoria,' Chisholm said. 'Other side of the park.'

'I know it,' Joe said.

Chisholm moved off towards one of the unmarked cars. Joe waited a few seconds. Crawford had gone back inside the tent and was out of sight. Joe made the most of the opportunity, walking quickly over to the man by the van.

'Joe Verdi, *The News*,' he said, his pen and notepad poised. 'I gather you found the body.'

The man nodded. He was in his thirties, medium height but with a lean, leggy build that made him seem taller. He was wearing a navy blue tracksuit and Nike trainers.

'Could I take your name?' Joe said.

'Simpson. Dave Simpson.'

'How old are you, Dave?'

'Thirty-eight.'

'You live around here?'

'No, I live over near Hornsey. But I work just by Springfield Park.'

'What do you do?'

'I'm a graphic designer.'

Joe gestured at the man's clothes.

'Let me guess, you were out jogging when you found him.'

'That's right. I go for a run at lunchtime, two, maybe three times a week.'

'Always across the marshes?'

'I do a circuit. Round the park, then over the bridge and along the river.'

'You saw the body from the track?'

'I saw the birds. A whole flock of them. Crows. I knew something was wrong. I went to take a look. I thought it was probably a dead fox. I didn't expect . . . well, it was a bit of a shock, I can tell you.'

'What did you do?'

'I chased the crows away. They were, you know . . .' He winced. '. . . pecking at the body. Then I rang 999 on my mobile.'

'What time did you find him?'

'About twelve-fifteen, twelve-thirty.'

'You been here since then?'

'The officer in charge – the woman – asked me to stay. I think they want to take a statement from me, but they seem to have . . .'

Simpson's voice petered out. He was looking at something over Joe's left shoulder. Joe turned round. Louise Crawford was right behind him.

'No, we haven't forgotten, Mr Simpson,' she said. 'Thank you for being so patient. I'll get one of my officers to take your statement now.'

'OK. I was just, you know. 'Simpson gave a guilty shrug. 'Answering a few questions.'

'That's fine,' Crawford said.

She turned her gaze on Joe. From a distance her dark blue eyes looked soft and warm. Close up they were cooler, intimidating.

'Mr Verdi was just going. Weren't you?' she said.

Irena and Anwar took the bus to the East End. Anwar didn't have a car, or a British driving licence, though they were both things he aspired to. Not being able to drive was a drawback – it closed off all manner of job opportunities – but they simply didn't have the money for driving lessons, never mind a car of their own. He could have called on a friend – another Kurd living in the same block of flats – to give them a lift, but Anwar was naturally cautious. He didn't want anyone else to see Irena, to ask questions about her. He was frightened – for Irena, but also for himself and his family. Memet Dil was not a man it was wise to cross. Anwar had never met him, nor any of his associates in the local Turkish underworld, but he knew of his reputation. In a community as small and tight-knit as theirs, it was impossible not to be aware of the criminal minority, the drug dealers and thugs, the extortionists and people-smugglers whose activities impinged to a degree on everyone's lives, even the quiet, law-abiding ones like Anwar.

He and Sara had had a long discussion about what to do. They hadn't involved Irena in their deliberations – at least not initially. She was too traumatised by Ismail's death to be able to think clearly, much less make decisions about her future. They'd wondered about going to the police, getting Irena to tell them what had happened, but decided against it. Irena was in Britain illegally. She'd be detained, sent to some secure establishment and then, ultimately, deported back to Turkey. That was not something any of them wanted. Besides, they were wary of the British police. They were better than the Turkish police, certainly, but they were still the police, the agents of the state. Anwar and his wife had seen too much injustice and brutality in their homeland to believe that the police, or any other official body, would protect them effectively against a man like Memet Dil. Whatever happened, Dil would find some way to get to them.

Anwar knew that Irena couldn't stay with them in their flat. It was too dangerous. Even remaining in Stoke Newington was not an option. There was only one course of action: Irena had to be taken away from London, somewhere Dil couldn't find her. That was all very well in theory, not so easy in practise. Anwar and Sara knew no one outside the capital. There were Kurdish communities elsewhere in Britain, but Irena couldn't simply go to one of them and expect to find protection and acceptance. How would she support herself? What would she live on? Where would she find accommodation, a job?

'What about Rafiq Khan?' Sara had said.

Anwar had already thought of Khan, but had reservations about going to him, about introducing Irena to a world that Anwar knew from his own experience was hard and depressing.

'What choice do we have?' Sara had said.

So Irena and Anwar took the bus down Stoke Newington High Street, then Kingsland Road and Shoreditch High Street, getting off near Liverpool Street Station and continuing on foot to an address in Whitechapel. It was a strange, unnerving experience for Irena – the red bus with its upper and lower decks, the passengers sitting neatly together in orderly rows, the traffic outside roaring past in an incessant, belching stream – but she took in little of it. She was in a daze, her mind fixed on Ismail to the exclusion of almost everything else.

The previous few hours had passed in a blur. Sara had given her a meal – some rice and lamb – and she'd taken a shower, standing in the bath, the water from the shower mixing with her tears as it flowed down her face. She'd found it hard to stop weeping. Even on the bus she'd had to make a deliberate effort not to cry, to draw attention to herself. Anwar had held her by the arm, guiding her as if she were blind. She did as he said without thinking. She trusted him to take care of her. She was still in deep shock. There was a desolate emptiness inside her. Her life had been torn apart by Ismail's death. Everything she loved, all her hopes and dreams had been destroyed in that one terrible instant.

Rafiq Khan's office was in a dingy sidestreet off Commercial Road, the wide, dreary main route east to Limehouse and the London docklands. It was a mixed area – Bangladeshi restaurants, Middle-Eastern kebab houses, Bollywood video rental stores and any number of Asian clothing retailers occupying premises adjacent to those great Western cultural icons, McDonalds, KFC and Ladbrokes. There was a room at the front of the building from which Khan's mini-cab business was run – a poky little place with a desk and radio console and a couple of wooden chairs that were usually taken by drivers waiting for customers to phone in. But through a door at the back was a second office in which Khan ran his other business – or rather one of his other businesses for Rafiq Khan, a Pakistani immigrant with trading in his blood, was not a man who was content with a mere two money-earning enterprises.

This other business was an employment agency that catered for both the local resident population and migrants who had come to England looking for work. All the people on Khan's books – although he didn't actually keep anything so formal as a 'book', unless you counted the entirely fictitious set of records he maintained for the benefit of the Inland Revenue and other official dupes – were non-white and many were in the country illegally. Khan had never found work for a white English person. The jobs he specialised in were not the kind that a white resident either needed or wanted to undertake – cleaning, catering, or agricultural work in the rural counties outside London, jobs which were all different, but all equally unpleasant, exploitative and low paid.

The Pakistani man at the desk in the front mini-cab office was speaking in Urdu into the radio mike as Anwar and Irena came in. A second man was slumped on one of the chairs, watching the television high up on the wall – an old black and white film showing – with studied indifference.

Anwar waited for the deskman to finish his conversation, then asked for Mr Khan.

'What you want?' the deskman asked curtly.

'Work.'

The deskman looked at them and sniffed. Then he went to the door behind the desk and opened it, exchanging a few words in Urdu with someone in the back office.

'He'll see you,' he said to Anwar, walking back to his chair.

The back office was as shabby as the front. Rafiq Khan didn't believe in ostentation, or even moderate window-dressing. Everything in the room was functional and cheap. If it didn't have a purpose, it had no business being there. The desk was scratched grey metal, the chairs grey metal, the filing cabinets grey metal. There was dirty grey lino on the floor, and though the walls were painted magnolia, that was probably only because the warehouse had been out of grey.

Mr Khan was better dressed than his office, but then that

wasn't difficult. He was wearing a light grey suit so shiny it seemed to be coated in grease and an open-necked collarless white shirt. He was a small man, with a smooth, silky complexion that belied his age, which was close to sixty. He glanced briefly at Irena, then looked at Anwar, addressing himself solely to him.

'So you want work?'

Anwar nodded.

'Not for me. For my friend here.'

'What kind of work?'

'Something outside London.'

'Agricultural work? If it's outside London, it will have to be agricultural work.'

'That's all right.'

Khan rummaged through a pile of dog-eared papers on his desk. Anwar let this gaze rove around the office. It hadn't changed much, if at all, since he'd last been there some five years earlier. A political activist in his native land, he'd come to England with Sara and Khaled, seeking asylum. They'd been granted temporary leave to stay, the immigration authorities persuaded that his life would be in danger if he was returned to Turkey. But it had taken several months for his case to be finally decided and in that period they had struggled to survive. The state benefits paid to them didn't cover their living costs and yet Anwar was forbidden to work. Desperate to earn some money, he'd come to Rafiq Khan – Khan's name given to him by a fellow Kurdish asylum seeker – who'd found him a job with a contract cleaning agency, working the night shift in West End hotels, a gruelling and demeaning experience for an educated man like Anwar.

Khan obviously didn't remember him. There was no reason why he should. He must have seen thousands of foreign migrants over the years he'd been running his employment agency. They were statistics to him, not people.

'You done agricultural work before?' Khan said to Irena, taking a sheet of paper from the pile. Irena looked at him blankly.

'She doesn't speak much English,' Anwar explained. 'She'll be able to do whatever is required.'

'I've got a mini-van going up to Norfolk this evening,' Khan said. 'Twelve-hour shift in a packhouse, 8 p.m. to 8 a.m. You want it?'

'Yes, we'll take it. What if she wanted to stay there, in Norfolk? To work.'

Khan shrugged.

'That can be arranged.'

'You can find her accommodation?'

'For a fee.'

'How much?'

'Twenty per cent of her shift pay. That doesn't cover the cost of the accommodation, you understand. That's the arrrangement fee. The gangmaster will sort out the accommodation charges and deduct them from her wages.'

'What will she be paid – for tonight's shift?'

'Minimum wage, £5.35, less tax and national insurance and my agency fee.'

'Which is what?'

'Twenty per cent.'

'Another twenty per cent?'

'You want the work, or not?'

'Yes, we want it.'

Khan tossed an A4 form across the desk.

'I'll need a name,' he said.

'A name?'

'Doesn't have to be her real one. You could put Marilyn Monroe, for all I care.'

Anwar studied the form.

'What about the rest, the address, date of birth?'

'I'll fill those in later. Just give me a name.'

Anwar turned to Irena.

'I'm going to put a false name on the form,' he said in Kurdish. 'No one will know who you are.'

'Where am I going?'

'A place called Norfolk. It's the countryside north of London. Someone will fix you up with a place to stay, work. You'll be safe.'

'How long will I be there?'

'I don't know.'

'What about the Turks?'

'They won't find you there. What name shall I put?'

'Anything.'

Anwar thought for a moment, then wrote Sakar Ali on the form. Sakar had been his mother's name, and Ali was a common Kurdish surname. The rest of the form he left blank. He knew Khan was cheating them. The whole form was a fiction. The so-called tax and national insurance deducted from Irena's pay would simply go into Khan's pocket. But that was how the system worked.

'Be outside at six o'clock,' Khan said.

That gave them a few hours to kill. Anwar considered going back to Stoke Newington, but decided against it. It was better to keep Irena away from the area, from any-where she might be spotted and recognised. But she would need some luggage – a few spare clothes, toiletries – to replace the personal possessions she had left behind in Memet Dil's garage.

Anwar telephoned his wife, then put Irena on to talk to Sara about what she needed.

'Send Khaled with the things,' Anwar told Sara before he rang off, giving her Rafiq Khan's address.

The rest of the afternoon they spent wandering around Whitechapel, an hour of it drinking tea in a dismal café. By half-past five, they were back at Khan's office. Khaled was already there waiting for them. He'd brought with him a small hold-all containing the items his mother had selected from her own belongings to give to Irena. Anwar gave the hold-all to Irena, then took three ten pound notes from his wallet.

'This is all I have. Take it, you'll need it. Now, you remember our address?'

'Six, Alexandra Court, Murray Road, Stoke Newington, London,' Irena recited.

'This is our phone number.'

Anwar wrote the number on a scrap of paper and handed it to her.

'Let us know where you are.'

A white mini-van with no windows in the back pulled in to the kerb next to them. The driver – a Pakistani youth in jeans and T-shirt – climbed out and opened the rear doors, disgorging a dozen exhausted-looking passengers: Indians, Sikhs, Pakistanis, Blacks, a woman who might have been North African and a boy, almost certainly her son, who looked too young to go out to work.

The passengers stumbled away from the van on weary legs and disappeared into the side streets. As they departed, a new batch arrived, more Blacks and Asians appearing out of nowhere and scrambling into the back of the van. There were no seats inside, just a couple of dirty mattresses on the floor.

Rafiq Khan came out of his office and gestured impatiently at Irena.

'This is it. Get in.'

Irena clutched the hold-all to her chest and stared at the other people in the van – eleven of them crammed together, bodies touching, legs intertwined. Twenty-two dull, uninterested eyes turned to gaze at her for a second, then looked away. Irena clambered inside and squeezed on to one of the mattresses. She saw Anwar and Khaled watching her from the pavement, Anwar trying to give her a smile of support and encouragement. Then the doors slammed shut, the engine turned over and the van pulled off.

5

Memet Dil took a sip of the thick, sweet coffee in the cup on his desk and lit up a cigar, inhaling slowly, enjoying the raw, throat-burning taste of the tobacco. He imported his cigars from Istanbul. The coffee too was from Turkey. He'd lived in England for three decades, but never assimilated with the natives of his new home. The English, of course, with their innate xenophobia, would never have accepted him, but Dil didn't mind that. He didn't want to belong in England. He wanted to remain what he was: the ambitious son of a shopkeeper from Diyarbakir who, through hard work and ruthlessness, had built himself his own fiefdom – not exactly an empire, but certainly a minor province, a world that functioned entirely according to his rules and his whims.

That this kingdom was founded on crime and violence was irrelevant to him. He made no moral distinction between legitimate and illegitimate enterprise. The whole concept of legality was artificial, in any case, manufactured by those in power to suit their own ends. Memet traded in cigarettes and alcohol, which were both legal goods – or legal provided you paid the requisite excise duty on them, a bureaucratic stipulation that Dil had never been too scrupulous about following. But he traded also in heroin and cocaine, both illegal. Yet what was the difference? They were all drugs, all addictive, all potentially harmful. In

Memet's eyes, the only reason some were legal, some not, was because cigarettes and alcohol were made and distributed predominantly by the West, whereas heroin and cocaine came from the Third World. It was just another example of the developed world's hypocrisy, its racism. If something made money for an American tobacco corporation, it was good. If it made money for peasant farmers in Afghanistan or Colombia, it was bad.

Memet was a businessman. He bought and sold. His business was subject to the same laws of supply and demand as any other business. He didn't make anybody buy his products or services, he simply supplied what his customers demanded. A bag of crack? Certainly, no problem. A passage to England in the back of a lorry? That can be arranged, at a price, of course. If you ignored the ethical dimension, he was really little different from British Airways or Coca-Cola – although neither of those companies was unfortunate enough to have an employee as stupid as Hasan Mustafa.

Hasan was sitting on the other side of the desk, fingering his moustache nervously. Farok was there as well, seated a couple of metres away from Hasan, as if he didn't want to be too closely associated with him – an understandable desire given Memet Dil's current mood.

Memet was angry. To an outsider that might not have been obvious. He didn't rant and scream when he was furious. He didn't lash out or foam at the mouth. He simply assumed an icy calm, an even greater self-control than he normally exhibited, that to those who knew him was more terrifying than the most explosive tantrum.

'Well?' he said, that one word loaded with a chilling menace.

Hasan swallowed.

'No sign of her, Memet bey,' he said, looking down at his hands, which were clasped tightly together in his lap.

Memet said nothing. He waited for Hasan to fill the uncomfortable silence.

'We've looked everywhere, Memet bey. We've driven round all the streets, the shopping centre, the community centre. We've talked to dozens of people, you know, spread the word. No one's seen her.'

Memet looked away across his office. It was a big room, furnished with heavy Turkish rugs and dark, brass-inlaid wooden furniture – a desk, chairs, an ornate glass-fronted cabinet – that he'd had shipped over from his homeland. How these two imbeciles sitting opposite him had let the Kurdish woman escape the previous night was a mystery to him. He'd already let them feel his displeasure when they'd returned to the garage without her. Going over that ground again now seemed a pointless waste of time.

'The trouble is, we don't know what she looks like,' Hasan went on, trying to make excuses for their failure.

He was right. None of them could describe Irena with any clarity. They'd only seen her briefly in the garage, her face partially hidden by her headscarf.

'And without a name . . .'

He didn't finish the sentence. They didn't know the names of any of the people they smuggled into Britain. They didn't give a toss who they were. That kind of detail was taken care of in Turkey, where the money changed hands and the travel arrangements were organised. Even the thirteen other Kurds who'd been in the lorry didn't know what their fellow passengers were called.

'We'll get a name,' Memet said. 'I've emailed Diyarbakir. They'll know who she is.'

'She won't say anything,' Hasan said, trying to sound confident.

'No?'

'She'll be too frightened. Like the others.'

The thirteen Kurds, also witnesses to the killing, had been made graphically aware of the consequences of sharing their knowledge with anyone else. Memet knew he could rely on their silence. The woman was different though. He didn't think she'd go to the police, but she might talk and others might use the information. That wasn't a risk he was prepared to take. Damn that idiot, Hasan. He was a loyal, reliable employee, but the stabbing had been so unnecessary. Why couldn't he control himself? That hot temper, that violent streak that Memet found so useful to him in the right circumstances, was in danger of ruining everything.

There was still time to recover, however. The Kurdish woman obviously had friends or family in London. People who were sheltering her. Once Memet had a name, it would be relatively easy to track those people down, to find the woman.

'Do you want us to keep making enquiries?' Hasan asked tentatively.

'Get on with your normal deliveries,' Memet replied. 'When I hear from Diyarbakir, I'll let you know.'

Joe put a pan of water on the stove to boil and poured himself a glass of wine – an Australian Shiraz that he'd picked up at the local off-licence on his way home from the office. Drinking a non-Italian wine still gave him the guilty feeling that he was doing something slightly wicked. His father refused to stock even a single bottle of what he called 'foreign' wines in his restaurant, and he'd brought up his children to believe that even sniffing the cork of a non-Italian vintage was somehow a sin.

Joe was continually surprised by how his father's opinions and prejudices had lodged themselves so firmly in his brain. Even when he didn't agree with them – and that was fairly often – Alessandro's views seemed to be irritatingly pervasive, little nagging cankers that gnawed away at Joe's subconscious. It wasn't just the wine. Alessandro's convictions about food and cooking were equally contagious. Joe had grown up with them, had had them drummed into him from an early age with a sort of Jesuitical fervour. The restaurant wasn't just a job to Alessandro, it was a calling. Throughout his childhood, Joe had regarded the restaurant as a living entity – like a sixth person in the family. It was always there, its demands and requirements always taking precedence, continuously absorbing his father's time and energy. When Joe became old enough to know what a leech was, the restaurant meta-morphosed in his mind from a shadowy, omnipresent relative into a voracious blood-sucking animal, then much later – when he knew about such things – into his father's mistress.

Joe hated the restaurant, resented its very existence, the power it had over his father and the way it made his mother miserable. It was their living, but it was also their millstone, a burden that none of them could cast off. When Joe was ten, old enough to be trusted with crockery, he was put to work in the dining room, clearing and wiping tables. A couple of years later, he graduated to waiting, taking customers' orders, and in his mid-teens – at weekends and evenings after he'd done his homework – he had to help his father in the kitchen, doing the menial jobs like cooking the pasta or washing salad.

Alessandro had always hoped that his eldest son would follow him into the business, but Joe had had other ideas. Well, actually just one idea – a fierce determination to do anything *except* work in the restaurant. Exactly what he was going to do instead Joe didn't know. He was vague about things like that. Getting away from Alessandro's was his primary objective. Beyond that, he was unclear about his career ambitions, a state of mind that had remained with him for the best part of a decade – his Walkabout Years, as he called them, encompassing leaving England at 18 to explore his Italian roots, a failed university period in Bologna, a failed marriage three years later and various failed jobs until he returned to London in his late twenties and drifted, almost by accident, into journalism.

Joe regarded the legacy of his teenage years in the restaurant as largely negative, but there was one positive aspect of those evenings of drudgery – he had learnt how to cook. For teaching him that invaluable skill, Joe would always be grateful to his father, even though the circumstances of the tuition had not been to his liking at the time. Alessandro Verdi was a perfectionist in the kitchen. He believed in quality and excellence. Even now, at sixty-five, he still got up at five every morning – just as he had done for forty years – and went down to the wholesale markets to buy his fresh fish, meat and vegetables for the restaurant. He could have had the provisions delivered, but he didn't trust anyone to select only the best. The English had an indifferent attitude to food that appalled him. They didn't seem to care what they ate. How else did you explain the under-ripe, tasteless tomatoes they bought, or the green, sour apples, or the peaches that were so hard you could have used them as cricket balls? Even the most feckless Italian housewife would not have tolerated such third-rate produce.

That particular conviction of his father's was one with which Joe wholeheartedly agreed. The English were lazy and unbelievably undiscriminating about what they put in their stomachs. Joe didn't regard himself as a 'foodie' – only the English could have loaded that word with so much contempt – but he was particular about what he ate, and how he prepared it. Cooking wasn't difficult. It just took a little time and thought. It didn't have to be complicated. Simple food was always the best. If those sentiments made him some kind of food zealot, then so be it.

The water in the pan was boiling now. Joe added salt and then a few handfuls of penne and a dash of olive oil to stop the pasta sticking together. From the fridge, he took a plastic container of homemade arrabbiata sauce that was left over from the previous evening and poured some into a pan to heat. Into the sauce, to make it more interesting, he tossed a few slices of pepperoni and some pitted black olives. Ten minutes later, with chopped basil and Parmesan sprinkled on top, it was ready to eat.

Joe took his plate over to the table in the open-plan dining area that was next to the small kitchen. The table top, and most of the floor underneath it, was covered with stacks of books and newspapers. Joe was organised about his food, but the rest of his life, and particularly his flat, was a chaotic mess. The books had been cluttering up the place for more than two years, but he hadn't got round to doing anything about it. His spirit was willing, but his body had so far proved woefully lacking. He had bought a couple of flat-pack bookcases from Ikea three months previously, but hadn't assembled either of them yet. He'd opened one of the boxes and glanced at the instructions and the fearsome collection of parts and decided that it was well beyond his DIY skills to even attempt to put it together. How pathetic was that, a man who couldn't even knock up an Ikea bookcase? Actually, he probably could have given it a go, but only at the expense of much swearing, several bruised knuckles and possibly a stress-induced stomach ulcer. Much better to resort to Plan B, which was to do nothing until the bookcases rotted in their packaging, or Plan C, which was to invite Ellie round for dinner and get her to assemble the bloody things. Ellie was a dab hand with a screwdriver.

The meal over, Joe slipped his jacket back on, checking to make sure his pen and notebook were in the pocket. He went out to his car and drove to the Victoria public house, near Walthamstow Marshes. The Victoria was an old-fashioned traditional sort of pub with no pretensions to being anything other than a rather seedy drinking den. The wine bar revolution had passed it by; so had the modern trend for good pub food. You could dine out at the Vic, but only if you liked pork scratchings and bitter. It was the perfect place for a bunch of off-duty coppers to unwind.

Danny Chisholm was there, sitting at a table with three of his plainclothes colleagues. Joe went to the bar and ordered himself a pint. There was an exchange of loud banter followed by a burst of ribald laughter from the detectives' table. Homicide cops, supposedly all buttoned-up Alpha males, were the biggest gossips Joe had ever encountered – journalists excepted, of course. Drinking with them was like being a bystander at a particularly rowdy hen night.

Joe was a quarter of the way through his pint when Chisholm sidled up alongside him and slid on to the adjacent stool.

'What'll it be?' Joe said.

'A pint, thanks,' Chisholm replied. 'I'll have a shot of whisky too. The single malt.'

The barman went to get the drinks. Joe took out his wallet, wondering how many thousands he'd spent over the years on 'hospitality' for police officers. He put a ten pound note on the counter for the barman, and another ten and two twenties next to it. Danny Chisholm didn't hurry, didn't even look around to see if anyone was watching. He put his hand casually over the notes and palmed them like a conjuror.

'Where are we?' Joe said. 'You know who he was, the dead guy?'

Chisholm took a sip of his beer, waiting for the Macallan to be served.

'He had no i.d. on him.'

'Nothing at all? No wallet. You think that's why he was killed, robbery?'

'We're keeping an open mind,' Chisholm said.

'Anyone been reported missing?'

'No.'

'What about the knife? You found it?'

'No. He wasn't killed on the marshes. Time of death was somewhere in the small hours. Between midnight and 2 a.m., the doc reckoned. There was almost no blood at the scene. He was killed elsewhere and dumped on the marshes.'

'Witnesses?'

'We're making enquiries. It's pretty isolated over there. No one about at night. No doubt that's why it was chosen. I don't hold out much hope of finding anyone who saw anything – maybe a vehicle driving along the track. They must have had a van or a car to transport the body. There are a few houses on the other side of the river, but, you know . . .' Chisholm shrugged. 'Who's looking out of their window at two o'clock in the morning?'

'You releasing a photo of the guy?' Joe said.

'Not a photo, a digital likeness. Basically a doctored photo. He was in a bad state. The crows had been at him. They start with the face, the eyes and mouth in particular.'

Joe grimaced.

'That's going to make it even harder to identify him, isn't it?'

'We don't think he's English. He had dark skin, Mediterranean or Middle Eastern, and his clothes weren't English. We're having them checked. From the labels, I'd guess they were Turkish. He was a Muslim, or maybe Jewish. He'd been circumcised. And no, I didn't verify that fact personally. It was in the autopsy report.'

'There are plenty of Turks in that area. You think he's a local man?'

'The clothes are a puzzle. If he was local, I'd expect him to be wearing something – shoes, a shirt, some item at least – that was bought here. He could be a new arrival.'

'Illegal?'

'Not necessarily. He might have come in on a visitor's visa. We're checking immigration records at ports and airports. He could've been a courier.'

'Drugs, you mean?'

'You know what Stoke Newington's like. The fucking Turks pretty much control the heroin trade. There are at least three or four established Turkish mafia families and lots of small gangs underneath them. Killings aren't unusual.'

'You think he was murdered because of a drugs squabble?'

'It's possible. We really don't know at the moment.'

Chisholm picked up his glass of whisky and downed it in one. He looked at Joe.

'As you're asking,' he said. 'Yeah, I *will* have another. And why don't you get in a round for the lads while you're here?'

Joe sighed and took out his wallet again. It was going to be another expensive night.

6

The journey out of London in the mini-van had been un-comfortable – though nothing like as bad as the trip across Europe in the back of the lorry. The twelve of them were packed tightly together. Irena could smell the bodies around her, feel their warmth, their breath wafting over her. With every corner, every movement of the van they were jolted against one another, knees and elbows clashing, soft flesh squeezing into other soft flesh. Irena hated it. She kept her bag on her lap, her arms wrapped around it, and closed her eyes, trying to sleep, to shut out the unpleasant surroundings. But it was impossible even to doze. It was too cramped, she could feel every rut in the road through the thin mattress – and she couldn't get Ismail out of her mind. His vivid image would not allow her to rest.

The short duration of the journey was its only redeeming factor. After an hour and a half the van came to a halt, the engine died and the rear doors were thrown open. The passengers climbed out. They were in a floodlit carpark outside a large green metal-sided building that was surrounded by fields. Another mini-van was pulling in next to them and more workers were getting out. They all seemed to know where they were going. Irena followed them into the green building where a foreman, an Englishman in grubby overalls, made them line up by the door. He divided them into four groups, gave them each a pair of yellow rubber gloves and barked some instructions that Irena couldn't understand. The groups moved off. As Irena came past, the foreman stopped her and pointed to her bag, saying something. She looked at him blankly. He reached out, trying to take the bag away from her. Irena clung on to it doggedly until, realising that he was simply going to store it somewhere out of the way, she let him take it.

The building was a vast industrial shed. The walls were the same on the inside as the outside – great sheets of green metal riveted together on an exposed framework of steel pillars and girders. Bluish fluorescent lights hung from the steel rafters, illuminating the production line in the middle of the shed, but leaving the outer reaches of the building in darkness. It reminded Irena of Memet Dil's garage, only this was much bigger and it didn't reek of petrol. It had an earthy, vegetable smell, a strong smell despite the fact that the shed was air-conditioned. There were big silver ducts in the roof sucking air out and pumping it back in through metal grids. Irena could feel the draught on her arms. It was cool, much cooler than the temperature outside.

The day shift workers were still at their positions along the conveyor belts that ran the full length of the shed. There was no break between shifts, no period of shutdown, however brief. The conveyor belts kept running, the produce kept coming. One group simply stepped aside and the new arrivals, Irena included, took their places.

A continuous stream of potatoes was moving past, fed on to the conveyor belt from a massive hopper at one end. Irena was standing in between a sallow-skinned woman and a pale, pasty-faced man who smelt of sweat. The man had been in Irena's van, but the woman she didn't recognise. She must have come in the other van. They'd both obviously done this job before for they immediately started picking potatoes off the conveyor belt and throwing them into a couple of metal vats behind them. Irena watched for a moment, trying to work out what they were doing.

The sallow-skinned woman glanced at her in irritation.

'No stand. Work,' she said in fractured English.

Irena gave her a bewildered look. The woman gestured impatiently at the potatoes, then picked one off the conveyor belt and held it up to show Irena.

'This bad,' she said, tossing the potato over her shoulder into the vat. She picked up another potato. 'This too small. You understand?' She threw that one away too.

Irena nodded. She had enough English to work out what she was being told. She studied the potatoes spread out across the conveyor belt, all different sizes and shapes, the earth from the field still clinging to them. She spotted a black one and picked it up and threw it into the vat. A half-rotten potato was next. It was soft and squashy. A smear of yellowish pulp stuck to the palm of Irena's rubber glove.

The pasty-faced man said something to her, clearly annoyed. He was jabbing a finger at the numerous sub-standard specimens she'd let past and that he had had to remove and discard.

'Too small, too small,' he said.

Irena forced a smile, trying to placate him. The bad potatoes were easy to spot, but how was she to know exactly which ones were too small? She picked up two she thought were borderline and held them out to the man, asking for guidance. He took the one in her right hand and tossed it back on to the conveyor belt.

'That OK,' he said.

The one in her left hand he threw into a vat.

'That not OK.'

Now she knew. Anything smaller than a hen's egg had to be rejected, even if it was a healthy potato. Exactly why she couldn't fathom – they were certainly good enough to eat – but it wasn't her business to question the system. It was all she could do to keep pace with the production line. She'd worked in an office in Diyarbakir, a clerical job that had had

66

its demands, its dull moments, but nothing like this. She'd never had to do anything as repetitive and monotonous as sort potatoes. It was mindless, but physically exhausting. There was nothing to it, yet you couldn't relax, you had to concentrate, stay alert. After a couple of hours she had sore feet from standing up, back ache from continually leaning forward to remove potatoes, and a headache from the noise of the machinery and the harsh lighting.

Occasionally there was a short break when the flow of potatoes temporarily dried up – one hopper emptying and a new one coming on stream – but they were never more than a couple of minutes long.

After four hours of this hard, tedious grind, the conveyor belt shuddered to a halt. Irena looked round, wondering what was happening. Workers were moving away, some heading outside into the carpark, others slumping down to the floor to rest. The pasty-faced man took a dog-eared sandwich out of his pocket and began to eat it. The sallow-skinned woman looked at Irena, peeling off her rubber gloves.

'Break,' she said. She held up her fingers. 'Fifteen minutes.'

Irena nodded, showing she'd understood. The woman pointed at herself and said, 'Yasmin.' Then she pointed at Irena. Irena got the message. She was about to give her real name, but then remembered what Anwar had put on the form in London.

'Sakar,' she said.

'Sakar?' Yasmin said. 'You come.'

She gestured at Irena to follow her and walked away across the shed. They went through a door at the side of the building into the ladies' toilets. Yasmin disappeared into one of the cubicles. Irena looked at herself in the mirror. The artificial lighting was unflattering, but even so she was surprised at how drawn and haggard her face was. Her eyes seemed to have sunk into their sockets, her skin was pale and blotchy. She filled a basin with warm water and immersed her hands in it. She was cold. Her long dress kept her lower half reasonably warm, but her arms and shoulders – even with her shawl wrapped around them – had been chilled by the air conditioning. She bathed her face, then dried herself, by which time Yasmin had emerged from the cubicle.

'This your first time?' Yasmin asked as she washed her hands.

Irena struggled to piece together a simple reply.

'English, no,' she said.

'You don't speak English? Where you from?' Yasmin pointed to herself again. 'Me, from Yemen. You know Yemen? In Middle East.' She pointed at Irena. 'You? Where you from?'

Irena shrugged. She couldn't follow what Yasmin was saying.

'Don't matter,' Yasmin said. 'You want?' She indicated the toilet cubicle. 'Time to go. You late, foreman get angry. He shout.'

Yasmin turned away and started to talk to another woman who'd just entered the room. Irena took the opportunity to use the toilet. She felt sick with fatigue. She wanted to rest her head against the wall of the cubicle and go to sleep. She wasn't even halfway through the shift. How was she going to survive to the end?

'You OK?' Yasmin said, knocking on the door.

'Yes, OK,' Irena replied.

'I go back now. Don't be late.'

For the next four hours, Irena continued to sort potatoes. The gruelling monotony of the task didn't change, but she found a way of coping with it, a way of conserving her resources so that she used only the absolute minimum amount of energy to carry out the work. The secret was to think of nothing while you did it. You had to let your mind relax into a zombie-like trance. All your movements had to be reflex, an automatic action devoid of conscious thought. Your eyes saw a sub-standard potato, your hands reached out and removed it from the conveyor belt. There was nothing in between. The whole process had to bypass the brain or it would drive you insane.

At the end of the four hours there was another fifteen minute break. Irena went to the toilets again and warmed her frozen hands up in a basin of hot water. She was stiff and tired, but less so than she'd been the previous break. She was pacing herself better, building up a greater stamina.

The final part of the shift, the production line swapped from potatoes to onions, though Irena's job remained pretty much the same. She was still picking out bad or undersized specimens and throwing them away into metal vats. What happened to the other onions, the ones that stayed on the conveyor belt, she didn't know. They passed through some enclosed machinery in the centre of the shed – she could see that from where she was standing – but she had little idea of what became of them after that. Presumably they were packed into boxes or sacks to be transported to market. There were more people down at the far end of the line – Irena caught glimpses of figures moving, forklift trucks reversing in and out – but they were too distant for her to work out exactly what they were doing. The industrial scale of the whole operation astonished her. In Diyarbakir there were no packhouses like this. The local farmers simply brought their fruit and vegetables in every morning on carts and set up stall in the market square. The produce they sold had been in the field the day before, sometimes it had been picked that very morning. No one cared how big or small the onions were so long as they were fresh and good to eat.

It was only when she heard movements behind her, glanced round and saw the foreman lining up a new group of workers, that she realised the shift was over. A great wave of relief engulfed her. Thank goodness! She could rest now.

She collected her bag from the corner where the foreman had deposited it and followed the other night shift workers outside. After the gloomy artificial environment of the packhouse, the sunshine was dazzling. Irena squinted, letting her eyes get used to the light.

The Pakistani youth who'd driven them up from London was standing beside his mini-van, chatting to the driver of the van parked alongside. From their body language, the way the Pakistani youth nodded at her as she came out of the packhouse, Irena guessed they were talking about her. The youth waved her over.

'You're the one who wants to stay, aren't you?' he said.

Irena stared at him helplessly.

'You . . . want . . . stay . . . yes?' the youth said, breaking the sentence up into pieces and speaking slowly and loudly, as if he were dealing with a half-wit. When Irena still didn't understand, he reverted to his normal East End vernacular.

'Stupid bitch. Doesn't speak fucking English. She's the one, I know. You got room for her?'

'Probably,' the other driver replied. He was English, a stocky, pockmarked man with short, tightly-curled blond hair. 'She got a name?'

'You care?'

'No. What about the shift she's just done? The money.'

'Khan will take that.'

'He going to send it on to her?'

The Pakistani youth laughed cynically.

'What do you think?'

The other driver grinned.

'What is she? Her nationality, I mean.'

'How the fuck should I know? Turkish, Iraqi, Arab, who gives a toss? You taking her, or not?'

The English driver looked at Irena and jerked his thumb towards the back of his van.

'Get in. You're coming with us.'

Yasmin and the other workers were already inside the van. It was just like the other van – no windows, bare metal sides, no seats. Instead of mattresses on the floor, this van had slabs of foam rubber that had originally been yellow but were now a dirty brown colour. Irena squeezed in next to Yasmin. Yasmin glanced at her and gave a tired smile, but didn't say anything. No one else was talking. Some were already dozing off, their heads lolling on their chests.

Irena leant back on the metal side and closed her eyes, trying not to think about her aching muscles, the pain in her legs and back. It was warm in the van, a welcome change from the frigid interior of the packhouse. The motion was soothing, soporific. Irena was drifting into unconsciousness when the van came to a halt. The rear doors banged open and the male workers – five of them – clambered over the seven women and out on to the street. The women were dropped off a few minutes later outside a shabby terraced house.

'You're staying here,' the driver said to Irena.

He turned to Yasmin.

'Sort her out, will you? I'll come back later and do the paperwork.'

There were two rooms on the ground floor of the house: a grubby kitchen at the back and a living room at the front that had been turned into sleeping accommodation – not strictly a bedroom for there were no beds, just three stained mattresses on the floor.

'We go upstairs,' Yasmin said.

There were two more bedrooms on the first floor, again with mattresses rather than beds, three crammed together in each tiny room so that there was barely space to walk between them.

'You take that one,' Yasmin said, pointing at a mattress.

Irena slumped down. There were no curtains in the room, but a sheet had been pinned over the window to keep out the light. Yasmin was already stretched out on her own mattress, her eyes closed. Irena pulled a dirty blanket over her legs and curled up on her side, her hold-all under her head as a pillow. Almost immediately, she was asleep.

'Nice piece this morning,' DCI Louise Crawford said acidly, pausing to talk to Joe before she went into the press conference. She had a bundle of newspapers and a grey cardboard file under her arm.

'Thanks,' Joe said.

'You're very well informed.'

She looked at him coolly, then glanced at Danny Chisholm who was standing next to her. Chisholm kept his face inscrutable.

'I'm surprised you're here,' Crawford continued. 'What can I possibly tell you that you don't know already?'

'Oh, I'm sure there'll be something. Did I get anything wrong?'

'No. You were pretty much spot on about everything. That's what worries me.'

'I like to get my facts right.'

'A journalist who's concerned about accuracy. Now there's a first,' Crawford said.

She moved on past him. Danny Chisholm swung open the door to the conference room and held it for her. There were fewer than a dozen journalists inside the room: the crime correspondents of the national dailies, reporters from the *Evening Standard* and Press Association, a young lad from the local Hackney weekly and a camera crew from the BBC – their regional, not national news department. A body on Walthamstow Marshes, a foreign, unidentified male, possibly a victim of a drugs turf skirmish, was not going to be the lead on the Ten O'Clock News.

Joe sat at the back, his notebook open on his knee, but he

didn't take many notes. He already knew most of the key facts about the case, had covered them in the story he'd filed the previous evening. Nothing much had changed overnight. The dead man's identity was still unknown. No witnesses had been found who could shed any light on where and why he'd been killed, or how his body had come to be dumped on the marshes. The real purpose of the press conference was for the police to try to rectify that situation by appealing for witnesses to come forward and by issuing a photographic likeness of the deceased to see if anyone recognised him.

Joe studied one of the sheets of paper Danny Chisholm had handed out to everyone in the room, the computer-enhanced electronic reconstruction of the dead man's face. It was a young man's face, a strong, handsome face. Joe wondered who he was – who he'd been, rather. Did anyone care? To the police, to the journalists in the room, he was just another corpse. A puzzle to be solved, a story to fill a few column centimetres. If no one knew who he was, did it really matter how and where he'd died?

Even with questions from the assembled reporters, the conference was over in less than forty minutes. Joe slipped his notebook into his pocket and left New Scotland Yard, handing in his visitor's pass at the front desk. He went back to his car and called the newsdesk, telling Ed Preston about the press conference, saying he'd bring the photographic likeness in later. Then he drove up to Stoke Newington. The detailed, hour-by-hour progress of the police investigation was closed off to him. He had no access to forensic reports or other internal information, except for any dribs and drabs the Met's press office might release during the day, but what he *could* do was follow the inquiry on the ground, where it made contact with the general public.

A team of uniformed officers had been deployed in Stoke Newington to try to identify who the dead man was – Crawford had touched on that in the course of the press conference. Joe left his car in a side street and went out into the main shopping area on Stoke Newington High Street. He saw a couple of officers immediately, a male and a female constable equipped with clipboards and the photographic likeness of the murdered man. They were approaching pedestrians, showing them the likeness, asking if the face looked familiar in any way. It was a long shot, but worth a try. If the dead man was from the local Turkish community, or visiting from Turkey, then there was a possibility that someone might just recognise him.

Joe introduced himself to the two officers.

'Mind if I tag along for a bit?'

The officers shrugged indifferently.

'There's not much to see,' the male constable said.

'You making any progress?' Joe asked.

'Not so far.'

'How many of you are there?'

'Six. Spread out up the High Street. Another two are concentrating on the Turkish and Kurdish Community Centre.'

The female constable attempted to stop a passer-by, a dark-skinned woman in a jellaba. The woman reacted defensively, hostile, maybe frightened, veering around the WPC and hurrying away up the street.

'We're getting that a lot,' the WPC said. 'Particularly from the women. They don't like being asked questions.'

'They don't speak English, most of them,' the male constable said dismissively.

'It's not that. Some do. It's cultural. They're wary of strangers approaching them.'

'You need an interpreter with you,' Joe said. 'Or one of the community leaders.'

'Wouldn't make much difference,' the male constable said. 'They don't like the police round here, it's as simple as that.'

'I'll check the shops,' the WPC said.

She went into a Turkish grocers, the window full of dates and nuts and coffee beans, and showed the photo-likeness to the shopkeeper. The male constable stopped a couple of youths who were walking past. They looked at the photo-likeness and shook their heads.

'Waste of time, if you ask me,' the constable said to Joe. 'No one knows who the poor bastard is. And even if they do, they're not going to tell us. Not if it's some drugs killing.'

'Is this your patch?' Joe asked.

The constable nodded.

'Five years I've been at Stoke Newington. I know the area well enough to know that we'll get zip out of the Turks. They're a tight-knit, close-mouthed bunch. Don't like outsiders, especially the law.'

'Is something the matter, constable?'

A tiny elderly lady was blocking their path. She had a shopping bag in each hand, a concerned expression on her face.

'I've watched you stopping people, asking questions,' she went on. 'Has something happened?'

'Nothing to worry about, madam,' the policeman replied. 'We're showing people this picture, that's all.'

He turned his clipboard around to reveal the photo likeness.

'Who is he?' the old lady asked.

'That's what we're trying to find out, madam. He was found on Walthamstow Marshes yesterday.'

'What was he doing on the marshes?'

'Not a lot,' the policeman said dryly. 'He was dead.'

'Dead? Oh, my goodness. How awful!' She peered more closely at the clipboard. 'He looks foreign.'

'We think he may be Turkish.'

'Oh, I don't know any Turkish people. Even though there are a lot of them about. I'm not racist mind. It's just that, well, they do keep themselves to themselves, don't they?'

'Yes, madam, thank you.'

The constable started to edge away, but the old lady wanted to keep talking.

'I was speaking to one only yesterday morning,' she said. 'A Turk, I mean. Well, when I say speaking, I mean *I* was speaking. She didn't seem to know more than a few words of English. Why do they do that? Come over here and not learn our language?'

'I don't know, madam. Now, if you'll . . .'

'Of course, I don't think she'd been here long, so I suppose that's an excuse. She was quite lost, poor dear. I had to show her the flats she was looking for. She seemed on her last legs. Very pale and ill-looking. Stoke Newington's full of them, isn't it? When I was a child, you hardly ever saw a foreign face round here. Now they're all foreign. It's very – what's that word?'

'I don't know, madam.'

'Multi-ethnic. That's what they call it, isn't it? Not that I've anything against it. They work very hard, don't they? Where would we be without them?'

'Yes, well, we have to be getting on.'

The policeman stepped around the old lady and strolled off along the pavement.

'Daft old biddy,' he muttered under his breath as Joe caught up with him.

'You know her?' Joe said.

'Edna something-or-other. She's always hanging around the shopping centre. Nothing better to do.'

The female constable came out of another shop, a kitchen design business with signs outside in both English and Turkish, and joined them on the pavement.

'Nothing,' she said, shaking her head. 'No one has a clue who he is.'

'We could stand here till Christmas and we still wouldn't find out,' the policeman said. 'I told the Sarge that at the station and he agreed with me, but no one gives a rat's arse what we think. Orders from on high. The bloody MIT. They should've kept murder investigations local. What's wrong with our own CID, eh?'

'You take the next few shops,' the WPC said. 'I'll do the street.'

She walked over to a Turkish-looking man who was loitering by a lamp post, smoking a cigarette, and showed him the photo likeness. Her colleague gave an irritated sigh and headed reluctantly for one of the shops. Joe stayed where he was. He'd got enough of a feel for the investigation on the ground now. It would serve no purpose to hang around much longer. He glanced back up the street. The old lady was shuffling slowly away, her shopping bags swinging in her hands. Something about what she'd said bothered him, he wasn't sure exactly why.

He went after her, then reduced his pace to amble along beside her.

'It's Edna, isn't it?' he said.

The old lady stopped and tilted her head back to look up at him. She wore horn-rimmed spectacles with lenses as thick as a magnifying glass.

'Yes. Edna Bullivant. Oh, it's you. You were with the constable, weren't you? Are you a police officer?'

'Journalist.'

'Oh yes? Which paper?'

'*The News.*'

'I don't read it, I'm afraid. I take the *Daily Mail.*'

'Can I ask you something, Edna? When you were talking to us just now, you mentioned a woman, a Turk.'

'Yes, that's right.'

'Someone you met yesterday. You thought she'd maybe only just arrived here. Why did you think that?'

'Why? Well, she was wandering around. I saw her up there by the bakers, then down here. She didn't seem to know where she was. And she looked so unwell, poor thing. You know, distressed.'

'You showed her some flats, you said.'

'Alexander Court. Number six. It's a block on Murray Road, one of those horrible things the council put up in the fifties. That was all the English she knew – the address. I had to take her round there. It was the least I could do. She was only a girl really. She needed looking after.'

'Murray Road?'

'Yes, it's down there. You want me to show you too?'

'Thanks, but I can find it myself.'

Was there anything in it? Joe wondered as he went in search of Murray Road. Possibly, yes. More probably, no. But he'd learnt over the years to go with his gut feelings. Not because they were always right, but because if there was a choice between doing nothing and following his instincts he would always go for the latter, even though they might prove to be wrong.

A dead man on the marshes. Unidentified, probably Turkish, possibly newly-arrived in Britain. A Turkish woman, also possibly newly-arrived, wandering the streets of Stoke Newington in a state of distress. Was there a link? Joe didn't know, but what did he lose by taking a closer look?

Alexandra Court was typical of the post-war social housing that had been erected all over London. As council flats went, they were reasonably attractive buildings – brick, rather than concrete walls, low-rise construction, some thought given to creating open spaces around the blocks, though no thought whatsoever as to how those spaces might sensibly be used. There was a strip of grass along the front and down the sides of the block, but large notices on the walls, reading, NO BALL GAMES. The only patch of potential recreational space for miles around and kids were prohibited from playing on it. No wonder they just hung around on street corners looking for trouble.

The hallway inside was pervaded with the lingering smells of cooking. Not English cooking, but the richer, more exotic aromas of the Middle East – onions, garlic and spices. The door to flat number six was opened by a plump, heavy-boned woman in a long dress. A silk headscarf was wrapped tightly around her head and under her chin so that only the centre of her face was visible.

She stepped back abruptly as she saw Joe outside. She seemed surprised, or maybe she was just uncomfortable being visited by a male stranger, an Englishman she'd never seen before.

'I'm sorry to bother you,' Joe said politely. 'My name's Joe Verdi. I'm a reporter for *The News*.'

The woman frowned.

'Reporter?' she said, as if it were a word she didn't know.

'A newspaper reporter,' Joe said. 'I wanted to ask you about a woman who came here yesterday.'

The woman gave a start. Her eyes narrowed and she backed away. She twisted her head round and called to someone in the flat.

'Khaled!'

A boy emerged from a door along the corridor. The woman said something to him in their own language and the boy came forward. He was about fourteen years old, slightly-built with a thin face and wary eyes. He was wearing jeans and a red T-shirt. He stood protectively in front of his mother, shielding her.

'What is it you want?' he asked Joe. He didn't look English, but he spoke the language with a north London accent.

'I'm asking about a woman who, I believe, came here yesterday.'

'Yeah? A woman?'

The boy's mother said something to him, apparently giving him instructions. He nodded impatiently, gesturing at her to keep out of it, he could handle this.

'You know who I mean?' Joe said.

'No, sorry,' the boy replied. 'We don't know anything about any woman.'

'You sure? She was brought here by an elderly Englishwoman.'

'You must have the wrong flat.'

'She was Turkish.'

'We're not Turkish, we're Kurdish.'

'Maybe she was Kurdish then.'

The boy's mother said something else. Joe couldn't understand the words, but her tone sounded agitated. Her body language alone was giving a clear message to her son: get rid of this man.

'Can't help you,' the boy said. He started to close the door.

'You know a man's body was found on Walthamstow Marshes yesterday?' Joe said.

The boy paused, the door still half open.

'What's that to me?'

'The police think he might have been Turkish – or maybe Kurdish. He was murdered.'

'So?'

Joe took a business card out of his pocket and offered it to the boy. Khaled didn't want to take it, but Joe persisted and in the end Khaled had no choice.

'My number's on there,' Joe said. 'Just in case you want to give me a call.'

The email from Diyarbakir came through in the early afternoon. Memet Dil studied the short message on his computer screen, then printed off a hard copy and deleted the original. There were fifteen names in the message. Thirteen of them Memet already knew. The remaining two were what interested him: Ismail Hourami and Irena Hourami. Husband and wife, one dead, the other on the run somewhere.

Memet called Hasan and Farok into his office and handed them the print-out.

'Hourami,' he said. 'Make enquiries. They must have

80

family in London. Find the relatives, and we find the woman.'

Hasan looked up from the print-out.

'And then?' he said.

Memet gave him an icy stare.

'You know what to do then.'

7

'I want to talk to you.'

It was a boy's voice, tentative, a little nervous. Joe sat up in his chair, paying attention. He pressed the phone tighter against his ear, trying to obliterate the background noise of the newsroom.

'It's Khaled, isn't it?'

'Yes.'

'Where are you, Khaled? At home?'

'No. I'm out in the street, on my mobile. I want to meet.'

'Where? I'll come and pick you up.'

'Not here. Not in Stoke Newington. I'll come to you.'

'You sure?'

'Yes. Where?'

Joe thought about the office, but ruled it out immediately. There was no privacy. It was too big, too intimidating for a youngster like Khaled. Joe sensed he had to take this gently, find some neutral ground on which to meet.

'Can you get a bus into town?' he said. 'There's a café near Liverpool Street Station – the Primrose Café.' Joe gave him directions. 'I'll meet you there in, say, half an hour, forty minutes. Is that okay?'

'Okay,' Khaled said.

Joe made sure he got to the café early. He didn't want Khaled showing up and finding him not there, then getting cold feet and leaving. Joe needed to be waiting, a reassuring presence, when Khaled arrived.

He'd chosen the Primrose Café to put the boy at ease. The name was somewhat misleading for there was nothing remotely flowery or twee about the café. The only blooms in evidence were the dusty carnations in vases in the centre of each table, and they were made of plastic. The real things would have wilted in a matter of hours, overcome by the potent mixture of fried food fumes and grease in the atmosphere. The café had been in business, under various proprietors and several different names, since the end of the Second World War. The décor had changed every decade or so to keep abreast of changing fashion, but the food and the kind of customers the café attracted had remained largely the same. The all-day breakfast, an epicurean delight of staggeringly unhealthy ingredients, was still the most popular item on the menu, followed closely by sausage, egg and bacon on toast – the all-day breakfast by another name – and sausage, egg and bacon in a bap – the all-day breakfast you could eat with your hands, which, given the state of the Primrose's cutlery, was probably the most advisable option. The words 'diet', 'slimline' and 'low-cholesterol' were unknown in the café, if only because the owner – a gargantuan sixteen-stone advertisement for his own cuisine named Eddie Corbett – didn't know how to spell them.

Joe paid for a tea at the counter and sat down at a table facing the door. The tea came in a half-pint mug made of china so thick you could've bounced it off the floor. Joe's father couldn't abide traditional English greasy spoon cafes like the Primrose. He couldn't comprehend how such places survived when there were infinitely superior eating establishments – like his own, for example – just around the corner. But Joe liked the no-frills, unpretentious nature of the Primrose. It was very close to the City. The buildings surrounding it contained banks and insurance companies, most of whose employees would never have dreamt of setting foot in a place like the Primrose. Yet the cafe, that smelly, insignificant, old-fashioned little hole with vinegar and brown sauce bottles on the tables, somehow managed to keep going, to serve its clientele of van drivers and couriers and porters and tradesmen whose unsung labours kept the whole financial district functioning.

Khaled wouldn't feel uncomfortable here. It was relaxed, friendly. No one bothered you if you didn't want to be bothered. Customers came and went all the time, but you could sit at a table for several hours undisturbed if that's what you wanted.

Joe had nearly finished his tea when the youngster arrived. Khaled pushed open the door and came in un-certainly, pausing to look around, then nodding as he saw Joe.

Joe let him get settled in the seat opposite before he asked him if he'd like something to drink. Khaled shook his head.

'You sure?' Joe said. 'You don't want a tea, or a Coke or anything?'

'No.'

Khaled's eyes flickered around the café. No one was taking any notice of them. A man in paint-stained overalls was sitting alone at a table, eating pie and chips, two men in dirty jeans and work boots were chewing on sandwiches and discussing the sports' pages of *The Sun*. Behind the counter, Eddie Corbett was putting a couple of burgers and eggs on the hotplate to fry.

'What about a snack?' Joe said. Khaled was a skinny kid. He looked in need of fattening up, something the Primrose was more than adequately equipped to undertake.

'No.'

Joe didn't push him. He drank some of his tea and waited. Let Khaled begin when he was ready.

Khaled studied him. He saw a man about the same age as his father. Tall, thickening out a little around the waist, but still – unlike Anwar – with a full head of dark hair. He was on the scruffy side, his clothes well worn, but Khaled felt at ease with him. There was something reassuring about his manner, about his gentle voice.

'You're a journalist, yeah?' Khaled said, checking his facts.

'That's right. For *The News*. It was on my card.'

'That's a serious paper, isn't it? Not some crappy tabloid.'

'Yes.'

'So I can trust you?'

'Yes.'

'If someone tells you something, you can keep it secret, can't you? You can protect them.'

'That depends on what they tell me. But yes, I'll always do my best to keep a source confidential.'

Khaled mused on that for a moment. Then he gave a slight nod, seemingly satisfied with Joe's reply.

'OK. What I'm going to tell you, I don't want anyone else to know it came from me. I mean that. This is just between the two of us.'

'How old are you, Khaled?' Joe asked.

'Fourteen.'

'Does your mother know you're here?'

'No. She thinks I've gone round to a friend's.'

'I don't want to make you promises I can't keep,' Joe said. 'That's not the way I work. Why don't you tell me whatever it is you want to say, and then we'll talk about what we might do with that information. How does that sound?'

Khaled hesitated. Joe sensed the youngster badly wanted to talk, to get something off his chest, but he needed to be prompted before he lost his nerve.

'It's about the woman, isn't it?' Joe said. 'The one who came to your flat yesterday.'

'Yes.'

'Who was she?'

'My aunt.'

'What's her name?'

'Irena. Irena Hourami.'

'I'll just make a note of that.'

Joe checked the spelling with Khaled and wrote the name in his notebook.

'Is that your surname too, Hourami?' he asked.

'Yes,' Khaled said. 'My father and Aunt Irena's husband, my Uncle Ismail, are brothers. *Were* brothers,' he corrected himself.

'Were?'

Khaled swallowed. He glanced around the café again.

'That body on the marshes. I think it's my Uncle Ismail.'

'Go on,' Joe said gently.

'My aunt, when she came to the flat, I heard her telling my mum. How it happened. How Uncle Ismail was killed.'

Joe listened intently while Khaled repeated the conversation he'd overheard. The youngster seemed composed, but there was a tremor in his voice that gave away his underlying anxiety.

'You think these men, these Turks, dumped your uncle's body on Walthamstow Marshes?' Joe said.

'I don't know for sure, but it fits. The man on the marshes was stabbed – I heard that on the news this morning. So was Uncle Ismail.'

'You know who the Turks were?'

'Aunt Irena heard a couple of names. Hasan, he was the one who killed Uncle Ismail.'

'Hasan? Nothing more?'

'Just Hasan.'

'And the other name?'

'Memet Dil. He's the boss. A bad man. You wouldn't have heard of him, but everyone round where we live knows who he is. You know, in the Turkish-Kurdish community.'

'What do you mean, "a bad man"?' Joe said.

'Drugs. He runs the drugs business, supplies the dealers, the people who push drugs on the street.'

'How do you know that?'

'I just do.'

'You ever taken drugs?'

Khaled looked shocked at the suggestion.

'No way. Never.'

'So how come you know who supplies them?'

'You think I'm a user?'

'I don't know you, Khaled. You're giving me information about a murder. I'm just trying to find out whom I'm dealing with.'

'You know about the Turks and the Kurds?' Khaled said. 'About what's going on in Turkey – has been for many years.'

'You mean the Kurdish struggle for independence? The PKK, the Turkish repression, all that?'

'You do know then. That's why my uncle and aunt came here. To get away from the Turks, from the police and soldiers back home. They lived in Diyarbakir. You've heard of Diyarbakir?'

Joe shook his head.

'I don't think so.'

'It's in the south-east of Turkey, in the Kurdish area. The Turks, they burnt all the Kurdish villages around Diyarbakir. There's a name for it, for what they did.'

'Scorched earth?' Joe said.

'Yes, that's it. The village people were forced to leave their homes and go to Diyarbakir. There are no jobs there, no decent houses. People my age are joining the *serhildan* – that's what we call the uprising against the Turks. It's terrible. Uncle Ismail was a journalist, like you. He wrote things the Turks didn't like. They arrested him loads of times, beat him up. You English think we're all the same – Kurds and Turks – but we're not. Everything's different, our history, our culture, our language. We don't get on in Turkey. And we don't really get on here either. A Kurdish kid like me, I wouldn't have anything to do with a Turk like Memet Dil, or any of his pushers. But they try to sell drugs to kids like me, younger children too. They don't care who you are – Turk, Kurd, English – you're just a customer to them. You know what they do? They give you a free taste, a couple of free tastes. Heroin, crack, whatever they've got. They get you hooked, then they start to charge.'

'Yes, I know,' Joe said. 'That's standard practice, what all dealers do.'

'Sometimes they force it on you. I have a friend, a Kurdish friend my age. Masoud. He got hassled by a pusher – one of Memet Dil's men. The pusher tried to make Masoud try some drugs. Masoud refused. There was an argument. The pusher came after him, beat Masoud up. He was in hospital for two weeks.'

'And one of Memet Dil's men, this Hasan, killed your uncle?'

'That's what Aunt Irena said.'

'Over money. An argument about extra payment for smuggling them into Britain?'

'Yes.'

'Where's your Aunt Irena now?'

'I don't know. My dad took her to this place in Whitechapel. Bourne Street. A man called Rafiq Khan. He finds work for people. She went in a van up to Norfolk. I don't think even my mum and dad know where she is now.'

'To Norfolk? Why?' Joe said.

'To get her out of London. Dil's men are looking for her.'

Joe picked up his mug of tea and took a sip, giving himself a moment to think. The tea was almost stone cold. He studied Khaled. It was an extraordinary story the boy had recounted. Joe had learnt to be cautious. He'd been told extraordinary tales before that had turned out to be false, but there was an innocence, a directness about Khaled that made Joe sure he was telling the truth.

'You should go to the police with this, you know.'

'No!' Khaled said vehemently. 'No police.'

'It might be the best thing for your aunt.'

Khaled stared at him accusingly.

'You lied to me. You said you could protect a source. You said you'd keep this to yourself.'

Khaled pushed back his chair and started to get up. Joe grabbed his wrist.

'Sit down. Please, Khaled. Just sit down.'

Joe pulled on the boy's arm. Khaled sat down again without offering any resistance.

'Why did you telephone me?' Joe said. 'What did you think I would do with this information?'

Khaled shrugged.

'I don't know. I thought . . . I thought maybe you could put it in the paper. That the Turks would be caught and punished.'

'The police aren't going to arrest and charge these men on the basis of an unsubstantiated newspaper article. An article in which the allegations come from an unnamed "source". It doesn't work like that, Khaled.'

'If I go to the police,' Khaled said. 'They will send my Aunt Irena back to Turkey. She's here illegally. If she goes back to Turkey, she will be killed. Memet Dil will make sure of that.'

'If she gives evidence against him, he won't be in a position to harm her. He'll be behind bars.'

'That makes no difference. He'll find a way. He has contacts in Turkey, people who will do it for him.' Khaled leant over the table. 'Don't you understand, that's why I came to you. I thought you could get the truth out into the open without putting Aunt Irena, or my family, in danger.'

'The police can do nothing to catch Memet without your aunt's evidence,' Joe said. 'She's a witness to a murder. You've given me information that is crucial to the police investigation.'

'You're going to go to the police?'

'I want *you* to go to the police. I'll come with you, if you'd like me to. I know the police officer in charge of the murder investigation. She'll look after you and your aunt, I can promise you that.'

Joe gave the youngster a few moments to think about it. Khaled looked down at the table, chewing on the tip of his thumb, his body tense.

'I don't know,' he said eventually.

'I could call her now,' Joe said. 'We could go straight to her office.'

Khaled said nothing.

'Look,' Joe said. 'I didn't lie to you. What you've told me is confidential, and I will always protect my sources. You have my word on that. I will go to jail rather than reveal a source. But I'm thinking of you and your aunt, Khaled. You've given me information about a serious criminal offence. I won't give that information to the police, but it might be advisable for you to do so.'

Still Khaled said nothing. Joe was acutely aware that he was only a boy. A minor being questioned by a journalist in the absence of his parents. It was perhaps putting undue pressure on him to ask him to make a decision on the spot.

'You want to talk to your mum and dad first?' Joe went on. 'Tell them what I said. Then call me, or go to the police together, the three of you. You're only a teenager. Your parents should be part of this.'

Khaled nodded.

'Yes, OK. Maybe I should talk to them.'

'Give me your mobile number. I'll call you later.'

Joe scribbled down the number, then took out his wallet and gave Khaled a five pound note.

'To cover your bus fares,' he said. 'Take it.'

They went out of the café on to the street.

'You OK?' Joe said.

'Yes.'

'It's the right decision, Khaled. Talk to your parents. Then go to the police.'

* * *

The moment he opened the door, Anwar knew he was in trouble. The two men outside – Turks, he could tell by the look of them – had the hard, pitiless faces of hired thugs. Cold, empty eyes, cruel mouths twisted into permanent snarls, an aggressive manner that betrayed their underlying anger, a violence that threatened to explode at any second.

'Is your name Anwar Hourami?' one of the men demanded. He was speaking Turkish.

Anwar guessed who they were. The realisation filled him with such terror that he panicked, stopped thinking clearly. He tried to slam the door in their faces, but they were too quick for him. The one with the moustache came in first, pushing Anwar back. The other followed, closing the door behind him. Anwar started to protest, but the first man hit him hard in the stomach. Anwar doubled up, gasping, and felt the two men grab hold of him and haul him down the corridor into the living room where Sara was sewing. She leapt up in alarm as she saw the men dragging Anwar in and throwing him to the floor.

'Anwar!' Sara almost screamed the word. 'Anwar, are you . . . who are these people? Anwar?'

She crouched down by her husband. He was too winded to speak. He moaned, wheezing for air. Sara straightened up and faced the two men.

'Who are you? What do you want? You can't just come in here and . . .'

Hasan hit her. Hit her across the face with the flat of his hand so forcefully that she staggered backwards.

'Shut up,' Hasan said. 'Let's start again, shall we?' He looked down at Anwar. 'Is your name Anwar Hourami?'

Anwar nodded, still struggling to breathe. Trying to close the door had been a mistake. It had simply confirmed to these men what they suspected. He had something to hide.

He tried to get to his feet, but Hasan pushed him back down with his foot.

91

'You stay there.'

Hasan looked at Sara. She was rubbing her cheek, in pain and shock from the blow.

'And your name?' Hasan said.

'Sara Hourami.'

'Good. Now we're getting somewhere. We're looking for Irena Hourami. Where is she?'

Anwar gazed up at the Turk. Maybe it wasn't too late to try to bluff their way out of this.

'Who?' Anwar said. 'We don't know any Irena Hourami.'

Hasan glanced at Farok. Their partnership was so well-established, so intuitive, that no words were necessary. Farok stepped behind Sara, his left arm whipping around her waist, pulling her to him. His right hand ripped away her headscarf to expose her neck. Sara felt the edge of a knife on her throat.

'I'll ask you once more,' Hasan said calmly. 'Where is Irena Hourami?'

8

It was late afternoon when Irena awoke. She'd slept for nearly eight hours, but she still felt tired. It was warm in the bedroom, the bright sunlight penetrating the thin cotton sheet over the window. Yasmin wasn't there, but the third mattress was occupied by another sleeping woman Irena had never seen before.

Irena lay on her back and stared up at the ceiling. There was a yellowish patch in one corner where water had obviously leaked through the roof. The wall was also marked by damp, the paper peeling off to reveal a mottled pattern of mould on the plaster underneath. The woman on the mattress was breathing noisily, submerged in the deep, heavy sleep that only the truly exhausted really experience. Her face was tanned, her hands brown and leathery, the fingernails chipped and ingrained with dirt.

The bedroom door was ajar. The smell of cooking drifted in and, faintly, somewhere downstairs, Irena heard the clatter of a metal spoon on a saucepan. She rolled off her mattress and stood up. She found a bathroom at the end of the landing, a cramped little room with a toilet, a basin and an old cast-iron bath with rusty sides and a bluey-green streak beneath each of the taps where dripping water had stained the white enamel.

She fetched her hold-all from the bedroom and washed herself. Then, feeling refreshed and more awake, she went downstairs into the kitchen. Yasmin was standing by the stove, stirring a pan of spiced vegetables. She turned her head as Irena came in.

'Hi, you want drink?'

She pointed to a mug on the table. Irena understood the sign language and nodded, but when she looked in the mug she saw that it was empty.

'No pot for tea,' Yasmin said. 'You make in cup.'

Irena gave her the bewildered shrug that was becoming her stock response to anything said to her in English.

'You no understand?' Yasmin said.

She lifted a pan of boiling water off the stove and filled the mug. Then she took a teabag from a box in a cupboard and immersed it in the hot water.

'This how they make it here,' she said.

Irena watched the colour leaching out of the teabag, turning the water brown. She'd never seen a teabag before.

'Tea?' she said. That was one word in English she did know.

'Yes, tea,' Yasmin said.

She went back to her stirring. Whatever it was in the pan, it smelt good. Irena was hungry, thirsty too. She sat down at the table, picked up the mug of tea and sipped it. The flavour was weak, but the liquid was what she needed.

'No, no,' Yasmin said. 'You take out.'

She removed the mug from Irena's grasp and scooped out the teabag with a spoon.

'English way,' she said, handing the mug back. 'You sleep good?'

She put her palms together against her cheek and made a loud snoring noise. Irena couldn't help laughing. As she heard the sound, she realised it was the first time she'd laughed since she'd left Turkey. Immediately she felt guilty. Ismail was dead and here she was drinking tea and laughing.

'When you arrive?' Yasmin asked.

'Uh?'

'When you arrive in England?'

When? Irena knew that word too. She held up her fingers.

'Two day,' she said.

'Today? Oh, two *days*. OK.'

Yasmin tried the question she'd already asked in the packhouse toilets.

'Where you from?'

'Where?' Irena said.

'Yes, where?' Yasmin pointed at her. 'Where from? Which country?'

Irena nodded, pleased with herself. She'd understood the question. The problem was she didn't know the English for Kurdistan, or even Turkey. So she gave the name of her home town.

'Diyarbakir.'

Yasmin screwed up her face.

'Where that?'

'Diyarbakir,' Irena repeated.

'Don't matter,' Yasmin said. 'You want some of this? I make lots.'

She put the pan of vegetables down on the table and took a couple of plates and two forks from the draining board next to the sink. The kitchen was sparsely furnished. There was the cooker, the table and three cheap wooden chairs and that was about it. There was no refrigerator or washing machine and only one cupboard on the wall.

Yasmin spooned the vegetables out on to the plates.

'You eat,' she said.

Irena tried a mouthful. The dish was mainly potatoes and onions mixed with chunks of fennel and flavoured with garlic and chillis.

'Good?' Yasmin said.

'Yes, good,' Irena replied.

She ate some more, trying to control the urge to bolt the food she was so ravenous. Yasmin sat down at the end of the table and concentrated on her own plate. She was probably ten years older than Irena, a slight, narrow-shouldered woman with a careworn face.

'What language you speak?' Yasmin asked.

When Irena didn't reply, Yasmin repeated the question in her Arabic dialect. Irena looked even more confused.

'Don't matter,' Yasmin said. 'We speak English. You here alone? You have husband? I have husband, two children. They in Yemen. I work here, send money to them. You understand? No, don't matter. You eat.'

When they'd finished the meal, Irena took out one of the ten pound notes Anwar had given her and offered it to Yasmin.

'For food,' she said.

Yasmin waved the money away.

'You keep. Buy food another day, OK? Today, I cook.'

They washed up and stacked the plates neatly on the draining board to dry. Yasmin was wiping the table when the pockmarked driver of the mini-van, Lenny, arrived. He came through into the kitchen, pulled out a chair and sat down. He placed the file he was carrying on the table and gestured at Irena to sit down.

'I need some information from you,' he said.

Irena frowned at him, then shrugged.

'You know what I'm saying?' Lenny went on. 'Paperwork. You got a passport?'

'She don't speak English,' Yasmin said.

Lenny didn't take any notice.

'A *passport*,' he said, emphasising the word.

Irena shook her head blankly.

'You got any papers at all?' Lenny said.

'No English,' Irena said.

Lenny gave a sigh of annoyance. These fucking towel-heads, it was always the same. He looked at Yasmin.

'You know anything about her? Like her name.'

'She called Sakar,' Yasmin said.

'Sacka?' Lenny said. 'Sacka what? Sacka shit?' He laughed at his own joke. 'Where's she from?'

'She say something, but I don't know what is. Diyarbakir. Where that?'

'You're asking me? I don't even know where fucking Norwich is.'

Lenny opened his file and riffled through the papers inside. He pulled out a sheet that had already been filled in for a Portuguese woman named Ligia Moreira – a woman who'd done a few weeks' work and then vanished, Lenny had no idea where. She'd probably gone elsewhere in Britain, the Portuguese were all over the place, or maybe back to her own country. Lenny was used to it. Very few workers stayed for long – the work was too hard and badly paid. Most of them were illegals, but the Portuguese were different. They were EU, legitimate. Making this woman – Sacka whatever – Portuguese simplified things. Lenny could easily get her a Portuguese i.d. card – forging Portuguese documents was a thriving industry in Thetford. It saved him filling in a new form and would satisfy the wankers at Immigration if they ever came calling.

'You're Ligia Moreira now,' Lenny said to Irena. 'OK?'

'Uh?' Irena said.

Why was he bothering? She had no idea what he was saying.

'You're Portuguese.' Lenny glanced at Yasmin, still standing over by the sink. 'Tell her she's Ligia Moreira, from Portugal.'

'How I do that?' Yasmin said. 'You just tell her. She no understand.'

OK, fuck that, Lenny thought. Simply tell her the rest, then he was covered with his boss: not that Frank – the gangmaster, a fifty-five-year-old lardarse who never left his office – would give a shit.

'I'll get you papers, an i.d. card,' Lenny said. 'The cost will be deducted from your wages. You can stay here with

Yasmin and the others. We'll deduct £50 a week for rent, OK? That's it.'

He put the sheet of paper back in his file and stood up.

'I'm coming earlier tonight,' he said to Yasmin. 'Six o'clock.'

'Six?' Yasmin said.

'We've a job up near King's Lynn. Make sure you're ready.'

Joe watched the figures in the glass-walled office at the far end of the newsroom and checked his watch again. The early evening editorial conference was usually over by this time. What the hell were they doing in there? He could see the editor at his desk, the chief sub and the other editors spread around the office: Features, Sports, Financial, International and Home news. Ed Preston, the Home news editor, was slouched in the corner of a modern, steel-framed sofa, his bald pate glistening in the low sunlight that streamed in through the gaps in the window blinds behind his head. Joe wondered if he could attract his attention, but Preston wasn't looking his way.

Joe stood up from his chair and wandered over to the water cooler, filling a plastic beaker and sipping it, trying to contain his impatience. It was half an hour since he'd left Khaled at the bus stop outside Liverpool Street Station, ten minutes since he'd got back to the office to find the news editor in conference. He needed to speak to Preston, speak to him urgently, but the conference was showing no signs of ending.

Joe stared hard at Preston's profile, willing him to turn his head. The news editor was talking now, his hands moving theatrically, emphasising some point he was making. The editor, small and neat in his black leather chair, nodded, then looked sideways. One of the other editors was joining in. Joe could bear it no longer.

He dumped his beaker of iced water in the bin and marched purposefully across the newsroom. There were reporters at their desks, on the phone or tapping away at their keyboards. Ellie Mason looked up and said, 'hi', but Joe didn't pause. He knocked on the door of the editor's office and went in. He apologised for interrupting.

'Ed, could I have a word, please? It's important.'

Preston looked at him, noting the tight expression on Joe's face, then he collected his papers together and followed Joe out of the office.

'What is it?'

'Not here,' Joe said.

They went into the interview room, a small office at the side of the open-plan newsroom that reporters could use when they needed somewhere quieter, more private to talk.

'Sorry to drag you out,' Joe said.

The room contained a rectangular desk and phone and four chairs. Joe took one of the chairs. Preston sat down opposite him. He was a tall man, with a heavy, pear-shaped body. He was in his shirtsleeves, his tie and collar loosened. Joe could smell the faint odour of sweat that always hung about the news editor at this stage of the day.

'That's OK,' Preston said. 'I was getting bored in there anyway. What's the problem?'

Joe told him about Khaled, their conversation in the Primrose Café. When he'd finished, Preston leaned back in his chair and said, 'Jesus.'

'What do we do?' Joe said.

Preston massaged the nape of his neck with one hand. He had thick mats of dark hair on the backs of his hands and on his forearms and chest, tufts poking out from beneath his shirt cuffs and collar, as if his body were compensating for the lack of hair on his head.

'This woman, the boy's aunt,' he said. 'She actually witnessed her husband's murder?'

'It happened right in front of her, according to Khaled. She took off into the night, slept rough in the cemetery, then went to the kid's house.'

'And this guy – Ismail Hourami? – he's the body on the marshes?'

'I'd put money on it. What's our position, Ed? Khaled came to me in confidence. He's only fourteen. He was obviously in a state of turmoil, didn't know what to do. He wants to protect his aunt and have the killers caught, but he doesn't want to go to the police.'

'Because his aunt's an illegal.'

'And because he's wary of the police, I think. He's Kurdish. He seems to have grown up here – sounds like a Londoner – but you know how it is. Ethnic minorities and the Met. You can understand why he might not be too keen on popping into Stoke Newington station.'

'You make him any promises?'

'I told him I'd protect him. But I also told him to talk to his parents, then go to the police. His uncle's been murdered, his aunt's in danger. Only the police can help her.'

'You think he *will* go to the police?'

'I don't know. I've never had to deal with anything like this before. I know what the PCC Code of Practice says – 'Journalists have a moral obligation to protect confidential sources of information'. But that usually applies when revealing the source will harm them – compromise them, get them sacked or jailed, something like that. This is different. What's our moral obligation in this case?'

'The same,' Preston said. 'A moral obligation has to be absolute. We protect our sources, whatever the circumstances. If Khaled wants to go to the police, that's his decision, not ours.'

'But he's just a boy. I'm worried for him, Ed.'

'Are you absolutely sure he was telling you the truth?'

'Yes, I'm sure.'

Preston rubbed his neck again, staring pensively across the room.

'I'll talk to the editor, see what he thinks.'

The news editor started to get to his feet. He was halfway

up when Joe's mobile phone rang. Joe pulled the phone out of his pocket.

'Joe Verdi.'

It was Khaled, though it took Joe a few seconds to realise it. The youngster was sobbing, clearly in distress, his words garbled and incoherent.

'They're dead . . . I got home . . . found them . . . blood everywhere . . . my mum, my dad . . . they're dead . . .'

'Khaled,' Joe interrupted. 'Take it easy. I'm listening. You say your parents are dead?'

'Didn't you hear? They're . . . fuck, it's awful. The blood. They're dead.'

He broke off into another fit of sobs. Joe could hear him choking, gulping for air.

'Khaled, where are you? In the flat?'

Khaled didn't reply.

'Are you in the flat?' Joe repeated.

'Yes.' The word was barely audible.

'Have you phoned the police?'

'The police? No.'

'I'll call them for you. I'm coming over too. Khaled, stay where you are, you understand. Don't touch anything. The police will be there very soon.'

Joe rang off, then immediately punched in 999. He asked for the police, and ambulance – just in case Khaled was wrong about his parents – gave the emergency operator the details, the address. He jabbed the 'off' button with his thumb. Ed Preston hadn't moved.

'His parents have been killed,' Joe said.

'Murdered?'

'Sounds like it.'

'Shit!'

'I'll call in, let you know what's happening.'

Joe pulled open the office door and sprinted across the newsroom.

9

A line of police cars and an ambulance were already parked outside Alexandra Court when Joe got there. He left his car further up the street and walked back to the main entrance to the flats. A uniformed constable stopped him from going inside the building. Joe showed his press card.

'I'm the person who called you,' he said. 'There's a young boy, the son, Khaled Hourami. Is he OK? Where is he?'

'The son?'

'He phoned me when he found his parents.'

'I'm sorry, sir, I can't tell you anything.'

'I need to know how Khaled is. Is he still inside the flat?'

'I don't know who's inside.'

'Who's in charge?' Joe said. 'Is it DCI Crawford, this is her patch?'

The name seemed to have an impact on the constable.

'DCI Crawford?'

'From the Homicide Command. Is she here? This is important.'

'I believe she is.'

'Would you let her know that Joe Verdi's here.'

The constable hesitated for a moment, reluctant to leave his post. Then he opened the half-glazed door behind him and went into the block of flats. Another marked police car arrived and two more uniformed officers got out. Joe drifted away from the entrance, not wanting to hinder the police operation. The ambulance was at the kerb right next to him, its rear doors ajar. He could hear a voice inside. A man's voice, soft, calming, talking to someone. Of course. They wouldn't have left him in the flat.

Joe eased open one of the doors. Khaled was sitting on the edge of a wheeled stretcher, leaning forward with his arms on his legs. He was breathing heavily, panting as if he were ill. There was a paramedic on either side of him. One was ready with a disposable paper sick bag.

'Just breathe out, try to relax,' one of the paramedics was saying. 'That's it, you're doing fine.'

The paramedic turned his head and saw Joe. Khaled did-n't look up. He was gazing at the floor, his body rigid, his eyes barely blinking.

'How is he?' Joe said.

The paramedic nearest the door stood up and climbed down from the ambulance. Joe followed him a few metres along the pavement.

'You a police officer?' the paramedic asked.

'I know the boy, Khaled,' Joe replied. 'How's he doing?'

'Khaled, is that his name? We haven't got a word out of him since we arrived. He's in shock. Badly shaken up. Who wouldn't be?'

'His parents . . . he phoned me when he got home.'

The paramedic shook his head.

'There was nothing we could do for them. You're not a relative?'

'No.'

'You know if he has family nearby?'

'I don't know. He may have. What's going to happen to him?'

'We'll take him to hospital. Get him checked over. They'll probably keep him in overnight. Maybe longer.'

'Can I talk to him?'

'Better not for the moment.'

'Have the police spoken to him yet?'

'Not so far. He's not up to answering questions, poor kid. What he saw . . . Christ, it doesn't bear thinking about.'

'Let me talk to him,' Joe said. 'Just a quick word. He knows me.'

'Well, I'm not sure . . .'

'I won't push him, don't worry.'

Joe went back to the ambulance and climbed inside. This time Khaled looked up. Joe crouched down in front of the boy. Khaled stared at him with blank, vacant eyes. He showed no sign of recognition.

'It's me, Khaled. Joe Verdi. You called me, remember?'

Khaled didn't reply. Joe wondered why he'd asked to speak to him. What was he going to say to the boy? Ask him how he was? Maybe he didn't really want to speak to him. What he wanted was for Khaled to know he was there. That he'd come. And that he cared.

'Khaled,' Joe said. 'You're going to be OK. The paramedics will look after you. So will the . . .'

Joe stopped. What was the point of words? There was nothing to say. He could see that Khaled wasn't registering anything. It was as if he were concussed, in a daze. Joe took the boy's hands in his own, then, impulsively, put his arms around him. Khaled was a child. What he needed was someone to hug him. The physical contact seemed to break the trance. Khaled gave a start. His arms came up around Joe's back and he began to sob, his whole body shuddering. Joe held him, Khaled clinging tight to him, until the spasms subsided.

'We'd better get him to hospital,' one of the paramedics said.

Joe pulled away. Khaled's face was wet with tears, his eyes tormented by an unbearable pain.

'I'm going to talk to the police,' Joe said. 'Tell them what you told me. It'll help them catch the people who did this. Is that OK?'

Khaled didn't seem to hear what Joe had said.

'Khaled, is that OK?'

'That's enough,' the paramedic said, pushing Joe gently back. 'He needs to see a doctor.'

Joe nodded.

'I'll be in touch, Khaled.'

Joe climbed out of the ambulance. One of the paramedics came after him and closed the doors, then went round to the front and got into the driver's seat. Joe watched the ambulance pull away. He thought about Khaled in the back, wondering how anyone, never mind a fourteen-year-old child, could get through the traumatic ordeal he'd just experienced.

Louise Crawford and Danny Chisholm were coming out of the flats. Chisholm broke away, heading for one of the police cars, but Crawford walked straight over to Joe. She looked tense, the colour had drained from her face. Whatever had happened, Joe knew it must be particularly harrowing.

'Let's go to my car,' she said curtly.

Joe waited until they were inside the car, Crawford behind the wheel, before he said, 'How were they killed?'

'Their throats were cut,' Crawford said.

'Jesus. And Khaled found them.'

Joe closed his eyes, trying to get the image out of his head. Crawford looked at him.

'Let's start at the beginning,' she said. 'First, the emergency call you made.'

'Khaled – the son – phoned me,' Joe said. 'He'd got home and found his parents.'

'Why you? Do you know the family?'

'No. But I met Khaled earlier this afternoon.'

'Met? Why?'

'He wanted to talk to me.'

'About what?'

Joe hesitated. He was in a dilemma. He was being asked for information that Khaled had given him in confidence.

How far should he take his moral obligation to protect a source? Was that obligation really as absolute as Ed Preston had claimed, or were there circumstances when public duty, when a personal sense of responsibility had to override journalistic principles? Khaled's mother and father were dead, murdered in the most horrific way. If Joe had information that might lead to the killers being caught, did he not have a moral obligation to give that information to the police?

Crawford was waiting impatiently. Joe could sense her simmering in the seat beside him. His mind was being torn in two. Keep a confidence, or share it? The ethics were too complex for him to analyse right now, so he did what his heart said was the right thing – what he believed Khaled would have wanted, what he felt the boy himself would have done if he'd been in a fit state.

'About the body on the marshes,' Joe said.

'Go on,' Crawford said.

Joe told her what he knew. About the old lady, Edna Bullivant, about his visit to the Hourami's flat, Khaled calling him, their conversation in the café. Everything. Crawford listened in silence, not interrupting once. Even when he'd finished she didn't say anything. Then she let out a long sigh, staring straight ahead through the windscreen.

'What the fuck were you playing at?' she said. 'Why didn't you come to us straight away?'

'I'm not a police officer, I'm a journalist,' Joe replied.

'You wanted the story, didn't you? The story, your "exclusive", was more important than our investigation.'

Joe was guiltily aware that there was some truth in that accusation.

'Two people are dead, Mr Verdi,' Crawford said. 'You want to go in there and take a look at them?'

Joe bridled at that. His anger flared momentarily.

'Don't put that on me. I didn't kill them.'

'You don't feel responsible in any way?'

'Yes, I do. I do feel responsible, even though I know I'm *not* responsible.'

'You should've called us after you met Khaled. We could've prevented this happening.'

'Listen, I was standing right next to a police constable when Edna Bullivant mentioned the woman she'd met. The constable heard every word she said. He could've picked up on it, followed it up, but he didn't.'

'You think that's an excuse?'

'I don't need an excuse. I've done nothing wrong.'

'No?'

'I have codes too, you know. Rules, guidelines I work by. I talk to a lot of people in the course of my job. Sometimes they're dodgy individuals, criminals even, but I don't shop them to the police. I couldn't survive as a journalist if people thought I was a copper's nark.'

'This isn't the same thing, and you know it.'

'Isn't it? Khaled came to me in confidence. He gave me information in confidence. That has some meaning to me. I urged him to talk to his parents and then go to the police.'

'You should have done that yourself. You withheld vital evidence in a murder inquiry. I can't overlook that fact,' Crawford said.

'Withheld? What the hell do you mean by that? Let's look at the timescale here, shall we? I met Khaled in the café at about four-thirty. I left him at around five, got back to the office at five-twenty. My boss was in conference so I couldn't speak to him immediately, but I did as soon as it was possible – about five thirty-five. And that's when Khaled called. Where's the "withholding evidence" in that?'

'We could've got to the flat before the killers.'

'You don't know that. You can't pinpoint the time of death to the exact minute. The Houramis may well have been killed when I was in the café with Khaled.'

'And they might have been killed after you left the cafe.'

'Don't be so bloody self-righteous. This is all hindsight.

How was I to know that in that short period someone would kill Khaled's parents? And another thing, while we're examining our consciences, have you asked yourself why Khaled didn't come to you in the first place? Have you thought about that? A frightened 14-year-old boy whose uncle had been murdered. Why didn't he go to the police instead of to a journalist? You want to know why? Because he didn't trust you. Because he's grown up in London, a Kurdish immigrant, and his view of the Met isn't as rosy as you'd like it to be.'

Joe looked away. A couple of white transit vans were pulling in to the kerb ahead of them. The scene-of-crime officers had arrived.

'I'll want a full statement from you shortly, so don't leave the scene,' Crawford said coldly. 'Right now I want names. Khaled's too distressed to help. You'll have to provide the information we need.'

She took a notebook and pen out of her jacket pocket.

'The one who allegedly killed the uncle first.'

'Hasan. No surname. That's all Khaled knew,' Joe said. 'He said he worked for another Turk, Memet Dil. Khaled said Dil was big in the drugs trade around here.'

'I know him,' Crawford said. 'Now the other name. The one in Whitechapel who organised the van to take Irena Hourami out of London.'

'Rafiq Khan. He has an office in Bourne Street, that's what Khaled said.'

Crawford wrote the names in her notebook, then clicked open her door.

'Let's see if we can salvage something from this fiasco,' she said wearily.

She didn't look at him. She climbed out on to the street and walked along the pavement to meet the Socos.

There was something about the two men that made Rafiq Khan immediately wary. He knew they hadn't come to his office looking for work. Most of the people who came to him had an air of desperation about them – they had to be desperate to even consider the kind of employment Khan offered – but these two, though they clearly weren't English, were sleek and confident, like a couple of well-groomed panthers. Turks, or maybe Arabs, Khan guessed. They didn't look like the poor, wretched foreigners who were the usual beneficiaries – or victims, depending on how you viewed it – of his recruitment expertise.

'What do you want?' Khan asked bluntly.

One of the men sat down in the chair across the desk from Khan. He had a thick moustache, a crescent of black hair curving around his upper lip. He was wearing an expensive light grey suit and hand-made leather shoes. A heavy gold ring glinted on the middle finger of his left hand.

'To ask you a few questions,' he said.

'About what?'

The second man had remained standing just inside the door. He took out a nasty-looking double-edged knife and began to pick his nails with it. He said nothing, but Khan didn't miss the threat that was implicit in the action. Khan felt a sudden dryness in his mouth.

'A man and a woman came here yesterday,' Hasan said. 'Kurds. You remember?'

'Maybe.'

Hasan stared at him. His eyes were black and lifeless, like chips of anthracite.

'I said, you remember them?'

'Yes,' Khan said.

His gaze went to the man with the knife. He was still picking his nails, running the sharp tip around the ends of his fingers.

'What happened to the woman, Irena Hourami?'

'She went in one of my mini-vans.'

'Where?'

'To Norfolk.'

'Where in Norfolk?'

'A packhouse near Thetford.'

'What's its name?'

'Wintertons.'

'Wintertons?' Hasan repeated the name, lodging it in his memory. 'Where is she now?'

Khan shrugged.

'I have no idea.'

Farok stopped picking his nails and walked over to the desk. He rested the flat of the knife on the edge of the desk.

'That's the truth,' Khan said, trying not to look at the knife. 'She didn't come back.'

'Why not?'

'She wanted to stay in Norfolk.'

'Where?'

'I don't know. The lad who drove the mini-van up there, he had a word with a local gangmaster. I don't know who it was.'

'This lad, where is he?'

'Out on a job. He won't be back tonight.'

That wasn't true, but Khan didn't want these two hanging around the office, waiting for Zahid to return. He wanted to get rid of them now.

'That's all I know,' he said. 'She wanted work, I found her some. I don't know who she was, don't care.'

Hasan looked at him for a time, then he got slowly to his feet.

'If you've lied to us, we'll be back,' he said.

Farok held his knife up in front of Khan's face and grinned.

'The three of us,' he said.

Khan stayed in his seat after the two men had left. He was a tough businessman, working in the black economy with all the risks that entailed, but violence – or the threat of violence – frightened him. The two men's visit had unnerved him. He took it as an omen, a presage of something worse to come. He had a nose for danger that had served him well in the past. In his line of work, it paid to know when to disappear for a few days, longer if necessary. Maybe it was time he took a holiday.

He went to the filing cabinet and removed a folder. He couldn't remember what name the Kurdish woman had given, but he knew it wasn't the name the man with the moustache had mentioned. He found the sheet of paper in the folder. Sakar Ali, that was it. He blanked the name out of his mind. He'd never met her. She didn't exist.

Taking the paper through into the small lavatory next to his office, he burnt it in the washbasin and flushed the ashes down the plughole. Then he went back to his desk and collected up his belongings. There was a safe built into the office wall. Khan opened it and removed three thick envelopes full of cash which he placed inside an attache case. He locked the inner door that communicated with the mini-cab office at the front of the building, picked up the attache case and left through the back door, locking it behind him. His black BMW was parked in the rear yard. He drove out on to Bourne Street and turned right. He was a quarter of a mile away, heading west towards Aldgate, when the two police cars, roof-lights flashing, sirens screaming, raced past in the opposite direction.

Joe phoned Ed Preston on his mobile, standing beside his car in Murray Road, one eye watching the activity outside Alexandra Court. The front door to the flats had been propped open and the ghostly white shapes of the Socos were coming and going from their vans. A small crowd of curious spectators had begun to gather on the pavement. Joe saw Crawford come out of the flats. She spoke to a couple of the uniformed officers and they headed towards the group of onlookers, moving them out of the way, ordering them to disperse.

'I'm outside the flats now,' Joe told Preston. 'I've had official confirmation that the parents are dead – throats cut.'

'How's the kid?' Preston said.

'In shock. An ambulance has taken him to hospital.'

'You speak to him?'

'Briefly. He's in a bad way. I'm going to need some help on this one, Ed. I'm not sure how much time I'll have to cover the story. I've talked to the DCI in charge. She wants me to make a statement.'

'Are the police hassling you? You need a lawyer?'

'I'm OK. But I could be tied up with paperwork for hours.'

'I'll see who's free. Hang on a second.'

Joe heard Preston bawling across the newsroom, a fainter voice responding. The news editor came back on the line.

'I'm sending Ellie out. What's the address?'

Joe gave him the details and some directions to pass on to Ellie, then he rang off and climbed into his car, leaning back in the seat with his eyes closed, thinking about what had happened – thinking about Khaled, about the boy's parents, about his own involvement.

He ran back over his acrimonious conversation with Louise Crawford. She clearly felt that he was partly to blame for the deaths of Anwar and Sara Hourami. Joe was feeling defensive about his role, tormented by those two haunting words, 'what if?'. What if he'd called the police the moment he'd left Khaled by the bus stop? What if the police had got to the flat in time to prevent the killings? What if . . . You could dwell on the possibilities for a lifetime. But it had all happened so quickly, so unexpectedly. As he'd said to Crawford, Joe knew that he wasn't responsible, that no reasonable assessment could attribute blame to him, but that didn't stop him feeling in some way at fault. Those deaths were on his conscience, and they always would be.

He could picture Khaled in the back of the ambulance.

112

See his face, that excruciating look in his eyes. He could still feel him shaking when he'd held him. Joe was trembling himself now. His hands were unsteady, there was a vague sensation of nausea in his stomach. Tears pricked at the corners of his eyes. He lifted a finger and wiped the moisture away. He'd witnessed some disturbing events in his years on the crime beat, but nothing that had touched him quite like this.

Ellie Mason's red and black Mini came crawling past. She saw Joe sitting in his car and pulled in to a parking space further along the street. She walked back and slipped into the passenger seat next to him. She brushed her hair away from her face and looked at him sympathetically. He was hunched over, his hands clasped tightly together in his lap.

'Ed told me,' she said. 'You OK?'

'Yes.'

'You don't look it.'

'I'll be all right.'

Ellie reached out and squeezed his hand affectionately. She could see the moisture glistening in his eyes, the slight quiver of his mouth.

'You want to talk about it?' she said.

'No.'

'A problem shared . . .'

'Is a problem doubled,' Joe said, and he glanced at her, almost smiling. It was an old joke between them, going back to the time when they'd been more than just colleagues.

'It's me,' Ellie said. 'You don't have to pretend.'

Joe was silent for a moment. Then he said, 'He's just fourteen. Just a kid. To come home and see that . . . how do you deal with something like that?'

Ellie didn't say anything. It wasn't a question that had an answer. She knew Joe didn't expect one.

'Is it my fault?' he went on. 'Am I to blame?'

She couldn't let that one pass.

113

'Don't be stupid. Of course you're not to blame.'

'I should've called the police straight away.'

'You weren't to know, Joe. It's not your fault.'

'So why do I think it is?'

'You didn't kill them,' Ellie said. 'No one's blaming you.'

'The police are.'

'Then they're wrong.'

'Are they?'

'You're getting emotionally involved.'

'Is that a bad thing?'

'Sometimes no, But on this occasion, yes. Khaled confided in you. You had a duty to protect him. You'd have been in breach of that duty if you'd gone to the police. You know that.'

'What's going to happen to him now? Who's going to look after him?'

'That's not your concern. There are other people – people much better qualified than you – who will make that decision. Now, why don't you fill me in on the facts I don't already know?'

Joe unclasped his hands and straightened up. He took a deep breath.

'OK.'

He outlined what had happened. Ellie scribbled notes on a pad on her knee.

'Thanks for coming out,' Joe said. He gave a wan smile. 'This isn't a story I want to write up.'

'You'd do the same for me,' Ellie said. 'Who's the SIO?'

'DCI Louise Crawford.'

'She inside the flat?'

'Yes.'

'Anyone see or hear anything?'

'I don't know. They've sealed off the building. They're probably interviewing the neighbours now. You won't get anything from Crawford, I can tell you that now.'

'I've enough to be going on with,' Ellie said. 'Just leave it . . .'

She broke off as a figure loomed up outside on the pavement. The figure – a young man in a sports jacket and tie – peered into the car. Ellie wound down the window.

'Mr Verdi?' the young man said, looking across at Joe. 'DC Nolan. DCI Crawford wants me to take you over to the station now, to make your statement.'

Joe was there for the best part of an hour, sitting in a stuffy interview room at Stoke Newington police station, giving his version of events while Detective Constable Nolan wrote it all down slowly in long hand. Joe could have typed it himself in half the time, if they'd given him access to a computer, but that wasn't how the police did things.

When he finally got away, it was nearly eight o'clock. He went back to Alexandra Court. The block of flats was still sealed off. The white transit vans and police cars were still parked outside, but Joe saw no sign of Ellie's Mini. He called the office and found her at her desk, writing up the story.

'You coming back in?' Ellie asked.

'Maybe later,' Joe replied. 'You don't need me, do you?'

'No, I've got it all sorted.'

'Any queries?'

'I don't think so. Why don't you go home, Joe? Or do you want to go for a drink instead? I think you could use one.'

'No, I'm OK,' Joe said. 'Thanks for the offer.'

He rang off and returned to his car. He drove back into town. Ellie was right, he *could* use a drink, something to ease the tension in his stomach. But he wasn't going to have one. He had things to do before he finished for the day. Irena Hourami was the key to this whole messy business, he knew that. She had to be found. He could have left the search to the police, but that wasn't how Joe saw his job. He wasn't a passive bystander, an ordinary member of the public. He was an active participant in the events he covered. In this case, in particular, he felt he had a personal stake. It was dangerous to allow his own feelings to intrude on a story, but it was too late now for him to step back into the role of an objective observer. He was involved, there was no escaping that fact. His conscience, his nagging sense of guilt, wouldn't allow him to simply sit back and wait to see what happened next. He had to *do* something.

He found Bourne Street on the A-Z he kept in the glove compartment and drove there. He wasn't surprised to see the police cars outside the mini-cab office. Procrastination wasn't one of Louise Crawford's weaknesses. She'd have wasted no time in getting a warrant to search Rafiq Khan's premises.

This wasn't a crime scene so the area wasn't taped off. There wasn't even a police officer outside on the pavement to stop Joe walking in. The mini-cab office was deserted. The television screen on the wall was blank, the radio console switched off. The door at the back of the office was open. Joe moved closer and saw from the splintered wood that the lock had been smashed.

There were three men in the rear office – two uniformed police officers and DS Danny Chisholm. They were empty-ing filing cabinets, piling documents on the desk and sorting through them. One of the uniformed officers saw Joe watching from the doorway and came forward.

'Can we help you, sir?'

Danny Chisholm looked up from a file he was reading and scowled.

'It's OK,' he growled to his colleague. 'I'll handle this.'

Chisholm came out into the mini-cab office and lit up a cigarette, flicking the match away into a waste paper bin by the desk.

'You're in deep shit, mate,' he said, his tone of voice implying that he wasn't overly concerned by that fact. 'Crawford wants your bollocks to stuff and hang on the wall of the police canteen.'

'Yeah?' Joe said.

'If I were you, I'd keep a very low profile over the next few days.'

'Where's Khan?'

'Not here,' Chisholm said.

'You got his home address?'

'A couple of the boys went over there. He's not there either. His wife says she doesn't know where he is.'

'Convenient. What about the mini-cab business?'

'There was a bloke here when we arrived, manning the radio. Asian bloke. Said he was just an employee, didn't know where Khan had gone. He said Khan took off around six, drove away in his black BMW.'

'You believe him?'

'For the time being.'

'What about Irena Hourami? You know where she went yet?'

Chisholm inhaled on his cigarette and blew smoke out through his nostrils.

'You've some nerve, you know,' he said. 'Coming here sniffing around after what happened in Stoke Newington.'

'You blame me for that too?'

'I saw the bodies. Very nearly threw up. Anyone who could do that to someone . . . shit, they must be fucking animals.'

'You know I told Crawford about Khan?'

'That's the only reason I haven't thrown you out on your arse. Pity you didn't come clean earlier.'

'So what about Irena Hourami?' Joe said.

Chisholm shrugged.

'We'll see.'

'You found anything?'

'I'm not sure there's anything to find. I've been in offices like this before. There's a ton of paperwork – files, forms – but most of it's bullshit, a screen to cover up what really goes on here. I'll bet a month's pay that most of the names on Khan's so-called "books" are false and not one of them is working legally in this country.'

Chisholm stubbed his cigarette out on the top of the desk and tossed the butt into the bin.

'And that's all you're getting from me,' he said. 'Don't bother to hang around.'

He went back through into the rear office. Joe stepped out into the street. It was getting dark, the street lamps beginning to glow a dull red. Rather than hiding the shabby characteristics of the area, the twilight seemed to accentuate them. The buildings appeared more rundown, the brickwork dirtier, the roofs and windows more dilapidated. The premises across the road were un-occupied, the windows boarded up with plywood. A warehouse down the street had charred window frames and smoke-blackened walls from an outbreak of fire – maybe accidental, but in this area more likely an arsonist's handiwork. There was the distant sound of traffic on Commercial Road, the unsavoury smell of kebabs wafting over from the same direction.

Joe walked to his car and sat for a time in the driver's seat, wondering whether to go back to the office, or find something to eat. As he pondered his options, he noticed a white mini-van turning into the far end of the street. The van came towards him. It slowed outside Khan's office. Joe saw the driver, a Pakistani youth, looking at the police cars parked by the kerb, then the van accelerated. It came past Joe. In his rear view mirror he saw it disappear around a corner.

Joe started his car engine and did a quick U-turn, head-ing after the van. He was just in time to see it turning into another side street. He followed. The van was fifty metres in front of him. It had pulled in and a number of people were scrambling out of the back. The Pakistani youth was holding the door open, urging his passengers to hurry.

Joe drove past and stopped round the next corner. He got

out of the car and waited in a doorway, taking a ten pound note out of his wallet. An Asian woman in a skirt and blouse, a bag swinging from her shoulder, walked by without noticing him. Joe gave her a couple of metres, then emerged from the doorway.

'Excuse me, I believe you dropped this.'

The Asian woman gave a start and turned. Joe knew she'd come from the mini-van. An area like this, at this time of night, the offices and workshops long closed, she couldn't have come from anywhere else. She looked at the ten pound note he was holding out.

'Uh?'

'I think you must've dropped it.'

She stared at him.

'Take it,' Joe said.

'I drop it?' the woman said.

'I think so,' Joe said. 'You work for Rafiq Khan, don't you?'

The woman eyed him warily, licking her lips.

'Why you ask?'

'Don't worry, I'm not a policeman, or any other kind of official. The van back there, that belongs to Khan, doesn't it?'

'Who are you?'

'I'm looking for someone. A woman, a Kurdish woman.'

'Kurdish? I don't know any Kurdish woman.'

'The van, where was it coming from this evening?'

The Asian woman kept looking at the ten pound note in Joe's hand, tempted. Joe thrust it into her fingers and she slipped it away into the pocket of her skirt.

'Norfolk,' she said.

'Whereabouts in Norfolk?'

'Thetford.'

'You been working in the fields?'

'A packhouse.'

'The name?'

'Wintertons.'

'This woman I'm looking for, she went to Norfolk yesterday evening, in Khan's van. Would she have been going to this packhouse?'

'Maybe. I don't know. That's the night shift. I work days.'

Joe let the woman walk away, the sky almost black now, the streetlamps on full, then went back to his car and drove to the office. The newsroom was virtually empty, most of the reporters gone home. The subs were at their keyboards, putting the last few pages together. There was a note on Joe's desk from Ellie, telling him where to find her copy. He logged on to the system and read through her story, knowing it would be good.

Leaving his computer on, he got himself a coffee from the vending machine. When he returned to his desk, he went on line and looked up the phone number of the packhouse in Thetford. There it was – A.P. Wintertons, Honey Lane, Barnthorpe, near Thetford. He punched in the number on his extension and got an answering machine informing him that the office was closed and would he please call back between 8 a.m. and 6 p.m. There was only the one number listed. Joe suspected there had to be more; a packhouse working around the clock, almost certainly for the supermarkets, wouldn't be incommunicado for half the day. He rang Directory Enquiries, but they only had that one number too.

Would Irena Hourami be working in the packhouse tonight? Joe couldn't get through to them by phone to ask, so there was only one way to find out. He turned back to his computer, to one of the on-line location finding services and printed off a map to help him find Wintertons. Then he finished his coffee and went out to his car.

10

Ellie stopped off at the shops on her way home to buy herself something to eat for dinner. Well, 'shops' was how she thought of it, a part of her still remembering the distant days when there had actually been some shops near where she lived. It was only a few years ago – five, six, maybe – that the fifty-metre stretch of retail units on the main road close to her flat had contained a bakers, a greengrocers, a butchers and an open-all-hours corner shop. The first three had all closed within two years of one another, their business taken by the giant supermarket that had opened a mile away. The corner shop had survived longer than the others, kept afloat by the Bangladeshi owner's prodigious work ethic, but even Mr Ahmed had succumbed eventually, unable to compete with the superstore on his doorstep. That retail monster, not content with simply destroying its rivals, had then rubbed salt in their wounds by buying up their former premises and merging them together into what they called a 'local convenience store', a mini-supermarket selling the same bland, industrialised food as the mother store, only at inflated prices.

Ellie didn't like the place. She had fond memories of the small, intimate shops that had been there before – of conversations with shopkeepers who knew her name, of bakers who knew how their bread was made, butchers who could recommend a joint of meat and had the skill to cut it from a carcass, greengrocers who could recognise a ripe pear, who could actually 'serve' you, as opposed to scanning barcodes through a machine. It wasn't just nostalgia, some sentimental longing for a past which had never really existed. Those shops genuinely had been better than this garish, impersonal, characterless emporium that had taken their place. Ellie shopped there because she had no choice – there was nowhere else to buy food. But she never lingered when she went in – what was there to linger over? She filled her basket as quickly as she could and fled the plastic environment, the over-bright lights, the piped music and the blank-faced assistants.

The old way of shopping – buying different ingredients in different places – had been inconvenient in many ways, but it had forced her to think about food, to plan how she was going to make a meal for herself. Now she simply let the supermarket do the thinking for her. She let them choose the ingredients and mix them all together into a ready-prepared package that she could throw into the oven or the microwave and have on the table in minutes. It was quick, effortless, but it took the pleasure out of eating, turned food into mere fuel. It suited her busy schedule, her lack of time, yet she knew that by aiding and abetting this supermarket takeover she was complicit in the destruction of a more communal, healthier, more sociable way of living that would never come again.

She tossed a few items into her basket – a carton of milk, some cheese, a loaf of wholemeal bread. Then she paused by the refrigerated display containing the cook-chill ready meals. The packages on the shelves looked uniformly tempting. Ellie ran her eyes over the glossy photographs of succulent chicken in cream and white wine sauce, lamb curry, 'Italian-style' lasagne, knowing from experience that the packaging was the most appetising thing about these dishes. Whatever mouthwatering treat the outside promised, she knew the inside would be a disappointment. The meat – what little there was – would be spongy and the sauces, regardless of their names and ingredients, would all taste the same – metallic and saturated with salt to give them some flavour. But it was food. She was tired, it was gone nine o'clock. The last thing she wanted to do was prepare a meal from scratch. She dumped a microwave lasagne into her basket and headed for the checkout.

Her flat was on the first floor of a late-Victorian terraced house that had been converted into two apartments in the 1980s. The ground floor was occupied by a 79-year-old widow named Hilda North who'd lost her husband to cancer ten years earlier and now lived alone, childless and isolated in her poky one-bedroom flat.

As Ellie opened the front door from the street and stepped into the hall, she saw Hilda emerge from her flat. The old lady must have been waiting close to her door, listening for Ellie's key in the lock. Ellie sighed inwardly. She didn't feel like being sociable. She wanted to eat and go to bed. But Hilda obviously needed to speak to her.

'Hello, dear,' Hilda said. 'Had a good day?'

Ellie noticed that her neighbour was flushed and slightly out of breath. She often wheezed, but it seemed worse this evening.

'Hello, Mrs North. Yes, thanks. Are you OK?'

Ellie felt obliged to ask the question, though she dreaded the answer. Hilda North's various ailments and the medication she took for them were enough material for a full evening's conversation – or rather a full evening's monologue, for Mrs North, when she got started, was almost impossible to interrupt.

'I'm not too bad, dear,' Hilda replied, a remark that Ellie knew from innumerable other occasions was generally a prelude to a long and tedious contradiction in which 'not too bad' somehow metamorphosed into 'virtually at death's door'.

'I didn't sleep very well last night. I've been getting these headaches. These nagging pains that won't seem to go away. And the rheumatism in my knees, it's getting much worse . . .'

Ellie nodded automatically, edging towards the stairs, hoping that Hilda might take the hint and let her go – although she never had in the past. Please, not tonight, Ellie thought, and immediately reproved herself for her lack of charity. Hilda was on her own, depressed a lot of the time. She didn't get out much. Ellie knew that these exchanges in the hall, however irritating to her, were an important social contact to Hilda.

'. . . whether you might be able to fix it for me?'

Ellie became aware that Hilda had stopped talking, that her last words had been a question that required some kind of response.

'I'm sorry. What was that?'

'The light bulb in my kitchen,' Hilda repeated. 'It's gone. I was wondering whether you could change it. I've got a new one.'

'Of course,' Ellie said. 'I'll do it now.'

She followed Hilda into her flat, glad to have something to do, to be able to give some practical assistance to her neighbour. She liked helping where she could – posting letters, doing shopping, giving Hilda a lift to the doctor's. It was the passive listening she found wearing.

The television was flickering in the corner of the cluttered living room, the sound on too loud as usual. The kitchen was in darkness. Ellie left the door open to allow light from the adjoining hall to filter in.

'When did the bulb go?' she said.

'A couple of hours ago,' Hilda replied. 'Just after I'd finished my tea. I didn't even have time to do the washing up,' she added apologetically, pushing a dirty plate to one side on the surface next to the sink, ashamed by its presence. Her joints were seizing up and her eyesight going, but she prided herself on her cleanliness. Her flat was always neat and tidy, dishes washed up immediately and put away in their proper place in the cupboard.

'It's ever so good of you,' she said. 'I'd do it myself, only I find it hard to get up there these days.'

'You shouldn't even attempt it,' Ellie said. 'You don't want to have a fall.'

She checked the switch on the wall was turned off, then climbed on to a kitchen chair and reached up to remove the old lightbulb.

'Where's the new one?' she said.

'Here you are, dear.'

Hilda picked up a bulb from the worktop and handed it to Ellie.

'Try the switch,' Ellie said, after she'd clicked the new bulb into place. 'There you go. That should last you a while.'

Ellie jumped down from the chair.

'Now, while I'm here, is there anything else I can do?'

'No, it's all right, dear, I can . . .' Hilda let out a sudden cry of pain. She bent over, holding her stomach.

'Mrs North!' Ellie said in alarm. 'What is it? What's the matter?'

Hilda straightened up slowly, one hand still pressed to her stomach.

'I don't know,' she said, a little breathlessly.

'Is something hurting?'

'No, not now.'

'But it was?'

'I had one earlier. Like a cramp. I think it's just a touch of indigestion.'

She took her hand away from her stomach, the movement tentative, as if she were waiting for another spasm.

'It's gone now.' She exhaled with relief. 'That must be it. Just indigestion. I think I'll have a glass of water.'

'I'll get it,' Ellie said. 'You go and sit down. I'll bring it through for you.'

Hilda shuffled into the living room. She was settled in

her armchair in front of the television when Ellie came in with her glass of water.

'Are you sure you're all right?'

Hilda nodded.

'I think so. My stomach's settled down now. It's this headache that's really bothering me. I seem to have had it for days.'

'Have you taken anything for it?'

'I had some paracetamol earlier, but it didn't seem to do anything.'

'Would you like me to get you some more?'

'No thank you, dear. I'll watch a bit of television, then go to bed, I think. You get along now.'

Ellie retrieved her bag of shopping and let herself out. She wondered whether she should have called a doctor for Mrs North. The old lady's stomach pains worried her, but then Hilda suffered from so many medical conditions that it was difficult to know which ones to take seriously and which could safely be ignored. Maybe it *was* just indigestion. Hilda had had indigestion before and it usually passed in a couple of hours, leaving no adverse effects behind. That's probably all it was. There was nothing to be concerned about.

Ellie climbed the steep flight of stairs to the first floor and went into her flat, turning on a couple of lamps and the television to make it more welcoming. She didn't feel that she had a strong nest-building instinct, but she'd always made an effort to imprint her taste and personality on her flats – this the fourth one she'd lived in since moving to London, but the first she'd owned rather than rented.

The flat had been old-fashioned and tatty when she'd bought it three years ago. She'd stripped off the patterned wallpaper with a steamer, had the plaster skimmed and painted it herself. The threadbare carpets had been ripped up and she'd hired a machine for a weekend to sand down the floorboards before treating them herself with stain and wax. The kitchen and bathroom were still in need of work. She would have loved to have gutted both rooms and started again, but that would have to wait until she managed to save some more money. Ellie wasn't good at saving money. She was careless about her finances, always living beyond her income. When she wanted something, she bought it, slapped it on her credit card and didn't worry unduly about how she was going to pay off the debt.

She emptied her bag of shopping, stowing the milk and cheese away in the fridge, then put the lasagne in the microwave. By the time she'd got herself a plate and fork and poured herself a glass of red wine, the lasagne was ready. She tipped the meal out on to her plate. It was a small portion, considering the price she'd paid for it, and very slushy, the bechamel sauce oozing all over the place. But it would satisfy her hunger, which was all she required of it.

She went through into the sitting room and settled herself down in front of the TV. There was a psychological thriller on BBC1. She'd missed the first twenty minutes of it, but she gave it a try anyway, pretty sure that she could catch up with the plot. Ten minutes later, she hadn't just caught up with the plot, she was way ahead of it, the whole thing was so implausibly predictable. Single woman meets handsome, mysterious stranger who turns out to be not quite what he seems. Oh *please*. Ellie had seen it all before in a dozen television dramas and the fundamental premise of them still annoyed her – women were stupid, that was about the long and short of it. They could be intelligent and independent, women with good careers and plenty of experience of the world, yet the moment they fell in love their brains somehow stopped working, they suddenly started doing unbelievable things and their eyesight, as well as their knees, went all wobbly so that they seemed unable to see that the man they'd fallen for had psychopath written all over him.

It was so patronising. Television seemed to have only two images of women, both offensive stereotypes. Either they were gullible victims, unable to control their own lives and prey to irrational emotions and dangerous liaisons, or they were half-wits pining for a husband.

Ellie didn't identify with either image, though she was aware that others were happy to pigeonhole her. Ed Preston, for instance. The dinosaur. He categorised her as a single professional woman in her thirties, ergo she had to be looking for a man. Why else did she get crappy assignments like weddings, or the speed dating feature he'd sent her on last month – a dispiriting experience that she'd found deeply humiliating even though she was doing it for her job. The organisers had portrayed it as a bit of fun, but where was the fun in advertising your desperation to forty complete strangers?

She was quite content the way she was. She liked living alone, liked being single. She could hear her biological clock ticking, but so what? The bloody thing could blow up for all she cared.

She'd finished her lasagne by now, and her wine. She could still taste the garlic and onion in her mouth. There was something overpoweringly artificial about the flavours, as if they'd been chemically produced in a laboratory rather than taken from vegetables grown in a field. She went into the kitchen and poured herself another glass of wine to wash away the pungent after taste. She regretted not cooking herself a proper meal. She would have enjoyed it much more, it would have been more nutritious and it would have tasted infinitely better. But she disliked cooking, especially for one. Where was the pleasure in spending time preparing food when there was no one else to appreciate it?

She took the bottle of wine through with her and sat back down in front of the television, staring at the screen without absorbing either the images or the words. She thought about Joe Verdi. In the car outside the Hourami's flat, he'd looked so distraught that Ellie had wondered about inviting him back to her flat for a meal. Joe was the perfect dinner guest – you bought in all the ingredients and he'd do the cooking for you. They could've shared the bottle of wine and . . . well, just seen what happened. But she'd pulled back. All that was in the past. There were too many complications she didn't want to revisit.

Ellie didn't like complications. She liked to keep her relationships simple, her men at a distance where they couldn't interfere too much in her life. She set the terms, laid down the parameters, and if the guys didn't like it, that was too bad. She'd had boyfriends who'd accepted that arrangement, but Joe wasn't one of them. He couldn't put up with that kind of detachment. He'd always wanted more than Ellie was willing to give.

The sharp ring of the telephone interrupted her day-dream. She heard Mrs North's voice on the other end of the line.

'I'm sorry to trouble you,' Hilda began, her voice weak, out of breath. 'But I'm not . . .' She gasped with pain, unable to complete the sentence.

'Mrs North?' Ellie said quickly. 'What is it? Your stomach again?' She could hear the old lady wheezing, almost moaning. 'Mrs North?'

'Yes . . .' The voice was fainter. 'My stomach.'

'I'll be right there.'

Ellie raced downstairs and knocked on the door of the ground floor flat. The old lady didn't answer. Ellie knocked harder.

'Mrs North! It's me, Ellie.'

She waited a few seconds longer, her ear pressed to the door, listening for any sign of movement inside. Then, when Hilda still didn't respond, she ran back upstairs and got the key to the old lady's flat from a drawer in the kitchen – the spare key Mrs North left with her for safekeeping.

Dashing back downstairs, Ellie let herself into the flat. Mrs North was slumped in the armchair in front of the television, where Ellie had left her an hour earlier. She was conscious, but obviously in too much pain to get up.

'Where does it hurt?' Ellie said, crouching down by the armchair.

Mrs North had her hands pressed to her stomach.

'Here . . .' She struggled to get the word out.

'Worse than before?'

Mrs North nodded. There was a sheen of perspiration on her face. Ellie put her hand on the old lady's forehead. It was burning hot.

'Does it hurt anywhere else?' Ellie asked.

'My head . . . and . . . I think I . . . feel sick.'

'Hang on.'

Ellie darted into the kitchen, whipping open cupboards, looking for some kind of receptacle. She found a plastic bowl under the sink and brought it out into the living room – only just in time for Mrs North was almost immediately sick. Ellie held the bowl under Hilda's mouth until the spasms subsided. Then she got some tissues and wiped the old lady's face. She noticed that there were flecks of blood in the vomit.

'Has that helped at all?' she said.

Mrs North shook her head.

'My stomach . . . it . . .'

She grimaced with pain again, then retched, bringing up more sick. Ellie screwed up her nose at the sour odour. The blood traces in the vomit were no longer flecks, but small clots. Ellie went to the phone and dialled 999.

The paramedics were calm, soft-spoken men who radiated an aura of competence. They examined Mrs North in her armchair, talking to her gently, their voices re-assuring. Then they brought in a stretcher and lifted her on to it.

'What's happening?' Hilda asked, gazing up at the two men in their green uniforms.

'Nothing to worry about,' one of the paramedics replied. 'We're just taking you to hospital. Get a doctor to check you over.'

'Hospital?' Hilda said.

She was turning her head from side to side in an agitated manner. Her face was flushed, streaming with sweat. She seemed delirious, not sure where she was.

'Best to be on the safe side,' the paramedic said.

The two men wheeled the stretcher out of the flat and into the ambulance. One of the paramedics stayed in the back with Hilda, the other climbed out to go round to the cab. Ellie watched him anxiously from the pavement.

'Are you her daughter?' the paramedic said.

'No. I live in the flat upstairs. Is she going to be all right?'

'We'll see what the doctors say,' the paramedic replied non-committally. 'Do you know if she has any family?'

'Not nearby. She lives alone. She's a widow. I know she doesn't have any children. I believe there's a nephew somewhere.'

'You coming to the hospital too?'

'I think I should. I'll follow you in my car. Which hospital are you going to?'

'Whittington. She may be in for a few days. You might want to throw her wash things, some clean underwear in a bag and bring it with you.'

'I'll do that.'

Ellie watched the ambulance pull away, then returned to Mrs North's flat. She disposed of the vomit in the toilet and took the bowl through into the kitchen and washed it thoroughly in the sink. The dirty plate from Mrs North's dinner was still on the worktop. A barely-touched chicken leg, a few potatoes and some congealed sauce were stuck to the plate. Ellie scraped the debris into the bin and washed the plate too. It was the least she could do to help out. Mrs North wouldn't want to come out of hospital to find the washing up needing to be done.

There was a small travel case on top of the wardrobe in the bedroom. Ellie collected together some underwear, spare clothes and toiletries and washing kit from the bathroom and packed them into the case. Then she locked the flat, fetched her shoulderbag from upstairs and went out to her car, parked, as usual, a hundred metres away outside someone else's house.

She had the same trouble parking at Whittington Hospital, eventually finding a space off Highgate Hill and walking the quarter of a mile back to Casualty. Hilda North had already been taken through into the emergency room, but the nurse at the reception desk took the old lady's case from Ellie and said she'd make sure it was taken to the ward.

'She's being kept in then?' Ellie said.

'Oh, yes. A lady her age, in her condition, she won't be released tonight. Are you family?'

'A neighbour.'

'Perhaps you could help me with some information for the file? It may be some time before she comes round.'

'Comes round?' Ellie said. 'You mean she's unconscious?'

'I'm afraid so. Her name and address first, please.'

Ellie gave the details the nurse requested, including her own name and contact numbers.

'Do you know if Mrs North's on any medication?' the nurse asked.

'A lot, I think. But I couldn't tell you what.'

'Is she allergic to penicillin or any antibiotics?'

'I don't know, I'm sorry.'

'Who's her GP?'

That Ellie did know. She'd driven Hilda there enough times. She gave the nurse the doctor's name and surgery address.

'She thought it was indigestion,' she said. 'How can she be unconscious?'

'It's not indigestion, I can tell you that now,' the nurse replied.

'Can I speak to a doctor?'

'I'll see what I can do. Just take a seat over there.'

Ellie sat down in the waiting area, alarmed now about Mrs North. What had happened to her in the short space of time since she'd left her flat? Unconscious? Dear God, what was the matter with her?

The Accident and Emergency Department seemed quiet. Ellie gave thanks that it wasn't a Friday or Saturday night, when the drunks, the car accident and pub brawl victims generally came in. A young man with blood on his face from a nasty gash above the eye was led in from the street by a young woman in a tight skirt and high heels. The young man was taken away into a treatment room by a nurse. His companion pulled a packet of cigarettes from her clutch bag and went outside for a comforting smoke. Nurses and auxiliaries came and went through doors. There was no running or shouting, no stretchers racing in from ambulances, no sense of urgency. Everything was unhurried and ordered.

An hour and a half had elapsed before a doctor finally came to talk to Ellie. He was a gangly Senior House Officer with ginger hair and spectacles, a stethoscope poking out from the pocket of his white coat.

'How is she?' Ellie asked.

'She's in intensive care.'

'Is she conscious?'

'She's come round, yes.'

'Do you know what's wrong with her?'

'Not yet. We're going to do some tests. Do you know if she has any heart or chest conditions? Or any history of stomach problems?'

'The nurse asked me that. I'm afraid I don't know.'

The doctor nodded, but said nothing. He didn't seem the garrulous type.

'Is there anything else I can do?' Ellie asked.

'Not really,' the doctor said. 'You might as well go home.'

Ellie returned to her car and drove back to her flat. The television was still on in her living room – in her hurry to get to the hospital she'd forgotten to turn it off. She flicked the switch and unplugged the set, then went to bed, still worrying about Mrs North.

11

Louise Crawford paused outside the interview room and looked in through the small glass pane in the door. Two men were seated at the table inside. One was Memet Dil, the other was his solicitor – an English lawyer of Turkish extraction named Peter Erdogan. Crawford had encountered both of them before. Dil's name had come up in connection with a homicide she'd worked on a few years previously – a shooting outside a pub in Harringay. He'd been questioned by the police, but not charged with any offence. Erdogan had been Dil's defence solicitor on that occasion too. He was a familiar figure at Stoke Newington police station, always on hand whenever a Turk was arrested. He had a reputation for confrontation and slipperiness.

Crawford didn't generally conduct these kinds of interviews herself. She left them to the junior members of her team while she concentrated on the overall management of an investigation. But she wanted to get the measure of Memet Dil. She wanted to see his face, his reactions, get a picture of the man that a transcript of an interview could never provide.

She pushed open the door and walked into the room. Erdogan glanced round, beginning his attack before Crawford had even sat down.

'Ah, at last,' he said. 'Chief inspector, I really must protest about the treatment of my client. There was absolutely no need to arrest him and bring him here tonight, especially at this late hour. If you have questions for him, he would happily have answered them at his home or his office in the morning.'

Crawford took no notice of him. She put her file down and inserted two tapes into the recorder on the table.

'Did you hear what I said?' Erdogan asked tersely.

'I did indeed, Mr Erdogan. But I think it's better to have everything on tape, don't you?'

'My client has nothing to do with this affair.'

'We'll let him speak for himself, shall we?' Crawford said.

She set the tapes recording and went through the interview formalities – time, date, persons present – before cautioning Memet Dil.

'You've been brought here on suspicion of involvement in the murders of three people,' she went on. 'Anwar Hourami, Sara Hourami and a man we believe to be Anwar's brother, Ismail Hourami.'

Memet Dil spread out his hands, palms up, in a gesture of innocent puzzlement.

'I've never heard of any of those people,' he said. 'I'm a respectable, law-abiding businessman. I'm astonished that you might think I know anything about such criminal activities, but, of course, I will do my best to assist you in your investigation.'

He gazed at her coolly. Crawford stared back, appraising him dispassionately. He was immaculately dressed in a dark suit and crisp white shirt, his red and white checked tie held in place by a gold pin inset with rubies and diamonds. His dark hair was sleek and oiled, his jowls showing only a faint trace of stubble though it was nearly eleven o'clock at night. A gold Rolex watch peeped out from beneath his jacket sleeve, the cuffs of his shirt fastened together with ruby and diamond links that matched his tie pin.

Crawford tried to get a feel for him from his appearance,

his manner, the look in his eyes. There was something calculating about him, something arrogant and utterly ruthless. Crawford had interviewed hundreds of people over the course of her career, some of them violent or dangerous. Even the worst had had the occasional redeeming feature, a human weakness or a hint of warmth. But Dil struck her as a man without feelings, a man with ice water in his veins.

'Ismail Hourami's body was found on Walthamstow Marshes yesterday afternoon,' she said. 'But we have reason to believe he was killed in a garage belonging to you. And that you were present at the time.'

Dil's eyes opened wide.

'I? Present? Chief inspector, I assure you I know nothing at all about this. My garage? That's ridiculous. Who gave you this information?'

'Where were you the night before last between midnight and 2 a.m.?'

'I was home in bed, of course. I'm a family man with a wife and four children. I don't keep late hours.'

'I put it to you that you weren't at home. You were at your garage in Honiton Street. A lorry arrived containing a number of illegal Kurdish immigrants, including Ismail Hourami and his wife, Irena.'

'Illegal immigrants?' Erdogan said. 'Are you accusing my client of smuggling immigrants as well as murder now? This gets more and more preposterous.'

'If you'd let me finish,' Crawford said. 'Shortly after the lorry arrived, there was a dispute and Ismail Hourami was stabbed to death by one of your employees – a man called Hasan. Can you confirm that you have an employee named Hasan?'

'Just a minute,' Erdogan broke in. 'What kind of a question is that?'

'A very simple one, I'd say. Does your client employ someone called Hasan? Is that so hard?'

'I find your tone unhelpful, chief inspector. You are accusing my client of a very serious offence. Do you have a shred of evidence to back up these outrageous allegations?'

'Just answer the question, please,' Crawford said, looking at Dil.

Memet shrugged.

'Do you have any idea how common a Turkish name Hasan is?'

'I'm not interested in how common it is. I'm asking if you employ someone of that name?'

Dil's brow furrowed and he squinted, making a show of thinking hard.

'I believe I may have an employee named Hasan, yes.'

'Hasan what?'

'I'm not sure I recall his second name.'

'You don't know his full name?'

'I have many business interests. I can't possibly keep track of everyone who works for me.'

'Where is he now?'

'I don't know.'

'What do you employ him to do?'

'Is this relevant to anything, chief inspector?' Erdogan said.

He put a very slight emphasis on her rank, an edge of mockery, of incredulity in his voice, as if he couldn't quite believe she was such a senior officer. Crawford was used to the sexist nuances of the male officers in the Met. She'd developed a very sensitive ear to their put downs and insinuations, then learnt to desensitise herself and ignore them.

'As we have information indicating that this Hasan killed Ismail Hourami, I'd say it was pretty relevant to everything,' Crawford said. 'Wouldn't you?'

'What "information"?' Erdogan said.

'I'll ask you again,' Crawford said to Dil. 'What job does Hasan do in your organisation?'

'I believe he was a delivery driver,' Dil replied.

'Was?'

'Yes. Now you mention it, I seem to recall that he went back to Turkey last week.'

'You remember that he went back to Turkey, but you don't remember his surname?'

'I think it might have been Mustafa. Hasan Mustafa. He was only a very menial employee.'

'When did he go back to Turkey? Which day?'

'I'm afraid I couldn't tell you. It's probably on file somewhere in my office.'

'We'll find it, if it's there,' Crawford said.

Memet glanced at his solicitor.

'You're going to go through my files?'

'We're doing so as we speak. We have search warrants for both your office and your garage. My teams will probably be there all night.'

Crawford watched him carefully as she replied, looking for any sign of uneasiness or agitation. But Dil's composure remained unruffled. A confident little shit, Crawford thought.

Erdogan leaned across the table. He licked his fleshy lips.

'This is serious and blatant harassment, chief inspector. My client is a leading and respected member of the Turkish community in London. I'm sure you wouldn't want your actions to be misinterpreted.'

Crawford turned to look at the solicitor. He was a small man with a plump, round face and a thick layer of hair that made his head seem too big for his body. Behind his rimless glasses, his eyes were vigilant, but somehow shifty.

'What do you mean, "misinterpreted"?' Crawford said.

'Let's just say that an impartial observer might consider your questioning of my client to be racially motivated.'

'I'm asking him about a killing that we believe took place in his garage. In what way would you say that was racially motivated?'

'I'm saying you should be careful, chief inspector. After all the hard work the Metropolitan Police have put into race relations over the last few years it would be unfortunate if the actions of one officer were to bring the force into disrepute.'

'Mr Dil's background is irrelevant to me,' Crawford said. 'All I'm concerned with is the facts.'

'Very well,' Erdogan said. 'Let's look at the facts, shall we? You send officers to confront my client in his home. You arrest him, haul him down here in the middle of the night and then make all manner of unfounded allegations against him. Do you have any evidence to substantiate those allegations? It would appear not. You say you have "information" about these killings. I ask you again, what information? Who is supplying this information? Whoever it is, they are obviously motivated by malice. My client has told you that he was at home in bed when this killing in his garage allegedly occurred. That is a simple fact to check. Ask his wife. She will confirm that he was with her all that time.'

'We will be checking,' Crawford said.

'Why didn't you check before you dragged my client out of bed and subjected him to this unnecessary interrogation? Would you have done this to a white man? Your conduct leaves a lot to be desired, chief inspector, and I should warn you that I shall be making a formal complaint to the Commissioner.'

'That is your choice,' Crawford said calmly. 'Now if we could get back to the matter in hand.'

She turned to Dil.

'Anwar and Sara Hourami were murdered earlier this evening. What were you doing between about 4 p.m. and 5.30?'

'My client has already told you,' Erdogan said impatiently. 'He has never heard of these people.'

'Mr Erdogan, we could get through this a lot quicker if you stopped interrupting,' Crawford said.

'We could get through it a lot quicker if you stopped asking pointless questions,' Erdogan retorted.

'If your client has nothing to hide, he should welcome the opportunity to clear this matter up. Mr Dil?'

'I was in my office. My secretary and several of my staff will be able to confirm that.'

'And your employee, Hasan Mustafa, where was he between those times?'

Dil's mouth curled into a contemptuous sneer.

'Really, chief inspector, such tricks are quite unworthy of you.'

'Oh, yes, I'm sorry, I forgot. He went back to Turkey last week.'

'This has gone far enough,' Erdogan said. 'My client has nothing further to say. You must charge him, or release him, chief inspector.'

Crawford looked at her watch.

'Interview terminated at 11.05 p.m.'

She pressed the stop button on the tape recorder and ejected the tapes.

'Well?' Erdogan said.

Crawford was tempted to prolong their wait, maybe even detain Dil overnight in the hope that some more concrete evidence against him might materialise. But her professionalism was stronger than her dislike of Dil and his slick lawyer. Memet's alibi would be watertight. She was sure of that. Without a witness to testify that he'd been present in the garage when Ismail Hourami was killed, or some forensic evidence, she had no case against him. The Socos would be going over Dil's garage with a microscope. One spot of Ismail Hourami's blood, or one of his fingerprints, one hair from his head, one fibre from his clothes, that was all she needed to wipe the smirk off the Turks' faces. But she knew that kind of evidence – if it was found at all – would take days to verify.

'You're free to go, Mr Dil,' she said.

Dil got to his feet and straightened his jacket. The diamonds and rubies in his cuff links sparkled as they caught the light.

'It was a pleasure to meet you again, chief inspector,' he said sarcastically.

'It won't be the last time,' Crawford replied. 'I can promise you that.'

Joe pulled into the carpark outside Wintertons packhouse and turned off the car engine and lights. It was nearly midnight. He'd taken his time driving out from London, stopping off for half an hour at a service station to have something to eat, then coming on to Thetford. He hadn't had to go into the town itself. The packhouse was on the southern fringes, fields all around it. It was bigger than he'd expected, a long, green metal shed like a factory. The carpark was big too, though there weren't many vehicles in it at this time of night – just a couple of cars over by the entrance.

Joe climbed out and walked across to the building. The outside was well lit, a spotlight on the wall illuminating a sign which read, 'All drivers must report to Reception before unloading.' Joe pulled open the door and went inside, finding himself in a small square vestibule with a counter and window along one side. Behind the window was a security guard in a black uniform lounging back in a swivel chair. A CCTV screen on the desk in front of the guard showed pictures from both the outside and the inside of the building, the image changing every few seconds as a different camera came on line. The guard must have seen Joe arrive – there was a camera covering the carpark – but he seemed in no hurry to find out what he wanted. Joe went to the window and waited for the guard to stand up and slide back the glass pane.

'Yeah?' the guard said. He was young, but overweight, his stomach bulging out over his trouser belt.

Joe told him who he was, showed his press card. The guard didn't look very impressed.

'Is there a manager here?' Joe said. 'Someone I can speak to.'

'It's midnight, mate,' the guard said. 'You think the management work nights? They're not that stupid.'

'Who's in charge then?'

'There's a foreman out on the production line.'

'Can I have a word with him?'

'About what?'

Joe considered telling him to mind his own business, but he restrained himself. The guard was typical of his breed: surly, rude, officious. Getting his back up was not the best way to obtain his cooperation.

'I'm trying to find a woman,' Joe said. 'I believe she might be working here tonight.'

'A woman?'

'Yes.'

'You with those other blokes?'

'What other blokes?'

'Came a couple of hours ago, asking about a woman too.'

Joe kept his face impassive.

'What did these men look like?' he asked casually.

'Foreign-looking. You know, Arabs or something.'

'Turks?'

'What's the difference?'

'They mention the woman's name?'

'Yeah, but I don't remember what it was.'

'Irena Hourami?'

'Could be.'

'What did you tell them?'

'Well, I didn't like the look of them. I told them we didn't give out that kind of information – on employees, you know. I said they should speak to Frank Parnell, he's the local gangmaster, takes care of most of the casual labour they use here.'

'What did they do?'

'They hung around in the carpark for a while. I went out, told them to clear off or I'd call the police.'

'And did they?'

The guard nodded.

'Haven't seen them since.' Something occurred to him. 'They weren't journalists, were they? They didn't look like journalists.'

'No, I don't think so. Any chance of talking to the foreman?'

The guard gave it some thought.

'You'd be doing me a big favour,' Joe said.

'This for some newspaper article?'

'Yes. I just want to check a few facts. It won't take long. A quick word and I'll be on my way.'

'I'll see if he's free.'

The guard picked up the phone and spoke briefly to someone at the other end. A couple of minutes later, the foreman came out into reception. He was a short, middle-aged man in blue overalls, the company logo on the left breast, dirt on the knees and elbows. Joe explained to him why he was there. The foreman shook his head doubtfully.

'I can't give out confidential information about our work-force, I'm afraid,' he said. 'I'm sorry.'

'I don't want confidential information,' Joe said. 'I just want to know if Irena is working here tonight. A simple yes or no. It's important.'

'Maybe you should come back in the morning. Speak to someone in the management.'

'I really need to know now,' Joe said. 'She's Kurdish. She may be in the country illegally. I know the police want to speak to her. You wouldn't want the police to raid this place, would you? I'm sure your management wouldn't. It wouldn't look good. A.P. Wintertons caught employing illegal migrant labour.'

That seemed to swing the foreman. He sniffed and rubbed his nose pensively.

'Wait here, I'll get the paperwork.'

He was back in under a minute, a thin sheaf of papers clutched in his hand.

'What was the name again?' he said.

'Irena Hourami.'

He scanned one of the pieces of paper.

'No. No Irena Hourami here.'

'Are you sure? What about last night?'

'No, she wasn't here last night either.'

'She came up in a mini-van from London. A van belonging to Rafiq Khan. You know Khan?'

'Of course. We use his people all the time. But none of them are illegal, we make sure of that.'

'She's Middle Eastern looking, young. She'd probably have been wearing a headscarf,' Joe said.

'A lot of the women here wear headscarves. But there's no Irena Hourami on my list. There are other packhouses around here, you know. Maybe you've got the wrong one.'

'Do Wintertons have other sites?'

'No, this is the only Wintertons. But there are other companies operating around Thetford. This is a big agricultural area.'

Joe thanked the foreman and went back out to his car. He drove away, out of the carpark and up the narrow country lane to the main road. Thetford was five miles to the north, Bury St Edmunds not much further to the south. On the other side of the road, just beyond the junction, was a small dirt pull-in area at the end of a track leading to a field, a five-bar farm gate blocking the access to the field. Joe reversed his car up the track so that it was off the main road and turned off the engine. In the distance, across the fields, he could see the floodlit packhouse, but the CCTV cameras on the building were too far away to see him.

Had he come to the wrong place? He believed the

foreman had been honest with him – there was no Irena Hourami working at A.P. Wintertons. That left two options. She was at another packhouse. That was quite possible. Maybe Rafiq Khan sent workers to other companies in the area. The second option was also a possibility: Irena was working at Wintertons under a different name.

The dashboard clock read 12.33 a.m. Joe could do nothing more right now. It was too late to drive into Thetford and find a hotel. In any case, he wanted to stay close to the packhouse, to see who came and went at the end of the night shift. He pulled his jacket close around himself, slouched lower in his seat and tried to sleep.

Hasan and Farok left their car in the carpark next to what the sign called, 'Thetford Bus Station' – a somewhat exalted term for a patch of potholed tarmac with a couple of stops and a tatty shelter at one end. They walked across the footbridge over the Little Ouse and through a ghastly 1960s shopping centre and pedestrian precinct, emerging into a street of old brick and flint buildings that served only to remind the passer-by of how attractive the town had been before the local planners had been allowed to indulge their passion for concrete.

Frank Parnell's office – the address helpfully provided by the security guard at Wintertons – was up the hill, in a predominantly commercial district that was deserted at this time of night. There were offices and small businesses, but very little residential property. That suited the Turks. They didn't want any light-sleeping neighbours hearing what they were about to do.

Farok had a torch in his pocket, Hasan a pair of heavy pliers and a crowbar concealed under his jacket, both implements selected from the collection of tools he kept in the boot of his car. The two men's function in Memet Dil's organisation was undefined and flexible. They did whatever was required of them. They were a versatile pair, though only within certain limits. Memet never called on them for tasks that needed subtlety or diplomacy or political skills, he did all that himself. But they were perfect for the cruder, more physical side of the business: distributing goods, collecting money, enforcing what Memet liked to call his 'company policy' and, occasionally, undertaking a little bit of breaking and entering.

Hasan glanced around, feeling exhilarated rather than nervous. This was going to be easy. He'd never been in any urban area that was so quiet. He was a creature of the metropolis, of a London where there were always people and cars about, even at one o'clock in the morning, where there were always clubs or drinking dens or brothels open. A town that closed down at 11 p.m. and reopened at nine the next day was a novelty to him.

They went into the yard at the back of Parnell's office and approached the one-storey modern brick building, both of them slipping gloves on their hands. There was an alarm box on the rear wall, just above head height, but that proved no obstacle to experienced burglars like Hasan and Farok. A leg up from his companion and Hasan had the box disabled in no time at all. The back door of the office was even less of a problem. One quick wrench with the crowbar and the lock snapped open.

They went inside. There was a storeroom and toilet at the back of the building, a larger office at the front through a connecting door that wasn't locked. They drew the blinds across the window overlooking the street and, using the torch to guide them, began to search through the desk and filing cabinets.

The personnel files – the details of all the workers Parnell contracted out to his customers – were in one of the tall metal cabinets, arranged in alphabetical order. Hasan lifted out a handful and stacked them on the desk, leafing through the documents while Farok directed the torch beam at them. There were plenty of surnames beginning with the letter H – Habacha, Hadiri, Horthy, Hussein, half a dozen others, none of them looking English to Hasan – but no Hourami. Hasan checked the letters on either side – G and I – in case the file had been accidentally misplaced, but Irena wasn't there either.

'Maybe she doesn't have a file yet,' Farok said. 'She only came here yesterday, after all.'

'Maybe.'

'The Paki could've been lying, told us the wrong pack-house.' Farok fingered the hilt of his knife in his pocket. 'Why don't we go back and talk to him again?'

'Let's check the other files,' Hasan said.

'What, all of them?'

'Hold the torch steady.'

Hasan went through the cabinet, drawer by drawer, document by document. There was no file on Irena Hourami.

'How're we supposed to find her now?' Farok said.

He clicked the torch off, just in case any of the light was leaking out through the window blinds. Hasan leant back in his chair. They'd gone to the trouble – and risk – of breaking in. He didn't want to go away empty handed.

'Let's go through the files from the beginning again,' he said.

'What for?' Farok demanded. 'She's not there.'

'She's not in the files. But that doesn't mean she's not in Thetford.'

'What do you mean?'

'She's not sleeping in the fields, is she? Khan said his boy had a word with a local gangmaster. Parnell's our man, I'm sure of that. So where is he keeping her? One thing I noticed as I went through the files – the same addresses cropping up time and time again. I reckon Parnell puts his workers up in houses. Let's make a list of where those houses are.'

Hasan went back to the first drawer and looked through

the files again, writing down the addresses of the workers on a sheet of paper. It took them nearly an hour – there were more than two hundred files to examine – but by the end they had a list of twenty-one properties in which the workers were living, sometimes ten or more to a house.

'We going to check all those?' Farok said.

'You got a better idea?' Hasan replied. 'As soon as it's light, we go round them all, see what we find.'

They left the files scattered across the desk – why bother to put them back when it was obvious from the door and alarm that someone had broken in? – and went out into the yard, pulling off their gloves as they walked back to their car.

12

Joe didn't sleep much that night – it was too cold and uncomfortable in the car. He dozed fitfully, waking every so often to look at his watch and wonder why the time was passing so slowly. When, finally, the morning came, he was stiff and shivering, longing for a hot cup of coffee. He turned the engine on and flicked the heater dial round to maximum, letting the warm air revive him.

Outside, the hazy dawn light was creeping across the landscape. The grass on the verge beside the road and the crops in the field opposite – they looked like potatoes to Joe – were glistening with dew. Over by the packhouse, the floodlights were still on, but there was no sign of life.

Joe switched on the radio and listened to the Today programme. The double murder of Anwar and Sara Hourami was one of the headlines. The news report told him nothing he didn't already know. There was no mention of any arrests, though the report did include a voice clip of Louise Crawford appealing for witnesses, anyone who might have seen the killers arriving at the Hourami's flat.

It was 7.45 a.m. when the mini-van came along the road from Thetford. The driver was a pockmarked white man with short curly blond hair. Joe watched the van turn left into Honey Lane and head across to Wintertons packhouse. The building was half a mile away, but with no trees or hedges to block his view Joe could clearly see the van coming to a stop in the carpark, the driver getting out and going round to open the rear doors. Indistinct shapes – ten, maybe a dozen people – emerged from the interior of the van and followed the driver into the packhouse. Ten minutes later, more figures came out of the building – different figures too far away to identify. They climbed into the van. The driver secured the doors and got back into the cab.

Joe slid down low behind the steering wheel of his car and waited for the van to come up the lane and pull out on to the main road. It turned right towards Thetford. Joe gave the van a few seconds head start, then went after it, keeping his distance. The road was flat, dead straight so it was easy to keep the vehicle in sight.

Entering the outskirts of the town, Joe closed the gap a little, following the van as it turned off the main road into a residential area that looked like a council estate. The houses were grouped together in short terraces, the brickwork faced with grubby grey pebbledash from which – with few exceptions – satellite dishes protruded. The van made three stops at three different houses, all within a mile or so of one another. At the first house, five men got out, at the second four women. Joe studied the women, close enough now to make out their faces. He didn't know what Irena looked like, but he was certain she wasn't one of these four. Three of them were too old – in their forties at least – and one was black. At the final stop, outside a semi whose front garden was littered with rubbish, three more women emerged from the back of the van. One was oriental, a small, Chinese-looking woman, and one was white. The third was wearing a headscarf and Joe thought for a moment that she might possibly be Irena. Then the woman turned her head and he saw that her colouring was all wrong – not the skin tone of a Kurd, but the much darker hue of the Indian sub-continent.

The van pulled off again. Joe followed it into the centre of Thetford where it turned into a yard at the rear of an office

151

building. Joe drove past and parked, then walked back to the building. The rear door was wide open, the lock clearly broken. Joe gave a perfunctory knock and went in, through a storeroom and into the front office. There were two men in the room – the blond curly-haired van driver and an older, fat man with a couple of strands of greasy hair slicked down across his balding head.

'I'm sorry,' Joe said. 'The door was open.'

He looked around the office. One drawer of a metal filing cabinet was open and there were cardboard files and papers strewn across the desk – so many that a few had slipped off on to the floor.

'You had a break-in?' Joe said.

The fat man looked at him with small, hostile eyes.

'Who the hell are you?'

'You must be Frank Parnell,' Joe said. 'The security guard at Wintertons gave me your name.'

'Wintertons?'

'I'm looking for someone. A Kurdish woman named Irena Hourami. I believe she came up from London two days ago in one of Rafiq Khan's vans, did a night shift at Wintertons, then stayed on. Youngish, probably wearing a headscarf, doesn't speak much English.'

Out of the corner of his eye, Joe saw the blond-haired man give a start. Joe turned to look at him.

'You know the woman I mean?'

Before the blond-haired man could reply, Frank Parnell butted in.

'Hang on a minute, what *is* this? You walk in here, asking questions, nosing around. Who the fuck are you?'

'I should've introduced myself,' Joe said. 'Joe Verdi, *The News*.'

'A journalist?' Parnell said. 'Piss off.'

Joe looked at Lenny.

'You know the woman?' he asked again.

'Never heard of her,' Lenny said, gazing back coolly.

'Did you hear me?' Parnell said. 'I don't talk to fucking journalists.'

Joe wandered around the desk, fingering one of the files, glancing at a loose sheet of paper.

'Anything taken?' he said. 'In the break-in, I mean. You called the police? No, I don't suppose you have, have you? You probably don't want the law taking too close an interest in your business.'

'Kick this wanker out, Lenny,' Parnell said.

'I still want to know about Irena Hourami,' Joe said. 'Where is she?'

'You weren't listening, were you? We've never heard of any Irena Hourami.'

'I'll give you a tip, Frank,' Joe said. 'The Met want to find her as well. You tell *me* where she is and it might save you a visit from the flatties. Do you really want them going through your files?'

'This is private property,' Parnell said. 'You're trespassing. You don't leave, I'm entitled to use force to eject you.'

Lenny took a step towards Joe. He was light on his feet, like a boxer. Solidly built too, his shoulders and upper arms bulging beneath his tight T-shirt. The fingers of his right hand curled into a fist.

'OK, I'm going,' Joe said.

He edged away behind the desk, taking one of his business cards from his pocket.

'You change your minds, give me a call,' he said.

He placed the card on the desk and exited through the rear door. Lenny followed him out, making sure he was really leaving, then returned to the front office.

'Who's the woman?' Parnell said.

Lenny shrugged.

'There was one, came up from London. But her name wasn't Irena Whatever, it was Sacka Something.'

'Illegal?'

'What do you think, she came from Rafiq Khan.'

'What you do with her?'

'Put her down as Portuguese. Same name as one who disappeared a few months back. Save on paperwork.'

'Which house is she in?'

'Melrose Street. Number thirty-three. There was space.'

Parnell rubbed a hand over his fleshy face, making his jowls vibrate, the tremors passing down through his flabby neck.

'I don't like it,' he said. 'It all smells too fucking fishy to me. Someone breaks into the office, goes through the files, then a journalist shows up asking questions about this woman. A coincidence? I don't think so.'

'The police too,' Lenny said. 'You think that scumbag hack was being straight about the Met?'

'Who knows? But why take a chance? It's trouble. Whatever it is, I don't want to be involved in it. Get rid of her, Lenny. Take her somewhere else, as far away as you can.'

'Where?'

'See if Jimmy will take her. I don't care. Just get her the fuck out of here.'

Irena's second nightshift had been as hard as her first. She'd been taken to a different packhouse, an hour's drive from Thetford. The building was similar to A.P. Wintertons, a long industrial shed, but it was older, the metal walls starting to rust. It was set in the middle of what seemed an endless plain – the Fens, Yasmin called them, though Irena didn't know what that meant. The countryside around Wintertons had been gently undulating, the landscape broken up by low hills and patches of woodland, but the land around this new packhouse was unremittingly flat. Irena, accustomed to the dry hills and small fields of south-eastern Turkey had never seen such a broad, open terrain. The fields were huge, a vista of lush green vegetation stretching to a horizon so far away it seemed like the very edge of the world. There were no hedges, no walls to

154

relieve the monotony of the scenery, just a network of drainage ditches and a few lonely roads. The packhouse was the only building in sight. When Irena climbed out of the mini-van and looked around, she wondered where the villages were. Where did all the people who tended these fields live?

The work was as boring and repetitive as it had been at Wintertons. Not potatoes or onions this time, but carrots. Twelve hours sorting carrots, discarding the ones that were too small or the wrong shape – a chart on the wall showing pictures of how a 'correct' carrot should look – and packing the remainder into small polythene bags, only a few carrots in each bag. It seemed an extraordinarily wasteful operation to Irena – so many carrots thrown away when they were clearly fit to eat – but maybe they had so much food in England that they didn't care.

Her arms, shoulders and back were aching painfully by the time they returned to their house in Thetford. Yasmin made them tea in the kitchen and shared some bread and butter with Irena, the bread a strange English variety – very white and tasteless and so soggy it stuck to the roof of the mouth like putty.

They'd finished eating and were about to go upstairs to sleep when Lenny arrived, walking into the house without knocking, taking them by surprise. Another driver had brought them back from the packhouse in the Fens so Irena hadn't seen Lenny since the previous evening. He'd been relaxed, almost pleasant then, but now he seemed tense.

'Get your stuff,' he said brusquely.

'Uh?' Irena said.

'Your stuff. Your bag. Get it. Now.'

'What happening?' Yasmin said.

'She's leaving.'

'Leaving? Why?'

'None of your fucking business.' Lenny looked at Irena. 'Your bag, your things. Get them.'

He jabbed a finger towards the ceiling, but Irena still didn't understand.

'Oh, sod it,' Lenny snapped. 'Which room is she in?' he asked Yasmin.

'Same as me. The front.'

Lenny beckoned to Irena.

'Come with me. Upstairs.'

Irena squinted at him uncertainly. Why did he want her to go with him?

'It's OK,' Yasmin reassured her. 'You get your bag. I come and help you. You leave it to me,' she added, glancing at Lenny.

Yasmin took Irena upstairs and helped her gather up her belongings and pack them in her hold-all. When they came back down to the kitchen, they found Lenny pacing impatiently around the room.

'Is that it?' he said. 'Everything?'

'Where she going?' Yasmin said.

Lenny stepped close to Yasmin. He took hold of her arm, gripping it tight, looking her hard in the eyes from only a few inches away.

'You've never seen her, you understand?' he said.

'What? What you mean?'

'She was never here. You got that?'

'Let go. You hurting me.'

Yasmin tried to break away, but Lenny tightened his hold on her arm, his fingers digging into her flesh.

'Listen to me, you stupid bitch. If anyone asks you, this woman was never in this house. You've never heard of her, never met her, OK?'

Yasmin stared at him, frightened by his aggressive manner.

'Why?' she said. 'Why you say this?'

'It doesn't matter why. The police might come here.'

'The *police*.' That frightened her even more.

'You want to be deported, sent back to whatever shithole

it is you come from? Then keep your mouth shut. You understand what I'm saying?'

Yasmin nodded.

'I understand.'

Lenny released her. Yasmin rubbed her arm where his fingers had left bright red marks on the skin. Lenny gestured at Irena to follow him. She hesitated. She didn't know what was going on, hadn't understood any of the exchange between Yasmin and Lenny.

Yasmin touched her on the shoulder.

'It OK. You go.'

'OK?' Irena said.

'Yes, OK.'

Lenny took her out to the van and put her in the back. She could've ridden in the cab with him, but he didn't want her next to him, this foreign woman who didn't understand a word he said. Irena sat on the foam rubber mattress, bewildered by the turn of events. She wondered where they were going. Was she going off to do another shift? She hoped not, she was far too tired to work. Maybe they were going to pick up more people and someone might explain to her what was happening. But after twenty minutes, it became clear to her that, for whatever reason, she was going to be the only passenger in the van.

She stretched out on the mattress, making the most of the space. There was a knot of anxiety in her stomach, but she was getting used to that. She was worn out, too weary to think any more. She closed her eyes and went to sleep.

Joe retraced the route he'd taken through Thetford, going back to the houses where the mini-van had dropped off workers – or two of the houses, at least. The one the male workers had gone into he decided to ignore. The migrant workers would almost certainly be segregated, put up in single-sex accommodation.

He stopped outside the last of the houses – where the

three women had alighted – and knocked on the door. The white woman answered. Joe could tell immediately from her complexion, her features, that she wasn't English. Her accent, when she spoke, sounded Eastern European.

'Yes, what you want?'

'I'm looking for a Kurdish woman,' Joe said.

'Kurdish? What that?' the woman said. She was in her forties. Her skin was pale and unhealthy-looking, blotches of red on her chin and cheeks.

'Turkish then,' Joe said. 'Her name's Irena. Irena Hourami.'

'Who?'

'Are there any Kurds living here?'

'Who are you?'

The woman was nervous. Joe could guess why. She was foreign, maybe working in England illegally. He was a white Englishman in a jacket and tie. To the woman that would mean officialdom, authority. Bad news.

'Can I come in?' Joe said.

The woman backed away, making no attempt to stop him entering. The first door off the hall was ajar. Joe caught a glimpse of mattresses on the floor inside the front room, but no one sleeping on them.

'How many people live here?' Joe said.

He knew the three women he'd seen dropped off earlier wouldn't be the only occupants of the house. Gangmasters were notorious for packing large numbers of migrant workers into very small spaces. There'd be eight, maybe more in a semi like this.

'Ten,' the woman replied.

'From where?'

'Don't know.'

'Is there a woman called Irena? Young, Muslim, wearing a headscarf.'

'No, no Irena.'

'Show me upstairs,' Joe said.

The woman didn't move. She eyed him suspiciously.

'Who are you?' she asked again.

Time for a harmless bit of subterfuge, Joe decided.

'I'm from the council,' he said.

'Council. What the council? Immigration?'

'Not immigration. Health and Safety. I don't want to see your papers, OK?'

'No papers?'

The woman looked relieved. She moved aside and let him go upstairs. There were three bedrooms on the first floor, more dirty mattresses with no sheets or pillows. Two of the rooms were empty. In the third, at the back of the house, the oriental woman and Indian-looking woman were asleep, still wearing their day clothes. They didn't stir when Joe glanced in on them. Joe went back downstairs.

'Where are the others?' he said.

'Working,' the woman replied.

'Where?'

'Fields. They back tonight.'

'OK. Thank you.'

Joe went out to his car and drove the quarter of a mile to the next house – where the four other women had been dropped off. As he went through the gate into the tiny front garden, he noticed that the door of the house was open. He walked in and paused in the hall. He could hear voices at the back – a man's voice shouting, then a woman replying, clearly distressed. They were speaking English, but both had foreign accents.

Joe padded cautiously down the hall and peeped into the room. It was a kitchen, worktops and cupboards around the edges, a small table in the centre, a sink in front of the window that overlooked the rear garden. A black woman – the one Joe had seen earlier leaving the van – was backed up against the sink, staring in terror at a dark-skinned man with a moustache who was looming over her menacingly. The man took hold of the woman's face, gripping her jaw with his powerful hand and squeezing so hard she cried out.

'You lie to me,' the man said. 'And I hurt you bad. You understand?'

The woman nodded, tears in her eyes.

'You know any woman looks like that?' the man said.

'No.' The woman forced the word out, struggling to speak with the man's fingers digging into the sides of her mouth. 'No.'

Joe stepped into the room.

'Let her go,' he said quietly.

The man released the woman and spun round, his gaze coming to rest on Joe, his eyes hard, malevolent. It was only then that Joe guessed who the man was. He felt suddenly exposed, vulnerable. His fingers groped behind him on the worktop, searching for a weapon.

He caught a slight movement over to his left. There was a second man in the room, half hidden by the open door. A man with a beard, a knife glinting in his right hand. Joe picked up the first thing he touched – a heavy dinner plate – and hurled it at the man. The edge of the plate hit the man on the bridge of the nose. Blood spurted from his nostrils. He lifted his left hand to his face, his eyes momentarily closed in pain. Joe kicked out with his foot, knocking the knife from the man's grasp. The knife skittered away into a gap beneath one of the cupboards.

The first man was coming for him now. Joe picked up another plate and swung it round, shattering the plate against the side of the man's head. The man swayed, dazed by the blow, but he didn't fall. The black woman over by the sink started to yell, a piercing scream that must have been audible two streets away. Joe threw a punch, his knuckles sinking into the man's cheek, then backed away. He snatched a frying pan from the stove and brandished it in front of him. The black woman was still screaming.

The man with the moustache shouted something to his

companion in a foreign tongue – Joe knew it had to be Turkish. He braced himself for an attack, but instead the men fled, ran out of the kitchen and away down the hall. Joe went after them. He grabbed hold of the bearded Turk before he could get out through the front door and dragged him back. The Turk lashed out. His elbow hit Joe in the face. Joe toppled over and as he fell, his head crashed into the wooden post at the bottom of the stair rail. A sharp stab of pain knifed through his skull. His vision blurred, a kaleidoscopic pattern of shapes passing across his eyes before everything went black.

13

He was out for no more than a few minutes, but it was long enough for the Turks to get away. When he opened his eyes, he saw the black woman crouching beside him in the hall.

'They've gone,' she said.

Joe struggled to sit up. There was a dull, throbbing ache in the side of his head. He lifted his hand and touched his temple. The skin was tender, but unbroken. He got to his feet, pausing for a moment to let his vision settle down. Then he went to the open front door and looked out. The street was quiet, a few cars parked along the kerb but no traffic moving past. A woman in the house opposite was standing in her front window, staring across at him. There was no sign of the two men.

'Did you see their car?' Joe said to the black woman.

'No.'

'Are you OK? They didn't hurt you?'

'Not much.'

'They were asking about Irena Hourami, weren't they? A Kurdish woman. Do you know her?'

'She don't live here. She don't work where I work. I don't know who she is.'

'She's new to the area,' Joe said. 'Came up a couple of days ago from London. A young woman, wears a head-scarf. You seen anyone like that around?'

'No.'

Joe looked back up the street. A police car was coming

towards him, pulling in outside the house. He guessed that the woman opposite must have called them. There was a second car following close behind, a dark green Ford saloon. Joe gave a start as he recognised the driver and his passenger: DS Danny Chisholm and DC Nolan, the detective who'd taken his statement at Stoke Newington police station. How the hell had they caught up with him so quickly?

Two uniformed officers climbed out of the marked police car and came through the gate and up to the house.

'We've had a report of a disturbance,' one of the officers said. 'A woman screaming.'

'Come in,' Joe said.

They interviewed him and the black woman in the kitchen, one of the uniformed constables asking the questions, the other taking notes. Chisholm and Nolan leaned against the worktop, looking on in silence, waiting for the local boys to finish before they took their turn. They had the air of scavengers about them, a couple of hungry hyenas skulking patiently on the sidelines, watching for the right moment to move in and eat their share of a kill.

The black woman – Elspeth Onwubiko was the name she'd given – told her story first, how the two men had forced their way into the house, searched all the rooms and then cornered her in the kitchen, threatening her, asking her about a woman she'd never seen or heard of.

'They had me over there against the sink,' she said. 'One of them was holding me – like this.' She demonstrated. 'Hurting me. Then this man arrived.' She nodded at Joe. 'He saved me.'

The police officer turned to Joe, who completed the rest of the story.

'Can you describe these men, sir?' the officer asked.

Joe gave them a description. He noticed Danny Chisholm making notes discreetly in the background.

'There's a woman across the street,' Joe went on. 'She

might have seen the Turks leave, seen what kind of car they had.'

'You say Turks, sir. What makes you think they were Turkish?'

Joe looked across at Chisholm, the detective scribbling a few last words before he glanced up.

'You want to tell them, Danny?' Joe said.

The uniformed officer swivelled round in his chair and gazed at Chisholm.

'You know each other?'

'Unfortunately, yes,' Chisholm replied sardonically.

'The one with the beard came at me with a knife,' Joe said. 'I kicked it out of his hand. It skittered away under that cupboard there. He wasn't wearing gloves. You might get some prints.'

DC Nolan dropped to his knees and peered under the cupboard. He nodded at Chisholm, then left the room, returning shortly after with a transparent plastic evidence bag and a pair of thin rubber gloves. He slipped a glove on one hand and felt under the cupboard, pulling out the knife by the blade and depositing it in the evidence bag.

'You're taking that?' the uniformed officer enquired.

'We need it more than you,' Chisholm said. 'I don't want to pull rank on you, but I think you've done all you can here. Why don't you go and talk to the woman across the street?'

'What about this?' the uniformed constable said. 'The assault on this woman.'

'Let's catch the guys first,' Chisholm said. 'We do, they'll be going down for a lot more than assault. Thanks for your help.'

Chisholm came forward, leaving the two local bobbies in no doubt that their time was up.

'You can go too,' Chisholm said to Elspeth.

'Those men . . .' she began.

'They won't come back. You don't need to worry about that.'

Chisholm waited for the Thetford cops and Elspeth to leave, then sat down at the table with his notebook. Nolan remained standing, his eyes fixed on Joe.

'That was a lucky coincidence,' Joe said. 'You arriving at the same time as the Norfolk boys.'

'It wasn't a coincidence,' Chisholm replied. 'They were with us over at Frank Parnell's office. A courtesy escort for visiting out-of-town colleagues. They took the emergency call – a disturbance at an address we'd just discovered was one of Frank's houses – so we thought we'd tag along.'

'You've talked to Frank Parnell?'

Chisholm nodded.

'And you know what is a coincidence?' he said. 'We get there and find that you've been there before us. Amazing, eh?'

'Did Parnell tell you that?'

'I saw your card on his desk. Parnell wouldn't tell us the time unless there was something in it for him. A tight bastard? Camels' arses and sandstorms have got nothing on him. But let's stick with coincidences for a while, shall we? Because we went to a packhouse earlier – A.P. Wintertons – and what do you know, you'd been there before us too. How about that then? You want to share with us your source of information?'

'No,' Joe said.

'You're making a bit of a habit of this, aren't you? DCI Crawford's going to be really pissed off when she hears.'

'Is she with you?'

'DCIs don't do the legwork themselves, you know that. She has a triple murder investigation to run, remember? Lucky for you I'm such an understanding, easy-going bloke. If Crawford was here, she'd have you swinging by your dick from the light fitting by now.'

'You have such a colourful turn of phrase, Danny.'

'I know. I could've been a journalist, only I have too strong an idea of right and wrong.'

'Do I sense a point here?'

'You're fucking up our investigation, Joe. Is that a good enough point for you?'

'I'm doing my job. You got a problem with that?'

'Yes, if it interferes with a case I'm working on. You're muddying the waters. Scaring away witnesses, scuffing up tracks, obliterating the scent we're following.'

'Can I help it if I get somewhere before you?'

'Who told you about Wintertons?'

'Does it matter now? Irena wasn't there.'

'Yes, it matters. Maybe whoever told you has other information that could be of use to us.'

'I'm not going to reveal my sources, Danny. You know me better than that. What did Parnell tell you?'

Chisholm stared at him incredulously.

'Oh, no, don't try that one. You're getting nothing out of me unless I get something from you first.'

'I've given you the knife, haven't I?'

'True,' Chisholm conceded. 'Quite the hero, aren't you? Tackling a couple of armed thugs with nothing more than a dinner plate.'

'It may be the knife that killed Anwar and Sara Hourami. Maybe Ismail Hourami too. That should earn you some brownie points.'

'Even you wouldn't keep a potential murder weapon from us. But let's face it, you only gave us the knife because it's no use whatsoever to you. Information, though, is different. You hoard that like a miser.'

'I've nothing to tell you, Danny. That's the truth. You know as much as I do now.'

'Try me.'

Joe shrugged.

'I know Irena came here in one of Rafiq Khan's vans. I told you that in London. I could find no record of Irena at

Wintertons. Maybe she went to a different packhouse. I haven't tried any others.'

'We found no record of her at Wintertons either,' Chisholm said. 'Her name wasn't on the worksheets. The foreman was vague, said he saw a lot of different casual workers passing through, couldn't remember any one woman in particular.'

'You found Khan yet?'

'No.'

'What about his staff? There's a kid – a Pakistani lad – drives his van. There may be more than one.'

'We know about him. We picked up a bloke hanging around Khan's office last night, a Romanian, said he'd gone up to Norfolk a few times in the van. He's the one told us about Wintertons. But the Pakistani kid's disappeared, like his boss.'

'What does Parnell say?'

'He's never heard of Irena Hourami. But he's a gang-master. Lying's his stock in trade. We'll check his records, see what he's hiding.'

'If the records are there,' Joe said. 'You know he had a break-in last night? Someone went through his files.'

'Is that so? He didn't tell us that. The Turks?'

'Has to be. How else did they get this address?'

'They thought Irena was here?'

'Elspeth says she isn't. I think she's telling the truth. I reckon the Turks were just going round Parnell's properties, hoping to pick up a lead.'

Chisholm glanced at Nolan.

'See if the local boys are still outside. We could use some help. Ask them to have Parnell's properties checked out. I don't think the Turks are stupid enough to hang around, but you never know, we might get lucky.'

Nolan nodded and left the kitchen. Chisholm's penetrating gaze came back to Joe.

'And?'

'That's it,' Joe said. 'That's all I know.'

Chisholm didn't look convinced.

'You sure?'

'Yes. Can I go now?'

Joe stood up. Chisholm stayed seated, his notebook open on the table in front of him.

'You're going back to London now,' he said.

'Maybe,' Joe replied.

'It wasn't a question. It was a statement of fact. You follow me?'

'And if I don't?'

'I don't want any more coincidences. Finding Irena Hourami is police work. I bump into you again in Thetford, or near here, and I'll nick you.'

'On what charge?'

'I'll think of something. Have a safe journey.'

Joe looked down at him, a faint smile of resignation on his lips. Chisholm was bluffing, of course. They both knew that. He couldn't stop Joe from staying on in Thetford, or from doing anything else in the furtherance of his lawful business. But the letter of the law wasn't what mattered here. There was the spirit to consider too. Maybe a few practical issues as well. Chisholm was right. Finding Irena was the police's job, not a journalist's. They had the manpower and resources to do it. Joe could stick around and watch, but tenacious though he was, he knew it would be irresponsible to get in their way. Questioning the police, holding them to account was part of his job, but hindering them wasn't.

He was tired, feeling the effects of the night in his car. His head was aching, and he was only just becoming aware of the mental impact that the confrontation with the Turks had had on him. He was shaken, there was no denying it. He'd been attacked and had responded with a violence that was alien to his nature. It had been in self-defence, but that didn't lessen the feeling of repugnance it gave him. Smashing plates on other men's heads, drawing blood, was not something he took lightly. It was time to step back from the fray and leave the police to get on with the fight.

'I'll see you around,' he said.

He nodded at Chisholm and walked out of the kitchen.

'I'm afraid I have some bad news for you . . .'

Ellie listened to the woman's voice on the telephone, the nurse calling from Whittington hospital, and felt a cold shiver pass through her body, knowing what was coming next.

'. . . Mrs North has died.'

Ellie's fingers tightened around the receiver. She closed her eyes for a moment.

'Hello? Miss Mason?'

'Yes, I'm here,' Ellie said.

'I'm very sorry.'

'When was this?' Ellie said.

'About half an hour ago.'

'What was the cause?'

'We don't know for certain yet. There'll have to be an autopsy. It appears to have been some kind of an internal haemorrhage. Are there any relatives we should notify? A next of kin. Your name is the only one we have on file.'

'I don't know. She had a nephew. He lives somewhere in Yorkshire, I think. But I don't have an address or phone number for him.'

'She had some things with her. A bag. Is there someone who could collect them?'

'Yes, I'll come and get them. Thank you for letting me know.'

Ellie hung up, and for a few seconds sat motionless in her chair. The news had stunned her, left her feeling breathless. She hadn't been particularly close to Hilda North, but she'd been fond of the old lady. They'd been friends – not intimate friends the way you could be with people your own age, but friends nonetheless, their relationship the more formal, more reserved kind that could span the generations. Mrs North had been lonely, and alone. Ellie had felt sorry for her, had done what she could to help her, occasionally – to her shame now – with irritation or resentment, but usually willingly. She was glad of that, glad that in some small way she had comforted Hilda in her final years.

She found it hard to believe that Hilda was gone, that never again would she come home to find the old lady waiting for her in the hall, or share a cup of tea with her in her living room, or drive her over to the local library to exchange her books. Those small, banal, everyday acts seemed to take on a greater importance now that they would never happen again.

Ellie finished the story she was typing and saved it, then went across to the newsdesk and explained to Ed Preston about Hilda, asking if she could have a couple of hours off.

'You filed your piece?' Preston said.

'It's all done. I'll come back in later, make sure there are no queries.'

Ellie drove to Whittington Hospital. The receptionist at the main desk didn't know anything about Hilda North or her belongings, but she rang the Intensive Care Unit and spoke briefly to someone there.

'If you'd like to go to the ICU,' she said to Ellie. 'They're dealing with it.'

The nurse in intensive care was the one who'd rung Ellie earlier.

'Thank you for coming in,' she said. 'I'm so sorry about Mrs North.'

'I don't understand. What happened?' Ellie asked. 'She was obviously ill yesterday evening, but for her to die . . .'

'It was very sudden. We'll know more after the autopsy,' the nurse said. 'Now, you mentioned a nephew, Mrs North's next of kin. Is there any way we can get in touch with him? Someone will have to make the arrangements for the funeral.'

'His name's Jeremy, I think. Jeremy North,' Ellie said. 'I'll see if I can find a phone number for him in Mrs North's flat and let you know.'

'Thank you, that would be most helpful.'

The nurse reached behind a desk and pulled out the travel case Ellie had packed for Hilda. It hadn't even been opened.

'This is Mrs North's bag. And these are the clothes she was wearing.'

The nurse handed Ellie a parcel, then produced an envelope from a drawer.

'Her watch and jewellery are in here. If you could sign for them, please.'

Ellie scribbled her signature at the bottom of the form and lifted the flap of the envelope. Mrs North's gold watch was inside, with her diamond engagement ring and gold wedding band. Ellie had never known Hilda's husband, though Hilda had talked of him often. Seeing the gold ring now, detached from Hilda's finger, gave Ellie a pang of sorrow. It seemed a poignant reminder of the old lady's marriage. Hilda's husband had died many years before. Now Hilda too had gone.

Ellie slipped the envelope into her shoulder bag, then picked up the case and parcel of clothes and left the hospital.

14

Irena had no idea whereabouts in England she was. She didn't know how long the van journey had taken – she had no watch and had slept the whole way – but she guessed it must have been a couple of hours. When they finally came to a stop and Lenny opened the rear doors, Irena could tell from the light, from the position of the sun high in the sky, that it was the middle of the day. Lenny said something to her and beckoned her out of the van. Irena picked up her bag and climbed out. They were parked on a street in the centre of a town. Irena looked around and saw pavements crowded with people, rows of shops – English shops – with names and facades that were entirely foreign to her.

Lenny took her arm and led her through a door next to a burger bar. A steep flight of stairs took them up to a first-floor office where a thin, wiry man in jeans and a T-shirt was talking on the phone. The man nodded at Lenny, as if they knew each other, then finished his phone conversation and held out a grubby hand. The two men shook.

'How're you doing, Jimmy?' Lenny said.

'OK, mate, not too bad. Yourself?'

Lenny sat down by the desk and the two men chatted for a few minutes. Neither of them offered Irena a seat. She stood near the door, watching them talking, knowing they were discussing her, but not understanding what they were saying. She listened for a time, trying to pick out individual words in their rapid exchange, then gave up, it was too hard. She waited patiently, passively, feeling as if all her free will had been taken away. She was like a piece of flotsam floating on the sea, powerless to control the water around her, simply going helplessly where the tide and currents chose to take her.

'Jimmy's going to look after you now,' Lenny said, and Irena realised he was speaking directly to her. 'OK?'

She didn't reply. She didn't know what she'd been asked.

'She doesn't speak English,' Lenny said.

'What's her work like?' Jimmy said.

'Good. You know these towelhead peasants, they're used to manual labour. She won't let you down.'

'What's her name again?'

'Ligia Moreira.'

'How'd you spell that?'

Jimmy wrote the name down on a scrap of paper.

'She's Portuguese,' Lenny said. 'But doesn't have any papers. Lost them somewhere.'

Jimmy looked at him and grinned, exposing a mouthful of uneven, yellowish teeth.

'No kidding, eh?'

'You can get her an i.d. though, can't you?'

'For a price, yeah.'

'You're doing us a big favour. Next time you're down Thetford way, Frank says he'll buy you a drink.'

'That'll be the day,' Jimmy said. 'How is the old bastard, anyway?'

'Same as ever.'

'And Marge? I should ring her more often, but you know how things are.'

'She's OK.' Lenny gave a lopsided smile. 'Well, as OK as you can be being married to a shit like Frank.'

Jimmy laughed.

'Give her my best.'

The two men shook hands again and Lenny left. Jimmy came out from behind the desk.

'You come with me, Ligia,' he said.

He took her outside to his van and made her get into the front.

'So you're Portuguese? *Falo um pouco de português. De onde é?*' he said. He employed a lot of Portuguese workers – and Brazilians who came into the country on fake Portuguese i.d. cards. He'd picked up a smattering of the language.

Irena didn't respond.

'Didn't think so,' Jimmy said.

He didn't care. In his world, everybody had something to hide.

The house was very like the one she'd left behind in Thetford – a small brick terrace with mattresses on the floors of all the rooms except the kitchen and bathroom. Jimmy took her upstairs and showed her where she could sleep. They were the only people in the house.

'The others are out working,' Jimmy explained. 'You'll start tomorrow. Tomorrow . . . you work. OK?'

Irena wandered around the house after Jimmy had gone, looking in all the rooms, noting the carrier bags of possessions next to the mattresses, wondering what the people she'd be sharing with were like. The house felt cold, though it was a warm summer day outside. It wasn't the temperature that made the place chilly, it was the atmosphere. The bare walls, the lack of furniture, the empty rooms with their pathetic little bundles of belongings – evidence of transient human habitation, of residents who lived there yet had failed, or chosen not, to turn it into a home.

Irena missed Yasmin. They'd known each other for only a couple of days, could barely communicate with each other, but Irena had regarded her as a friend. Yasmin had taken her under her wing, made her feel welcome, shared her food with her. To Irena, those small acts of kindness had meant a great deal. Without Yasmin, those first days would have been unbearable. Lost, homesick, grieving for Ismail, Irena didn't know how she would have survived without Yasmin keeping her company – in the house and on the packhouse production line. Now she was alone again, Irena could feel depression taking hold of her once more, dragging her spirits even lower, demoralising her. She hadn't had time to dwell too much on her loss, but now the memories of Ismail came flooding back and her eyes filled with tears. She couldn't stop them, didn't want to stop them. She sat at the kitchen table and wept.

They were meant to be together. That was the only reason they had come to England. To be with each other, to start a new life, a family. Ismail had been so strong, strong enough for both of them, a real fighter. He wouldn't have given in to adversity, he could endure anything. Irena thought of the newspaper articles he'd written back home in Diyarbakir, courageous, provocative pieces that he'd known would arouse the ire of the Turkish authorities. But then that had been their point. To throw down the gauntlet, to challenge what he saw as unjust oppression by an illegitimate government. He was a Kurd. He regarded the land he lived in as part of Kurdistan, not Turkey. The aims of the PKK – a free and independent homeland for his people – were Ismail's aims too, though he abhorred the methods of the Kurdish Workers' Party. He was a journalist, not a soldier. He chose the pen rather than the sword to wound his opponents, judged the effectiveness of his campaign by the ferocity of the response it aroused.

And the response had been gratifyingly harsh. Irena had lost count of the number of times Ismail had been arrested during their five-year marriage. How many times the police had kicked in their door during the night and hauled Ismail off to jail. She knew he'd been tortured while in custody, knew he accepted that the ill treatment came with the territory, though he never talked about it to her. He saw the pain he endured as a small victory, the police's brutality as evidence of their desperation, their moral bankruptcy that would eventually bring them down.

Irena had lived in fear that one day Ismail might not come back. She believed that he could have faced that possibility with equanimity, but he knew that she could not. So for Irena they had fled to Europe. They had abandoned their home and their families and the fight for independence that meant so much to Ismail and trekked west to England, a country they dreamt of as a peaceful, civilised haven for refugees – an illusion that had lasted only minutes before the Turk's knife had ripped it savagely away.

In time, the tears stopped flowing. Irena wiped her eyes with her handkerchief and chided herself for her weakness. She must pull herself together, try to be as resilient as Ismail had been. That was what he would have wanted. She went to the kitchen sink and bathed her face. She felt drained, relieved that – for the moment, at least – there were no more tears to come.

She was tired, but she didn't want to sleep just yet. She had shelter, a roof over her head, but she had no food. In Thetford, Yasmin had shared her meals with her, but Irena couldn't rely on her new housemates being so altruistic. She had to provide for herself now. She had the money Anwar had given her. All she needed to do was find somewhere to spend it.

She checked that the three ten pound notes were safe in the pocket of her skirt and went out of the house. There was no key to lock up – the door had been open when she and Jimmy had arrived. Irena pulled the door to and paused on the step, looking both ways up the street. She could see a taller building in the distance, a church tower rising up above the surrounding roofs. She guessed that must be the centre of the town and set off towards it. There would be a market somewhere, she thought. Somewhere she could buy food.

It was a longer walk than she'd expected – a good twenty minutes along streets of neat semi-detached houses and well-kept front gardens before she found herself in the middle of the town. There was a central square that, in Turkey, would almost certainly have been crammed with stalls, with traders touting their wares. But here it was filled with parked cars. Irena wandered past the shops that fronted on the square. There were jewellers and newsagents, clothes and shoe retailers, but no shops selling food. Irena drifted into a side street, then across a busy main road and found herself in a carpark outside a huge supermarket. She knew these places existed in the West, but this was the first time she'd set eyes on one. She lingered by the entrance for a time, looking in through the big glass doors, watching other people going in and trying to summon the courage to follow them. The sheer size of the shop intimidated her. What did you do once you were inside? How did you find your way around it?

Finally, she decided she'd waited long enough. It was time to take the plunge. She walked through the doors, half expecting someone to leap out and accost her, to tell her she had no right to be there. But no one took the slightest notice of her. The store was cool, brightly lit, soft music playing somewhere in the background. Irena wandered past the trays of fruit and vegetables, puzzled by the layout of the shop. There was plenty of produce on display, but no one seemed to be on hand to serve the customers. Irena moved to one side to make herself less conspicuous and watched what everyone else did.

A woman came in from the carpark and picked up an orange plastic basket from a stack by the door. Then she went to the shelves of fruit, selected her own apples and bananas and put them in plastic bags. So that was how you did it – you helped yourself. Irena followed the woman at a distance and noted how she went down different aisles putting items into her basket before going to a row of counters manned by women in uniforms to pay for her goods. There were other customers, she noticed, who didn't have baskets but were pushing metal trolleys full of groceries, presumably to feed large families. She didn't need that much food. A basket would do her just fine. She went back to the entrance and collected one.

There was a huge variety of fruit and vegetables to choose from. She hardly knew where to begin. She put some onions in a bag and deposited them in her basket. Then she moved on to the salads. There were four or five different kinds of lettuce and stacks of cucumbers that, for some reason she couldn't comprehend, had been sheathed in plastic. The tomatoes came in several different sizes – big fat ones, medium-sized ones and tiny ones in plastic containers. Irena picked up one of the medium-sized tomatoes. It felt hard and wasn't fully ripe, the skin orange rather than red. When she lifted it to her nose, it didn't smell of anything. The apples didn't have a scent either, which Irena found curious. The English must like their fruit under-ripe and odourless, she thought.

She kept going along the aisle, putting a few potatoes into her basket, a korm of garlic and a glossy aubergine. Then she went off to explore the rest of the shop. She was astonished by how many different things were on sale, how beautifully it was all packaged. Nothing was loose. The rice, the sultanas were all sealed in bags. Even the bread was wrapped in plastic, some of it already sliced for you. She chose carefully, not selecting too much. She had thirty pounds, but she didn't know how far that would stretch. England was an expensive country, she knew that.

When she'd got all she wanted in her basket, she went to the counters where you paid and copied the other customers, putting the items on a conveyor belt and watching as the shop assistant passed the goods over a machine that seemed to know all the prices. It all seemed very clever and it had the additional advantage – as far as Irena was concerned – of not requiring any kind of communication between her and the shop assistant. The language barrier wasn't a problem here. A total came up on a little electronic screen and Irena held out her money for the assistant to take. Eight pounds and thirty-seven pence. Irena didn't really know whether that was good value for money or not. She was just happy that she had enough food for a few days now and still had two of the ten pound notes Anwar had given her.

She walked home with her plastic carrier bags, feeling proud of herself for coping with such an alien way of shopping, feeling for the first time since she'd arrived in England that she had regained some small measure of control over her own life.

She ate some sultanas and an apple in the kitchen of the house, which she still had to herself, then took her groceries upstairs to the bedroom. She placed the carrier bags next to her hold-all at the head of her mattress and lay down. The man who'd brought her here – she didn't know his name – would come back when it was time for her to go to work. She didn't know when that would be. But in the meantime it was sensible to rest, to conserve her energy. She closed her eyes and went to sleep.

'My name is Greenwood, Alan Greenwood,' the man's voice on the telephone said. 'I'm an environmental health officer with Islington Borough Council.'

'Oh, yes?' Ellie replied warily, a part of her brain already switching off, thinking, 'Oh, God, not some council health story.' Environmental health, that was dirty restaurants and takeaways, wasn't it? Or drains. Please don't let it be drains, she thought. I'm on a national newspaper now. I don't have to do stories about drains any more.

'How can I help you?' she went on.

'The hospital gave me your number,' Greenwood said.

'The hospital? What hospital?'

'Whittington.'

'I'm sorry, you're losing me. Why would Whittington Hospital give you my phone number?'

'It's about Mrs North, Hilda North,' Greenwood said. 'I'm speaking to the right Ellie Mason, aren't I? You are – were – Mrs North's neighbour?'

'Yes, yes I am – was. Did you say you were from environmental health?'

'Yes, that's correct. I'm looking into the circumstances surrounding Mrs North's death. The hospital tests and post mortem examination have revealed that she died of typhoid fever.'

'*Typhoid?*' Ellie said incredulously. 'Typhoid? Are you sure?'

'There's no doubt about it.'

'But people don't die of typhoid any more, do they? Not in this country.'

'It's certainly rare,' Greenwood admitted. 'But it happens. There are a couple of hundred cases of the disease annually in the UK, most contracted overseas, in countries where typhoid is more of a problem.'

'Mrs North had typhoid?' Ellie still couldn't fully absorb the information. 'But how? How did she get it?'

'That's what I'm trying to establish. As I'm sure you know, typhoid is a notifiable disease. The Health Protection Agency has passed the case on to us and we have a duty to investigate it. Would you mind if I ask you a few questions about Mrs North?'

'Not at all.'

'Did you know her well?'

'That's hard to say. I live in the flat above hers. I saw her frequently, often every day, but it was mostly in passing. You know, coming in and out of the house.'

'Had she been abroad in the last few weeks?'

'No.'

'You can be certain about that?'

'Absolutely. I'd know if she'd been out of the country. She didn't go anywhere much, in fact. Apart from trips to the shops, the doctor's, she was virtually housebound. I'd say she never went further than a couple of miles from her flat in all the time I knew her.'

'What about contact with other people? Had she met anyone recently who'd been abroad and might have been carrying the disease?'

'Not that I know of,' Ellie said. 'How exactly do you catch typhoid? I thought it was from dirty water.'

'That's probably the most common way of contracting it,' Greenwood said. 'Certainly in countries where hygiene and sanitation standards are not very high. But you can, of course, catch it from people who already have the disease. Or people who've had it and recovered. Some people are carriers. They don't show symptoms of typhoid, but they can still spread it to others.'

'You mean she could've caught it from a stranger in the street?'

'Not that easily. Typhoid is a bacterial infection, a form of salmonella. It's not an airborne disease like, say, flu. You usually contract it by drinking contaminated water or handling or eating contaminated food, or by direct contact with a person who is infected with the bacteria. Had she had any visitors in the last three weeks – the incubation period is one to three weeks?'

'I don't remember her having any,' Ellie said. 'I'm sure she'd have mentioned it if she had. She didn't get many visitors.'

'What about contacts outside the home? Did she have any regular appointments? A lunch club, perhaps, or any other kind of social activity?'

'No. As I said, she didn't go out much. She didn't seem to have many friends. She was a widow, she lived alone.'

'She didn't have any family?'

'Not close. I never saw any relatives at the house.'

'So you were probably the person who had the most to do with her?'

'I suppose I was,' Ellie said.

She'd never looked at it like that before, but it seemed terribly sad now that she – a neighbour who'd known the old lady only a few years and didn't give her much thought – had been Hilda North's closest contact.

'Have *you* been abroad recently?' Greenwood asked.

'Me? No.'

'How's your general health?'

'You think Mrs North might have caught typhoid from me?'

'We have to explore all avenues.'

'What're the symptoms of typhoid?'

'Usually a headache to start with, followed by fever, then joint pain, sore throat and loss of appetite. Often there's a feeling of soreness in the stomach area and constipation that can change to diarrhoea as the disease progresses.'

'I've none of those. I feel fine.'

'Nevertheless, it would be advisable for you to be tested.'

'In hospital?'

'A visit to your GP with a stool sample is all it takes. I can give you a sample container.'

'Give me? When?'

'Do you have access to Mrs North's flat?'

'I have her spare keys, yes.'

'I'd like to visit the flat, if possible. Check her kitchen, her water supply, her sewage outlet. Do a few tests. Would you be able to let me in?'

'Well, I'm not sure. I'd feel a little uncomfortable about that unless I had the permission of Mrs North's nephew, Jeremy – he's her next of kin, but he lives in Yorkshire.'

'Do you have a contact number for him?'

'Yes. I rang him last night to tell him his aunt had died. He's coming down in the next couple of days to sort out her affairs.'

'Could you ring him, ask his permission?'

'I suppose so.'

'It would simplify matters. We really need to act quickly on this. Typhoid is a serious disease. We need to trace the source of the infection, to stop anyone else catching it.'

'I'll call him now,' Ellie said. 'And get back to you.'

Memet Dil wasn't a religious man. The constitution of his native land described Turkey as a democratic secular state, and Dil regarded himself as a democratic secular citizen. He was a Muslim, but not a practising one. He observed some of the tenets of his faith, at least the ones that suited him. He didn't drink alcohol and he didn't gamble – though his abstinence was based less on religious stricture than on personal preference. Both those vices held no appeal for him. They were debilitating weaknesses, indulgences that clouded the judgement, and Dil despised weakness.

He never prayed. Breaking up his busy schedule to go down on his knees five times a day seemed an unnecessarily onerous commitment to a faith he had never considered a primary driving force in his life. His visits to a mosque were infrequent and usually expedient, having some purpose other than communing with God, but despite this casual adherence to Islam he felt that Allah had been good to him.

He had only to look around him to see the numerous ways in which he had been blessed. He had a house in an affluent area of north London, a large detached residence with seven bedrooms, a tennis court on which he rarely set foot and three garages to house his trio of Mercedes, a car he liked so much that he had bought himself a dealership. He owned two Turkish restaurants – in Stoke Newington and Harringay – a hotel on the south coast near Brighton and a nightclub and pub in the West End of London. He didn't drink himself, but he had no objection to others doing so, particularly as supporting their intoxication was such a profitable business.

He enjoyed running these various enterprises for their own sake – the process of accruing money had fascinated him since he was a boy helping out in his father's shop – but the main reason he had diversified into these different trades was money laundering. He made so much through his illegal activities that he needed some legitimate way of cleaning up and disposing of the proceeds. The car dealership and all the rest were fronts, the legal face he presented to the world, but the foundations of everything were drugs.

He'd discovered the allure of heroin when he was only a teenager. Not as a user, but as a tiny link in the supply chain from the poppy fields of Afghanistan to the streets of western Europe, a chain that passed directly through his home province in south-eastern Turkey. His family had had ties to the cartel that controlled the flow of raw opium through Iran and Iraq. One of Memet's uncles had owned a laboratory where the opium was refined into heroin and, being childless himself, had brought his nephew into the business and groomed him to take over, a role Memet had duly, and willingly, inherited when his uncle died. The laboratory was a profitable undertaking, but Memet was ambitious. He wanted more than a life in provincial Turkey – however prosperous – was ever going to offer him. The big money, he realised early on, was not in refining drugs but in distributing them, so he came to England and set up his own network of dealers and pushers, modelling his organisation on the corporate idea of vertical integration. He was no longer a small part of the chain from Afghanistan to England, he was a whole section of it. He owned laboratories in Turkey, had a fleet of lorries and teams of couriers to transport the heroin across Europe, and he controlled the distribution of the drug to the customer in London and a dozen other major continental cities.

He had a lot to be thankful for, not least the fact that – so far – he'd never been caught. He'd had brushes with the law in the past, but they'd never amounted to a serious threat to either his livelihood or his liberty. He was too careful to incriminate himself, too cunning to leave any trail of criminal activity that could be easily traced back to him. His direct employees, the people next to him in the chain of command, were too frightened of him to even contemplate turning him in to the authorities. When they were caught – and a number of them *had* been caught, casualties were inevitable in an organisation as large as his – they kept their mouths shut and took their punishment without a murmur, knowing that if they didn't, the penalties would be far more severe.

Having a good lawyer and enough money to pay off officials was helpful, of course, particularly in Turkey where baksheesh was still a way of life. But Memet was uncomfortably aware that no lawyer, and no amount of backhanders would save him from a British jail if Irena Hourami were to testify against him in court.

Memet's interview with the police had unsettled him more than he cared to admit. His initial reaction to the female officer who'd questioned him had been contemptuous. What could a woman do to threaten him? But as the interview progressed, he'd been struck by her tenacity and warned himself mentally not to underestimate her. She'd been at a disadvantage. There was no solid evidence to warrant charging him with any offence. But Memet knew that the moment she got that evidence, Louise Crawford would act swiftly and ruthlessly.

'We didn't find her, Memet bey,' Hasan said. 'But we intend to go back,' he added quickly. 'There was a setback this time.'

They were in the small office next to Dil's distribution centre, a cellar underneath a clothing warehouse where the heroin that arrived in bulk from Turkey was broken down into smaller packets for sale on the street. Only a handful of trusted people knew the cellar existed.

'A setback?' Dil said frostily.

'It won't happen again, you can be sure of that. We were questioning a woman, looking for information, when this man interrupted us. He attacked us.'

Hasan glanced at Farok, who had an ugly purple bruise on the bridge of his nose.

'The woman started screaming her head off. The neighbours would have heard her so we got out fast. It was a good job we did. A couple of streets away from the house we passed a police car coming the other way.'

'This man who attacked you?' Dil said. 'He was a policeman?'

'I don't think so. We could have dealt with him, but it seemed wiser to retreat.'

Hasan didn't say anything about Farok losing his knife. That was one fact it seemed prudent to withhold.

'That was sensible,' Dil said, adding – just in case these two numbskulls thought he was paying them a compliment – 'It's a pity you don't exhibit that kind of judgement all the time. I want no more bodies, you understand? Three is enough.'

Hasan looked at him, puzzled.

'But the Hourami woman. You said . . .'

'Excluding her, of course.'

'We'll go back, Memet bey,' Hasan said. 'We'll find her. It seemed better to leave Thetford for a while. We didn't want the police picking us up.'

'They're looking for you here too,' Dil said. 'They can tie you in to the Ismail Hourami killing.'

'They have proof?' Hasan said. 'How?'

'I don't know. Maybe the others said something before you got to them – the other Hourami and his wife. There's a son too. Maybe he knows something.'

'The son . . .'

186

'The son is irrelevant just now,' Dil said. 'Irena Hourami is what counts. She saw the killing. She's the danger. I want her out of the way.'

'You're telling us to go back to Thetford now?' Hasan said.

Dil gave the question some thought, assessing the risks in the calm, dispassionate way he looked at all his business decisions. There was no sense in panicking. The police hadn't found Irena Hourami yet. Maybe they wouldn't for some time. What was the greater immediate threat? The woman being located? Or Hasan and Farok being caught and questioned? It was a difficult one to call.

'I want you to keep out of sight for a couple of days,' Dil said, making his choice. 'I mean that. You find somewhere to hole up. You don't go out, you don't go near any of your usual haunts, you keep away from your friends. It might be better if you found somewhere outside London. If you need to contact me, don't phone. Leave a message here and I'll pick it up. Give it forty-eight hours, until the heat's off, and then go back to Thetford and start looking around again for Irena Hourami. You understand?'

Hasan nodded.

'What if the police get to her first?'

'You'd better hope they don't,' Dil said.

15

Alan Greenwood was waiting for her outside the house, standing by the open rear doors of his Islington council van, pulling on a pair of white overalls over his office clothes. He was in his forties, a slightly-built man with a pencil moustache. Ellie opened up Mrs North's flat and let Greenwood in. Jeremy North had had no objections to the environmental health officer examining his aunt's flat – quite the opposite. It was clearly in his own interests to discover whether the flat was contaminated by typhoid bacteria.

Greenwood was carrying a large case, like a doctor's surgical bag, in each hand. He unfastened one of the cases and handed Ellie a small opaque plastic container no bigger than a 35mm film cartridge.

'For your sample,' he said. 'Drop it off at your GP and he'll send it away to be tested.'

Ellie fingered the tiny container, wondering how exactly she was supposed to get a stool sample into it.

'The typhoid bacteria,' she said. 'You think there'll still be some around the flat?'

'They're resilient little buggers,' Greenwood replied. 'Proper cooking kills them, but they can survive refrigeration, freezing and drying. Abroad, there've been cases of people catching the disease from an ice cube in a drink.'

He slipped a pair of sterile rubber gloves on to his hands and took a box of swabs out of his case. Ellie watched him, remembering suddenly the details of the night Mrs North had been taken to hospital.

'She was sick when I was here,' Ellie said. 'I got her a bowl, washed it out afterwards. Could I have contracted typhoid from that?'

'From her vomit? Yes, that's possible. Did you wash your hands thoroughly?'

'Yes.'

'You may be all right then. You get most typhoid bacteria in the urine and faeces of infected people. The bacteria accumulate in the bowel, then penetrate the lining of the intestines into the bloodstream.'

'If I have got it?' Ellie said.

Greenwood glanced at her.

'We're not a Third World country – although I know that's hard to believe if you ever travel on the Northern Line. Early diagnosis and prompt treatment with antibiotics and you should be fine. It's only in countries with poor medical services, no drugs and insanitary living conditions that large numbers of people die of typhoid.'

'Mrs North died.'

'She was elderly, not in good health – or so I understand. I don't have the clinical details of her case, but I gather there were complications. She had an internal haemorrhage, liver failure. You're a young woman. You look fit. Typhoid's not going to kill you.'

'I hope you're right,' Ellie said.

'If I'm not,' Greenwood replied, his mouth twitching briefly into a smile, 'you won't be around to argue with me.'

He picked up his swabs and a tray of plastic containers.

'Kitchen, bathroom and toilet,' he said. 'If they're lurking anywhere, that's where they'll be.'

'I'll leave you to it,' Ellie said. 'I'll be upstairs if you need anything.'

Ellie retreated upstairs to her flat, relieved to get away.

Every minute she remained in Mrs North's flat had only increased her sense of unease, the feeling that she was risking her life in a contaminated zone. She knew she was overreacting, but that didn't stop her being genuinely worried. Hilda North had died of typhoid. *Typhoid!* That was a disease you got in Africa or India, not England in the 21st century.

She went into her bathroom and washed her hands in the basin, scrubbing her skin and nails hard with a brush, using more soap and hot water than she'd ever done before. Even then she still felt unclean. Greenwood's confidence in her ability to fight off the disease had not reassured her. She'd been exposed to typhoid bacteria, might possibly be carrying the infection. She had no symptoms, but Greenwood had said the incubation period was between one and three weeks. The bacteria might be living inside her now, multiplying by the hour, these nasty little killer germs building up in her gut, waiting to strike, waiting to . . . Calm down, Ellie told herself. You don't know you've got it. Even if you have, it's a treatable disease. But Mrs North had died. That was different. I'm not Mrs North. Just stop worrying.

She put the plastic container Greenwood had given her on top of the toilet cistern – she'd take her sample in to her GP first thing in the morning – and went into the kitchen to make a pot of tea. What were the symptoms Greenwood had mentioned on the phone? Headache, sore throat, fever. She swallowed. Her throat felt fine. She didn't feel feverish. Was she imagining it, or could she detect the beginnings of a headache? Don't be stupid. If it is, it's probably a stress headache, not typhoid.

She drank her tea at the kitchen table, thinking back two days to the night Mrs North had been taken ill, trying to recall exactly what she'd done in the old lady's flat. She'd held the bowl while Mrs North was sick, wiped her mouth afterwards, then later, after the ambulance had gone, she'd flushed the contents of the bowl down the toilet and rinsed it out. She'd washed the bowl in the kitchen sink. She'd been thorough, she remembered that. She'd only used washing up liquid, not disinfectant. Was that sufficient to kill any bacteria? She'd washed her hands, she was sure. That would have got rid of any germs. Typhoid was a contact disease. You couldn't breathe the bacteria in, you had to ingest them – eat or drink contaminated food or water. That's what Greenwood had said. Ellie relaxed a little. She'd been careful in Mrs North's kitchen. She'd washed the bowl, then she'd tidied up, washed Mrs North's dinner plate. The dinner plate . . . Ellie recalled the almost untouched food, the chicken leg and potatoes. Chicken? Chickens carried salmonella, didn't they? It was endemic in the British poultry industry. And Greenwood had said typhoid was a form of salmonella. She'd mention it to him later, when he'd finished in the old lady's flat. Perhaps it was significant.

It was a good hour and a half later that the environmental health officer knocked on her door.

'All finished,' he said blithely, his demeanour much more cheerful than Ellie would have expected from someone who'd been exploring for potentially lethal bacteria.

She went downstairs with him and locked up Mrs North's flat again.

'It would be best if no one went in there for the time being,' Greenwood said. 'Until I get the results back from the lab.'

'How long will that take?'

'A priority case like this, less than forty-eight hours.'

'One thing I didn't mention,' Ellie said. 'Mrs North had chicken the evening she fell ill. She left most of it on the plate. You said on the phone that typhoid was a form of salmonella. I was wondering . . .'

Greenwood interrupted before she could finish.

'It's not the same bacteria,' he said. 'The salmonella you get in chickens is salmonella *typhimurium* or salmonella *enteritidis* or various other salmonella serotypes. There are about 1400 different ones. Typhoid fever is caused by salmonella *typhi*. Chickens don't carry that, it's a human disease. Poultry would only be infected with it if somewhere in the food chain their carcasses had been handled by a person with typhoid or a typhoid carrier who was shedding bacteria. Besides, Mrs North must have contracted the disease a few weeks ago. What she ate that last evening would have been irrelevant.'

He picked up his cases of samples. Ellie held open the front door for him. He paused on the threshold.

'How are you feeling?' he said.

'OK,' Ellie replied.

'If you start to feel ill, you go straight to your GP. No sense in taking any chances.'

'I will,' Ellie said.

'I'll be in touch as soon as the results come through.'

Danny Chisholm put his plastic cup of coffee down on the desk and pulled out a chair. DCI Crawford looked at him inquiringly.

'Well?'

Chisholm shrugged.

'There's no trace of her,' he said. 'Not even a sniff.'

'Give me the details.'

Chisholm took a sip of his coffee. He was dying for a cigarette, but smoking was banned in the mobile incident room. He'd worked with superior officers who smoked themselves, who turned a blind eye to lighting up in the office, but Crawford wasn't one of them. She didn't approve of smoking. She didn't approve of much really, except breaking the balls of her male officers. And results. She liked results. Chisholm was uncomfortably aware that a result was not something he was going to be able to give her.

'We've been round every one of Frank Parnell's properties,' he said. 'The Norfolk boys gave us a hand.

Irena Hourami isn't in any of them. Parnell says he's never heard of her. So do all the migrant female workers in his houses.'

'You check his records?'

Chisholm gave a cynical snort.

'His records? Now there's a great work of fiction. Parnell could win the Booker Prize for his records.'

'He's lying?'

'I looked him up on the PNC. He has form. A couple of assaults a long time ago – brawling outside pubs on a Saturday night when he was a young man. More recently, a few offences under the Companies Act. He's made quite a career out of it. He sets up a company, calls it an "employment agency" and registers for VAT. Then he hires out labour to farmers and packhouses and charges them £7-8 for an hour's work, plus VAT, of course. Not that the workers get that amount. Frank claims to pay them the minimum wage, but after he's deducted his extortionate rent for providing accommodation – if twelve to a house with one blocked toilet and no heating can really be called accommodation – and taken tax and national insurance off too, the workers are left with about £2 an hour, if they're lucky.

'Frank salts the VAT and tax and NI deductions away in some offshore bank account the Revenue can't touch, then goes bust, owing the taxman a fortune. It's a nice little scam. Business difficulties, he claims. Cash-flow problems, economic downturn. His company just couldn't keep trading. And what happens to him? Nothing. Going bust isn't a criminal offence, not unless you can prove fraud or dishonesty or something else – which is bloody difficult. Frank cries a few crocodile tears for the Revenue inspectors, but is back in business next day under a different name. He's an undischarged bankrupt so, in theory, he can't be a director of any company, but that doesn't stop him. He uses fronts, aliases, a web of sub-contractors to shield himself and he gets away with it. Free enterprise, it's a wonderful system, isn't it?'

'You think he knows where she is?' Crawford asked.

'If he does, he's not going to tell us.'

'You check the farms and packhouses around Thetford?'

'Every one within a ten mile radius. There's no record of her at any of them. Have we got a photo of her yet? That would help.'

'We're still trying to obtain one from the authorities in Ankara.'

'So all we've got is a vague description. A young, Middle-Eastern-looking woman. There are probably thousands of migrant women who look like that in Norfolk and Lincolnshire, all working casually in the agricultural sector. Most of them are here illegally, working on false papers, probably under false names too. They're all terrified of being caught by Immigration and deported. No one is going to come forward and help us.'

'What about the Turks? Any sign of them?' Crawford said.

'Not in Thetford. The Norfolk boys are supposedly keeping an eye on Parnell's houses, but it's a pretty hopeless task. He's got 21 properties. What would you need to watch them properly? Two officers a shift, three shifts a day for each house. That's 120 or more men, not to mention vehicles for them all. Norfolk don't have the resources to mount a surveillance operation like that. Who does? You ask me, I'd say the Turks have come back to London. Disappeared into the Turkish underworld where we'll never find them.'

Crawford nodded.

'That would be my guess too. No one's going to give them away. They're all too scared of Memet Dil.'

'What's the score with Dil's garage?'

'I got the forensic report this morning.' Crawford picked up a file on the desk and tossed it aside dismissively.

194

'There's nothing to indicate that Ismail Hourami was ever there.'

'Nothing?'

'They must've cleaned the place with a jet wash. He's a careful man, our Mr Dil. That's why he's still walking the streets. He doesn't do his own dirty work and he makes damn sure he has a watertight alibi for every occasion he might need one.'

'And the knife?'

The knife was the one piece of good news they'd had. Joe Verdi was a pain in the proverbial, but Crawford had to acknowledge that he'd done them a big favour.

'There were minute traces of Sara Hourami's blood on it,' she said.

'Just hers?'

'Yes.'

'And fingerprints?'

'We got a match. Farok Gurcan. Two convictions, one for ABH, one for distributing a Class A drug.'

'He's done time?'

'Two years for the assault. The Class A conviction was overturned by the appeal court on a technicality.'

'So we've got names for the pair of them now.'

'For all the use it is. We need Irena Hourami. Without her we have no case. We've got nothing from Alexandra Court. No one saw the killers arrive or leave. No one heard a thing. Irena's our only witness.'

'What about the kid, Khaled?'

'He didn't see his uncle killed. Hearsay's no use to us in court.'

'If we had a photo of her, we could put out an appeal. TV, the newspapers, see if anyone comes forward.'

'I'm pushing the Foreign Office to put pressure on Ankara, but there's a lot of bureaucracy involved. It could take weeks to get a photo – if there even is one.'

'The Houramis don't have a picture of her?'

'I asked Khaled – talked to him in hospital. He says no.'

'How is he?'

'Still in shock. But he's young, resilient. I think he'll pull through, given time.'

Chisholm drank some more coffee. His craving for a cigarette was getting stronger. He was longing for the interview to end so he could sneak outside and light up.

'What do you want me to do?' he said.

Crawford chewed on a fingernail. The strain was beginning to show on her face, Chisholm thought. No bloody wonder. Three murders to investigate, the key witness missing. Who wouldn't be worried?

'Find Irena Hourami,' Crawford said.

'Is that all?' Chisholm nearly replied, but restrained himself. 'How?' he said instead. 'She could be anywhere in East Anglia. Further afield, maybe. We can't check every farm, every packhouse in Eastern England. We can't search every house rented out by a gangmaster. It's just not possible.'

'You got an alternative?' Crawford said. 'Get back up to Thetford, Danny. I'll talk to the Norfolk force, get you the help you need. I don't care what it takes, but I want Irena Hourami found. And found soon.'

Ed Preston stared at Joe in disbelief.

'Run that by me again. You want to do *what*?'

'Go undercover as an illegal migrant worker,' Joe said. 'There's a good story there. Maybe a series of articles on what it's like being a foreign worker in 21st century Britain.'

'Now, look, I'm not . . .'

'Hear me out,' Joe broke in. 'I've already got a couple of pieces of the picture. There's Rafiq Khan, who runs a so-called employment agency from the East End, transports workers out to packhouses and farms in places like Norfolk. Then there are the gangmasters who actually live in the countryside who supply agricultural labour. I met one in Thetford, went to a couple of the houses he keeps his workers in. We all know about gangmasters, but the conditions in those houses were horrendous. Mattresses crammed into every room, ten people to a terraced house. No doubt the gangmaster exploits the workers, rips them off at every turn. What are they going to do about it? They're foreign, don't speak much English. A lot of them are illegal. Even the legal ones probably don't know their rights, or are too scared to assert them.

'I said 21st century Britain, but really it's not much different from 19th century Britain. Then it was women and children the gangmasters exploited, underpaying them, cheating them, abusing them. Now it's foreign workers. They're the only people who'll do this kind of work. But the way they're treated, the conditions they live in, are a disgrace.'

'OK, I accept there's an issue here,' Preston said. 'But why go undercover? Why not just talk to the workers, get their stories?'

'Because I won't *get* their stories. Most of them won't talk to a reporter. Even if they do, I won't get a true picture of what it's really like being an illegal worker. I need to experience it first hand, actually live the kind of life they have to lead. That's the only way to get an accurate feel for it. I have to become one of them.'

Preston sucked on the end of his pen.

'So what are you proposing? Going out to Norfolk and getting a job on a farm?'

'It's not that simple. All the labour in these agricultural areas is contracted out to gangmasters. If I walked into a gangmaster's office and asked for work, he'd smell a rat immediately. That's not how he gets his workers. Most of them come through illegal channels. I have to come the same way.'

'Meaning?'

'There's another side to this. It's not just about the

197

working conditions of migrant workers, it's about people-smuggling. The two are inextricably linked together. I need to get inside that illegal supply chain, expose the whole system from start to finish. It's a massive global business. These workers come from all over – Africa, the Middle East, China, every part of Europe.'

'You're going to pretend to be a foreigner and get some-one to smuggle you into Britain. Is that what you're saying?'

'Look at my colouring. I could pass for a Turk or maybe even an Arab, something like that. No one would suspect I was English.'

'You're proposing to start in Turkey?'

'Not that far back in the chain. I could start on the other side of the Channel. Calais and Boulogne are packed with illegal workers looking for an opportunity to get to England.'

'And how much will all this cost?'

'I don't know. Not a fortune. A couple of grand, maybe. Whatever it is, don't you think it's worth it? I could get some great material.'

'Two thousand pounds?' Preston said.

'What's that to *The News*? Look at what we spend money on. That feature last week in the Arts section, for instance. We sent someone to Los Angeles to interview a British film director – a director who lives in London, I might add. What did that cost? The airfare, the hotel bill, food. I bet it wasn't far off two grand, and what did we get for it? A vacuous profile that was little more than a puff for the director's new movie.'

'What Features spend their budget on is their business.'

'You know what I'm saying, Ed. The crap we sometimes publish, it's embarrassing. I'm sick of the way we're becoming a pliable offshoot of the PR industry. That's not what journalism should be about. We should be better than that.'

'Two thousand is a lot of money, Joe.'

'It's peanuts. I'll take unpaid leave to do it, if you like. And think what you'll save on my expenses.'

'Is that the ones you claim, or the ones you actually spend?' Preston said dryly.

'We're a newspaper, not some frivolous lifestyle magazine,' Joe said forcefully. 'This is exactly the kind of story we should be covering. Taking risks, showing what's really going on in this nasty corrupt little island of ours.'

The news editor pursed his lips, gazing around the interview room to which they'd retreated to escape the constant interruptions of the newsroom. He liked Joe Verdi. He liked his commitment, his determination, the passion he put into his work. Of all the reporters on the paper he was probably the most empathetic, the one Preston would choose first for any human interest assignment, particularly ones concerning the underdog or socially disadvantaged. But Joe also had a tendency to get over-emotional, to get too personally involved in the stories he covered. In journalism, you had to maintain a delicate balance between heart and head. That wasn't something Joe was always able to do.

'This wouldn't have anything to do with finding Irena Hourami, would it?' Preston said, turning his gaze back to Joe.

Joe decided to come clean.

'Maybe at the beginning,' he admitted.

'It wasn't your fault that the Houramis were killed. Guilt – it's not a sound basis for good journalism.'

'I know,' Joe said. 'But I can't help feeling I was in some way responsible.'

'That's crap, Joe.'

'The son, Khaled. I feel an obligation towards him. I know that's irrational, but some feelings *are* irrational. I was with him when his parents were killed.'

'Thank God for that,' Preston said. 'If he hadn't been

199

with you, he'd have been in the flat and had his throat cut too. You thought of it that way? You saved his life.'

'It's a different country out there, Ed. People like us, the people who read our paper, we have no idea what really goes on, how some people live. There are tens of thousands of them. Hidden away in our big cities and in grotty houses in the country. It's the black economy that keeps the rest of the economy going. The people who clean our offices, who wash the dishes in our hotels, who pick the fruit and vegetables we eat – they're mostly foreign, mostly illegal. We try to keep them out, the rightwing press and politicians rant on about how these people are coming here to scrounge and abuse our benefits system, but the truth is, these workers are the ones who are being abused. They're not on benefits, they work bloody hard for very little money and without them our whole economy would collapse.'

'And Irena Hourami?'

'This other economy is big enough, and secretive enough, to swallow her up.'

'You think you can find her?'

'No. I did initially, but I don't think it's realistic now. The police, with all their resources, have been looking for her for three days. They know she went to Thetford, that's a town of only about 20,000 inhabitants, but they can't find her. They might never find her – if she doesn't want to be found. But going up there myself, it's opened my eyes to this other world. I think it's something the paper should investigate more thoroughly.'

'It sounds a tough assignment to me, Joe. Are you sure you're up to it? Physically, I mean.'

'What do you mean?'

'Well, you're not getting any younger.'

'You saying I'm old? Jesus, why does everyone think I'm about to peg out? I'm a fit young man.'

'You're a middle-aged asthmatic. And you're proposing

200

to sneak into the country in the back of a lorry and pick vegetables in Lincolnshire. That's pretty much what you're suggesting, isn't it?'

'I suppose so,' Joe conceded. 'I've done agricultural work before, you know. I've picked grapes and olives in Italy.'

'That was twenty years ago.'

'I can still do it.'

'And what about the other risks? These people-smugglers are a vicious bunch. They guess, or even suspect, you're a journalist and you're dead meat.'

'I know the risks,' Joe said. 'I'm prepared to take that chance. I want to do it. This is an important issue. OK, it won't be easy. But worthwhile stories never are. You have to work at them. I'm up to it, you have to believe me, Ed.'

Preston mulled it over for a time. Joe didn't press him for a decision. He sensed the news editor was favourably disposed towards his request – if he hadn't been he would already have rejected it – but he was weighing up the pros and cons.

'I'll talk to the editor,' Preston said eventually. 'It'll be up to him.'

'Now?'

'If he's free.'

Joe went back to his desk while Preston went to see the editor. Having the news editor on his side would be a big advantage in any negotiations with the editor. Preston was a persuasive advocate when he was selling a cause he truly believed in.

Joe hadn't been entirely honest with the news editor, and he suspected Preston knew it. He wasn't being entirely honest with himself either. He'd said he wasn't going to try to find Irena Hourami because that was an unrealistic ambition. That was half true. It *was* an unrealistic ambition. But that wasn't going to stop him looking for Irena. He hoped he was wrong, but he wasn't optimistic about the police's chance of locating her. If they hadn't managed it now, while the trail was still fresh, how would they succeed when the scent became weaker?

Maybe he was deluding himself, but he was convinced that going undercover into the illegal migrant world would give him a chance of tracking Irena down. A slim chance, he knew that, but it was better than nothing. His main aim – he told himself – was journalistic. To write an accurate, truthful exposé of the people smuggling racket. But if in the process he found a lead that might take him to Irena, well, it would be foolish not to follow it up, wouldn't it?

Ed Preston came out of the editor's office and walked across the newsroom to Joe's desk.

'You've got the okay,' Preston said. 'But you take some back up, someone who knows where you are, who can raise the alarm if anything goes wrong. The editor was adamant about that.'

'Another reporter, you mean?'

'Yes, but I'm not sure I can spare anyone.'

'I'll ask Henry,' Joe said.

'Weaver?'

'He's got nothing better to do.'

'He's got his column to write.'

'That's what I mean,' Joe said.

16

They took Henry's Mitsubishi Shogun Sport – a big black four-wheel drive Goliath of a car that had been designed for crossing the world's most inhospitable deserts and was thus ideally equipped for the London suburbs – and drove south, heading across Kent towards Dover. At a service station on the M20, they stopped to fill up with petrol. Joe watched the electronic indicator on the pump racing around and stopping at £104.86.

'It costs a hundred quid to fill this thing up?' he said incredulously when Henry got back in behind the wheel.

'Only does eighteen miles to the gallon,' Henry replied. 'Keep the engine running and it would use up the fuel as fast as I could pump it in. Extravagant, I know.'

'Wouldn't it be cheaper to drive around in a Chieftain tank?'

'They're excellent cars. Very reliable. They test them on Mount Fuji, you know.'

'Henry, they're made in Sunderland, or some place like that,' Joe said. 'That's a long way from Mount Fuji.'

'You know what I mean. I know it's a gas guzzler and I'm destroying the planet with it, but Ginnie likes it for collecting the kids from school.'

'The school's in the middle of a ploughed field, is it?'

'And it's very useful for when we go down to the cottage.'

Joe had been to Henry's 'cottage' a few times. It was a

five-bedroom Queen Anne house in Hampshire, with half an acre of garden, a stretch of river for fly fishing and a billiard room in the old stable block. The only thing Henry used the Shogun for when he was there was for driving the quarter of a mile to the village pub.

'Thanks for coming with me,' Joe said. 'I couldn't have done it without you.'

'You think I'd pass up a few days in France on expenses? It gives me a chance to stock up my wine cellar.'

'We're supposed to be working, not shopping.'

'You can get a lot of booze in a car like this, you know. Last time I nipped across the Channel, I drove down to Reims, came back with twenty cases of champagne. Saved an absolute fortune.'

'Twenty cases?' Joe said. 'That's 240 bottles.'

'Well, I need something to do in the evenings,' Henry replied.

The cross-Channel ferry left just before noon. They could've taken the train through the tunnel, but Henry had insisted on going by sea – ostensibly because he got claustrophobia at the very idea of the tunnel, but in reality because he wanted to have lunch on the boat.

It was only a short crossing – an hour and ten minutes – but that was long enough for Henry to order a full four-course meal. Joe had a salad and a coffee and watched while Henry worked his way through soup, grilled steak, cheese, apple tart and half a bottle of burgundy. By the time he'd finished, the ferry was docking in Calais.

They disembarked and drove straight through Calais, heading down the coast to Boulogne where they checked into the hotel they'd booked in advance. Joe left Henry to have an afternoon nap in his room and went out into the town. His first stop was the bank, a Credit Agricole, where he changed the crisp new fifty euro notes he'd been given in England into smaller used denominations – grubby twenties and tens that were more consistent with the cover story he had prepared for himself.

He'd thought long and hard about the new identity he was going to assume. The most difficult part had been deciding on his nationality. With his Mediterranean skin and black hair he could pass easily for a Spaniard, an Italian, a Portuguese or a Greek. But all four of those countries were in the European Union and their citizens could work legally in the UK. To enter Britain as an illegal, he had to originate from somewhere outside the EU. The Middle East and North Africa had been possibilities. Joe thought he might just be convincing as a Moroccan or an Egyptian, but in the end he had opted for Albania as his country of origin. It was in Europe, but not the EU. He couldn't speak Albanian, of course, but he thought it unlikely that he would encounter many people in England who would be able to catch him out. Albania was a mysterious country that very few western Europeans knew much about and it had the advantage of being close to Italy. There was a steady stream of Albanian refugees and economic migrants coming across the Adriatic to the heel of Italy. It was entirely plausible that he might have come across by that route and then worked his way up through France to the Channel.

Joe had already adjusted himself mentally to his new role. What he needed to do now was make the physical changes that were required to support his cover story. He had the correct basic colouring for the part he was going to play, but nothing else about him was right. His clothes were English and far too smart for an Albanian refugee, and his hands and face weren't dirty and weatherbeaten enough for someone who had been doing hard manual labour for the past few months. He hadn't shaved that morning, which was a start. By the following day, at the rate his beard grew, he would have a decent covering of stubble on his jawline. His clothes were easier to deal with. He could keep nothing that had an English label in it, even his underwear, but if he'd supposedly been working in France for a while, it was not stretching credulity too much for him to be wearing French clothes, provided they were cheap and grubby enough.

He wandered around the centre of Boulogne for a time, steering clear of the expensive designer shops, and in a backstreet near the station he found what he was looking for – a second-hand clothes shop. He picked out a well-worn pair of trousers, a couple of shirts, a sweat top and a soiled jacket and tried them on to make sure they fitted. A pair of scuffed work boots and a peaked cap completed the outfit. The shopkeeper – an emaciated young man with a gold stud in his nose – showed no obvious interest in him or the clothes he was buying, but Joe was taking no chances. That was why he'd come to Boulogne first – to equip himself so that when he moved on to Calais he was already in character when he arrived.

He packed his purchases into a carrier bag and went to a department store to buy some French underwear. The second-hand clothes shop had stocked a few tatty pairs of underpants, but Joe drew the line at wearing used Y-fronts. His final call was at a pharmacy where he bought a tooth-brush and toothpaste. He didn't bother with soap or a razor. He wasn't planning on doing much washing or shaving over the next few days. That was it: he had every-thing he needed for his illegal entry into England – everything, that is, except his passage across the Channel, but that would be arranged in Calais.

Henry had emerged from his room after his nap and was having tea and cake in the hotel lounge. Joe joined him on the elegant high-backed sofa and ordered himself a mineral water from the waiter.

'Had a good sleep?' he asked Henry.

Henry nodded.

'Very refreshing. You want some of this cake, it's very good.'

'No, thanks.'

Henry eyed the carrier bag Joe had placed on the floor by his feet.

'You get what you wanted?'

'Yes.'

Joe pulled the jacket out of the bag and held it up. Henry grimaced.

'My God, that is horrible. You intend to wear that thing?'

'You should see the shirts I bought,' Joe said.

'That's a French jacket?'

'The label's French.'

'I didn't think the French could bring themselves to manufacture anything quite so ghastly. How much did it cost?'

'Five euros.'

'You were done.'

Henry refilled his cup with tea from the pot and added a fresh slice of lemon.

'It's funny, I never drink lemon tea at home,' he said. 'Always milk. But the minute I get across the Channel it seems the right thing to do. Like coffee and croissants for breakfast. You're not planning on wearing that jacket in here, are you?'

'I'll change tomorrow morning, when we leave.'

'That's a relief. This hotel has a reputation to maintain. I'd hate to see you thrown out for being a vagrant. This cake is really excellent, you know. Are you sure you don't want any?'

'There doesn't seem to be much left.'

'I'll order some more.'

They stayed in the hotel lounge for the rest of the afternoon, then Henry went upstairs to his room to shower and change. They could have dined in the hotel, but Henry said he knew a restaurant just outside the town – a 'cosy little bistro', he called it – that one of his old school chums at the Garrick Club had recommended. The bill for dinner, including the two bottles of claret Henry consumed almost single handedly, came to 250 euros.

'Ed Preston will have a heart attack when he sees that on our expenses claim,' Joe said. 'Try to be frugal, he said.'

'Well, we only had two bottles of wine,' Henry replied indignantly. 'I'd call that pretty frugal. I mean, there's a limit, isn't there? Are we supposed to starve ourselves?'

'I don't think there's much risk of that,' Joe said.

'If it makes you happier, I'll submit it separately. Put it on my exes. No one will make a fuss. I'm sure I'll get a column out of this little jaunt. Can't think what at the moment, but something will come to me. Now, what do you say to finding a bar and having a couple of cognacs before bed?'

Joe was up early the following morning. He had breakfast alone in the hotel dining room, then returned to his room and changed into his second-hand clothes. He studied himself in the mirror, impressed by the transformation a threadbare shirt, faded trousers and dirty jacket could bring about. His face looked different too. His beard was growing nicely, a dark shadow over his chin and upper lip, and if he messed up his hair with his fingers, it added to the impression of scruffy unkemptness that he was trying to create. His hands were still too soft and clean for a labourer, but he intended to do something about that after he left the hotel.

He folded up his English clothes and packed them neatly into his travel case with his other personal belongings – his mobile phone, his passport and his Italian leather wallet from which he'd removed his wad of creased euros. That left only two items – his reading glasses and his asthma inhaler. The reading glasses weren't a problem. They were a cheap pair he'd bought off the shelf at his local chemists. There was nothing on them, or their case, to identify their country of origin. They might have been French, or even Albanian spectacles.

The asthma inhaler was more difficult. The canister of

salbutamol bore a label on which various instructions were printed – shake before use, store below 30 degrees, do not exceed the stated dose – all in English. Joe slid the canister out of its plastic casing and peeled off the label. The casing itself was embossed with the words 'Ventolin Evohaler', but he could do nothing about that, short of filing away the plastic letters. He had either to leave the inhaler behind, or hang on to it and hope that no one bothered to look too closely at it. He went for the second option. The conditions in which he was likely to be living over the next two weeks, he could see that he was going to need his inhaler.

The transformation was now complete. He was no longer Joe Verdi, the London journalist, he was Alban Cobani, an Albanian migrant with no papers – an uneducated peasant who'd picked tomatoes and olives in Italy, worked on building sites in France and was now looking to get to Britain in search of a better life.

Leaving his room, Joe went down the corridor and knocked on Henry's door. It was a while before Henry answered. When he finally opened the door – tousle-haired in his pyjamas and a silk dressing gown – he stared at Joe and yawned.

'Yes?'

'It's me,' Joe said.

Henry blinked.

'My God, I didn't recognise you. That's good, bloody good. Come in.'

Henry pulled the curtains back and sat down on the edge of his bed. He brushed his floppy blond hair out of his eyes.

'What time is it?'

'Half nine,' Joe said.

'*Half nine?* Do you have to be up so early? You had breakfast?'

'Yes. These are my things.'

Joe put his travel case down on the floor.

'Everything's in there. My clothes, passport, the lot.'

'What if the French police stop you, ask for i.d.?'

'I'll take that chance. How many times have the French police stopped you and checked your passport?'

'Well, never. But then I don't look like you. Is it my imagination, or do those clothes smell?'

'It's not your imagination. I'll leave you to settle up here.'

'You're going? Now?'

'I'll see you in Calais. You remember the arrangements?'

Henry nodded

'I'll come and find you this evening,' Joe said.

He slipped the carrier bag containing his spare shirt, towel, toothbrush and toothpaste under his arm and left the room, going downstairs to the foyer and out into the street. On his way to the railway station, he made a detour into a small municipal garden and picked up a handful of soil from one of the flower beds. He rubbed the earth into his palms and the backs of his hands, working it into his skin and under his fingernails. Then he wiped off the excess on his trousers and inspected the end result. Not bad. They looked more like labourer's hands now. They weren't sufficiently rough and calloused to pass a close examination, but they were good enough for his purposes. First impressions, his general aura of uncleanliness, were what counted.

At the station, he bought himself a single to Calais, paying cash for the ticket and speaking bad French the way he imagined an Albanian immigrant might. The accent wasn't crucial at the moment, but it would be later. It was sensible to put in some practice, to get in character and stay in character from now on. He sat by the window in a second-class compartment for the short journey up the coast. No one sat next to him. A smartly-dressed middle-aged woman who got on after him had paused momentarily in the aisle as if she were considering the vacant place beside him, but she'd taken one look at Joe's clothes and unshaven face and hurried past to another seat. The reaction had reassured him that his appearance was convincingly unprepossessing. I look the part, he thought. I now have to concentrate on acting the part, on actually *being* an illegal migrant.

The station concourse in Calais was bustling with people – some queuing for tickets or waiting for passengers to arrive, others simply loitering about. Joe shuffled across to the exit, neither hurrying nor dawdling. Railway stations, particularly ones like Calais through which foreigners were continually passing, were rife with dubious characters – lowlife criminals such as pickpockets and conmen, but also hotel touts and other semi-legitimate opportunists who preyed on innocent travellers. That was one of the prime reasons Joe hadn't wanted to arrive with Henry. Looking inconspicuous, blending into the background, were not two of Henry's more obvious characteristics. Joe didn't want anyone to notice him. He kept his head down, avoided eye contact with the people around him and slipped anonymously out into the city.

He'd studied a map of Calais in detail before he left England and knew exactly where he was going – not to the old town, which was where most tourists headed, but to the seedy area down by the waterfront. He found a café close to the lorrypark for the cross-Channel ferries and went inside. He was surprised by how full the place was for eleven o'clock in the morning. There were groups of men sitting at most of the tables and other men leaning on the bar, chatting desultorily and sipping coffee or beer. There were no women. Joe guessed that the customers were almost all lorry drivers killing time while they waited for their car ferry to England. As he walked to the bar, he heard at least four or five different languages being spoken – English, French, Spanish, Italian, a couple of others that might have been Polish or Czech. Some of the men were playing cards or flicking through newspapers. There was an air of restless boredom about everyone. Tired men who

211

were used to waiting, but still found it frustrating to hang around doing nothing when their ultimate destination was only 22 miles away across a narrow stretch of water.

Joe ordered a coffee from the barman – the *café noir* that an Albanian would drink rather than the milky *grand crème* the English favoured. He added sugar and stirred the drink slowly, watching the men at the tables, trying to identify their nationalities. The English were the easiest to spot. There were more of them and they clustered together, keeping themselves apart from the 'foreigners' in the café. Joe knew that if he approached some of these drivers he might find one who was willing to take him across the Channel in the back of his lorry, though probably no more than one – most wouldn't risk losing their jobs and a criminal prosecution to smuggle in an illegal immigrant, no matter how much money Joe offered them. But Joe didn't want an individual driver who was willing to take a chance. He was looking for something more organised – one of the professional smuggling gangs that operated out of Calais. He had to be cautious, not try to hurry things. You couldn't just walk into a bar and ask to speak to the local crime boss, book your passage across the water as if you were on a package tour. He had to take his time, try not to arouse suspicion.

He finished his coffee and attracted the barman's attention.

'I look for place to stay. Cheap,' he said in faltering, heavily-accented French.

The barman gave a classically exaggerated Gallic shrug of indifference, a contemptuous 'pouf' exploding out from between his pursed lips.

'You know place?' Joe went on.

The barman didn't deign to reply, but simply gestured towards a noticeboard on the wall at the end of the bar and turned away without a word. Joe walked over to the noticeboard. It was covered with a few official-looking notices and a lot more unofficial ones – items for sale, flats to rent, advertisements for local builders, electricians and other tradesmen and a whole section of brightly-coloured cards advertising services of a rather more personal nature. In one corner – looking as if they'd been there a long time – were a few dusty business cards for hotels and pensions, including a couple that just read '*Chambres*'. Joe found a pen and a scrap of paper on the bar, wrote down the names and addresses and went off to find somewhere to stay.

Most of the hotels were close to the port, a couple of them on the same street. It wasn't an area of Calais Joe would normally have considered visiting. It was rough, rundown. The buildings had a dilapidated, seedy appearance. Outside one of the hotels, three North African men were hanging about idly, chatting and smoking. Their eyes followed Joe as he walked past. He felt uncomfortable, threatened, and had to remind himself that he was no longer a white middle-class English journalist. He was an Albanian labourer who would feel at home in an immigrant area like this.

Joe went round a few of the hotels and pensions on his list, assessing them from the outside. None of them had any kind of star or other recommendation from the local tourist board and it wasn't hard to see why. They were all uniformly dirty and uninviting. The building containing the rooms to rent was particularly insalubrious. Joe went through a passageway into a courtyard at the back of the building and saw mounds of decaying rubbish piled up along the walls. There were discarded hypodermic syringes scattered over the paving stones, a used condom stuck to a windowsill. The stench of rotting refuse turned his stomach. It was just what he was looking for.

He went back into the passageway and climbed a gloomy flight of stairs to the first floor. A bellpush next to a battered wooden door had a handwritten '*chambres*' sign over it. Joe pressed the button. A buzzer sounded and the door clicked open. As Joe went through, a young North African-looking man – Algerian or Moroccan – came up the stairs from the street and followed him inside. A fat man in a soiled vest and baggy trousers was standing behind what passed for a reception desk. The North African ignored him and headed straight for the corridor off the hall. The fat man called him back.

'Hey, you, Abou, I want a word.'

The North African paused and turned.

'You've been smoking that shit again, haven't you?' the fat man said. 'That fucking weed you darkies like. I told you not to. You hear me?'

The North African nodded automatically, gesturing wearily with a hand as if he didn't give a damn.

'How many times do I have to tell you?' the fat man continued. 'It stinks the place out. I smell that shit again and you're back on the fucking street. You and your fucking mates. You got me?'

The North African shrugged, his mouth turning down at the corners. What did he care? He'd heard it all before. He kept going along the corridor. The landlord's eyes, sunk deep into his pudgy face like currants in a bun, swung back to Joe.

'What do *you* want?' he snapped.

'Room,' Joe said in his Albanian French. 'You have room?'

'What d'you think the sign outside says? How long?'

'Uh?'

'How long do you want the fucking room for?'

'Don't know.'

The landlord looked Joe over, taking in his clothes, his dirty hands. Joe kept his eyes lowered, his shoulders bent, trying to give the impression of a timid labourer, a migrant who knew his place.

'Fifteen euros,' the landlord said.

'Fifteen? OK.'

'You have luggage?'

'*Quoi?*'

214

'Luggage. Bags.'

'No.'

'Pay upfront then. Two nights minimum. You understand?'

The landlord held out a fleshy hand, wiggling his fat fingers as if he were tickling a trout. Joe felt in his jacket pocket and pulled out three crumpled ten euro notes. He handed the money to the landlord who lifted a key down off a hook on the wall and held it out.

'Number six. Down there.'

The room was as bad as Joe had expected – a small rectangle about the size of a walk-in cupboard, with a single bed against one wall and a window high up at the far end that was so grimy the glass was opaque. Joe sat down on the edge of the bed. There was only just room for his legs. His knees were almost grazing the wall which was painted what appeared to be a pale brown colour, but it might just have been ingrained dirt. The light was so dim it was hard to tell. There was a damp, musty smell. Joe could feel it beginning to irritate his throat, his lungs.

He examined the bed. The pillowcase was stained and smelt of body odour. The sheets had a creased, slept-in look. If they were changed, it was probably only twice a year. What do you expect for fifteen euros a night? Joe said to himself. He stretched himself out on top of the tatty duvet. It was still early in the day. The kind of people he wanted to meet only came out after dark. He'd wait until the evening before he ventured out in search of them. But what to do until then? He didn't fancy walking the streets aimlessly. He didn't feel like sleeping, or going to a café. He wished he'd brought a book to read, but that would have been foolish. Albanian manual workers didn't read books. That didn't leave him many other options for passing the time. He stared up at the ceiling, noting the cobwebs in the corners, the dust on the cornices. He ran over his plans in his mind, going through them step by step, working out exactly how he was going to pull them off.

17

Ellie was at her desk, putting her pen and notebook in her bag, getting ready to go home, when her phone rang. She thought about ignoring it, just walking away and forgetting about work, but she couldn't do it. Her years in the business had turned her into a telephone slave, a minion at the beck and call of the ring-tone. She lived by the phone, even more so since she'd acquired a mobile. It was with her twenty-four hours a day now, almost always switched on, permanently waiting for the next call. There was something about the sound that was seductive, a Siren's song that she was incapable of resisting. She picked up the receiver.

'Yes?'

'Ellie Mason?'

'Speaking.'

'It's Alan Greenwood, Islington Environmental Health Department.'

The name gave her a jolt, reawakening her fears about typhoid. She reminded herself to call her GP, to find out if the results of her test sample had come back yet.

'Hi,' she said. 'What's happening about Mrs North's flat? Any news?'

'I've had the lab analysis,' Greenwood said. 'Every sample I took has proved negative.'

Ellie gave a sigh of relief.

'That's good, isn't it?'

'In some ways, yes. The flat seems to be clear. No trace of typhoid bacteria in any of the most likely places.'

'You have reservations?'

'I was hoping for a positive somewhere. Hoping to pinpoint the source of the infection. That would make it simpler to deal with. The negative results just leave unanswered the question of where and how Mrs North caught the disease. That's worrying.' Greenwood paused. 'Particularly as there's been a complication. Another case.'

'Another case of typhoid? Where?'

'A couple of miles from Mrs North's flat. Similar circumstances. A 75-year-old man, a widower, living alone in a flat. He was admitted to hospital two days ago. The HPA's just rung me to say the preliminary tests have confirmed the presence of salmonella *typhi* in his body.'

'Hang on a second.'

Ellie sat down at her desk and retrieved her notebook and pen from her shoulderbag. She found a clean page and scribbled a few notes.

'I'm putting this on the record, Mr Greenwood,' she said. 'What's the victim's name?'

'You're going to do a story on this?' Greenwood said apprehensively.

'You know I'm a journalist. I've already done a piece on Mrs North's typhoid. Surely you don't expect me to ignore this?'

'No, I suppose not. There'll probably be a press statement tomorrow morning – from the council press office.'

'I don't want to wait for that,' Ellie said. 'What's his name?'

Greenwood hesitated, then said, 'Goodwin. Joseph Goodwin.'

'Which hospital is he in?'

'Whittington. The same as Mrs North.'

'What's his condition?'

'Serious, but stable.'

'You think the two cases are linked?'

'You're going to quote me on this?'

'Yes.'

'It seems highly likely. Two incidences of such a rare disease in such a small geographical area. That's one of the reasons I'm ringing, to ask if Mrs North knew this man.'

'The name doesn't ring a bell,' Ellie said. 'Where exactly does he live?'

'Woodview Road. Number sixty-eight.'

Ellie knew the street. It was only a ten, fifteen minute walk from her flat.

'You never heard Mrs North mention him?' Greenwood went on.

'I don't think so.'

'Is there any point at which they might have had contact with each other in the last few weeks? They're close in age, both living alone. Some social event perhaps.'

'As I told you before,' Ellie said. 'Mrs North didn't have much of a social life. She never went out in the evenings and not very often during the day.'

'A mutual friend then. Could there be a third party who'd had contact with both of them and passed the disease on without contracting it themselves?'

'Is that possible?'

'In theory, yes. He, or she, might have got the bacteria on their hands, say, and touched some food or drink that was then ingested by Mrs North or Mr Goodwin.'

'I can't help you there, I'm sorry.'

'Do you know where Mrs North did her shopping?'

'For food? Yes, at the local supermarket.'

'Which one?'

'SupaMar Mini, on Colville Avenue.'

'Anywhere else?'

'There isn't anywhere else round where we live. It's pretty much a SupaMar monopoly. You think they might have been selling contaminated food?'

'Whoa, easy there,' Greenwood said hurriedly, a note of anxiety in his voice. 'I'm not saying anything about that, especially for publication. We have to be very careful before we start speculating, making allegations.'

'But typhoid is spread by infected food and drink, isn't it? It makes sense to check local food shops?'

'One thing at a time. I need more information about Mr Goodwin before we bring a supermarket into the equation.'

'You're going to check his flat, like you did Mrs North's, I suppose?'

'I'm going over there now.'

'You think there might be more cases?'

'I don't want to speculate about that either. I don't want to say any more, OK? Not if you're going to quote me.'

'What about off the record?'

'I have to go. Thank you for your help, Miss Mason.'

Greenwood rang off. Ellie picked up her notebook and bag and walked over to the newsdesk. Ed Preston was talking to one of the other reporters. Ellie waited for them to finish, then told the news editor about her phone call.

'I'm going to head up there, see what I can find out,' she said.

Woodview Road was a short street of two-storey yellow brick terraced houses. Alan Greenwood's white van was parked outside number sixty-eight. Ellie went up the steps and in through the open front door. The door to the ground floor flat was ajar. Ellie pushed it with her foot. She heard voices inside the flat, then Alan Greenwood came into view. He was wearing his white overalls. There was a woman with him, a dumpy, middle-aged woman with straight blonde hair and a central parting revealing black roots. Greenwood saw Ellie and started.

'Miss Mason . . . look, this isn't the . . .'

'I won't get in the way,' Ellie said. 'I know you've got a job to do. I'll wait out here.'

She retreated into the hall and sat down on the stairs leading up to the first floor flat. It wasn't long before the blonde woman came out. She glanced sharply at Ellie and headed for the front door. Ellie went after her.

'Excuse me . . .'

The blonde turned.

'Did Mr Greenwood tell you who I was?' Ellie asked.

'He said you were a journalist. I've nothing to say.'

The blonde kept walking. Ellie caught up with her on the step outside.

'Did he tell you I knew the other victim personally? That I lived upstairs from her. Hilda North, I mean. He's asked you about Mrs North, hasn't he?'

The blonde frowned. Ellie knew she had her attention, could try to break down the barrier of hostility she sensed in the woman.

'Are you a relative of Mr Goodwin's?' Ellie said.

'I'm his daughter.'

'I'm sorry he's been taken ill. How is he?'

'Not good. You knew Mrs North?'

'I called the ambulance that took her to hospital,' Ellie said.

She explained what had happened, her connection to Hilda North, her distress when the old lady had died.

'My name's Ellie Mason. I work for *The News*.'

'Trudy,' the blonde said. 'Trudy Morgan.'

'You live nearby?'

'A mile or so away. My dad . . .' She stopped.

'They can treat it,' Ellie said. 'Mrs North was unlucky. She wasn't a well person before the typhoid struck.'

'My dad's tough, quite fit for his age. Maybe he'll be all right,' Trudy said, looking anxiously at Ellie for confirmation.

'I'm sure he has a good chance,' Ellie said. 'Do you have any idea how he might have caught the disease?'

'No.'

'He hasn't been abroad recently?'

'Mr Greenwood asked me that. No, he hasn't been abroad for years.'

'And he didn't know Mrs North?'

'Not as far as I'm aware. Excuse me, but I can't stay. My kids are at home. I just came round to unlock the flat. I'll pop back later when Mr Greenwood's finished.'

'One last question,' Ellie said. 'Where does your dad do his shopping? His food, his groceries.'

'Well, I do a lot of it for him,' Trudy replied. 'Usually at the SupaMar Mini. You know, on Colville Avenue.'

'I know it. Thanks,' Ellie said.

She watched Trudy Morgan walk to her car and drive away, then took out her mobile phone and punched in the number of the newsdesk direct line.

At dusk, Joe put his jacket back on and got ready to leave his room. He wondered what he should do with his wad of money. He had more than two thousand euros distributed around his various pockets. He could leave it in the room, but there was no secure place to hide it and he didn't trust the landlord. He looked just the type of shifty rogue who would have no scruples about going through his guests' rooms when they went out. Taking the cash with him was risky too. He couldn't afford to lose it. But he felt happier if he could keep it on his person. He put a few ten euro notes in his trouser pocket and divided the rest into three packages, putting one in each of his socks and the third down the front of his trousers, tucked under the elastic of his boxer shorts.

He went along the corridor to the bathroom on his way out. It was a tiny room containing a dripping shower with green mould on the walls and a lavatory so stained and filthy Joe had to avert his eyes while he peed into it.

The door to one of the other rooms swung open as Joe walked past to the exit. The young North African came out. Joe caught a glimpse of the inside of the room – clothes hanging up around the walls, a big silver portable CD player next to the bed, clutter on the floor – and realised that Abou – if that was his real name and not some racist insult concocted by the landlord – wasn't a temporary guest in the house, but a permanent resident.

Abou nodded at him and Joe nodded back. Neither of them spoke. They went down the corridor, a few yards apart. Abou let himself out through the front door, but Joe lingered in the hall. The landlord had a sitting room behind the reception desk. Joe could see him through the half-open door, slumped in an armchair watching television, his belly sagging beneath his grubby vest. Joe knocked on the door. The landlord turned his head and saw who it was. He hauled himself reluctantly to his feet and came out into the hall, not pleased to be disturbed.

'What do you want?' he demanded curtly.

Joe cringed and backed away apologetically.

'Excuse me. I sorry. You help me maybe.'

'*What?*'

'Help me.'

'What're you talking about?'

'I look for place to eat,' Joe said. 'You know?'

'To eat? Do I look like a restaurant critic?'

Joe pretended he hadn't understood.

'Restaurant. You know?' he said, nodding his head vacuously like the dim peasant he was supposed to be.

The landlord gritted his teeth.

'There's a place round the corner. Zouzou's. Cheap. It's where all the darkies and Arabs go. You'll fit in there. I lock up at one. You come back later than that and you sleep in the courtyard.'

The landlord swung round and waddled back into his sitting room, closing the door firmly behind him. Joe went out and down the stairs. He was hungry, but he didn't go straight to the restaurant. He had to check in with Henry first.

It was a fifteen minute walk to the hotel where Henry was staying. It was an exclusive, rather old-fashioned establishment with the atmosphere and furnishings of a London gentleman's club, though, being French, probably rather better cuisine. Joe felt a little out of place walking into the wood-panelled foyer in his scruffy clothes and work boots and asking the liveried receptionist for Monsieur Weaver. The receptionist obviously thought Joe was out of place too, the look of distaste he gave him, but he picked up the internal phone and rang Henry's room. A few minutes later, Henry emerged from the lift and walked across the foyer towards Joe.

'Let's go in the bar,' Henry said.

They found a quiet table away from the other hotel guests and Henry ordered himself a Martini. Joe had a mineral water. He wanted to keep a clear head for later.

'Where are you staying?' Henry asked.

Joe told him.

'It sounds frightful,' Henry said. 'I'll make a note of the address. I checked in with Preston, by the way. He wants to know exactly what you're doing.'

'I'm going to a restaurant later,' Joe said. 'Then I'll find a bar, see what happens.'

'That's it? That's your plan?'

'There are a lot of foreigners near the port. A lot of illegals. Someone will know how you buy a passage to England.'

'Well, for God's sake be careful.'

They fell silent as the waiter brought their drinks, transferring their glasses and two little bowls of salted nuts to the table. Henry took a sip of his Martini.

'You could have dinner here with me.'

Joe shook his head.

'I don't think they'd let me in the dining room dressed like this.'

'Mmm, you have a point.'

'Besides, I want to make myself visible near where I'm staying. A new face. See who takes an interest in me.'

'And if you get nowhere tonight?'

'I'll try again tomorrow. You can wait another day, can't you?'

'In a hotel like this? Dear chap, I can wait a month. I wangled a suite, you know. I sort of let slip that I was an English travel writer. They upgraded me at no extra charge, same price as a double. You should see the bathroom. A few hundred gallons of ass's milk and Cleopatra would be right at home there.'

'I'll think of you when I'm being chewed alive by bed bugs,' Joe said.

Henry studied him pensively.

'I'm worried about you, Joe. What you're doing is very risky.'

'I can look after myself.'

Henry nibbled on a couple of salted nuts.

'You know why they made me a columnist on the paper?' he said.

'You mean, apart from the fact that you and the editor were at Oxford together?' Joe said dryly.

'That's just a coincidence.'

'Sure it is.'

'You were right the other day in your father's restaurant. That crack you made about zeitgeist being German for bullshit. That's what I do. I bullshit. I'm the literary equivalent of a rent-a-mouth. A rent-a-word, call it what you like. I have opinions on every subject under the sun, it doesn't matter what. Politics, the arts, crime, television, I can give you a trenchant view on them all.

'I know nothing about any of them, of course, but that's an essential requirement for the job. If you know something about a subject, you can't dissect and analyse it usefully in five hundred words. Ignorance is an absolute must. You have to be able to simplify everything. You'd probably get as valid an opinion on an issue if you went down the pub on a Saturday night and asked the first drunk you encountered. The difference is, I get the opportunity to air my ill-informed views in a national newspaper, and am richly rewarded for doing so.'

'Has this bout of self-flagellation got a point?' Joe said.

'The truth is,' Henry said. 'I was no bloody good as a news reporter. We all know that. I just didn't have what it takes. No sticking power, no tenacity, too lazy to put in the hours required. No guts basically.'

'That's bollocks, Henry, and you know it.'

'No, I'm being honest here. Asking questions, cross-checking the answers, digging for information, all that kind of stuff that news reporters have to do, it's just not me. But you, you're different. That's what you like – a challenge, obstacles to get round, dirt to discover, scandals to unearth. You've got guts.'

'If you're trying to embarrass me, you're succeeding.'

'You have to have guts to do what you're doing. Have you thought about it? You must be mad, trying to infiltrate the people-smuggling racket, a business run by some of the most dangerous criminals in the world. And all for the sake of a story.'

'I know what I'm doing.'

'I know you do. You know exactly what you're doing. Yet you're still going ahead with it. That's what I mean when I say you have guts.'

'I'll get some good material, if I can pull it off,' Joe said.

'You could also get killed.'

'Don't remind me.'

Joe drained his glass of mineral water and scooped up a handful of nuts.

'I'll be in touch,' he said, standing up.

'Good luck,' Henry said.

* * *

Zouzou's, the restaurant the hotel landlord had recommended – if recommended was the right word – was a small, dingy place hidden away down an alley between two concrete buildings that had been liberally sprayed with graffiti. Joe paused at the mouth of the alley, steeling himself to go on. Up till now, things had been relatively simple. He'd acquired a few new clothes, changed his appearance, found a place to stay. None of it had been difficult – or particularly risky. The dangerous part was all to come, and he wasn't sure how he was going to cope with it.

The criminal underworld wasn't unknown to him. He'd been a reporter in London for fourteen years, had covered probably hundreds of crime stories. But reporting crime was easy. It wasn't a frontline job. He didn't witness the harrowing things a police officer or social worker saw, he didn't suffer the crimes the way their victims did. By the time he got to the scene, everything had been sanitised. He was a privileged bystander, a recorder of facts, but his experience of the events was always second-hand. Now he was stepping outside that comfort zone, venturing into an area of which he knew little. He was descending into the underworld, and it frightened him.

The restaurant was only half full. It was dimly lit, a couple of dusty lamps glowing on the walls, but in the gloom Joe could make out a few people huddled around the tables at the back of the room. As far as he could tell, they were all black or North African. There was a reek of garlic and spices that was so strong it stung his eyes. A sort of African jazz music – drums and electric guitar – throbbed monotonously from the sound system.

Joe took a seat at an empty table at the front of the restaurant, pulled off his cap and stared at the tablecloth, the cap clutched in his hands. There wasn't a printed menu on the table and he hadn't noticed a blackboard on the wall. He waited. He didn't look at the other customers, though he sensed them looking at him. He wanted to create an impression of a man who was lacking in confidence, a stranger who was a little bit lost in an unfamiliar world – a potential target for the local villains who would be able to smell vulnerability the way sharks scent blood.

After a few minutes, a waiter strolled over from the bar and tossed a dog-eared sheet of card down on the table. He was young, olive-skinned with boyish Arab features.

'You want a drink?' he said.

Joe squinted up at him, pretending he hadn't understood.

'*Quoi?*'

'Drink,' the waiter said. 'You want?'

'Ah, yes.'

'What? Beer?'

'Yes, beer.'

The waiter sauntered away. Joe watched him, his gaze straying discreetly to the other customers. Abou was one of them. He was sitting with two other men in the corner near the kitchen, sprawling sideways against the wall with one arm draped over the back of his chair. Smoke drifted up from the cigarette in his hand.

Joe turned his attention to the sheet of card, putting on his glasses and reading down the list of seven or eight dishes that had been handwritten in French, some of the words misspelled. The cuisine was North African – couscous, merguez, chakchouka. Joe opted for the kefta mkaouara, giving the waiter his order when he brought his beer over to the table. The food took twenty minutes to arrive. No one took any notice of Joe in the interim, or while he was eating the kefta – a meatball stew with tomatoes and eggs and a fiery flavouring of hot pepper harissa sauce – but when he'd finished and the waiter had removed his plate, Abou came over and sat down opposite him. He stared at Joe for a time, his demeanour managing to combine both arrogance and shiftiness. Finally, he spoke.

'What's your name?'

He spoke French with a lilting, slightly nasal accent, the vowel sounds harsher than a native Frenchman's.

'Alban Cobani,' Joe said.

Abou's brow furrowed.

'What?'

'Alban Cobani.'

'You new?'

'Uh?'

'New. When you arrive in Calais?'

'Arrive? Today.'

'Where from?'

'South.'

'What are you? Where you come from? Which country?'

'Albania.'

'Albania?'

Abou repeated the word as if he'd never heard it before.

'Why you here?'

'Work. I look for work,' Joe said.

'Yeah?' Abou said sceptically.

Calais was not the most likely place in France to find work. But then the foreign workers who came there hadn't come to find work, and they certainly hadn't come for the sea air. They had only one reason for being on the Channel coast – getting to England.

'What sort of work?' Abou said.

'Anything.'

Abou sucked on his cigarette and exhaled. Joe breathed in the sweet, pungent aroma of marijuana.

'What work you do before?' Abou asked.

'What?'

'Before. What job you do?'

'Fields. Pick vegetable. Hotel. Building. I do all.'

'Where you want to work?'

'Where?'

'In Calais?'

'I work anywhere. You know job for me?'

Abou laughed, exposing a set of uneven teeth scarred by silver fillings.

'A job? Me?' he said. 'I have business. You want to buy cigarette?'

'No,' Joe said.

'Anything else? You know what I mean?'

Joe looked at him blankly.

'What?'

'You want ganja?'

'What ganja?'

'This.' Abou held up his cigarette. 'You want?'

'No. No smoke.'

'What about other drug?'

'Drug?'

Abou put his hand over his forearm and mimed the insertion of a hypodermic needle, depressing an imaginary plunger with his thumb. Joe shook his head. Taking drugs didn't fit his character. Alban Cobani was a simple working man – simple in every sense – from a predominantly agricultural Eastern European country. He'd have vices. He might drink to excess, even visit prostitutes, but he wouldn't take hard drugs.

Abou shrugged.

'You change your mind, you ask me, OK? I fix things.'

'OK.'

Abou pushed himself to his feet and slouched back to his own table. Joe paid his bill and left the restaurant. He thought about going round a few bars and making inquiries about work, but decided not to. He had to be careful, not rush things. The approach had to come from the other side. He'd been noticed, that was what mattered. Now he had to wait and see what they did next.

18

Joe stayed in bed late the following morning, then went out to a café and had a breakfast of coffee and bread and jam. He lingered in the café for as long as he could, watching the street outside, gazing idly at the cars, the pedestrians walking past – killing a few hours while he waited impatiently for the evening. When he began to feel he was outstaying his welcome – the waiter's sarcastic enquiry as to whether he wanted to order lunch spurring his exit – he left the cafe and drifted into the centre of Calais, wandering aimlessly around the streets, window shopping and taking in what few sights the city offered. There weren't many tourists in evidence. Twenty million travellers passed through Calais every year, but almost none of them stopped. They were all on their way somewhere else. That was how Joe felt too. He was marking time, waiting for the moment when he could continue his journey.

He had a ham baguette and a beer for lunch in a café near the town hall, then found a payphone and called Henry's hotel. The receptionist said that Monsieur Weaver had gone out after breakfast and had not yet returned. Joe tried Henry's mobile and found it switched off. He left a message saying simply, 'It's me. Where are you?' and rang off.

He went back to his room with a copy of the local newspaper and leafed through the job advertisements, ringing a couple of small classified ads that were seeking casual labourers. He had no intention, of course, of applying for the jobs, but the newspaper was part of his cover. The process of sifting through the vacancies helped to reinforce in his mind the role he was supposed to be playing. Everything about him, from his physical manifestations – his clothes, his appearance – to his mental state had to be consistent with the character of Alban Cobani. If he thought like an Albanian migrant, then he was much more likely to behave like one.

In the early evening, after a long nap to pass more time, Joe folded the newspaper and slipped it into his jacket pocket, then went out of his room. Going down the corridor to the bathroom, he could hear music playing – the same kind of African jazz he'd heard in the restaurant the night before. Abou's door was open and Abou was lying back on his unmade bed with a cigarette smouldering in the corner of his mouth. He glanced at Joe, raising a lazy eyebrow in greeting, before looking away, his hands fidgeting restlessly to the beat of the music. He didn't say anything, but when Joe passed back along the corridor, the North African waved him to a halt.

'You go eat?'

Joe nodded.

'*Oui.*'

'You go to bar later?'

'Maybe.'

'The Nautilus is good place,' Abou said.

'Where that?' Joe said.

'By the water. That way.'

Abou gestured vaguely over his shoulder and took a puff on his cigarette, half closing his eyes as he inhaled, his hands still moving rhythmically to the music as if he were playing an invisible drum. He seemed to have forgotten that Joe was there. The landlord hadn't though. He came out of his sitting room and demanded to know whether Joe was staying longer than two nights.

'I tell you tomorrow,' Joe said.

'Before ten,' the landlord said. 'Or I'll give your room to someone else. You understand?'

'I understand.'

Joe went downstairs and headed towards the city centre. Near the main post office, he stepped into a phone kiosk and paused, glancing around casually to see if anyone was watching before he punched in the number of Henry's hotel.

'I got your message,' Henry said.

'Where were you?'

'I took the car over to Cite Europe, near the Eurotunnel. To do some shopping.'

'*Shopping?*'

'There's a hypermarket there. You should see it, it's un-believable. This massive bloody great shed the size of an airport. I'm not kidding. You need a golf cart and a guide to get around the place. And it's absolutely packed with Brits. They all come over on day trips. Get off the Eurostar, spend a few hours in the hypermarket, then get back on the train and go home. I'm going to do a column about it. How the nation of shopkeepers became a nation of shoppers. That's all these people do. They don't see any of France, they don't experience anything of French life. All they're interested in is cheap booze. Calais has become the biggest shopping mall in the world. And I must say, the *foie gras* was very reasonable.'

'You've been buying *foie gras*?' Joe said.

'Only a few jars. And some wine. So what's happening? Are we going for dinner somewhere? I noticed a nice little place around the corner from here. A bit on the pricey side, but . . .'

'Henry, I'm supposed to be undercover. Impoverished Albanian labourers don't go for dinner in expensive French restaurants.'

'No, I suppose not. How's it going?'

232

'Hard to tell. I'll see after tonight. I'll be in touch again tomorrow so leave your mobile switched on this time.'

'I will.'

'Enjoy your dinner.'

Joe retraced his steps and found a cheap-looking restaurant close to the docks. He had chicken with chips, the chicken tough and stringy, bathed in a sauce that had the consistency and taste of glue. He'd intended to drink only mineral water, but changed his mind after his meal was served and ordered a quarter litre of red wine to wash away the taste of the chicken.

It was dark by the time he arrived at the Nautilus bar. There were tables outside on the pavement, but no one was sitting at them. It was an overcast night, a hint of rain in the air – too chilly for *al fresco* drinking. Joe went inside and bought a beer at the bar, taking his glass to a table near the window. If the bar had been christened after Captain Nemo's famous submersible – and Joe had his doubts that Jules Verne was much read in these parts – it was an appropriate name, for it had many of the characteristics of a submarine. It was dark, narrow, claustrophobic, the ceiling low enough to touch with a raised arm.

Joe pulled his newspaper from his pocket and spread it out on the table, pretending to study the job vacancies, though the print was almost indecipherable in the poor light. Gradually, the bar began to fill up with customers – seamen, port workers, a few obvious lowlifes. There was only a handful of women. The Nautilus wasn't the kind of place you took your girlfriend or wife for a night out – unless you were a pimp.

A figure sat down in the chair next to Joe. It was Abou. He looked at the newspaper open on the table.

'You find job?' he said.

'I look,' Joe replied.

Abou slouched lower on his chair, the ever-present cigarette stuck to his lower lip, the smoke curling up into

233

his eyes. He seemed relaxed, but watchful. His body was at rest, but Joe sensed a power in him, an energy that could explode suddenly if circumstances required it.

'You have papers?' Abou asked.

Joe regarded him warily, working out how Alban Cobani might respond.

'Papers?' he said.

'Work permit.'

'Why you ask?'

Abou grinned. His fillings flashed. He sat up abruptly and slapped Joe on the shoulder, his best mate now.

'*Mon ami*, don't worry. You think I care whether you have work permit or not? What's it to me? Do I look like a policeman?'

Joe forced a sheepish smile.

'No, OK.'

'Take it easy. Let's have a drink. You want another beer?'

'Yes, beer good.'

Abou swaggered away to the bar and came back with two bottles of beer. Joe accepted the drink politely, knowing that Abou was going to expect something in return.

'You new here,' Abou said. 'You need friend. You know why I ask about work permit? There people here – foreign, not French – lots of them. You know, Spanish, Portuguese, EU people. They have permits. Those jobs,' Abou waved a finger dismissively at the newspaper on the table. 'They go to people with papers. Not you.'

'Not me?'

'You illegal.'

'I work in France already. No one ask questions,' Joe said.

'You lucky. Where you work?'

'Marseille, Paris. Building work.'

'They big cities. Easy place to work. Why you come here, to Calais?'

'No reason.'

Abou smirked.

'I know why. You want to go to England, eh? That why everyone come here. Right?'

Joe shrugged.

'I don't know.'

'You think about going to England?' Abou said. 'There jobs there. Well paid. Easy life. You no work, you claim benefit, you know what I mean? Government pay you.'

'Yes?'

'England easy place to work. I know plenty people go there. Make big money. You interested?'

Joe drank some of his beer, trying to give the impression of a man mulling over the idea, intrigued but not totally convinced.

'Big money, huh?' he said.

'Better than here,' Abou said. 'The French, they all crooks, cheat you. The English, they straight, honest people. Get better deal.'

'How I get there? Through tunnel?' Joe said.

'Tunnel?' Abou gave a contemptuous sneer. 'No go through tunnel. You go over there, tunnel terminal, there hundreds of people like you. They climb fence, hide under trains, walk along tracks. Stupid. They get killed. Or caught and sent back home. You want to go back to Albania?'

'No tunnel?'

'You go ferry. Safer. I know man can fix it.'

'Yes?'

'You want to speak to him? He give you good price.'

'What price?'

'You speak to him. You got money?'

'Some.'

'You wait here.'

Abou stood up and pushed his way through the crowd of drinkers standing shoulder to shoulder down the length of the room. Joe gulped down some more beer, lubricating the dryness in his mouth and throat. His heart was beating faster. He could feel the creeping sickness of fear in his stomach. This was where things got dangerous.

The man who came back with Abou was short and barrel-chested. He had a broad, toad-like face, no chin and heavy-lidded eyes that were sharp and calculating. His hair was thick and long, hanging down over the collar of his workman's jacket and his complexion was blotchy, patches of dry red skin on his face and neck. There was another man with him, a big hefty guy who looked and acted like a bodyguard. He remained standing while the barrel-chested man sat down opposite Joe and gazed at him for a time without speaking.

'This is Janos,' Abou said, resuming his seat.

Janos? Joe thought. Not a French name, and the man certainly didn't look French. What was he? Eastern European? Hungarian maybe. Joe hoped to God he wasn't Albanian – that would blow his cover immediately.

'Abou says you want to go to England,' Janos said, and Joe was relieved that he'd spoken in French.

'Maybe.'

'Don't waste my time. Yes, or no?' Janos said, in the kind of tone you didn't argue with.

'OK,' Joe said. 'If price good.'

'You have three thousand euros?'

'That the price?'

'You have it?'

Joe licked his lips. He didn't want to seem too keen.

'That too much,' he said. 'I no have three thousand.'

Janos gave him a hard stare. Joe wondered if he was the first person to attempt to haggle with him. He hoped not. Janos scratched one of the sore patches on his cheek.

'How much you got?' he said.

'Maybe two thousand.'

'On you?'

'No.'

'You bring it tomorrow night. Abou tell you where.'

'How I go? To England.' Joe said.

'Ferry. In the back of a lorry.'

'That safe? I get caught?'

'That's the chance you take. You in?'

Joe looked away. Alban Cobani would be intimidated by this man, but Joe didn't have to put on an act. *He* felt intimidated.

'You in?' Janos repeated impatiently.

'Yes, I go,' Joe said.

'Two thousand euros.'

Janos stood up and walked away across the bar, his bodyguard trailing after him. Joe watched them go. He badly wanted another sip of beer, but Abou was still at the table. Joe didn't want him to see that he was nervous.

'Who that man?' Joe asked.

'Bad man,' Abou replied. 'You pay him, OK. You no pay him . . .'

Abou didn't bother to finish the sentence. He leant closer to Joe. Joe could smell beer and marijuana on his breath.

'You get money. Meet me here nine o'clock tomorrow night. OK?'

'OK. Nine o'clock.'

Abou pushed back his chair and disappeared into the throng. Joe picked up his bottle of beer and drained it in one go. He wiped his mouth and took a deep breath. So that was it. It was all fixed. It had been more straightforward than he'd expected, but then why should it have been complicated? Calais was full of immigrants wanting to get to England. The secure area around the Channel Tunnel terminal was infiltrated every night by would-be stowaways – people desperate enough to hide in freight wagons or even cling precariously to the couplings between wagons for the short trip under the water. Joe had seen it dozens of times on the television news – shadowy figures scaling the perimeter fences, scuttling for cover as the Eurotunnel security guards hunted them down and ejected them, both parties knowing that the following night the cat-and-mouse game would begin all over again.

With such huge demand for a passage to England, it followed naturally that various opportunists would move in to meet that demand. The poorest immigrants would continue to look for a free ride through the tunnel, taking their chances with the guards and the deadly wheels of the trains, but for anyone with enough money there was a safer way of achieving their ends. It wasn't foolproof, and it wasn't cheap, but a place in the back of a lorry on one of the car ferries to Dover was yours for the asking if you knew the right people. Joe had been surprised that Janos had shown no curiosity about who he was and where he'd come from. But then he realised he was still thinking like a journalist. Janos was a businessman. The only question that mattered to him was, could you pay?

It had started to drizzle outside. Joe came out of the bar and pulled up his jacket collar. Across the water, he could see the lights of the ferry terminal, the superstructure of a cross-Channel ferry towering over the port buildings.

He turned and walked away up the street, the fine rain sprinkling his hair, the droplets clinging to the sleeves of his jacket, glistening like tiny pearls in the light from the streetlamps. As he turned the corner to head away from the dock, he had a powerful sensation of being followed. He looked back, but there was no one there. He increased his pace, slightly unnerved. The streets were darker and narrower here, the lamps more widely spaced. It was hard to see clearly.

He was nearing a junction when he heard a movement in the shadows. He spun round, but too late. A thick, muscular arm hooked itself around his throat and a knife point pressed against the side of his face. Joe froze, offering no resistance. A second man stepped out from the blackness of an alley – Janos. His hands moved swiftly over Joe's body, checking his jacket pockets. He found the reading glasses case and flicked it open, glancing indifferently at the spectacles inside. The asthma inhaler interested him more.

'What this?'

'Drug. For chest,' Joe said, struggling to speak with the arm locked across his windpipe.

He took a couple of shallow breaths, mimicking a wheeze. Janos turned the inhaler around in his hand. Joe watched him, his pulse throbbing violently. If Janos saw the words on the plastic casing . . .

But it was too dark for reading. Janos shoved the inhaler back in Joe's jacket and felt in his trouser pockets, removing a couple of ten euro notes, the only cash Joe had brought out with him – the only obvious cash, that is. His three bundles of banknotes were still down his socks and boxer shorts, but Janos hadn't found those.

'This all?' Janos said, disappointed at the thin pickings.

'I have rest,' Joe said. 'Tomorrow, you said.'

Janos rapped out a command and the man behind Joe released him. Joe rubbed his sore neck, breathing heavily.

'You keep quiet about this,' Janos said. 'You tell no one you go to England. You never met me, you don't know my name. You understand?'

'I understand,' Joe said.

Janos held up the euro notes he'd taken from Joe's pocket.

'I keep these, as down payment,' he said. 'You pay rest tomorrow.'

The two men slid into the alley and were gone. Joe stumbled away up the street. He was still shaking when he got back to his room. His breath was coming in short gasps. He felt the familiar tightness in his chest. He took out his inhaler and held it up to his mouth, his hand trembling. He took two puffs, then lay back on his bed until his breathing returned to normal.

19

'Take a look at this,' Ed Preston said, throwing a couple of sheets of paper down on to Ellie's desk. 'Just came through from PA.'

Ellie glanced at the printout, stiffening as she read the opening paragraph of the Press Association story: '*Health officials in Norfolk are investigating a mystery outbreak of typhoid which has left an elderly woman seriously ill in hospital.*'

'You in a position to chase it up?' Preston said.

Ellie read a few more paragraphs before she looked up at the news editor.

'I'm clear.'

With Joe away in France, Ellie had been keeping an eye on the Kurdish murders case – the Hourami killings – but there'd still been no breakthrough in the investigation, she'd checked with the Met only that morning.

'Norfolk?' she said.

'It's more than a coincidence,' Preston said. 'Two in London, now one in East Anglia. Find out what's going on.'

Ellie read through the rest of the PA report, jotting down notes on her pad, then she went online and found phone numbers for the Norfolk Health Protection Agency and the Norfolk County Council Environmental Health Department. She called the HPA first. They were friendly, but unhelpful. They'd already passed the buck to the local authority.

'Try the county council press office,' the secretary at the HPA suggested.

Ellie went directly to the environmental health department instead. She hated press offices – and press officers. In any organisation they always seemed to be the last people to find out about anything. The decisions were made elsewhere, the personnel who knew what was going on were anywhere but the press office.

The environmental health department switchboard put her on hold while they tried to connect her to an officer, then cut her off. Ellie rang back. There was no one available to take her call, the operator said. Everyone was out, or in meetings. Or hiding under their desks, making signs against the evil eye, Ellie added mentally. A journalist's on the line, a *London* journalist. Time to get out the garlic and the sharpened wooden stakes.

'Try the press office,' the operator said coolly. 'They're supposed to handle press enquiries.'

The press office weren't sure exactly what was happening. They knew there'd been a case of typhoid in Swaffham, but that was about all they did know. The PA report must have been based on some local news agency story, written by a reporter with rather better contacts than the county council press officers.

'Is it just the one case?' Ellie asked.

'I think so,' the press officer replied.

'But you're not certain?'

'No.'

'Do you know the source of the infection?'

'No.'

'What's being done to investigate it?'

'I'm not sure. You'd have to speak to the environmental health people.'

'They told me to speak to you.'

'Did they? Oh. Leave it with us, we'll get back to you.'

Ellie gave them her mobile number and went across to the newsdesk.

'I'm not getting very far on the phone,' she told Ed

Preston. 'I'm going to go up there and stick my metaphorical foot in the door.'

The news editor waved her away, giving his tacit approval.

'Watch your metaphorical toes,' he said.

It was only eighty miles to Swaffham, but by the time Ellie had got through north London and then negotiated the rural by-ways of East Anglia it was early afternoon when she arrived in the town. She'd enjoyed the drive, the window wound down, the CD player on, the rolling fields of Norfolk passing by outside. She was glad of a chance to get out of London, to breathe in some air that, unlike in the capital, you couldn't actually see.

She'd printed off a map from the internet before she'd left the office so finding the house where the typhoid patient, Winifred Kirkpatrick, lived was relatively simple. It was a modest flint and brick semi on the western edge of the town, where the built-up area gave way to fields of corn. Ellie rang the doorbell, but wasn't surprised to get no answer. She knew from the Press Association report that Mrs Kirkpatrick, a widow in her eighties, lived alone. Out of curiosity – or sheer nosiness – Ellie wandered around the side of the house to the back garden. In the adjoining garden, separated from Mrs Kirkpatrick's by a waist-high wooden fence, an elderly woman was sitting out on the terrace beneath the shade of a blue and red striped umbrella. She was reading a book, but glanced up as Ellie came into view.

'Are you looking for Winnie?' the woman said, peering at Ellie over her reading glasses. 'She's been taken ill, I'm afraid.'

'I know,' Ellie said. 'Have the environmental health people been here?'

She'd expected to see more signs of activity around the house, someone inside carrying out the same kinds of tests Alan Greenwood had done at Hilda North's flat.

'They left, oh, about half an hour ago,' the woman said. 'Are you from the council?'

Ellie explained who she was.

'From London,' the woman said. 'You've come a long way.'

'Mrs Kirkpatrick's in hospital, I understand,' Ellie said.

'Yes, the Queen Elizabeth, in King's Lynn.'

'Do you know who let the environmental health people into her house?'

'I did. I have her spare keys. Winnie has mine. It's the best way, don't you think? Leave them with your next-door-neighbour. Then they're handy if you need them.'

'You must know Mrs Kirkpatrick well.'

'I do. Twenty-four years we've lived next to each other.'

The elderly woman closed up her book and placed it on the garden table. She removed her glasses and gazed quizzically at Ellie.

'A journalist, you say?'

'That's right,' Ellie said.

'There was another journalist here earlier. A man. From the *Eastern Daily Press*. I didn't take to him. He was rude, not at all friendly. But you look a nice young woman.'

Ellie smiled.

'Thank you.'

'Come round through the gate. I'll pop the kettle on and we'll have a cup of tea.'

Rosemary Wilson – as the woman introduced herself – retreated into her house and reappeared five minutes later with a tray of tea things.

'How do you like it? As it comes?' she asked, putting the tray down on the garden table.

'That'll be fine,' Ellie said.

Mrs Wilson passed her a cup of tea, then poured one for herself and added a spoonful of sugar. She was a tall, thin woman with a slight stoop and neatly-cut grey hair. She

243

was wearing clip-on earrings, some kind of yellow stone set in silver, and a sleeveless blue dress.

'It's not often I get to have tea in the garden,' she said. 'But it's so warm today. I love sitting out on the terrace.'

'I'm not surprised,' Ellie said. 'It's a very attractive garden.'

'Thank you. I do all the planting, but I have a man who comes in and takes care of the heavy stuff. Mowing the lawn, cutting the hedge, that kind of thing. I don't like machinery. My husband used to do all that.'

'You're a widow?'

She nodded.

'These past twelve years.'

'And Mrs Kirkpatrick?' Ellie said, steering the conversation on to the topic that really interested her. 'I believe she's a widow too, isn't she?'

'Yes, Winnie lost her husband, oh, about seven years ago.'

'When was she taken ill?'

'Two days ago. She hadn't been herself for some time. She complained of a headache, sore throat. She was off her food too. When I popped round the day before yesterday, I was shocked by the state she was in. She hadn't managed to get out of bed, which was very unusual for Winnie, and she had this raging fever. I called the doctor, of course, but he didn't come out. They don't, do they, these days. The receptionist at the surgery advised me to call an ambulance. Help yourself to a biscuit, by the way.'

Ellie took a digestive from the plate on the tray and waited for Mrs Wilson to continue. She knew she would. This was her moment centre stage. Something out of the ordinary, something newsworthy, had happened next door. She wasn't going to pass up the opportunity to talk about her role in the events.

'When the man from the council came round this morning and told me Winnie had typhoid, well, I was flabbergasted. Typhoid! It's not something you expect in this country, is it? How do you get typhoid? The council man was as puzzled as I was. He asked me all these questions, put on this white suit and went into Winnie's house to look for bacteria. He even asked me to go to the doctor for a check-up, in case I'd got it too.'

'That happened to me as well,' Ellie said, and she told Mrs Wilson about her experience with Hilda North.

'So you know all about it,' Mrs Wilson said. 'And your tests?'

'Negative,' Ellie replied. 'I got the results yesterday.'

'That must be a relief for you.'

'It certainly is.'

Mrs Wilson looked at her anxiously.

'Do you think it's possible I might have it too?'

'I don't know. Get the test done, that's the only way to be sure.'

'It's a nasty illness. Poor Winnie is in a very bad way. They won't allow her any visitors, you know. She's in an isolation room.'

'Did the environmental health man have any idea how she might have caught it?' Ellie asked.

'Well, he wanted to know if she'd been abroad, but of course she hasn't. Not for years. She and Jack, that was her husband, went to Spain once, but that was a long time ago.'

'And she has no connection with the two typhoid victims in London?'

'In London? Oh no, she never went to London. It's a complete mystery how she got it.'

'Can I ask where she did her shopping?' Ellie said.

'Her shopping? Well, it varied. We're lucky here, we still have some local shops. There's a newsagent and a greengrocer and a bakery. There used to be more, but they've all been taken over by building societies and charity shops now.'

'Did she ever use a supermarket?'

'Oh, yes. Well, you have to, don't you? Some things you can't get elsewhere. We have to buy our meat at a super-market now – since the butchers closed. I don't like it, but what can you do? They say supermarkets are convenient, but they're only convenient for people with cars. I don't have a car, nor does Winnie. The supermarket's a long way to walk, and then you have to get home with all your heavy bags.'

'They don't deliver?'

'Yes, they do. But you need a minimum order of £25. Winnie used it sometimes, every month or so. Order in bulk and then freeze everything. That's what you have to do these days. Winnie has a big freezer in her garage, but I've only got the little one in the fridge. You can't get much in there.'

'Which supermarket is this?'

'SupaMar. They opened a big place on the outskirts of the town a few years back. They sell everything – food, clothes, kitchen equipment. They have their own travel agency and insurance company too. Someone told me they're opening an estate agency soon, so you can buy or sell a house through them as well. It won't be long before they're doing everything. There won't be a small shop left in the country.'

'The man from environmental health, can you remember his name?' Ellie said.

'I think it was Walker. What was his first name? Alistair. Alistair Walker.'

Ellie put her empty tea cup back on the tray.

'Thank you,' she said. 'I hope I haven't imposed on you too much.'

'Not at all,' Mrs Wilson said. 'Are you going to write a story for the paper about this?'

'Just as soon as I've spoken to the environmental health people.'

Ellie took her leave of Mrs Wilson and went back to her car. She drove away from the house and pulled in to the kerb around the first corner. Removing her mobile from her bag, she punched in the number of the council's environmental health department. Alistair Walker was in the office, but on another line. Ellie rang off and called the Queen Elizabeth Hospital for a condition check on Winifred Kirkpatrick. The switchboard put her through to the ward and the sister told her that Mrs Kirkpatrick was 'seriously ill but stable', the same words Whittington Hospital had used to describe Hilda North's condition just before she died. It was hospital-speak for 'there's nothing we can do, we're just waiting to see what happens'.

Ellie tried the council again and this time got through to Alistair Walker. He had a soft growl of a voice, a gentle Norfolk accent that gave Ellie a mental picture of a big shambling man with a beard. Ellie told him who she was, mentioned her involvement in the London typhoid cases and her dealings with Alan Greenwood, wanting him to take on board the fact that she wasn't simply another journalist like all the rest: she had a personal stake in the whole business.

Walker was more than happy to talk, though he had nothing really revelatory to say. He had no idea how Mrs Kirkpatrick might have contracted typhoid. He'd taken samples from her house, but couldn't say whether he'd found any bacteria until the results came back from the laboratory.

'It's just the one case, is it?' Ellie said.

'Yes.'

'You checked Mrs Kirkpatrick's kitchen and bathroom?'

'Of course.'

'What about food? You can catch typhoid from contaminated food, can't you? Did you check her fridge?'

'There wasn't much in it, certainly nothing that was two to three weeks old which is when she must have first caught the disease.'

'What about her freezer? Typhoid bacteria can survive

freezing, can't they? Did you check the food in her freezer?'

'She doesn't have a freezer.'

'It's in the garage. Her next-door-neighbour told me.'

There was a short silence on the other end of the phone. Then Walker said, 'I didn't know that. Thank you for mentioning it.'

'Have you spoken to Alan Greenwood yet?'

'I tried earlier, but he was out.'

'The only thing the two London cases seemed to have in common was that both victims shopped at the same SupaMar store. Mrs Kirkpatrick also did some of her shopping at a SupaMar.'

'I'll go back and check her freezer.'

Ellie gave him her mobile number.

'I know it will take a couple of days for you to get the results, but when you do, will you give me a call?'

'Yes, I'll do that,' Walker said.

Abou was already waiting for him in the Nautilus bar, seated comfortably at a table, his legs stretched out, a cigarette in his hand. He was drinking beer straight from a bottle. Joe sat down next to him. Tucked under his arm was the plastic bag containing all his worldly possessions – his spare shirt, towel, toothbrush and tube of toothpaste.

Abou got straight down to business.

'You have the money?'

Joe nodded.

'Show me,' Abou said.

'Here?'

'Yes.'

Joe had the banknotes in his inside jacket pocket now. He didn't want to have to rummage in his socks and underwear to access the cash. He put the wad of euros on the table, looking around to see if anyone was taking an interest. Abou counted the notes.

'You're twenty short,' he said.

'Janos take twenty from me last night,' Joe said.

'You got another twenty?'

'Yes, but Janos say . . .'

'Who gives a fuck what Janos said?' Abou broke in. 'The price is two thousand. You want to go to England, or not?'

He gave Joe a hard stare. The easy-going affability slipped off him and Joe saw a different, nastier Abou.

'Give me the twenty.'

Joe felt in his trouser pocket and brought out the remainder of his cash – a little more than a hundred euros in small denominations. He selected a couple of fives and a ten and slid them across the table to Abou. Abou added the notes to the rest of the money and slipped the whole bundle into his own pocket.

'Janos say I give money to him,' Joe protested weakly.

'You give to me,' Abou said. 'What the difference?'

He drained his bottle of beer and stood up, signalling to Joe to follow him. They went out of the bar and along the street, turning off after fifty metres into a hidden yard where a small dark van was waiting. Janos and his bodyguard were sitting in the front, the bodyguard in the driver's seat.

Abou pulled open the rear doors of the van. Joe was on edge, his heart pounding. This was the point of no return. Once he was inside the van, he was entirely at the mercy of the smugglers. There was no walking away from them, no pausing for second thoughts.

'Get in,' Abou said.

Joe saw other people in the back of the van. Nine or ten of them. All men. Dark-skinned North African men with frightened eyes. The sight reassured him. He wasn't the only one. There were others going too. Joe climbed in next to the men. Abou joined them, pulling the doors closed and banging on the metal roof to tell Janos' bodyguard to move off.

No one spoke as the van turned out of the yard and

accelerated. Joe didn't even look at the other men. He was preoccupied with his own thoughts, trying to calm the fluttering sensation in his stomach. He'd telephoned Henry earlier, told him what was happening, about the nine o'clock rendezvous at the Nautilus. He'd given him Abou's name, and Janos', but it was just a formality really. Joe knew he was on his own. If anything went wrong, Henry wouldn't be able to help him.

But would anything go wrong? Joe had slept badly the previous night, wondering about his knifepoint encounter with Janos. What had been the point of that? To rob him? If they'd found his cash, would Janos and his accomplice have taken it? Why go to the trouble when Joe was going to hand it over freely the next evening? Did they suspect he wasn't what he seemed? Joe didn't think so. They didn't appear to care who he was. They'd certainly asked him no questions. Maybe they'd been frisking him for papers, for evidence of his identity. Or perhaps it was simpler than that. Perhaps they did it with all their 'customers'. A pre-emptive strike to threaten them, terrorise them and keep them cowed. They would be more pliable then, less inclined to cooperate with the authorities if they were caught.

It had crossed Joe's mind that once they had his money, the smugglers might kill him. But that didn't make sense. The presence of the other men gave him confidence. Killing so many people would have been madness. Janos and Abou weren't that stupid. Joe felt his nerves relax a little. He'd paid his money. There was no logical reason why the smugglers shouldn't now fulfil their side of the agreement.

The van turned a few times, then came to a halt. The rear doors were flung open and Janos waved them out. The van was parked beside a high wire-mesh fence. On the other side of the fence was the vehicle holding area for the cross-channel ferries – a huge carpark lined with rows of articulated lorries and trailers. The area was illuminated by floodlights, with the exception of the stretch of fence immediately by the van where the lights had been conveniently switched off, or broken. The ground was cloaked in a shadowy darkness that would hide any activity from prying eyes on the far side of the lorry park.

Abou went to the fence and pulled open a section of wire mesh that had already been cut through. He gestured at the group of North Africans.

'Quickly! Through here.'

The North Africans crossed over to the fence. Joe was about to follow when there was a sharp report, like a tiny explosion. Something pinged off one of the metal fence posts, sending tiny sparks into the air. Abou threw himself to the ground, yelling, 'Down!'

The North Africans dropped to the tarmac. Joe ducked down behind the van, realising suddenly what the noise had been: a gunshot.

'Fucking Bulgarians,' Janos snarled, flinging himself down next to Joe, his hand reaching under his jacket and pulling a pistol from his trouser belt. The bodyguard had a gun out too. He was peering cautiously over the bonnet of the van.

'You see them?' Janos said.

The bodyguard shook his head.

'Too dark.'

'They're over there,' Janos said. 'Near the warehouse.'

There was a second report. A bullet hit the side of the van. Janos raised his pistol and fired off a shot blind. An answering shot came back, then another.

'Fuck!' Janos said.

He twisted his head round.

'Abou!' he yelled. 'You OK?'

'Yes,' Abou called back. He was lying flat on the patch of dirt between the road and the fence.

'Get them to the truck.'

'Now wait a . . .'

'No fucking arguments,' Janos shouted. 'We cover you. You get them through. You got that?'

'The gunshots. Someone will have heard.' Abou's voice was high-pitched, shaking with fear.

'So move!'

Janos glared at the North Africans spread-eagled at the side of the road.

'You want to get to England, go with Abou. You understand? Abou, you ready?'

Janos nodded at his bodyguard. They knelt up, pistols resting on the bonnet, and fired off three shots each in quick succession.

Abou was on his feet now, crouching down low by the fence. He gesticulated urgently at the North Africans.

'Move yourselves. Hurry!'

The North Africans scrambled to their feet and snaked through the hole in the fence. Joe hesitated. This was crazy. A turf war between rival smuggling gangs and he was caught in the middle.

'Get over here.' Abou cried. 'Now!'

Joe knew he had no choice. He ran to the fence and wriggled through the hole. Behind him, Janos and his bodyguard were firing more shots. Abou grabbed Joe's arm and pulled him to his feet. The North Africans were already running across the lorry park, a straggling group of figures with bags clutched to their sides. Joe and Abou went after them.

A bullet hit the ground just in front of Joe and ricocheted off with a whine. Joe swerved, running in a zig-zag line, almost bent double to offer less of a target to the gunmen beyond the fence. One of the North Africans went down. Joe thought he was simply diving for cover, then realised with a sickening jolt that he'd been hit. He was lying ominously still on the ground. Joe slowed and changed course, heading for the body.

'Leave him,' Abou shouted.

'But we . . .'

'Leave him!'

Abou gave Joe a violent shove, pushing him to safety behind the first row of trucks. The North Africans were cowering against the trailer, looking back in terror at the motionless figure on the ground. Janos and his bodyguard had stopped shooting and were leaping into the van. The engine kicked into life and then the van was moving off, the tyres screaming as it turned and raced away up the road.

'Let's go,' Abou yelled. 'This way.'

He sprinted across the lorry park, cutting through the rows of vehicles until he reached a high-sided articulated lorry with French number plates. Abou flipped back the catch on the trailer doors and swung one open just wide enough to allow Joe and the North Africans to clamber inside. Abou climbed up after them.

'The man . . .' Joe began.

'Forget about the man,' Abou snapped. 'He's dead.'

Abou waved the men to one side, then bent down and lifted two trapdoors that were set into the floor of the trailer, their edges so finely tooled that they were invisible to all but the closest examination. Beneath the trapdoors, the chassis had been specially modified to accommodate a secret compartment a few metres square and just deep enough to contain a human body.

'Get in,' Abou said. 'Someone will let you out at the other end.'

The men looked down at the cavity by their feet, all of them apprehensive, hesitant. Abou gestured at them impatiently.

'Quickly! You want to go to England?'

One man took the lead. He crouched down and lowered himself into the compartment, stretching out on his back, his small travel bag by his feet. The other men followed, lying down next to one another like sardines in a tin. Joe

253

was the last. The mere thought of being entombed in that cramped little hole was enough to set his heart palpitating. Already he could feel his chest constrict, a cold sweat break out over his body.

'What the fuck are you waiting for?' Abou hissed. 'Get in.'

Joe wasn't going down there, no way. There'd been cases of smuggled immigrants suffocating to death inside sealed compartments. It was madness to even think about going to England like this.

Abou grabbed hold of Joe's arm and tried to force him into the hole.

'Get in!'

'No, I no go in there. I stay up here,' Joe said tremulously.

'You go in the compartment, or you don't go at all,' Abou said. 'Get in the fucking hole.'

Joe shrugged off Abou's grasp. He took a deep breath and licked his lips. His back was clammy with sweat yet his mouth was bone dry.

'Get in, or get off the lorry,' Abou shrieked. 'We don't have time for this shit.'

Joe was trembling all over. He'd just seen a man shot dead. It could so easily have been him. This wasn't what he'd expected – a gun battle, a cold blooded killing. It wasn't part of the deal. He wasn't a reporter any more, watching from the sidelines. He was in the thick of it in all its raw brutality, and he was terrified. This wasn't just about a story now. It was about staying alive. He wanted to walk away, get back to his safe, sheltered world. But he knew he couldn't. He had to finish what he'd started.

'OK, I go,' he said.

He dropped down into the compartment before he changed his mind. There was only just room for the ten of them. They were squashed together so tightly that Joe could feel the body heat of the man next to him. The trapdoors closed over them. The compartment was plunged into an oppressive darkness. Joe could sense the floor of the trailer above him, only a couple of inches from his face, but he couldn't see it. He heard Abou shuffling boxes around to hide the trapdoors. A sudden attack of panic swept over him. He couldn't breathe. He was going to die in here. They were all going to die. He started to pant, to hyperventilate. His heart was thumping, his face sweating. There was a vice around his throat and around his chest. He was choking. He wanted to cry out, to scream for help, but he couldn't get the air through his vocal cords. He tried to lift his arms, to claw at the trapdoor, but he couldn't move his shoulders he was sandwiched so tightly between the next man and the metal side of the compartment. He closed his eyes. The blood was surging through his head, hammering at his retinas. He was suffocating. This was it. This was the end. He blacked out.

It was the best thing that could have happened. As he lapsed into unconsciousness, his brain shut down and his body relaxed. His heart beat and breathing slowed. He was out for no more than half a minute, but as he gradually came round he realised that he could see the underside of the trapdoor, see the faint outlines of the other men. There was light filtering in from somewhere – a tiny crack or a hole. And if there was light, there would be air too. He could breathe. His body would cope. He just had to control his mind, stop it panicking again.

He focused on the rhythmic expansion and contraction of his lungs. At all costs, he had to avoid an asthma attack. In, out, in, out. He counted the cycles, concentrating on breathing to the exclusion of all other thought. He had to slow everything down, find a way of separating his mind and body like Buddhist monks did during meditation. And it worked. He found his limbs relaxing. The blood no longer pulsed through his skull. His breathing eased. Hang in there, he said to himself. You can get through this.

He heard the cab door of the lorry open and slam shut.

The engine turned over. The vehicle moved forward. Wheels crunched on concrete. Joe listened for the telltale change in the noise of the tyres – and there it was – the sudden hammer blow as the lorry hit the metal loading ramp and drove on to the ferry.

There were other sounds after that. Other engines around them, footsteps on the metal vehicle decks, men's voices, all fading away until Joe was aware of nothing except the muted stirrings, the soft breathing of the men beside him in the trailer.

Underpinning everything was the distant rumble of the ferry engines, the vibrations throbbing up through the hull and into the sides of the lorry. Then the sound changed, the frequency of the vibrations altered. The ferry was pulling away from its berth, heading out of port and across the Channel towards England.

20

Joe knew it was only a seventy minute crossing from Calais to Dover, but cooped up in the lorry's secret compartment it seemed much longer. It was stiflingly hot, the enclosed space and the heat of ten bodies squashed close together turning the compartment into an oven. The air was thin and low in oxygen. Joe took shallow breaths, lying absolutely still, avoiding any unnecessary exertion. The trickle of light seeping in through tiny cracks in the walls was too feeble to illuminate much of the interior. Joe couldn't see the other men's faces though he could hear and smell them. With his vision impaired his other senses seemed to have become more acute. He could detect every minute movement around him, pick up the faint scents of sweat, his own as well as the other men's.

He tried not to think about how vulnerable they were in this oversized coffin in case it induced another panic attack. What if the ferry were to sink? He imagined the ship going down, the vehicle decks flooding, the compartment slowly filling with cold sea water and shuddered. Think rationally, he told himself. How often do cross-Channel ferries sink?

How long had they been sailing? Fifteen minutes? Twenty? Joe was aware of the ferry engines chugging away in the background, but he felt no movement, no rolling or dipping in the waves. That was one consolation – at least he wasn't feeling seasick. He wondered who the other men were. Did they know the man who'd been shot, left behind in the lorry park in Calais? Was he their friend, or just another nameless casualty of the people-smuggling trade? How did these men feel, embarking on a hazardous sea crossing like this? And this was the easy bit. Stowing away on a lorry from Calais wasn't difficult. There were no immigration checks on vehicles *leaving* France. The French authorities didn't care how many illegal migrants were hiding in the backs of lorries – the more the better as far as they were concerned, it was a few less migrants for *them* to worry about. Stowaways were a problem for the English, and since when had the French been unduly bothered about creating problems for *les rosbifs*?

The hard part came at the other end when they landed in Dover. Immigration controls were much tighter there. Lorries were stopped at random and searched. The UK authorities had X-ray machines that could detect secret compartments like this one, they had dogs that could sniff out unauthorised human passengers. But it was a hit-or-miss affair. Only a tiny proportion of the thousands of vehicles coming across the Channel every day could be stopped. For every illegal immigrant caught, there were probably several hundred who got away.

Joe hoped he was going to be one of the latter, even though he knew that detection would result in no great hardship to him. A few hours in custody until he could prove his real identity, maybe a verbal reprimand from some angry immigration officer, but not much more. His companions wouldn't get off so lightly. They'd be locked up for months while the Home Office decided what to do with them, then almost certainly deported to their home countries, back to the poverty, injustice or strife they'd been trying so determinedly to escape.

The ferry was slowing. Joe could hear it in the engines. The other men had felt it too. They were shuffling around nervously, preparing themselves for what was to come. The minutes passed, then they heard the faint, very distant sound of the ship's Tannoy. The words were impossible to make out, but Joe knew they were the instructions to drivers to return to their vehicles on the car decks. Soon they heard footsteps outside the trailer, doors opening and closing. The cab door of their own lorry slammed shut. The ferry juddered, the engines reversing, manoeuvring the ferry into its docking position. Joe ran through the stages in his head, matching each one to the sounds he could hear outside. The ferry coming to a stop, the massive bow doors swinging open, the ramp descending gently on to the quayside. Then the lorry engine ignited and they were disembarking, rattling across the ramp on to the quay.

Joe was crushed against the side of the compartment as the lorry turned sharply, negotiating the road through the ferry terminal. He waited tensely for any sign that the vehicle might be pulled over for a customs and immigration check. Maybe they'd be lucky and go straight through.

Then he felt the lorry brake. Was it simply a traffic jam on the way to the exit, or something more worrying? The lorry slowed. It turned to the left and came to a stop. Shit! They were going to be searched.

Joe heard footsteps outside, the cab door opening, voices. Then the rear doors of the lorry were pulled back and someone climbed inside the trailer. Joe held his breath. He could feel the man next to him stiffen, sense the others doing the same. Feet scraped on the trailer floor. More than one set. Two men. Joe listened intently for the patter of dog's paws. If they brought a sniffer dog in, it was all over. They'd be detected immediately. But he heard only human feet, the voice of a customs officer as he asked the driver what was in the boxes he was transporting.

The footsteps moved deeper inside the trailer. Joe heard the sound of a cardboard box being opened, the customs officer saying something, the words too muffled to make out. Joe snatched a quick breath. The air inside the compartment seemed thinner, hotter. He felt perspiration on his forehead. No sniffer dog. Not so far, anyway. That was good. How did these things work? Was there a preliminary check on several vehicles and then only the suspicious ones went on for a further, more thorough examination? They couldn't X-ray every lorry, could they? They had to be selective.

'Thank you,' Joe heard the customs officer saying.

Had he imagined it? Thank you? Did that mean . . . He didn't dare to hope.

There was a scuffle of feet as the men clambered out of the trailer. The rear doors slammed shut and moments later the lorry moved off. It kept going, through the terminal and out on to the main road, heading away from Dover towards the motorway to London. Joe felt his body relax, the relief wash over him. He'd made it. He was back in England.

It was the early hours of the morning when the lorry finally came to a stop. The boxes that had been used to conceal the entrance to the secret compartment were moved aside and the trapdoors were lifted. A fresh, cool draught gusted over the bodies in the compartment and Joe gave a sob, gulping in the air, filling his starved lungs. Thank God. The worst few hours of his life were over.

He climbed out with the other men, shaking his arms and stamping his feet to relieve the stiffness in his muscles. They were in a lay-by at the side of a dual carriageway. Parked behind the lorry was a small white van. Joe and the other men were transferred to the van for the final few miles of their journey to London. The people-smugglers were well organised on both sides of the Channel. The transfer was effected with slick, professional ease, as if it were a nightly occurrence – which no doubt it was.

Ten of them in the lorry – that was twenty thousand

euros the smugglers had made at no real risk to themselves. The ten were probably only the tip of the iceberg. There'd have been others, hidden away in other lorries on the same ferry. The smugglers worked on percentages. Spread the load, send dozens of illegal immigrants over simultaneously in different vehicles. Some would inevitably get caught, but most would get through. There wasn't even a downside for the criminals, because all of the passengers – successful or unsuccessful – had paid their money up front.

The van brought them to a workshop – some kind of metalworking business, lathes and drills all around the edges, an open space in the centre with a winch in the ceiling above. The doors of the workshop were closed before the men were allowed out of the van so Joe couldn't see what lay outside. The only windows in the room were two skylights in the roof and all that was visible through those was an overcast night sky, an orange glow indicating that they were in an urban, street-lit area.

The van driver was a man of few words. After releasing them from the vehicle, he said simply, 'Stay here, OK? I'll be back in the morning.' Then he opened a small door in the workshop wall and disappeared through it. A key turned in the lock on the other side. Joe went to the door and tried it, just to make sure. Then he checked the main doors through which the van had driven in. They were locked too. There was a third door at the side of the workshop. That was unlocked. Joe pushed it open, but it led only to a tiny office and a toilet. He took a look around the office, opening the desk drawers, the cupboards on the wall. There was nothing in any of them. Nothing to indicate where they were, or what kind of business might be operating from the workshop. The whole place was probably a front, Joe guessed – no more than a staging post in the people-smuggling racket. The workshop didn't look, or feel, as if it were in use for its original purpose. The machinery was old, bits of it rusting, there was no work in progress on the bench tops, no debris on the floor. Times had changed. Nowadays there was a lot more money in illegal immigrants than there was in metalworking.

The North Africans had adapted effortlessly to this new environment. They were sitting on the floor of the workshop, their backs against the wall, seemingly quite happy to remain there until someone came to tell them what happened next. One of the men had opened his travel bag and was sharing out pieces of chocolate and dried fruit. He offered some to Joe who shook his head. He didn't want to take their food, they would need it more than he did. Looking at these men, genuine migrants who'd faced God knows what hardship and dangers on their journey to England, made him feel like a charlatan. He was only pretending, an actor playing a part. If things got tough, he could step out of his role, discard his costume and make-up and return to his real life. These men had no such choice. This *was* their real life.

'There's a toilet through there,' Joe said, still speaking in French. 'A tap for water.'

One of the men nodded, chewing on a handful of raisins. '*Merci.*'

'Where you from?' Joe asked.

'Libya.'

'All of you?'

'Me and my two friends here. The others, they from Morocco and Algeria.'

Joe sat down on the floor next to them. The concrete was cold and hard, but there was no alternative. There were no chairs in the workshop.

'The man who was killed,' Joe said. 'You knew him?'

The Libyan shook his head.

'No, he on his own. We don't know him. Don't know his name.'

'Was terrible,' Joe said. 'Seeing him shot like that.'

The Libyan shrugged.

'Yes, terrible. These things happen.'

These things happen? Joe thought. Was that all he could say? Was that what all the others would say too? Did they not feel anything? A man had died, but no one seemed to care. Certainly not Abou or Janos, or the Bulgarians who'd shot him. Nor, apparently, these men who'd witnessed the killing. But then why *should* they care? They were still alive. That was all that mattered.

'Where you go? You stay in London?' Joe said.

'We go Manchester. We have friend there.'

'Libyan friend?'

'Yes.'

'When you leave Libya?'

'Three month ago.'

The man took a sip of water from a plastic bottle and passed the bottle on to his companions.

'How you get to France?' Joe said.

'We go Tunisia first, then Morocco, then boat to Spain.'

'Was hard?'

'Hard?' The man shrugged. 'We do it, that's all.'

Joe was interested to know more, but he sensed the men didn't want to talk. Perhaps he'd asked enough questions already. He closed his eyes. He hadn't slept at all in the lorry, on the ferry or on the journey from Dover to London. He'd been too tense. He was weary. The workshop floor was uncomfortable, but before long he dozed off into a shallow sleep.

At intervals during the night, he awoke, feeling stiff and cold. On one such occasion he noticed the workshop was in darkness and had a brief panic attack, his heart racing, hammering against his chest until he realised that one of the North Africans must have switched off the light. He could hear them sleeping beside him, found the quiet sounds of their breathing a comfort.

The final time he stirred, it was morning. Watery grey sunshine was creeping in through the skylights. He stood up and stretched himself, walking around the workshop to loosen up. He shivered. He was wearing all the clothes he possessed, except his spare shirt, but he felt frozen to the bone. He went through into the toilet and tried the taps over the grubby basin. There was cold water, but no hot. Scooping cold water up with his hands, he bathed his face. It felt like ice on his skin, but it woke him up.

The Libyans were coming round when he returned to the workshop. They offered him some raisins from their dwindling supply and this time Joe accepted. He chewed slowly on the dried fruit, trying to recall when – if ever – he'd had such a meagre breakfast before, and wondering where his next meal might come from.

A key turned in the lock of the workshop door and two men walked in. One was the van driver who'd brought them there, the other was a thick-set man in a black leather jacket. He had the same colouring and similar facial features to Janos. Another Eastern European, Joe thought. The man's accent, when he spoke, supported that conclusion.

'What you do now?' he said in English, looking around at Joe and the North Africans.

It was one of the Libyans who replied, speaking English for the first time.

'We are in London?'

'Yes.'

'Where? Near Victoria bus station?'

'No. You want Victoria? You can get there on the tube.'

'Tube?'

'Underground train. You have place to go? Work?'

'Yes, we OK,' the Libyan replied.

'And the rest of you?' Leather Jacket said. 'You want work?'

The other North Africans shook their heads.

'We have friend,' one of them said. 'We go there.'

That left only Joe.

'I have no place,' he said, adjusting his Albanian accent from French to English. 'You have work?'

'What you do?' Leather Jacket asked.

'In Italy, France, I work on farm. Pick vegetable.'

'Farm work? You want farm work?'

'You have it?'

'I fix, no problem.'

Leather Jacket walked away and made a call on his mobile, speaking in a language Joe didn't recognise – Hungarian probably. The North Africans, meanwhile, were gathering up their things, preparing to leave.

'How we get to Victoria?' one of the Libyans asked the van driver, who gestured with his hands, giving them directions to the nearest tube station.

The Libyans conferred briefly with one another in their own language, then one of them looked at Joe.

'We go now.'

Joe shook hands with them.

'Good luck in Manchester.'

'Yes, thank you. Good luck too.'

They went to the door of the workshop, pausing for a moment to survey the street outside, to adjust to their first proper glimpse of London, then they were gone. The remaining North Africans followed.

Leather Jacket finished his phone call and came back across the workshop to Joe.

'I fix,' he said. 'There is man. He need people. Good worker.'

'Where?' Joe said.

'Countryside,' Leather Jacket replied vaguely.

'How I get there?'

'He take you.' Leather Jacket pointed at the van driver. 'It cost you, you understand? You have money?'

'Money? I have little bit.'

'Show me.'

Joe took a few euro notes from his jacket pocket, carefully

leaving some of the cash behind. He knew they'd clean him out, if he gave them the opportunity.

Leather Jacket snatched the money away and riffled through it.

'Sixty euros. Is this all? You have more?'

'That all,' Joe said. 'I have no more.'

Leather Jacket crumpled the notes between his fingers and shoved them away into his pocket.

'Get in van,' he said.

They made two stops in the first ten minutes of the journey, picking up four more people at two different locations. The four – all men, all obviously foreign – climbed into the back of the van clutching small bags. They sat down next to Joe, squeezing into the restricted space, glancing at him warily. Joe wondered if they'd all just arrived in London too, even if they'd come over on the same cross-Channel ferry as he had. Two of the men looked slightly oriental – not Chinese or Japanese, but maybe Thai or Malay. The other two – from their clothes and faces – could have been from Pakistan or Afghanistan. They seemed shy, withdrawn, nervous. No one spoke.

After half an hour, Joe made an attempt to converse with them.

'Me Alban,' he said. 'What you call?'

The men didn't reply. Joe tried again.

'You have name? Where you from?'

'Yes,' said one of the Orientals.

'You know where we go?' Joe said.

They avoided his gaze. They didn't feel like talking, or perhaps they simply didn't speak English. Joe left them alone.

The rest of the journey was passed in silence. Joe had no idea where they were going – there were no windows in the back of the van. There was no way of even working out the general direction in which they were headed. It could've been Surrey or Kent, there were plenty of farms in both counties, but he thought it more likely that they were going to East Anglia or Lincolnshire. Those were the really big agricultural areas of the country, where thousands of migrant workers were employed.

He was none the wiser when they finally arrived at their destination and were allowed out of the van. They'd stopped on the grass verge at the side of the road. There were fields stretching to the horizon all around them, but no indication of where they might be – no road signs, no landmarks, no buildings whose vernacular might have given away their location. As far as it was possible in an island the size of England, they appeared to be in the middle of nowhere.

On a track leading off the road, a tractor and a muddy Land Rover were parked. Standing next to the tractor was a group of three men and two women who were clearly migrant labourers. Two other men were present, both white and English. One was short, wearing blue overalls and thick-soled leather boots; the other was ten years older – in his mid fifties – a tall, gaunt man with a green Barbour jacket and a face that seemed creased into a permanent expression of worry. They were standing a little apart from the migrant workers. Joe guessed they were the tractor driver and his boss – the farm manager or foreman, maybe the farmer himself.

The older man in the Barbour jacket called Joe and the other four newcomers over and told them to leave their bags on the raised earth mound at the edge of the field.

'My name is Richard Hibbert,' he said brusquely. 'This is my farm, Coppice Wood Farm. You're picking courgettes today. Have you picked courgettes before?' His eyes roved over the blank faces. 'I'll show you anyway. Watch me.'

Richard stepped off the track into the adjoining field. He bent down to the plant at his feet and pushed aside the leaves. At the base of the stem, a number of shiny dark green courgettes were growing, some with their yellow flowers still attached to them.

'We're looking for good, healthy mature specimens,' Richard said.

Joe tried to identify his accent. There was a hint of a burr in the way he pronounced his 'r's. His vowel sounds, particularly the 'u' in 'mature' were rich and long. Norfolk, Joe guessed. We're in Norfolk.

'This one here, for example,' the farmer went on, 'is too small. The courgette needs to be about six inches long, no less than six inches, but not more than eight inches. We're looking for a uniform cylinder shape. If the fruit bulges or is misshapen, leave it. And it needs to be firm to the touch. If it's squashy, or it's been damaged in any way, don't pick it. Do you understand?'

No one responded, so Richard repeated the question.

'Do you understand?'

A few heads nodded. Not all, but enough to satisfy the farmer, who took a thin wooden-handled knife out of a bucket and showed them how to slice a courgette off its stem.

'Cut at the base,' he said. 'In the stalk of the courgette. One clean cut, that's all it takes. Then you place the courgette on the conveyor belt. Place, not throw. I don't want them all bruised.'

Richard glanced at the man in the blue overalls. 'OK, Alf, let's get going.' Then he turned back to address the workers. 'I want four of you on that side, four on the other, two in the middle doing the packing. Any questions? Good. I'll see you later, Alf. Give me a call if there are any problems. '

The farmer strode across to his Land Rover and drove away along the track. Alf climbed into the cab of the tractor and started the engine. Attached to the rear of the tractor was a trailer which had narrow conveyor belts projecting on either side like wings. The conveyor belts were suspended about three feet off the ground, just high enough to clear the leaves of the tallest courgette plants.

Joe took a knife from the bucket and found himself a place in the line of workers. One of the two women in the group was to his left. She looked European, but not English. She had dark hair, a tanned face and high, well-defined Slavic cheekbones. On Joe's right was a skinny black man in a T-shirt and jeans. The tractor moved off. Joe bent down, brushing aside the leaves of a plant to expose the growing courgettes. He slid his hand in among the stems and was surprised to feel a slight scratching sensation on his skin. He didn't know that courgette plants were prickly. The stems and the veins on the underside of the leaves were lined with tiny spines – not sharp thorns like a gooseberry bush, but unpleasant enough all the same. A few hours of this and Joe knew his hands would be raw, but they hadn't been given gloves to wear. He was tempted to ask for a pair, but had to remind himself that Alban Cobani wouldn't make a fuss, he'd just get on with the job. He sliced off a couple of ripe courgettes and put them on the conveyor belt which was an arm's length in front of him.

Each of the workers had their own row of plants to harvest. The courgettes they picked travelled along the conveyor belt to the trailer behind the tractor where two men, walking along the tracks left by the tractor wheels, packed the vegetables into cardboard boxes. By the time they reached the far side of the field, the trailer was full. The cardboard boxes were unloaded on to the track and more empty boxes assembled from the flatpacks stacked on a shelf at the back of the tractor. The workers moved aside to let the tractor swing round on to a fresh patch of plants, then took their positions again and followed the conveyor belts back across the field, picking as they went.

After an hour, Joe's lower back was aching from the constant bending and straightening and his hands were striated with minute scratches. He'd picked fruit before, in

Italy. But he'd been a younger, more supple man then. And grapes and olives were easier on the back than picking courgettes, which grew at ground level. It was physically the toughest job he'd ever undertaken. The most boring too. The relentlessly repetitive nature of the work was gruelling. The tractor kept going at a pace that allowed no respite from the grind. If you eased off for even a moment, the conveyor belt pulled away and you were left behind, having to pick even faster to catch up.

Joe glanced along the line. He was the oldest person in the group and seemed to be struggling more than the others. The Slavic-looking woman was quick and dexterous and, being small, didn't have so far to bend as he did. The skinny black man was slower, but he seemed to pace himself well, never hurrying, never getting behind. The legs of Joe's trousers were soaked through from the dew on the plants, his brow glistening with sweat as the morning passed and the sun got hotter.

There was no shade anywhere. By mid-day the heat was unbearable. They'd been working for almost four hours without a proper break. Joe was hungry and desperately thirsty, but he had no food or water with him. Not that that would have made much difference for there was no time to eat or drink. Alf was the only one who wasn't suffering. Seated comfortably out of the sun in his tractor cab, he had little to do except steer in a straight line, sip water from the bottle he'd brought with him and periodically shout at his workers to unload the boxes of courgettes.

Joe was beginning to wonder how much longer he could keep up when the tractor came to a halt and Alf turned off the engine.

'Break,' he shouted. 'Twenty minutes.'

The workers retrieved their bags and flopped down on to the ground on the perimeter of the field. Joe was exhausted. His shirt was sodden with sweat, his mouth parched. He stretched out his legs and closed his eyes. Every muscle in his body felt as if it had been tenderised with a steak mallet, his hands and wrists were red and itching from the scratches, his eyes aching from the dazzling sun. He wanted to sleep, but his body had only one imperative: liquid. Food he could do without, but if he didn't get something to drink he would pass out.

'You want some?'

Joe opened his eyes and turned his head. The skinny black guy was holding out a bottle of water. Joe blinked, half wondering if he were delirious and imagining it all.

'Have some,' the black guy said.

He thrust the bottle into Joe's hand. Joe took a gulp, swilling the water around in his mouth and letting it trickle slowly down his throat. That was how desert people drank, he'd read that somewhere years ago. Do it slowly, a little at a time.

'Thank you,' he said.

'Take as much as you want,' the black man said.

'You are sure?'

'I have more.'

Joe took another long gulp, feeling the water revive him. The black man watched him, taking in his worn clothes, his dirty unshaven face.

'You have worked on a farm before?'

'Yes.' Joe said.

'But you bring no water?'

'I only arrive today,' Joe said, careful to make sure he didn't lapse into his normal English. 'I come in van. I have no water, no food.'

'You arrived today? From where?'

'From France. I come on boat. Look for work.'

'This is your first day in England?'

'Yes, first day.'

Joe handed back the bottle of water. The two female workers were sitting just behind him on the earth embankment – the Slavic-looking woman and a plump, round-faced black woman with glossy skin and her hair tied up in a bright red scarf. The Slavic-looking woman had a chunk of wholemeal bread in her hand. She broke off a piece and handed it to Joe.

'Take it,' she said. 'What's your name?' Her English was good, though heavily accented.

'Alban. What your name?'

'Marina.'

Joe held out his hand. Marina shook it. Her palm was warm, her grip surprisingly strong.

'This is Grace,' Marina said, indicating the black woman next to her. 'And Kwasi.'

The skinny black man nodded at Joe.

'Where are you from, Alban?' he asked.

'Albania.'

'Albania, eh? You are on your own?'

'Yes, on own. Thank you for helping me.'

Kwasi gave a brief, mournful smile.

'I remember my first day in England,' he said. 'And I wish I didn't.'

Twenty minutes had never passed so quickly for Joe. He was nowhere near recovered from the morning's exertions before Alf was yelling at them all to get back to work. They stumbled into the field with their knives and resumed their positions behind the tractor and its conveyor belts. The tractor pulled off and the punishing cycle of bending, cutting and straightening began all over again. Joe performed the actions automatically now. He was getting adept at recognising which fruits to pick and which to leave on the plants. The prickly leaves and stems still scratched his skin, but he no longer cared. Keeping up with the tractor while using only the minimum amount of energy was his sole objective. Just get through the day, he said to himself. You can survive a day, for God's sake.

He was beginning to realise just how hard agricultural labour was, why so few English people were willing to do it. He'd eaten plenty of courgettes in his life, but he'd never given a single moment's thought to how they were picked. He'd had a vague idea that most farm jobs were mechanised these days. He knew that potatoes were harvested by machine, but of course you could do that with potatoes: lift the entire crop and scoop them up into a lorry. But courgettes still had to be picked by hand. They ripened at different rates, the plants kept producing for months and no one had yet invented a machine that could recognise a ripe fruit and cut it, leaving the immature fruits behind to be picked later.

There was a brief respite in the middle of the afternoon when they ran out of boxes and Alf had to phone the farmer on his mobile to bring out more. The workers took advantage of the hold-up by immediately dropping to the ground where they stood, lying flat out to rest on the bare soil between the rows of courgette plants. An image came to Joe of galley slaves collapsing over their oars when they were permitted to stop rowing. We're not slaves, he thought, but the work we're doing, the way we're treated, is surely closer to slavery than almost any other employment in modern Britain. He didn't even know whether he was going to be paid for his labour. The farmer hadn't asked for their names and there was no gangmaster present to record who was working and for how long.

It was 6 p.m. when the ordeal came to an end. The last few boxes of courgettes were unloaded from the trailer and deposited on the track next to the field. But even then the working day wasn't quite over yet. A flat-backed lorry arrived shortly after and they had to follow it along the track, loading all the boxes they'd filled during the day. Joe could hardly walk he was so tired. When the lorry had gone, he slumped down on to the earth mound beside the track and wondered whether he'd ever have the strength to get up again. The other workers seemed equally worn out. They were sitting down too, some eating snacks they'd brought with them, some lying back with their eyes closed. No one had the energy to talk. Kwasi was next to Joe. He offered him the last inch of water from his bottle and Joe downed it gratefully.

'Thank you.'

'Hard day, eh?' Kwasi said.

'Yes, hard. I tired.'

'Where are you living?'

'Living? I don't know. Man in London say he fix me work. He say nothing about place to sleep.'

'Maybe Barry's taking care of that.'

'Who Barry?'

'This is him now.'

Kwasi nodded up the track where a white transit van was speeding towards them, swerving from side to side to avoid potholes. The driver – a young man in his 20s with spiky hair and an earring – braked heavily and the van skidded to a stop.

'In the back,' Barry shouted through his open window. 'Get a fucking move on, I'm in a hurry.'

Joe hesitated, then scrambled into the back of the transit with the others. The doors weren't even closed properly before the van pulled off and accelerated away along the track. Joe couldn't see out, but he knew from the feel of the ride when they reached a metalled road. Five minutes later they were back on some kind of rough track but the van didn't slow down. The workers in the back clung on tight to the metal rails along the sides as the van bounced and rattled along, tossing the passengers around so violently that one man's head caught the edge of a stanchion, opening a cut on his temple that began to bleed profusely. He staunched the flow with his sleeve and, when finally the van came to a halt, took out a handkerchief and dabbed at the wound.

The rear doors opened and seven more men clambered in – seven more weary, sweaty migrant workers who'd been out in the fields all day. There were now seventeen of them in the back of the transit, crammed together on the bare ply- wood floor. There were no seats, not even any mattresses or foam rubber to cushion the jolts and bumps.

The second batch of passengers – the seven – were dropped off first. Joe saw a street of terraced houses when the van doors were opened to let the men out, but it gave him no clue as to where they were – one terraced house looked pretty much like any other. At the second stop, Marina and Grace got out. Marina smiled at Joe as she stepped over his legs.

'We'll see you, Alban.'

A few minutes later, the van stopped for a third time. Barry opened the doors to let Kwasi and two other men out. That left only Joe and his four companions from London.

'You the new lot?' Barry said. 'I want one out here, the rest stay put, you're in another house.'

Joe climbed out before the others had time to react. He wanted to stick close to Kwasi. He seemed like a useful person to know in this alien world he'd entered.

'What I do?' Joe said to Barry. 'You want name? Who I am?'

'I'll do all that shit later,' Barry said. 'Don't bother me now.'

Joe stood on the pavement with Kwasi and watched the transit van drive away.

'Barry?' he said. 'Who he?'

'He works for the gangmaster who pays our wages,' Kwasi replied.

'Gangmaster?'

'Eddie Tremain. He's the boss. Come on, I'll show you over the palace.'

They went into a narrow, three-storey terraced house. The other two men had already gone inside, but it was clear from the mattresses in the front room that more than three people lived there. Kwasi showed Joe the kitchen at the rear of the house, a small room about eight feet square with a window overlooking a walled backyard. Two men were seated at the table drinking tea, a third was standing by the stove, stirring something in a pan. Kwasi greeted the two at the table and introduced them to Joe as Marko and Stipe, both Croats. Kwasi didn't say anything to the third man, who poured the contents of his pan – a thick soup of some kind – into a bowl and shuffled out of the room with it, avoiding everyone's gaze. Joe asked Kwasi who he was.

'His name's Radu. At least, that's what everyone calls him,' Kwasi replied. 'No one knows much about him, he doesn't talk to anyone, doesn't mix.'

'How many people here?' Joe said.

'In total, fifteen. But we work different shifts so we're not all here at the same time. It would be hell if we were.'

'You good at English. Where you from?'

'Ghana.'

They went back out into the hall and up the stairs. The bathroom was poky, the floorboards bare. The bath and washbasin were chipped and stained and the area in front of the toilet was a darker colour than the rest of the floor, the wood damp with urine where people had missed the bowl. There was a sour, ammonia smell in the air that reminded Joe of a public urinal.

Kwasi looked around the room and shook his head resignedly.

'We try to keep it clean, but what can you do? Fifteen men in a house, one toilet.'

There were two bedrooms on the first floor. The two men who'd been in the courgette fields with them were in the front room, dozing on their mattresses on the floor.

'We're upstairs,' Kwasi said.

They climbed the stairs to the attic – the biggest room in the house, but with a sloping ceiling that made it impossible to stand upright except in the very middle. There were three mattresses on the floor. Radu was sitting cross-legged on one of them, spooning soup into his mouth, the bowl held directly under his chin to catch the dribbles. He had a wrinkled, leathery face and long greasy black hair. He was staring straight ahead, rocking back and forth as he ate. His eyes had a blank look.

'You can have that mattress,' Kwasi said, pointing. 'No one's using it.'

'Someone use before?' Joe said, looking down at the mattress, noting a brownish stain at one end.

'He left a couple of days ago,' Kwasi said.

'Why he leave?'

'People come and go, that's how it is.'

Kwasi put his bag down next to his own mattress. His possessions – what few he had – were arranged in neat piles beside the mattress: a couple of shirts carefully folded, a spare pair of trousers, underwear and socks and a toothbrush and toothpaste laid out on a green face flannel. Kwasi picked up his wash things and a towel.

'I'm going to clean myself up.'

Joe lay down on his mattress. His back was killing him, his arms and legs so tired he could barely lift them. He glanced across at Radu, who was slurping his soup, liquid seeping out from the corners of his mouth.

'Hello. My name Alban,' Joe said.

Radu didn't respond. He just kept staring into space and eating his soup. Joe closed his eyes. It was warm and stuffy in the attic. He could smell the rank odour of sweat on his body, on his soiled shirt. His hands were filthy, smeared with green pigment from the courgettes, his jaw line was black with dirt and stubble. He'd never felt so grimy and tired in his life. Yet he'd only done one day's work. *One day.* What had he let himself in for? he wondered. This was much harder than he'd expected. His body was creaking, struggling to cope. Maybe Ed Preston was right and he really was too old for manual labour. Maybe Ben

Montgomery, the manager of his Sunday League football team, had also been correct. Joe was over the hill, fit only for a quiet retirement. Don't be such a bloody wimp, Joe thought. Have some pride. You show them you've still got it in you. Some people do this all their lives, year in, year out. If they can do it, then so can you.

21

Kwasi shared his evening meal with him – a dish of onions and courgettes fried up with a chopped chilli that seared Joe's throat. The onions and chilli had come from a shop, the courgettes from the farmer's field they'd been working in that day.

'They must've fallen into my bag,' Kwasi said with a sly grin. 'Can't think how. Still, no one's going to miss them, are they?'

'I pay you for this,' Joe said. 'For food.'

Kwasi gave a dismissive shake of his head.

'Forget it.'

'No, I have money.'

Joe took a ten euro note out of his pocket.

'You can't use those,' Kwasi said.

'No?'

'You'll have to change them into pounds.'

'Where I do that?'

'A bank. But they're all closed in the evenings.'

'There is bank here?'

'In town.'

'What town we in?'

'You don't know? Downham Market.'

That was good, Joe thought. He was in the right area of the country. Downham Market was only twenty or so miles from Thetford.

'I never hear name before,' he said. 'Downham Market?'

279

He made a show of trying to pronounce the name in his cod Albanian accent. 'Is big?'

'Not very,' Kwasi said.

'How long you here?'

'Three months.'

'You work in fields every day?'

'Or a packhouse.'

'What a packhouse?'

'A building, like a factory. Where you sort vegetables, put them in boxes, wrap them in plastic to sell. You understand?'

'Yes, I understand.'

Joe took a mouthful of onions and courgettes. It wasn't the kind of meal he was used to eating, but he was grateful to Kwasi for providing it.

'This good,' he said. 'Thank you.'

'Any time.'

They were sitting at the kitchen table. They'd timed their meal just right for there were only two chairs in the room, probably in the entire house. The men who came in after them had to eat their food standing up or take it back to their bedrooms to eat on their mattresses. Kwasi told him the names of the residents and their nationalities. There seemed to be Lithuanians, Kosovans, Serbs, Poles and, of course, the two Croats Joe had met earlier and Radu, whose nationality no one seemed to know. There were no Albanians, Joe was relieved to learn.

'Many people,' Joe said.

'Too many,' Kwasi replied. 'When everyone's here, you can't move. We're all on top of each other. People lose their tempers. Sometimes it gets nasty.'

'Why you here?'

'For work. That's why I'm here.'

They'd finished eating when Barry arrived. He was accompanied by an older man – a big, smartly-dressed fellow in his fifties with receding hair and a coarse, weather-beaten face that had been outside in too many icy winds. Eddie Tremain, the gangmaster. Trotting at Tremain's heels was a small, wire-haired mongrel named Skipper.

'Off your chairs,' Barry said.

Joe looked at him.

'Uh?'

'Off your fucking chairs.'

Barry took hold of Joe's chair and pulled it out from under him. Joe fell backwards on to the floor.

'You stand up when the boss comes in,' Barry said. 'Show some fucking respect.'

Joe picked himself up and backed away, his head bowed, his hands cupped together in front of him, the epitome of servile deference.

'Excuse me,' he said apologetically.

Eddie Tremain lowered his heavy frame on to the chair. Skipper lay down by the gangmaster's feet. Tremain scratched the dog's neck affectionately, then looked Joe over.

'This the one?' he said to Barry, who'd taken Kwasi's chair.

'Yeah.'

'I like to take a look at everyone on my books,' Tremain said. 'See the whites of their eyes. Where you from?'

'Where from?' Joe said.

'You speak English?'

'A little.'

'Where do you come from?'

'From Albania.'

'Why didn't you say so the first time? Albania, now there's a shithole. We had any Albanians before, Barry?'

'A few.'

'We get them from all over. They queue up to work for me, don't they, Barry? We give 'em such a wonderful life. Lots of work, accommodation, plenty of healthy exercise in the fresh air. And we pay 'em too. We'll be giving 'em free health insurance and a fucking company car next.' Tremain gave a humourless laugh and Barry joined in obsequiously. 'What's your name?'

'Name?' Joe said.

'You repeat everything I say, I'm going to get really pissed off. What's your fucking name?'

'Alban Cobani.'

'Alban Cobani? What kind of name is that? You a Muslim?'

'No.'

'Good. I hate fucking Muslims. I don't want any of that praying shit. Not on my time, anyway. I've had some. Kneeling down in the fields, facing east and all that bollocks. Fuck that. You work for me, you work. You understand? You got any papers?'

'No papers,' Joe said.

'I can get you a work permit. It'll cost you a hundred quid. You got any money?'

'No.'

'What, nothing at all?'

'Maybe few euros.'

'Euros? They're no fucking use to you here.'

'I go to bank with them.'

'When are you going to do that, eh? You'll be working all day. I'll change 'em for you. 'Course I'll charge a commission for doing it. Let's say twenty per cent, shall we?'

'Twenty? That a lot.'

'I'm doing you a favour. Do you want a work permit, or do you want to go back to fucking Albania? See what he's got, Barry.'

Barry got up from his chair and reached out, trying to feel in Joe's jacket pockets. Joe stepped away automatically, starting to protest. But his words were choked off abruptly as Barry's fist sank into his stomach – a hard, penetrating punch that took Joe's breath away. He doubled over, gasping, and felt Barry's hands moving slickly over his clothes, removing the cash from his pockets.

'Forty euros, that's all,' Barry said, counting the money.

'Forty?' Tremain said. 'That's what, twenty-five quid? Give it here. We'll take the rest out of your wages. Plus the fifty quid a week rent, of course. You got that?'

Joe was too winded to reply.

'Mr Tremain's talking to you,' Barry said, his hand snaking out and slapping Joe hard across the ear. 'Didn't you hear him? You got that, he said.'

Joe nodded weakly.

'Well that's that sorted,' Tremain said.

He heaved himself up and leaned over towards Joe, who was still clutching his stomach.

'I like to get things straight right from the beginning,' the gangmaster said. 'I'm in charge. I make the rules. You don't like it, you can fuck off.'

Tremain adjusted his jacket, brushing his hands over the lapels, straightening his tie as if he were looking in a mirror.

'Nice to meet you, Alban,' he said as he walked out, the mongrel scampering along behind him.

The streets were quiet when Joe slipped out of the house to find a telephone. He headed towards the centre of the town, using his sense of direction, his feel for an area to guide him. He knew very little about Downham Market, had never been there before in his life. A small market town in Norfolk, that was the sum total of his knowledge.

It seemed a pleasant enough place. The houses were an eclectic mix of periods and styles – newly-built townhouses juxtaposed with sixties semis and a few much older cottages that must once have been surrounded by fields. The town had expanded out from its original core, but it still had the atmosphere of a small rural settlement. Joe caught glimpses of farmland in the distance between the houses.

The fruity odour of freshly-spread muck wafted in on the prevailing wind.

It took him fifteen minutes to find a payphone. He so rarely had call to use one that he hadn't realised how scarce they were becoming, how soon the Perspex BT booths would become museum pieces like the classic red-painted kiosks they'd replaced – curiosities for the social historian to treasure and schoolchildren to study with incredulity, marvelling at how crude and primitive their grandparents lives had been.

He picked up the receiver and dialled the operator, making a reverse-charge call to *The News*. Ed Preston answered.

'Where are you?' the news editor asked.

Joe told him.

'You OK?'

'Yes.'

'How was the trip?'

'Uncomfortable.'

'Good,' Preston said. 'It'll make a better story. You getting some good material?'

'I think so.'

'You'd better be. Two thousand plus euros is a lot of money. You spent it all?'

'Every cent. The gangmaster took my last few notes this evening. Cleaned me out.'

'You need more?'

'I should survive until I get paid.'

'What job are you doing?'

'Picking courgettes today. I'm bloody knackered, I can tell you.'

The news editor gave a cruel chuckle.

'It's about time you did a proper day's work.'

'I knew I could count on you for sympathy, Ed. I'll call in again in a couple of days.'

Joe hung up, then dialled the operator again and made

another reverse-charge call – this one to Henry's home number.

'Thank God,' Henry said when he heard Joe's voice. 'You all right?'

'Fine.'

'Where are you?'

'Downham Market.'

'I was worried. There was a shooting last night at the ferry terminal. It was in the paper this morning, before I left Calais.'

'I was there,' Joe said.

'What happened? The paper said it was rival smuggling gangs – Eastern Europeans. There've been shoot outs before, apparently.'

Joe hesitated. He'd tried to blank the incident out of his mind.

'It was pretty hairy. Bullets flying about, one of the group I was with killed. A North African. I don't know who he was.'

'Jesus, that sounds nasty.'

'It was.'

Joe didn't want to think about it. The images were still too vivid, too disturbing. He wanted to put Calais behind him and focus on other things.

'How are you fixed?' he said. 'We need to meet.'

'Just give me a time and place,' Henry said.

'How about tomorrow evening?'

Joe gave Henry his address and arranged a time and rendezvous, then rang off. He was pushing open the door to leave the phone box when he saw something outside and stopped abruptly. There was a short row of shops just along the street from the payphone – a Chinese takeaway called 'Wok This Way', a laundrette and a mini-market and off-licence combined. A woman was coming out of the mini-market with a carrier bag in her hand. It was Marina. She turned away without noticing Joe in the booth and began to walk up the street. She was passing the Chinese takeaway when a group of three youths who'd been loitering outside the shop stepped out to block her path. The youths grinned at one another. Time for some fun. One of them said something to Marina. A second kicked out with his foot, knocking the carrier bag from Marina's hand. Her shopping scattered all over the pavement.

Marina started yelling at them, waving her arms angrily. The youths encircled her, taunting her with racist jibes. Joe pushed open the door of the phone booth and ran to her aid.

'You bastards. You leave her alone,' he shouted furiously.

The youths saw him coming – this big, dirty, unshaven man with clenched fists – and scarpered, sprinting away up the street and down an alley.

'You OK?' Joe said to Marina.

She nodded.

'They no hurt you?'

'No, I'm OK. They just shitheads. Stupid shitheads.'

Joe bent down and helped her gather up her shopping.

'Where you live?'

'That way. Five minutes,' Marina said.

'I come with you.'

He took the bag from her and carried it as they walked to her house.

'They do that before?' he asked.

'Once, twice maybe. Not just me. They do it to others too. Other women in my house. They tell us to go home, say bad things. You know, "fuck off, you foreign whore." Stuff like that. They shitheads. Boys with no brains.'

Marina's house was a semi at the very end of a cul-de-sac. On a patch of wasteland adjacent to the house were two old caravans with dented sides and rusty roofs, their corners propped up on piles of bricks.

'You come in,' Marina said. 'I make you drink.'

They sat in the kitchen of the house while Marina boiled water and made tea.

'How many live here?' Joe asked.

'In the house, nine. There six more in the caravans.'

'You all work for Tremain?'

'Yes. You meet him yet?'

'He come round earlier. With Barry.'

'What you think of him?'

Joe's stomach still ached from the punch Barry had given him.

'I don't like,' he said.

'They both bastards,' Marina said. 'Nasty bastards. They come round here, sometimes drunk. They try to get women upstairs. You know what I say? They touch you.' She shuddered. 'They shitheads too.'

'Where you from?' Joe said.

'Ukraine. Kiev.'

'You here long time?'

'One year.'

'With papers?'

Marina laughed. She had small, slightly crooked teeth.

'You joking? No one here have papers.'

'Other women in house. Where they from?'

'All over,' Marina said. 'Lithuania, Russia, Middle East, China.'

'You have woman from Kurdistan?'

'Kurdistan?'

'In Turkey?'

'No, no one from Turkey. Why you ask?'

'I meet Kurds in France,' Joe said, fabricating a reason for his interest. 'They come to England too. Want job on farm. I think maybe they come here.'

'I don't know women from Turkey,' Marina said.

'You no meet any Kurds on farms?'

'No, never. You want more tea?'

Joe stayed until after nightfall, drinking tea and talking, Marina introducing him to some of the other women in the house as they came into the kitchen to cook and socialise.

When he left, Marina accompanied him to the front gate.

'Thank you,' she said. 'For what you do. Chasing those nasty boys.'

'It was nothing,' Joe said.

'Maybe we work together again tomorrow.'

'Yes, maybe. Goodnight.'

'Goodnight.'

Joe turned and walked away along the pavement, trying to remember the route home through the dark, unfamiliar streets.

22

Next morning, they were back in the fields at Coppice Wood Farm, picking courgettes. Joe was tired, his muscles still sore from the previous day's exertions. He hadn't slept well. He wasn't used to sleeping on a mattress with no pillow or duvet, sharing a room with three other men, two of whom snored and the third – the antisocial recluse, Radu – who spent half the night coughing.

He'd had a cup of tea and a piece of dry bread for breakfast – courtesy of Kwasi, who insisted on sharing what few provisions he had. His generosity made Joe feel guilty, but he accepted the Ghanaian's help with gratitude. He needed it. Joe had no food of his own, and no money to buy any. Eddie Tremain had taken the last of his euros. It was a strange, worrying experience for Joe. He had funds in his bank account, of course, but they were inaccessible in his current situation. Never before had he been completely without money.

'When we get paid?' Joe said to Kwasi.

'The end of the week,' Kwasi replied.

'I pay you then. For food.'

'Forget it, man. I've enough for two.'

'No, I pay you.'

'I don't want your money.'

'I make meal then. Share it, like you share with me.'

'OK, whatever.'

Marina was next to Joe in the picking line again. She was

wearing a navy blue T-shirt and jeans, her dark hair fastened back with a rubber band.

'You OK?' Joe asked her.

'Yes, fine. Why?'

'Those boys last night. They scare you?'

'They just shitheads. They don't scare me. You live here, you get use to all that. It happen all the time. They push you in street, call you names, things like that. Sometimes worse. Kwasi, they beat him up once. Didn't they?'

Kwasi, on the other side of Joe, gave a phlegmatic nod.

'A gang of kids. Drunk.'

'They beat you bad?' Joe asked.

'A few cuts and bruises.'

'Why they do that?'

'The English, they don't like us,' Marina said.

'Why not?'

Marina shrugged.

'Because we're different. They don't like foreign people.'

'We take their jobs?'

'They don't do work like this. It all foreigners. I pick vegetable for three month now. I never once see English person in field.'

'What you do before you pick vegetable?'

'In Ukraine, I work in factory. I come over here, work in hotel in Norwich. Cleaning room, changing beds, washing floors. It pay better than job in Kiev.'

'Why you leave hotel?'

'Manager, he bother me. You know, he chase me, want to get me in bed. Too much shit. I go, find work in countryside for summer. In fields, no one bother you.'

Joe could empathise a little with both Marina and Kwasi. He'd grown up in England, had an English mother, but had never felt truly accepted by the English. It was partly his name. His father had chosen Giuseppe as his son's Christian name because he wanted one part of him to be wholly Italian. It was Alessandro's way of clinging on to the homeland he'd left behind. To Joe, it was an embarrassment, a stigma that set him apart from his English peers. Giuseppe Verdi – what a name to be saddled with in Hackney. Joe's classmates, fortunately, were such cultural ignoramuses that they had no idea after whom he'd been named. But they picked on him anyway, called him an Eyetie, a wop. He was a mongrel, a cross-breed, a half-blood. Why was it that the names for mixed race people all had pejorative undertones? Joe had felt an outsider. His name was alien to the English, so was his way of life. His classmates went home to a waiting mum or, quite often, an unemployed dad. Joe went home to a restaurant, to a tiny table in the corner of the kitchen where he'd do his homework with the chefs bustling around him. Those things stayed with you, those childhood experiences. Joe was completely at home in England now, but a part of him still felt stateless.

He sliced off another ripe courgette and placed it on the conveyor belt. He knew what to expect from a day in the fields now, but that didn't make the work any easier, any less back-breaking. He'd brought a bottle of water with him today – an old plastic lemonade bottle he'd found lying around the kitchen – which he drank from at intervals, stopping the dehydration that had exacerbated the hardship of his first day picking courgettes. It was cooler, which also helped. The sky was grey and cloudy, presaging rain which, in mid-afternoon, duly arrived – a short, heavy downpour which they had no choice but to keep working through. There was nowhere to shelter, in any case, even if Alf had been inclined to let them.

The rain soaked them to the skin, leaving their clothes dripping, their hair in rats' tails. The soft earth of the field became an unpleasant quagmire into which their feet sank as they worked along the endless rows of courgette plants. Even when the rain had stopped, the sky remained overcast. No sun emerged to dry them off. Instead, a wind picked up, gusting across the flat terrain, biting into their wet clothes, gnawing at their exposed hands and faces until they were shivering with cold.

Radu, who'd come with them today, felt the chill more than the others. He started to cough, a harsh, racking cough that seemed to judder through his entire body, forcing him to stop work and wheeze for breath.

'You OK, Radu?' Marina said.

Radu didn't reply. He spat a gob of mucus out on to the ground. Joe noticed that there was blood in the mucus.

'You ill, Radu,' he said. 'You should go to doctor.'

Radu took no notice. He picked another courgette, trying to keep up with the conveyor belt. There was no time to pause, no time to rest. When they'd completed one row, there was always another row to start. When they'd finished a field, there was always another close by to harvest. Only when the flat-backed lorry came to pick up the bulging boxes of vegetables did Joe's spirits lift. The end of the shift was in sight.

They returned to their house in the back of Barry's transit van as before, twenty of them this time, all worn out, all still damp from the rain, their bodies exuding the unpleasant odour of wet clothes and sweat. The house was dank and chilly. Joe found himself short of breath and had to use his inhaler. He wanted nothing more than a hot shower to warm himself up and wash away the grime of the fields, but the house didn't have a shower, and it didn't have any hot water. There was no boiler, no water tank or immersion heater. If you wanted hot water, you had to heat it up in a pan on the stove, a time-consuming, laborious process that no one seemed inclined to undertake. Even attempting it would have led to strife, for there were fifteen hungry men in the house and only four rings on the hob. Hogging one ring just to heat water for washing would have been seen as a selfish, wasteful act, so Joe washed in cold water, stripping to the waist in the bathroom and using an old piece of soap he found on the basin to clean his body. He looked at himself in the cracked mirror, seeing a different Joe Verdi. In just two days of working outdoors his face seemed to have weathered. His hair was tangled and dirty and his stubble was turning into a beard.

Kwasi shared his evening meal again – more fried vegetables which they ate sitting on their mattresses in the attic because the table and chairs in the kitchen were already occupied. Radu was stretched out on his own mattress, his face turned away from them. He seemed exhausted and ill, the phlegmy cough still troubling him. Kwasi leaned over and pulled a blanket up over Radu's body.

'You want to keep warm,' he said. 'Get out of those wet clothes.'

Radu curled up into a foetal position and ignored them. Kwasi shrugged and dipped his fork into his fried vegetables.

'This food good,' Joe said. 'You good cook.'

'Not really,' Kwasi said. 'I do the same things all the time. I only have about four dishes – vegetable stew, vegetable soup, fried vegetables and boiled rice, that's about it.'

'You only eat vegetable?'

'No, I just can't afford meat.'

'Meat expensive here, eh?'

'On what we're paid, yes. What I'd give for a big piece of roast chicken. Sometimes I dream about it. Roast chicken with fried potatoes.'

'You very kind to me. I thank you,' Joe said. 'You good man.'

They ate their vegetables. There were chopped onions and chilli, but the main ingredient was courgettes – four of them that had once again managed to fall into Kwasi's bag.

'What do you think to England?' Kwasi said. 'You like it?'

'I don't know. I only here for two days. It OK. One day hot, one day it rain. Is like that all the time?'

'Yes. Except for the hot day. Usually it just rains.'

'I no like rain. Is cold.'

'When did you leave Albania?'

'One year ago. I go Italy first, then France. When you leave Ghana?'

'Three years ago.'

'You have family?'

'A wife, two children. Two boys.'

'Where they?'

'In Ghana. I send money home to them.'

'You no see them for three year?'

'No.'

'That sad.'

Kwasi looked away.

'Yes, it is,' he said.

'They no come over here?' Joe said.

'That's not possible. The British wouldn't let them in.'

'You have papers? Work permit?'

'No.'

'You illegal, like me.'

'Everyone here is illegal.'

'You always work in field?'

'Just since the spring. I worked in London during the winter. Cleaning offices.'

'Picking vegetable better?'

'Just different. I wanted a change. It's cheaper living out here. I can save more money.'

'Maybe save enough to go home?'

Kwasi frowned wistfully.

'That would be nice.'

Hasan braked gently and brought the car to a stop by the kerb. He turned off the ignition and surveyed the road ahead through the windscreen. There were small, nondescript terraced houses on both sides of the street, cars parked bumper to bumper outside them. Hasan glanced at the number of the nearest house and counted off the doors until he got to number fifteen.

'It's that one, with the red door,' he said.

In the passenger seat next to him, Farok wound down his window and threw the butt of the cigarette he'd been smoking out on to the pavement.

'Who's going to do it?'

'It's my turn,' Hasan said.

He waited for a moment. This was the third of Frank Parnell's houses they'd checked since they'd arrived back in Thetford. They were being careful, making absolutely sure the houses weren't being watched by the police before they went near them. They were being more subtle too. The violent, threatening tactics they'd used the last time had been counterproductive. It went against Hasan's natural instincts, but he was trying to adopt a softer, more devious approach to the job of locating Irena Hourami. He didn't know whether she was still in Thetford, but there was no other place they could begin their search. If she was hiding out in one of Parnell's houses, they would find her. If she wasn't, someone in the houses would know where she had gone.

Hasan pushed open his door and climbed out of the car. He walked slowly along the street, his posture relaxed but his eyes flickering continually from side to side, watching for men in parked cars, for faces in the windows of the houses opposite. He got to number fifteen and turned down the passageway next to it, going through to the yard at the rear of the house. There were three women in the kitchen, Hasan could see them through the glass pane in the back door. They were at the table eating. Hasan knocked on the door and went in.

The women looked round, their expressions hostile, wary, seeing this man they didn't know entering the house.

Hasan smiled and told them he'd come from Frank Parnell. The women's faces relaxed. Parnell was their landlord, their employer. None of them liked the gangmaster, but his name gave this stranger a reassuring credibility.

'Frank's doing a check on all his houses,' Hasan said glibly, repeating the story he and Farok had spun at the previous two addresses they'd visited.

He took a notebook and pen out of his pocket.

'Fifteen, Langton Street, that's right, isn't it? There are how many of you here?'

'Ten,' one of the women said. She was short and dumpy with a swarthy Mediterranean complexion, a couple of black moles on her cheek.

'Ten?' Hasan said. 'I have eleven down here.'

'No, only ten,' the woman insisted. 'There only ten mattresses, no room for more,' she added quickly, as if she feared that Parnell might be looking to increase the number of occupants.

'Are you sure?' Hasan said. 'What about the new girl, the Kurdish girl?'

'What new girl?' the woman said.

'Came a few days ago. What's her name again? Let me check.' He leafed back through his notebook. 'Ah, here we are. Irena Hourami. She's here, isn't she?'

'There no Irena here. No Kurdish girl. Everyone been here one, two month. No one come this week. We full. Mr Parnell, he know that.'

Hasan shook his head and sighed.

'Frank must have mixed up the paperwork. Typical. I'll make a note of that. Ten of you. Thank you. Sorry for interrupting your meal.'

Hasan slipped the notebook away into his pocket and left the house, walking back down the street to the car. Farok looked at him expectantly as he climbed into the driver's seat.

'Nothing,' Hasan said. 'Let's try the next one.'

'My God, you look awful,' Henry said.

'Thanks,' Joe replied. 'That's just what I want to hear.'

'You've aged. And you look so scruffy. That beard, your hair, those dreadful clothes.'

'Have you finished?' Joe said.

'It's just a bit of a shock.'

'I'm sleeping – or rather, not sleeping – on a mattress on the floor, in the attic of a house with no hot water and fourteen other occupants. I'm working twelve hours a day picking courgettes, one minute baking in the sun, the next dripping wet in the rain. In those circumstances, it's not easy to look like a male model.'

'I'm only thinking of *you*, Joe,' Henry said. 'I know how gruelling manual labour can be. I do half an hour in the garden and I have to lie down for the rest of the day. Are you sure you're up to this?'

'I'm fine,' Joe said.

'Only this kind of work . . . well, it's young man's work, isn't it?'

'I said I'm fine.'

'You don't look fine. Are you sure you're coping?'

'Of course I'm coping,' Joe snapped.

'Oh, touched a nerve.'

'You haven't touched a nerve. Yes, I'm tired and dirty and every muscle in my body aches, but I'm managing, OK? Now let's drop this subject, shall we? What's happening with Irena Hourami?'

Henry sniffed and looked away through the windscreen of his car. He'd picked Joe up from their prearranged rendezvous, well away from Joe's house, then they'd driven a short distance out of Downham Market and parked in a lay-by. There were fields next to them, a sprinkler watering the crops, the spray catching the light of the evening sun.

'I spoke to Ellie,' Henry said. 'She's covering the story

now. There's nothing to report. Irena still hasn't been found.' He looked back at Joe. 'You picked up any scent?'

'I'm asking around, but I'm not holding out much hope,' Joe said. 'I'm not going to bump into her by chance in some farmer's field. We have to go about this another way.'

'You have an idea?'

'Frank Parnell, the gangmaster in Thetford. He's the key. When I went to see him in his office, there was another man there – his assistant, Lenny something. A pockmarked guy in his thirties with curly blond hair. I mentioned Irena and Lenny reacted. He *knew* who I was talking about.'

'You think Irena's still in Thetford?' Lenny said.

'No, if she were, the police would have found her by now. But I think Lenny, and probably Parnell, know where she is.'

'You want me to talk to them?'

'You won't get anywhere, I can tell you that now. They won't talk to journalists.'

'So if she's not in Thetford, where do you reckon she is? Back in London?'

'Not London. It's too dangerous for her there.'

'She could be anywhere then.'

'I've been thinking it through,' Joe said. 'Irena came up to Thetford. We know that for certain. I'm pretty sure she worked at Wintertons packhouse, but there's no record of her there. I think she's changed her name, or someone's changed it for her. Parnell and Lenny are involved, I'm sure of that too.'

'You think they're hiding her?' Henry said.

'I don't know. Why would they do that? I think it's more likely they realised she was bad news and got rid of her. But they wouldn't just drive her somewhere and dump her at the side of the road. She needs a roof over her head, work, some way of supporting herself.'

'A friend, a relative?' Henry suggested.

'Or another gangmaster. That's their business, after all.

They must know other gangmasters in other towns – someone who could find Irena accommodation, a job, no
questions asked.'

'That's not going to be easy to find out.'

'See what you can dig up on Parnell and Lenny. Ask
around. Find out their backgrounds, where they come
from, who they know. And get a list of gangmasters – they
all have to be registered now. Not for the whole country,
just eastern England, the agricultural areas. Let's say,
Norfolk, Suffolk, Cambridgeshire and Lincolnshire.'

'There could be hundreds of them. What do we do then?'

'Not we, *you*. You ring round them, see if they know
Frank Parnell, see if they've taken on any young Kurdish
women recently.'

Henry pulled a face.

'That sounds like bloody hard work.'

Joe grinned at him.

'It'll be good for you. Doing some proper journalism
again. And it's a darn sight easier than picking courgettes,
believe me.'

Alistair Walker, the Norfolk County Council environmental
health officer, was as good as his word. As soon as he got
the results back from the lab, he phoned Ellie.

'Mrs Fitzpatrick's house was clear,' he said. 'No traces of
typhoid bacteria on any of the samples I took from her
kitchen or bathroom.'

'Oh.' Ellie was disappointed.

'But I'm glad you mentioned her freezer to me . . .'

Walker paused. There was something theatrical about the
silence. Ellie got her pen ready, her notebook open at a clean
page. She knew he was about to tell her something important.

'Yes?' she prompted.

She had the feeling he was enjoying this moment. Well,
in environmental health you had to take them when you
could.

'It was quite a well-stocked freezer,' Walker went on. 'Peas, beans, ice cream, some sausages, a loaf of bread. She'd frozen a couple of packs of chicken legs as well. Two legs in each pack. One of the packs was complete, but she'd taken a leg out of the other pack and left the second leg behind in the freezer. I took samples from that leg . . .'

'And?'

'Found traces of salmonella *typhi* on the skin.'

Ellie's pen moved quickly over her notebook, the short-hand outlines large and untidy.

'The chicken was infected with typhoid?' she said.

'The *surface* of the chicken. That's important. Chickens don't carry salmonella *typhi*, people do.'

'And your conclusion?'

'Somewhere in the supply chain – from the poultry farm to the processing and packing plant to the retail outlet – the meat was infected with typhoid bacteria. The most likely source is a human handler who was carrying the disease.'

'And Mrs Fitzpatrick, when she took the chicken leg out to cook, got the bacteria on her hands?'

'And somehow ingested them, yes. It wouldn't have been difficult. Just touching her mouth without washing her hands would have been enough to get the bacteria into her body.'

'You're sure that's the source of the infection?' Ellie said. 'A chicken leg.'

'The remaining chicken leg is contaminated. I think it's pretty likely that the other leg, which Mrs Fitzpatrick presumably ate, was also contaminated.'

'Only I want to be absolutely clear on that point, because of my next question,' Ellie said.

'Where did the chicken come from?'

'Yes.'

'SupaMar.'

'You're sure of that too?'

'The leg was still on its white polystyrene tray. The

300

plastic wrapping had been broken to remove the other leg, but the label was still intact, complete with barcode, price and sell-by date.'

'Have you told SupaMar?'

'I have indeed. That was the first thing I did.'

'What did they say?'

'If you want a quote, you'd better ask them direct. Let's say they were shocked. And concerned.'

'Do you know what action they're taking?'

'Again, I think you'll need to speak to them about that. I've specified certain things that they have to do – the minimum requirements, if you like.'

'Which are?'

'Obviously to trace the source of the chicken. They can do that with the barcode. All meat has to be traceable by law nowadays. They have to identify where it came from, where and when it was processed and packed, check every step of the supply chain to the shop where Mrs Fitzpatrick bought the product.'

'Check their employees too?'

'Yes. Everyone who might have handled this batch of chicken will have to be tested. The workplace and machinery will also have to be checked, samples taken. We've only had three cases of the disease so far, but it's highly likely there will be more. Two cases in London, one in Norfolk, the chicken products were obviously distributed over a large geographical area.'

'Are SupaMar withdrawing all chicken products from their stores?'

'I think they will, as a precaution. Obviously, this particular contaminated batch will all have been sold or taken off the shelves by now. The sell-by date on the pack in Mrs Fitzpatrick's freezer was almost two weeks ago. But there may be other, more recent contaminated batches out there.'

'You say it's highly likely there'll be more typhoid cases,' Ellie said.

'I think that's a reasonable prediction, given the facts.'

'An epidemic?'

Walker chuckled.

'Don't put words into my mouth. I think the public needs to be aware that there may be typhoid bacteria around and take extra care with their hygiene. I don't want to cause alarm. People need to make sure they wash their hands and kitchen utensils thoroughly when they've been in contact with raw meat. And they need to make sure that meat is properly cooked. It's just basic common sense really.'

Ellie looked at her watch as she made her notes. It was 8.30 p.m. – after hours in most offices other than a morning newspaper. She was wondering how she was going to get a quote from SupaMar.

'When did you speak to the supermarket?' she asked.

'About an hour ago.'

'Do you have a name and a number? I'll need to get a comment.'

Walker gave her the information.

'Have you spoken to any other journalists?' Ellie went on.

'No, and I don't intend to. This is all yours, Miss Mason. You told me about the freezer. One good turn . . .'

'Thanks. I'll keep in touch.'

Ellie rang off and pushed back her chair, barely able to contain her excitement. She headed across to the newsdesk, resisting the urge to run. Stay cool, you're an experienced reporter, she told herself. Try not to act like a rookie with their first scoop.

Ed Preston looked up at her as she drew near, seeing something in her face.

'This better be good,' he said.

Ellie perched herself on the corner of his desk, pushing her curly hair away from her face. Casual, as calm as she could manage.

'It's good,' she said.

23

On Joe's third morning in Downham Market, Barry picked them up in the transit van around 7.30. As Joe climbed into the back of the van, he saw Marina and Grace already inside. Kwasi sat down next to Grace. Joe squeezed in beside Marina. She smiled at him, her hair framing her tanned face. Joe could smell soap on her skin.

'Where we go today?' he asked.

Marina shrugged.

'Is a surprise.'

Barry never said anything when he collected them, never gave them any information, just shut them in the back of the van and let them wonder. No one seemed to care. No one asked any questions. They went wherever the van took them, did whatever they were told at the other end. It was easier that way. The nature of the work didn't matter to them – it was always going to be hard, they knew that. The best way to deal with it was to simply get on with it, put in the hours and be thankful when it was over.

As it turned out, Marina was wrong. Their destination wasn't a surprise. It was Coppice Wood Farm again. When the rear doors of the van were opened, Joe saw that they were in the main yard of the farm. On one side of the yard was the farmhouse, a traditional two-storey brick building dating from the mid-nineteenth century. On the other side was a modern metal-sided packhouse with wooden pallets and empty drums of agricultural chemicals stacked untidily outside it.

The workers climbed out of the van. Joe eased himself down gently. His muscles had stiffened up overnight and his joints were creaking. Had he really only done two days work in the fields? It felt like so much more. What a contrast it was to his normal life. In London, at this time of the morning, he'd only just be getting out of bed, making himself an espresso before heading off to the office and a day of phone calls and desk slouching. For all its dynamic, go-getting image, journalism was essentially a sedentary occupation. Joe used more energy in an hour picking vegetables than he did in an entire week at *The News*.

The office seemed a long way off now. So did the real Joe Verdi. He'd immersed himself so completely in the role of Alban Cobani that he didn't feel as if he were pretending any longer. He *was* Alban Cobani, and he had the sore back and blistered hands to prove it. It was easy to get sentimental about the English countryside, but there was nothing noble or romantic about toiling on the land. It was tough, dirty and bloody unpleasant.

'Come on, get a move on, we haven't got all fucking day,' Barry said, as Joe lowered himself awkwardly to the ground.

Marina was just behind Joe. Barry reached up with a hand and tried to help her down. She veered away from him, but he grasped hold of her arm as she descended and attempted to hold on to it. Marina knocked his fingers away contemptuously and strode across the carpark, seeking sanctuary in the group of male workers. Barry stared at her resentfully, his cheeks colouring. Then he saw Joe watching him.

'What you looking at, you wanker?' Barry said aggressively.

Joe turned away. He didn't want another confrontation with the gangmaster's assistant. One punch to the stomach was more than enough.

Coming across the yard was the familiar figure of the farmer, Richard Hibbert. His face, as usual, had an anxious set to it and there was something agitated about his manner this morning.

'How many are we today?' he asked Barry.

'Twenty. That's what you wanted, isn't it?'

'Yes, that's fine.'

Richard turned to the cluster of workers, drawing an imaginary line in the air with his hand.

'The ten on this side, go with Alf to the fields. The rest of you, come with me.'

Joe, Kwasi, Marina and Grace were in the second group. They followed the farmer into the packhouse. The inside of the building was cool, the air conditioning fans in the roof whirring noisily. The nightshift workers were just finishing, collecting up their belongings and shuffling out to the waiting van. Richard assembled the new arrivals and allocated them places along the production line. He outlined what they each had to do, then gave a brief health and safety talk, pointing out the potential hazards of the machinery and telling them what to do in an emergency.

It was a mixed salad production line. Whole lettuces – iceberg, kos, lollo rosso – and other leaves such as cress and rocket were fed on to the end of a conveyor belt where one group of workers broke them apart by hand, stripping the outer, less crisp leaves from the lettuces and discarding them before sending the remainder on through a rolling carpet of chlorine and water.

A second group of workers inspected the salad as it emerged from the wash, picking out any bad leaves that might spoil the appearance of the finished product, and a third group packed the salad into plastic bags and passed them through a machine that modified the air in the packaging, increasing the carbon dioxide content to give the lettuce a longer shelf life. At the end of the line, the last group of workers packed the plastic bags into boxes for dispatch to the supermarket whose own brand label and barcode had been pre-printed on the bags.

Joe was given a pair of rubber gloves and a place in the first group. Kwasi was next to him and, directly opposite, on the other side of the belt, was Marina. She'd tied her hair back with a rubber band, as usual, before putting on the white paper cap with which they'd all been issued.

The first lettuces came along the conveyor belt. Joe picked one up and ripped away the outer leaves, throwing them into a bin. Then he tore apart the remaining lettuce and put it back on the belt. After picking courgettes, it was relatively light work. True, it was boring and monotonous, but at least it was indoors, away from the vagaries of the English weather.

On the other side of the packhouse, behind Marina's back, Joe noticed the farmer looking at his watch and hurrying towards the door. His face was very pale, his shoulders bowed under some invisible weight. Joe wondered whether he was ill.

Richard certainly didn't feel well. As he left the pack-house, he paused for a moment. He was breathless. He had a knot of anxiety in his stomach, as if he were about to sit an important exam. It was a sensation he was experiencing with increasing, and discomfiting, regularity these days and it was particularly bad this morning for one over-whelming reason: the supermarket buyer was coming to visit him. Supermarkets gave their customers free offers and loyalty cards. They gave farmers ulcers.

Richard had never met the buyer before. He'd met other buyers, of course – they were an unavoidable blight in the farming business – but not this particular one. The super-markets changed their buyers every year or so, sometimes as often as every six months. They didn't want them getting too friendly with the suppliers, or too sympathetic towards them – any kind of rapport was seen as colluding with the enemy. Buyers were moved around from department to department so they never gained any real knowledge of their suppliers' businesses, never had a chance to understand the economics, the difficulties suppliers experienced in meeting the retail giants' onerous demands.

Richard walked away across the farmyard, feeling the change in atmosphere as he got nearer to his house. The packhouse had been built five years ago, but it still felt like an alien building to him. It didn't feel as if it belonged on a farm. Farms were about crops and livestock, about being in touch with the land and the seasons. They had distinctive noises, distinctive smells, the feeling of being part of the landscape. They were a powerful manifestation of the partnership between man and the soil that stretched back thousands of years. The packhouse, in contrast, was a factory. It didn't blend in with the landscape the way the farmhouse did. Its design, its purpose were more suited to an urban environment. It contained machinery, it was clean and sterile, it had a chemical smell. Richard hated it, even though he was the person who had had it built. It represented everything he loathed about 21st century agriculture – the mechanisation, the mass production, the industrialisation that had destroyed all the things he saw as good about farming.

His wife was in the big stone-flagged farmhouse kitchen, putting coffee cups and a sugar bowl on a tray in preparation for the buyer's arrival. She glanced at Richard as he came in from the yard, knowing how wrought-up he was about the visit. Soothing him with bland reassurances never worked, but she tried all the same.

'This one might be different,' she said.

Richard gave an incredulous snort.

'You know he won't be. They never are.'

'What's his name again?'

'Jason Carr.'

'I've got some of those chocolate shortbread bisuits. Maybe we can soften him up a bit.'

'Soften him up? We'd need a pile-driver, not a few biscuits.'

'They're doing well – their profits, I mean. Perhaps this year they can afford to be a bit more generous.'

'Generous? A *supermarket*?'

Richard snapped the word out like a gunshot and his wife turned away, understanding his anger, but feeling hurt by his tone.

'I was only trying to help,' she said. 'To cheer you up.'

'Nothing's going to cheer me up,' Richard retorted.

He knew he'd upset her, but he was too agitated to apologise.

'I'm going to go over my figures again. I'll be in the office.'

He marched out of the kitchen and along the hall to the small room at the back of the house where he kept his paperwork. His stomach was a ball of writhing worms. The short walk to the office had made him breathless again. Slumping down behind his desk, he opened the file containing his summarised accounts and cash flow forecast for the year. He knew the details of them off by heart. He'd spent hours reviewing them, looking for ways of increasing his income and reducing his costs. They made sobering reading. For each of the last five years he'd made a loss. He had assets in land and buildings, but his revenue wasn't enough to cover his overheads. Without bank loans and a hefty overdraft he would have been technically insolvent.

He wanted to show Jason Carr his accounts, but he had too much pride to actually do it. It wouldn't make any difference, in any case. The supermarket buyer wasn't interested in his finances. His sole concern was the targets he'd been set by his superiors. Richard knew from past experience that those targets would be completely unrealistic, achievable only if the buyer could drive down prices and screw even more concessions out of his suppliers.

What surprise would young Jason have in store for him today? Richard wondered. He knew the buyer would be young, they always were. Some ambitious twenty-something who wanted to get on and would carry out the supermarket's ruthless cost cutting with alacrity, even if it meant putting a farmer out of business.

There were many ways in which the buyer could boost his company's profits. Richard, like every farmer, had been a victim of a few in his time. The 'two for one' offers in the stores that were paid for by the farmer, not the super-market; the in-store promotions that had to be funded by the farmer; the payments to get a more prominent display inside a store, even donations to a charity that the super-market used to enhance its public image which had to be supplemented by contributions from suppliers. None of the payments was compulsory, of course. You didn't have to accept the terms if you didn't like them. But if you didn't play ball, the supermarket delisted you, refused to take any more of your produce, and then where did you sell it? Richard only had one customer, the big super-markets. If they delisted him, he was finished.

Judith Hibbert put her head round the office door and said, 'He's here,' in the sort of nervous, awe-struck voice normally reserved for a visit by royalty. 'Are you going to see him in here?'

Richard considered for a moment. The office was cluttered and cramped, too obviously a place of business. Better to go somewhere more comfortable, where the buyer could be put more at ease, in a better mood.

'We'll go in the sitting room,' Richard said.

'I'll let you get settled, then bring in the coffee.'

Richard tucked his file under his arm and went back along the hall to the kitchen. He was still tense, but the feel-ing of nausea in his stomach was easing. The waiting was over. The unexpected was always less daunting when it became a reality.

'Mr Hibbert?'

The man at the kitchen door was in his mid to late twenties. He had short, neatly-combed hair and was wearing a dark grey suit, white shirt and plain tie – as specified in head office dress regulations. He had the clean-cut, antiseptic look of a Mormon missionary.

'Call me Richard.'

'Jason Carr.'

Richard shook his hand.

'Pleased to meet you, Jason. You found us all right?'

'Yes, thanks. No trouble.'

'Come and sit down.'

Richard showed him through into the sitting room. He seemed a pleasant enough young chap. But then they always did, until you got down to business.

'Would you like a drink?'

'Thanks. A coffee would be nice,' Jason said.

He sat down in an armchair and placed his black attache case on the floor beside it.

'Did it take you long?' Richard asked, making small talk.

'An hour and a half.'

'You know this part of the country?'

'Not well.'

'Which department were you in before?'

'Household goods. You know, detergents, toilet cleaners, washing-up liquids.'

'It's a bit of a change for you, I expect. Moving into salads and perishables.'

'Not really. The fundamentals are the same across the business.'

No, they're not, Richard screamed inside his head. That's the problem with you people. You think lettuces are the same as soap powder. You think running a chemical plant is the same as running a farm. Can't you see that food is different? It has to be grown, it has to be nurtured, it's a living thing susceptible to weather and disease and pests.

You cannot treat it the same as toilet rolls or disinfectant.

Judith Hibbert came in with the tray of coffee and put it down on a table. Richard introduced her to the buyer.

'How nice to meet you, Jason,' Judith said. 'I hope we'll get on with you as well as we did with Tony. Where's he gone, by the way?'

'He's moved across to the home entertainment division,' Jason said. 'DVDs, CDs and books.'

'He's buying books now? I didn't think he was much of a reader.'

'Oh, he doesn't read the books,' Jason said. 'He just decides which ones to order.'

'How do you like your coffee, Jason?'

'Milk, one sugar. Thanks.'

Judith filled a cup and passed it to Jason. She held out the plate of chocolate shortbread biscuits and he took one, placing it carefully in his saucer. Judith poured a cup for her husband, then retreated towards the door.

'I'll leave you to it.'

The door closed softly behind her. Jason took a sip of his coffee and put his cup down on the floor. He lifted his brief-case on to his lap and took out a sheaf of papers.

'Shall we get started?' he said.

For the next hour they worked through the order sheets, the invoices, the delivery and quality specifications for the produce Richard supplied to the supermarket – not just the pre-packed salads the migrant workers were processing in the packhouse, but also the fresh whole lettuces, cucumbers, courgettes, radishes and other vegetables that were currently growing on the farm.

Richard was pleasantly surprised by how well the meeting was going. Jason was a personable young man. He was cooler, more reserved than his predecessor, Tony, who'd liked a joke to lessen the tension of their discussions, but he was efficient, competent, focused on the job in hand. He wasn't someone Richard warmed to, but then he didn't expect to. Theirs was a business relationship, not a friendship. All Richard wanted was a buyer who was straight with him, who negotiated in good faith and kept to the terms of the agreements they reached. That wasn't too much to ask for, surely? Afterwards, Richard wondered how – despite his experience – he could have been so ludicrously naïve.

He never saw it coming. They were nearing the end of the meeting, nearly all the points on their agenda covered, when Jason hit him with a blow that made Richard recoil – literally slam back into the cushions of his chair – though the buyer hadn't laid a finger on him.

'We won't be able to pay so much, of course,' Jason said.

'What do you mean?' Richard said, staring at him in disbelief.

'I need a five per cent cut,' Jason said, his tone so matter-of-fact that he clearly had no idea of the implications of that statement to a farmer like Richard.

'Five per cent? In which area?' Richard said.

'Across the board.'

Richard was momentarily speechless. The nausea in his stomach had come back with a vengeance. He wondered whether he was going to be sick, throw up here on his sitting room carpet.

'You're not serious?' he said eventually.

'Is there a problem?' Jason said.

Is there a problem? Richard yelled silently. Of course there's a fucking problem. He took a deep breath. Losing his temper was not the way to handle this.

'Do you know what that will do to my margins?' he said, feeling stupid even as the question slipped out from his lips. Jason Carr didn't give a damn about his margins. The supermarket's margins were all that concerned him.

'I'm afraid it's essential,' Jason said. 'We have to find a way of cutting our costs if we're to maintain our market share against the other supermarkets.'

Maintain our market share. It was doubtless one of those phrases the supermarkets drummed into their employees at sales meetings, along with all the other jargon about 'customer choice' and 'consumer-led purchasing parameters'. But could Jason Carr, in his nice grey suit and polished black shoes comprehend what all this company gibberish he was parroting so glibly meant to a farmer with dirt under his fingernails and bank loans big enough to sink an aircraft carrier?

'But we agreed a price at the beginning of the season,' Richard said.

'I know. This isn't a decision we've taken lightly, believe me. We value our suppliers, and we want to continue working with you. But that won't be possible, I'm afraid, without some slight adjustments in terms.'

He made it sound so simple, so painless. Richard wanted to slap him around the head.

'I planted on the basis of the price I agreed with Tony,' Richard said. 'A five per cent cut will wipe out my profit entirely.'

Jason nodded sympathetically. Did head office teach them how to do that too? Richard wondered cynically. Were all buyers issued with a manual instructing them how to show empathy with suppliers, a manual complete with a disposable sachet of crocodile tears?

'I'm sorry,' Jason said. 'But we have no choice. If you can't supply us at that price, we'll have to find someone else who can.'

There it was, out in the open. The threat to delist. The supermarket would carry the threat out too, Richard had no doubt about that whatsoever. Food wasn't a local business any more, it was global. Your chickens weren't cheap enough? The supermarkets could import millions from Thailand where health regulations were more lax and wages lower. Your cucumbers were too expensive? No problem. They could fly them in more cheaply from Spain and Florida.

Sourcing locally – unless it was part of some PR stunt to convince gullible consumers that their neighbourhood superstore had the best interests of the community at heart – was never a supermarket priority. Nor was keeping their side of a deal when they could save money by reneging on it.

Richard had agreed a price for his produce six months earlier, but he had no contract with the supermarket. No farmer did – it simply wasn't the norm in the business. Deals were made, but there was never any formal written agreement between the parties. Supermarkets liked, indeed insisted that their supplies, and suppliers, should be flexible. They wanted to be able to turn them on and off at will. It was a one-sided arrangement, of course. The supplier couldn't vary the terms of the deal, that was the supermarkets' prerogative. Richard had friends outside the farming business who found this arrangement extraordinary. The farmer went to the expense of buying seed, planting it, tending it until harvest and then the supermarket could say it didn't want the produce, or wanted it only at a reduced price, and the farmer had no legal recourse. What other business operated like that, with the terms so distorted in favour of one party?

'Five per cent,' Richard said. 'That's a huge cut. It means I'm losing money on every lettuce, every cucumber I supply you with.'

Jason shrugged.

'As you know, it's a very tough market out there. There's a lot of competition, particularly on prices. We can't afford to be undercut by our rivals.'

'But *I* can't afford to effectively give away my produce.'

'You can cut costs too, can't you?'

'I've already paid for the seed, the fertiliser, the pesticides. I have a lot of fixed overheads, debts. Where am I supposed to cut my costs?'

'What about your workforce?' Jason said. 'Can you not reduce costs there?'

'My workforce is already on the minimum wage. I can't go lower than that. Does it have to be five per cent? I've been a good loyal supplier to SupaMar for ten years and more. Can you not look at your figures again and give me the price I agreed with Tony?'

'Out of the question, I'm afraid. Five per cent is the absolute minimum cut we need. I don't have any say in the matter. I'm given my targets. I can't change them. I can't give preferential terms to you or any other supplier. I wish I could.'

'But there must be some room for manoeuvre. Can you not . . .'

'There's no point in discussing it,' Jason interrupted sharply. 'All I need to know is whether you agree to those terms?'

Richard could feel his whole body trembling with emotion – with anger, with indignation, distress, the feelings so intense that, if they were left unchecked, he was either going to explode with fury or break down in tears. He bit his lip, turning his head away so he didn't have to look at the buyer, at the young man's smug, complacent face. Richard knew he didn't have a choice. Jason knew it too – in this particular game he held all the cards. If Richard said no, he was ruined. The crops were already in the fields, most ready to be harvested. Selling them to the supermarket, even at a reduced price, was better than nothing. It wouldn't cover all his costs, but it was income, probably enough to meet the interest on his loans, enough to keep the bank at bay. The alternative – well, there wasn't really an alternative. He could say no, and a part of him longed to tell the supermarket where it could stick its five per cent cut, but that would have been foolish. He'd have been bankrupt before the summer was out.

He'd have to check his books later, find a way of cutting costs. His overheads and bank debt were fixed, there was no room for manoeuvre there. His wages bill was the only item that gave him any scope for savings. He could employ fewer people, but still expect them to do the same amount of work, and he could pay them less. The workers were on the minimum wage already – as he'd told Jason Carr – but perhaps he could negotiate some kind of deal with the gangmaster, Eddie Tremain. It would inevitably mean the migrant workers would be more exploited, it would probably entail some breach of employment regulations, but what alternative did he have?

Jason was waiting. Richard turned back to him, trying to summon as much dignity as was possible in the humiliating circumstances.

'Yes, I suppose I have to agree,' he said bitterly.

In the middle of the morning, they were allowed a fifteen minute break. Most of the workforce, including Joe, went outside into the yard for some fresh air or a cigarette. Joe stretched his arms and back and walked up and down a few times to relieve the stiffness in his legs. That was the trouble with the production line – you used only a few muscles, and those repetitively. Your upper body, your arms, shoulders and back were working continuously, but your lower body had nothing to do except gradually seize up.

Kwasi was leaning on the wooden fence, talking to Grace and Marina. Joe strolled over to them and rested his hands on the top strut of the fence, looking out over the fields of lettuces and courgettes. Marina had taken off her white cap and let her hair down again. It hung to just above her shoulders, a few strands blowing across her face in the breeze. She had an orange in her hand. She peeled the skin off and broke the orange into segments. She offered Joe a piece.

'You want some?'

'Thank you.'

Joe took the orange and chewed it, the juice sweet on his

tongue. Marina gave a segment each to Grace and Kwasi, then looked back at Joe. She had very dark eyes. Sad eyes, Joe thought as he gazed at her.

'You work in packhouse before?' she said.

'No,' Joe said. 'This first time. You been here before?'

'A few times.'

'You enjoy?'

She gave him a sardonic smile.

'Do you?' she said.

'Is boring. But better than work in fields. Fields harder.'

Marina gave him another segment of orange.

'It take away taste of packhouse,' she said.

'Taste?'

'Chlorine. You know chlorine? They wash lettuce in it.'

'Ah, yes.'

The packhouse was air conditioned, but the atmosphere was still tainted by chemicals. Where the salads came out of the wash, the stench of chlorine was so strong it stung the eyes. Even at the beginning of the production line, where Joe had been working, the packhouse smelt like a swimming pool.

'I don't know why they do that,' Marina said. 'Put that stuff on the lettuce. Would you eat it, soaked in chemicals? I see it in supermarket. You know what they charge? Two pounds for one of those bags. Two pounds for few bits of chopped lettuce. Why anyone pay that?'

'The English, they rich,' Joe said.

'Rich? Maybe. Stupid too. And lazy. Why not buy lettuce and chop up yourself? How hard is that?'

The packhouse foreman came out into the yard and called the workers back in. Marina scraped her hair away from her face with her fingers and secured it with the rubber band. Joe adjusted the paper cap on his head, making sure it was on tight. The hygiene regulations struck him as strange. The workers all wore hats to ensure that stray hairs didn't end up in the bags of salad. Yet the salad was doused with chlorine, a deadly poison. Joe knew which he'd rather find in his food.

As he walked across to the packhouse, he looked towards the farmhouse. Richard Hibbert was out in the yard, seeing off a younger man in a grey suit. The younger man got into his car – a gleaming dark blue Audi Quattro – and drove away. Richard watched the car depart, then turned, his shoulders slumping, and almost stumbled back into the farmhouse.

24

Ellie was getting nowhere with SupaMar. She'd been ringing the supermarket's press office all morning, trying to
obtain information to supplement the brief statement she'd
been given the previous evening – a statement that had only
been provided reluctantly when Ellie had made it clear that
her story was going in the paper regardless. But the press
officer was being evasive, attempting to stonewall Ellie by
telling her that a full press release would be issued later, the
exact time left irritatingly vague. The company had a major
food scare on its hands, Ellie told him. Did he think the
problem would simply go away if they said nothing?

'I can't add to the statement you were given last night,'
the press officer said.

'But all that says is that you're "taking the problem of
contaminated chicken very seriously" and will "do everything necessary to safeguard the health" of your customers.
What does that mean?' Ellie said.

'It means what it says,' the press officer replied. 'We're
taking steps to make sure all our chicken products are safe
to eat.'

'What steps?'

'We've withdrawn the products from all our stores and
are cooperating fully with the authorities in their investigation into the typhoid cases, that's all I can say.'

'Do you know where the contaminated chicken came
from?'

'We're investigating the supply chain.'

'Was it from this country? Was it imported?'

'We're investigating the supply chain.'

'All meat has to be traceable by law. You must know where it came from, where it was processed.'

'That's what we're looking into right now.'

'It's taking you a long time. Norfolk environmental health department has given you the barcode on the contaminated chicken wrapper. Put it into your computer and it should tell you instantly where the chicken originated, shouldn't it?'

'It's not quite that simple.'

'Why isn't it? Does SupaMar have its own processing plant? Does it get all its chicken from certain poultry farms? Can you give me the names of those farms?'

'That's commercially sensitive information. I can't give you that.'

'An elderly woman in London is dead,' Ellie said. 'Two more people are seriously ill with typhoid. Don't you think it would be best if you were absolutely open about this whole affair?'

'You don't know that the dead woman caught typhoid from our chicken,' the press officer said. 'There's no proof of that.'

'There's pretty good circumstantial evidence. She shopped at SupaMar, we know you've been selling contaminated chicken. It's a fairly persuasive link, don't you think?'

'Look, we don't want this being blown up out of all proportion. It's only three cases.'

'How many does it take to get you to come clean about the source of the chicken?' Ellie said.

'Come clean? You make it sound as if we've got something to hide. That's a very serious allegation.'

Ellie tried to contain her exasperation.

'If you've nothing to hide,' she said. 'Why don't you just give me the information I'm asking for?'

'I've told you, we'll be issuing a full statement later. I haven't been given all the details yet. When I get them, I'll release them to the press.'

'You've been most helpful,' Ellie said sarcastically. 'I'll look forward to this statement. If I'm still alive by then.'

She hung up and called Alistair Walker at Norfolk County Council. He was out of the office, as were all the other environmental health officers. 'It's this typhoid thing,' the departmental secretary told Ellie. 'They've dropped everything to concentrate on it.'

The secretary gave Ellie Walker's mobile number. When Ellie called it, the environmental health officer sounded hesitant. She could hear a strange discordant counterpoint of animal noises in the background.

'I'll call you back in a minute,' Walker said, almost shouting.

When he came on the line again, the background noise had faded noticeably, but was still there in the distance.

'Where are you?' Ellie asked.

'A poultry farm.'

'That was the noise I could hear? Chickens?'

'Yes.'

'It was very loud.'

'That's what 40,000 chickens sound like when you put them together.'

'*Forty thousand?*' Ellie said. 'Forty thousand chickens in one place?'

'One shed.'

'It must be a big shed.'

'Not as big as the chickens would like.'

'This is a farm that supplies SupaMar, I take it?'

'That's correct.'

'Where is it?'

'I'm not sure I should tell you that.'

'SupaMar won't tell me either. They're not being exactly forthcoming about all this.'

There was a moment's silence. Then Walker said, 'You didn't get this from me, OK?'

'OK.'

'It's called Gosling Hall Farm. It's near Fakenham.'

'You think it's the source of the typhoid?'

'I don't know. We're doing tests.'

'How long are you going to be there?'

'A few more hours.'

'I think I might come out and take a look for myself.'

'You won't get near the farm,' Walker said. 'SupaMar have brought in security guards. They've set up a check-point on the main entrance, stopping everyone coming in.'

'That sounds interesting,' Ellie said.

'You're not deterred?'

'I love a challenge.'

Ellie saw the security guards a quarter of a mile away as she drove across the plain towards Gosling Hall Farm. They were standing on the edge of the main road, where the track leading to the farm branched off. There were two of them, both in navy blue uniforms. An unmarked dark blue van was parked close by on the verge at the side of the track.

Ellie slowed as she reached the farm entrance, but she didn't stop. She glanced sideways out of her window. The guards were big men with thick necks and heavy thighs, the SupaMar golden logo on the shoulders of their uniforms. They were pacing restlessly across the track, bored but watchful. Ellie could tell at once that there was no point in trying to sweet talk her way past them. If the SupaMar press office was representative – and she believed it was – there was an endemic hostility to the media in the company. The security men were unlikely to be very - sympathetic towards a journalist wanting to gain access to the farm. They had presumably been posted there to prevent that very thing from happening. Ellie wondered what the supermarket was so worried about.

She had a map of the area with her, so she knew that Gosling Hall Farm had only one entrance. That didn't mean that there was only one way in though. Not to a resourceful press hound with a pair of stout shoes.

She drove on along the main road for another mile, then turned off to the right, taking a narrower, single-track road that brought her round to the back of the farm. Pulling off on to the verge, she switched off her engine and scanned the surrounding terrain carefully. The farm was half a mile or so away across a stretch of fields containing some kind of grain crop. Ellie's knowledge of agriculture was hazy, but she thought it was probably wheat. The farm buildings stood out against the skyline. There was a two-storey house with a red tiled roof and next to it, dwarfing the house, a massive shed like an aircraft hangar. That had to be the chicken shed. It was an impressively large edifice, but even so Ellie's mind boggled at the thought of cramming 40,000 chickens into it.

She picked up the digital camera she'd brought with her – not one of the expensive professional SLR cameras the staff photographers used, but a slim compact small enough to fit in her pocket. Then she climbed out of the car, slithered down the low embankment at the side of the road and began to walk across the fields, sticking to the edges where she wouldn't flatten the stalks of ripening wheat. There were three fields between her and the farm. The first two were sufficiently distant for her not to worry about being spotted, but as she entered the third she became more cautious, moving in a low simian crouch to make herself less conspicuous. Fifty metres from the farm buildings, she dropped to her hands and knees and crawled to the edge of the field, lying flat on the bank below a wire fence and studying the ground ahead of her. There was a dirt yard between the house and the chicken shed. It was a wide space, but it seemed smaller because a good two thirds of it was taken up by stacks of grey plastic mesh crates which

Ellie guessed were used for transporting the mature chickens to the slaughterhouse. In the remaining third of the yard, five or six vehicles were parked, including another dark blue van like the one at the farm entrance and a white van with Norfolk County Council emblazoned on the side. She could see no sign of any security guards.

As she watched, a man in a white boiler suit emerged from the shed carrying a tray of small plastic containers. It had to be Alistair Walker. He went to the council van, opened the rear doors and deposited the tray inside before heading back to the shed. Ellie moved quickly. She stood up, vaulted over the waist-high wire fence and flitted across the yard after Walker. Behind her, she heard a man's voice yelling, 'Oi, you!', but by then she'd whipped open the door of the shed and ducked inside.

The noise hit her first – a piercing, ear-splitting cacophony of clucking chickens – followed immediately by the stench. She'd never smelt anything like it before – a pungent, stomach-turning animal odour, a concentrated, overpowering farmyard smell that was tainted with something rank and unhealthy. It reminded her of off meat that had been left out in the sun too long.

The size of the shed stunned her. It must have been seventy or eighty metres long and almost as wide. It had no windows, but there were open vents in the high roof through which a small amount of natural light was seeping. The dirt floor of the shed was seething with so many chickens that they seemed like maggots feasting on a giant carcass. There were birds everywhere, packed tightly together. Barely a square foot of earth was uncovered. The chickens were in a constant state of agitation, their bodies jostling against one another, their necks jerking up and down in a repetitive pecking motion. They looked deformed their breasts were so swollen. From the ones nearby, Ellie could see that their legs were almost too weak to support the weight of their enormous bodies. Some had collapsed to the ground, simply too heavy to stand up.

The man in the white boiler suit was picking up another tray of containers from a shelf on the wall of the shed.

'Mr Walker?' Ellie said.

The man turned. But before he could reply, the shed door banged open and a security guard rushed in.

'You,' he said, pointing an accusatory finger at Ellie. 'Where the hell did you come from?'

'Me?' Ellie said ingenuously. 'I've just come to talk to Mr Walker.'

'How did you get here? I haven't seen a car arrive.'

'I came on foot.'

'Foot?' The guard looked at Walker. 'Is she with you?'

The environmental health officer was on the spot. Ellie didn't want to compromise him so she came clean.

'I'm a journalist,' she said.

The guard gaped at her.

'What? A journalist? Out! Now.'

Ellie ignored him.

'Have you found anything interesting?' she asked Walker.

The guard stepped in between the two of them. He wasn't particularly tall, but he had broad shoulders and biceps bulging beneath his tight uniform.

'I said out,' he snapped. 'You're trespassing.'

'I've got all my samples,' Walker said. 'We'll have to wait and see what the lab finds.'

'You're not to talk to her,' the guard said.

'I beg your pardon?' Walker said.

'She shouldn't be here. You're not to speak to her. You hear me?'

'Who are you to give me orders?' Walker said indignantly. 'I'll talk to whoever I like.'

'This is some chicken coop,' Ellie said, gazing across the shed. 'Is this an independent farm, or does SupaMar own it?'

'Don't answer that question,' the guard ordered.

He grabbed hold of Ellie's arm.

'I've told you, out. Or I'll call the police.'

The guard dragged Ellie roughly from the shed and flicked on his radio, talking to his colleagues up the track.

'We have an intruder. An intruder in the shed. Request immediate back-up. Over.'

Ellie shook off the guard's grip and stepped away from him. Walker came out of the shed and headed for his van. Ellie went after him.

'You stay here,' the guard said, reaching out to grab her again.

Ellie spun round, her eyes flashing.

'Don't you touch me!'

The guard backed off, momentarily shaken by her violent reaction. Ellie walked across to Walker's van. She had a clear view of the track now, could see the two other security guards running clumsily down from the main road. They stumbled into the yard, panting audibly, and stopped, looking around for the intruder, their expressions puzzled as they realised it must be this slip of a woman with the curly hair. What were they going to do with *her*?

Ellie took advantage of the guards' confusion.

'Have you finished here?' she asked Walker.

'Yes.'

The environmental health officer was pulling off his boiler suit.

'Any chance of a lift to my car?'

'Get in.'

Ellie slid into the front of the van and locked her door. The guards were conferring, glancing in her direction, unsure what to do next. Walker got into the driver's seat and started the engine. The guards came over and huddled together next to Ellie's door, three big, hard security guys who'd been humiliated by a woman. The first guard, the one who'd confronted her in the shed, jabbed his finger at her angrily. There was a touch of red in his cheeks.

'You don't come back here,' he snarled through the van window. 'This is private property. You keep away or you'll be in deep shit. You understand?'

Walker eased up the clutch and the van moved off, turning to head up the track.

'You seem to have got under their skin, Miss Mason,' he said.

'I do my best,' Ellie replied.

Alistair Walker took a long swig of his orange juice and put the glass back down on the table, looking across at Ellie.

'Thanks. I needed that. It was insufferably hot inside that shed,' he said.

They were in a pub on the west side of Fakenham, a few miles from Gosling Hall Farm. The environmental health officer had taken a bit of persuading, but he'd eventually agreed to let Ellie buy him a drink: ostensibly as a thank you for taking her to her car, but really – as they both knew – another opportunity for Ellie to pump him for information.

'I've never seen anything like that place,' Ellie said. 'Are all poultry farms like that?'

'Most aren't so big. A few are bigger,' Walker replied.

'Bigger? More than 40,000 birds, you mean?'

Walker nodded.

'Fifty thousand isn't uncommon,' he said. 'Occasionally a hundred thousand.'

'All in one shed? Jesus. What kind of life is that for a chicken?'

'Short,' Walker said.

He wasn't quite the big shambling man with a beard that Ellie had imagined when she'd first spoken to him on the phone. He wasn't remotely big – only an inch or two taller than she was – or shambling, and though he had a beard, it was a very neat, well-trimmed beard, not the bushy, unkempt variety she'd pictured.

'A lot of them couldn't even stand up,' Ellie said.

'They're Page 3 chickens,' Walker said dryly.

'Page 3?'

'Valued only for their enormous breasts. That's how they're bred, especially for the supermarkets.'

'Isn't that cruel?'

'It's modern poultry farming, the factory way. You go to a free range farm, the chickens are outside roaming around. They've got relatively small breasts and legs sturdy enough to support their weight. Broiler chickens, on the other hand, are all like the ones you saw back there. They're bred to put on meat very quickly, to develop huge breasts. They're not natural, basically, like bodybuilders on steroids.'

'You were testing them for typhoid?'

'Not the birds. I was checking the people who work there, the inside of the shed, the toilets, places where bacteria might breed. The chickens don't have typhoid. Other diseases, yes, but not typhoid.'

'The birds are diseased?' Ellie said.

'Don't get excited. It's not news. It's the norm in these broiler sheds.'

'What sort of diseases?'

'Salmonella, e-coli, campylobacter.'

'Campylobacter? What's that?'

'It causes food poisoning, severe diarrhoea. Half the chickens on sale in this country have it. I know, we've tested them for it.'

'Fifty per cent?' Ellie said. 'Fifty per cent of them can give us food poisoning?'

'More than that, if you include the other bacteria chickens commonly carry. If you cook the meat properly, it's not generally a problem.'

'And you say it's the norm on these big poultry farms?'

'You've seen how the birds are kept. They're brought in as young chicks from specialist hatcheries and shut away in a darkened shed for the next six weeks to be fattened up.

The sheds aren't cleaned out at all during that period so by the end the chickens are knee deep in droppings. If one bird gets an infection, it spreads like wildfire until they've all got it. There are antibiotics in the feed and water, but they don't eradicate the diseases. Some of the bacteria are resistant to antibiotics now, anyway.

'They're pretty grim places. Each chicken, when it's fully grown, has about a pizza-size piece of ground to stand up in, and some of them – as you noticed – can't even stand up. Others don't make it to the end of their six weeks. They keel over from disease. Some get heart failure – their hearts can't take the strain of pumping blood around those over-sized breasts. When they do finally peg it, the other birds often eat them.'

Ellie grimaced.

'Ugh, that's revolting. Don't they remove the dead birds?'

'You've been inside a shed,' Walker said. 'Forty thousand jostling chickens. Could you spot a dead bird in the midst of them? And would you then want to wade through all the shit, the stench of ammonia enough to knock you out, to remove the carcass?'

'I knew about factory farming,' Ellie said. 'But I didn't realise it was as bad as this.'

'You want cheap chicken in the supermarket, this is how it's produced,' Walker said.

'Does SupaMar own this farm?'

'No, it's independently owned and run. But SupaMar takes all the chickens. They go to a processing plant over near King's Lynn to be killed and cut up, then dispatched to the stores.'

'Which plant is that?'

'It's called Elliston-Jones Ltd.'

'Is that where Mrs Fitzpatrick's contaminated chicken came from?'

'The barcode has been traced back to the plant, yes.'

'So I assume you're going to test for typhoid there too?'

'Some of my colleagues have been there today. All the workers will have to be checked, the premises, the machinery. It will take a while to complete.'

'The factory is still operating?'

'We thought long and hard about that. We could have ordered it to shut down, but decided that keeping it open was the best way to catch all the employees, test them for the disease. There are a lot of foreign workers there, migrants. If someone is carrying typhoid, shedding bacteria, we want to identify them. Close the place and the workers will all disappear. We don't want them going underground, spreading the disease somewhere else.'

'Aren't you worried that chicken may still be being contaminated at the plant?'

'It's a calculated risk. But one more case of typhoid and we'll close Elliston-Jones down immediately.'

'And Gosling Hall? Are you going back there tomorrow?'

'No, thank God. I've finished there. Another day in that shed – the smell, the noise – would be more than I could take. How people work there is beyond me.'

'Are you testing anywhere else?'

'No. The typhoid bacteria have to have come from either here, or the processing plant. The plant is the more likely source, I'd say. That's where the chickens are stripped of their feathers, cut up, packaged – where more people handle the carcasses.'

'It's still just the three cases, isn't it?'

'Yes.'

'Maybe it was an isolated incident, a very small batch getting contaminated,' Ellie said. 'And the typhoid bacteria have disappeared now.'

'Bacteria don't disappear. Not for long anyway. Sooner or later they come back.'

Walker finished his glass of orange juice and got ready to leave.

'Do you eat chicken, Miss Mason, or are you a vegetarian?'

'No, I'm not a vegetarian,' Ellie replied. 'But I'm seriously considering becoming one.'

Ellie sat in her car outside the pub after Alistair Walker had driven away and contemplated what to do next. She could return to London immediately and write up her story. She had enough material for a short piece on the typhoid tests the Norfolk environmental health officers were conducting, but that wasn't enough to satisfy her. She'd come all this way. She didn't want to go back with just an interview with Walker and a fleeting glimpse of the chicken shed at Gosling Hall Farm. Her visit to the farm had been cut short before she felt she'd really had a chance to explore the site, to fully absorb what was going on there. She also wanted a few photographs to complement anything she wrote. One snap of the inside of that shed would be more powerful than any number of words. But the security guard had caught up with her too quickly – before she could use the camera in her pocket. That irritated her, left her with a nagging sense of unfinished business.

She started her car engine and drove back towards the farm, circling round to the rear again but not parking in the same place as last time. She took a different line across the fields of wheat, approaching Gosling Hall from directly behind the chicken shed, so that the bulk of the building hid her from anyone who might have been watching from the farmhouse or the yard. When she reached the back of the shed, she was pretty sure she hadn't been observed. She paused for a moment, then edged along the wall of the shed and peeped cautiously around the corner. The farmyard extended down the side of the building, a strip of dirt and gravel about ten metres wide. There was a forklift truck parked up against the shed and next to it a couple of large metal bins, each about the size of a builder's skip. There were no people in sight – no farm workers, who might well have finished for the day, and no security guards, who would certainly be staying on into the evening and maybe through the night.

Ellie slipped around the corner and ran down the side of the chicken shed to the big metal bins. She crouched down by the first bin to catch her breath. The noisome smell of poultry was strong here. Ellie thought at first that the reek was seeping out through the roof vents in the shed, then she realised it was emanating from the metal bins. She lifted the lid of the nearest bin a fraction. The stench of fetid chicken got suddenly stronger, unpleasant enough to make her step back and cup a hand over her mouth and nose. She forced herself to raise the lid higher and peer inside. The bin was almost full of dead chickens – dozens of them lying six or seven deep. They'd been tossed in one on top of the other. Ellie saw horny yellowish feet sticking out from shapeless bundles of feathers, beaks gaping wide, beady but lifeless eyes staring up at her. She let the lid drop and turned away, almost retching. It was half a minute or more before she could bring herself to lift the lid up again and take some photographs of the contents.

The second bin also contained chicken carcasses, presumably more of the birds that Walker said died regularly from disease and heart failure. Ellie took photographs of those too, then moved off, her hand over her face again, trying to shut out the foul stink.

Just beyond the bins was a side door into the chicken shed. Ellie tried the handle. The door wasn't locked. She pulled it open and stepped through, finding herself in a small vestibule with a second, inner door leading off it, the area obviously intended to prevent chickens escaping when the outer door was opened. As she pulled the first door to behind her, she heard a noise outside – an engine, tyres crunching on the rough surface of the farm yard. She left the door ajar and put her eye to the crack. An open-backed yellow lorry was coming down the side of the building, stopping next to the metal bins. Painted on the door of the lorry cab was the name, J. Hollings Haulage, with a phone number beneath it. The driver climbed out and flipped down the side gate of the lorry, stepping out of the way as a second man – in grubby blue overalls – walked around from the front of the shed and hauled himself up into the forklift truck.

Ellie watched as the two metal bins were loaded on to the back of the lorry. The operation only took a few minutes, then the lorry reversed away and the forklift truck operator headed back across the farmyard.

Ellie closed the outer door of the chicken shed and pulled open the inner door. She felt something brush against her leg and looked down to see a carpet of chickens at her feet, a moving carpet of heads and bodies that stretched into every corner of the vast building. The noise was deafening, the smell of ripe flesh and toxic droppings almost unbearable. Ellie prodded at the birds with her shoe, driving them back, but there was nowhere for them to go they were crammed together so tightly. They squirmed against her calves, pressing so hard that she could feel the warmth of their bodies through the material of her trousers. She focused the camera on the writhing mass of birds and snapped off a few photographs, zooming in to get close-ups of the chickens' cramped conditions and top-heavy frames. There was a dead chicken a few metres away, lying on its side in a slushy white puddle of excrement. Ellie photographed the carcass, recording the chickens around it pecking at the corpse, plucking away the feathers and eating the decomposing tissues underneath.

By now, the reek of the shed was nearly overpowering her. She stepped back into the vestibule before she was sick, having to strain to close the door against the weight of the chickens on the other side. She tore open the outer door and stumbled out of the shed, gulping in the fresh air.

Gradually, the wave of nausea that had swept over her started to ebb. She wiped her face with the sleeve of her jacket and turned to go. That was when she saw the man in blue overalls coming back down the side of the building. He saw her at exactly the same moment and stopped dead, his mouth dropping open in surprise. By the time he'd recovered, Ellie was already running, sprinting towards the rear of the chicken shed. She heard him shout out, but didn't catch the words, didn't know if he was yelling at her or calling for the security guards.

She scrambled over the wire fence and down the grassy bank into the field, racing along the edge where there was a narrow strip of uncultivated land. Only when she'd reached the other side and was crossing the second field did she dare to glance back. No one was pursuing her. She slowed to a jog, then a walk, panting for breath, her face damp with perspiration. They weren't coming after her, thank God. She exhaled with relief and made her way back to the road.

They were waiting for her by her car.

Two security guards, including the stocky one who'd dragged her out of the chicken shed earlier. They'd driven round from the farm in their blue van and were standing next to her Mini. Ellie hesitated for second, taking in the belligerent set of the men's faces, then climbed up the bank on to the road. She could feel her pulse rate increasing, but she wasn't going to let them intimidate her.

'I told you to stay away from here,' the stocky guard said. 'Don't you understand English?'

Ellie didn't bother to reply. She walked towards her car. The two guards stayed where they were, blocking her path.

'I said, don't you understand fucking English?'

'Would you move away from my car, please?' Ellie said.

'What were you doing over there?'

'That's none of your business.'

'It bloody well is when I'm employed to keep people out. What were you doing?'

'I've just told you, it's none of your business.'

'I warned you earlier. That's private property. You're trespassing.'

'So?' Ellie said.

'That's a criminal offence.'

'Sorry, it's not. It's civil.'

'You heard of aggravated trespass? That's a crime.'

'That's different,' Ellie said. 'Didn't they teach you that at security guard school? Aggravated trespass has to involve an element of intimidation, obstruction or disruption to a lawful activity. Did you see me doing anything to obstruct or disrupt the activity of the farm?'

'You're a smart little bitch, aren't you?' the taller security guard said.

'It's my business to know the law. Now would you get away from my car, please?'

'We'll see what the police have to say, shall we?' the stocky guard said.

'OK. You got a phone? Call them.'

The two guards exchanged glances.

'Go on,' Ellie said. 'I'll tell you what they'll say. They'll say, don't waste our time. Trespass is a civil offence. Bring an action for damages against the trespasser, that's all you can do. You want my name? It's Ellie Mason. I work for *The News*, in London. OK? Now, if you'll excuse me, I have to be going.'

Ellie took out her car keys and pressed the button to unlock the doors. The stocky guard leant back on the driver's door with his arms crossed, staring at her pugnaciously. Ellie wondered what they'd have done if she'd been a man. Roughed her up a bit? Given her a going over then claimed she'd attacked them first and they were only acting in self defence? There were two of them. They could corroborate each other's evidence, get away with something like that. But she was a woman. A journalist too.

She'd pissed them off, but they wouldn't get physical with her. There were taboos, things even a couple of thugs like this wouldn't stoop to.

'I'll ask you one more time,' Ellie said. 'Will you get away from my car?'

The guards didn't move. Ellie pulled her mobile phone out of her jacket pocket. She hoped they hadn't noticed the bulge of the camera in her other pocket. If they realised she'd been taking photographs, they might not be so restrained. They'd confiscate the camera, remove the memory card. It wasn't something they could lawfully do, but they wouldn't care about a technicality like that. Keeping Gosling Hall Farm's chicken rearing methods and its links to SupaMar out of the newspapers was more important than some nosey journalist's rights.

'I tell you what I'll do,' Ellie said. 'I'll ring the police myself. I'll tell them I'm on a public highway being stopped from driving away by a couple of private security guards. The coppers will love that. They hate people like you, amateurs in uniform. They'll be over here before you can pump up your biceps. And you know what'll happen after that? You'll be in custody for a few hours before you're charged, then the story will be in the papers – I know that because I'll write it myself, giving SupaMar the kind of publicity their PR people spend millions on trying to avoid – and tomorrow morning you'll both be out of a job. You want me to make the call?'

'You twat,' the stocky guard said venomously, but he moved away from the car.

Ellie pulled open the driver's door and slid in behind the wheel, locking the door as a precaution. The stocky guard hammered on the window with a clenched fist.

'You come back here again and I'll fucking have you,' he shouted.

'It was nice talking to you too,' Ellie murmured and turned on the engine.

'I'm checking up for Frank. He wants to make sure his houses don't get too overcrowded,' Hasan said.

He had his patter well rehearsed by now. This was the seventh of Parnell's Thetford houses he and Farok had visited. This one was very like all the others. Grotty, run-down, mattresses crammed into every available space. Hasan looked at the two foreign women seated at the kitchen table – one sallow-skinned and Middle Eastern-looking, the other Chinese.

'How many are living here at the moment?'

The sallow-skinned woman did a calculation in her head.

'Eight.'

'Just eight?'

'Is enough.'

'I have nine down here in the records,' Hasan referred to his notebook, making sure the women couldn't see that there was nothing written in it.

'Nine?' the Chinese woman said. 'There not nine. Eight only.'

'What about the Kurdish girl who came last week?' Hasan said.

Out of the corner of his eye he noticed the sallow-skinned woman stiffen, but he didn't look at her.

'Kurdish girl?' the Chinese woman said.

'Irena Hourami. I think that was her name.'

'Yes, there was girl. I no know her name. But she not here now.'

'She's not?' Hasan said. 'What happened to her?'

'Don't know. She only stay short time. One, two night.'

'Are we talking about the same person?' Hasan said. 'Young, with a headscarf?'

'Yes, she have headscarf.'

Hasan turned to the sallow-skinned woman.

'You remember this girl?'

Yasmin eyed him warily. There was something about him

337

she didn't trust. She knew Frank Parnell, knew Lenny and a couple of the other van drivers who took them to work, but she'd never seen this man before. Instinctively, she sensed she should be careful.

'You remember the girl?' Hasan asked again.

'What you say her name is?'

'Irena Hourami.'

'This girl she no call Irena.'

'Maybe I'm wrong about the name,' Hasan said. 'I've got so many in my book it's easy to get them mixed up. But you remember a girl in a headscarf?'

'Yes, I remember.'

'Do you know where she went?'

Yasmin recalled the day Lenny had come to take Sakar away, remembered what he'd said to her, the warning he'd given about keeping her mouth shut. Frank Parnell must have known what Lenny was doing so how come this man, who claimed to come from the gangmaster, didn't know where the girl had gone, didn't even know her name?

'No,' Yasmin said. 'I don't know where she go.'

'You're sure?'

'Yes, I sure.'

Hasan studied her hard for a moment longer, then he put away his notebook and stood up.

'OK, that's all. I'll tell Frank.'

He went down the hall and let himself out of the front door of the house. Farok was waiting in the car outside.

'Anything?' he said.

Hasan stroked his moustache with his thumb and fore-finger, smoothing the sleek black hairs down around the corners of his mouth.

'Maybe,' he said.

25

The poultry slaughterhouse, Elliston-Jones Ltd, was located on the outskirts of King's Lynn, in a depressing industrial park just off the A47 bypass that formed part of the main arterial route from Norfolk to Lincolnshire. There was nothing remotely distinctive about the area. It was like all the dozens of other industrial parks up and down the country – an ugly sprawl of access roads and carparks and buildings knocked up on the cheap from a standard design that required no imagination or architectural skill, just thousands of concrete breeze blocks, some sheets of metal and a planning authority willing to tolerate any number of hideous eyesores for the sake of a few jobs.

The slaughterhouse, from a distance, could have been mistaken for a cash and carry warehouse or a storage depot. It was only when you got closer and went round the back to the loading and unloading area that its true purpose became apparent. Stacked in long rows across the broad tarmac apron were hundreds of grey plastic mesh crates containing live chickens. Ellie recognised them as soon as she drove in. They were identical to the crates she'd seen at Gosling Hall Farm. She parked in a marked space next to the loading bay entrance and got out. A high-backed lorry had arrived just before her and more crates were being unloaded and deposited with all the others. She could see the birds flapping around agitatedly inside the crates, hear their frightened squawks. She could smell them too – that same noxious poultry odour she'd had to endure the previous day at Gosling Hall.

There must have been sixty crates on the lorry. As one forklift truck was unloading them and stacking them four crates high on the apron, two more forklifts were working at the other end of the line, picking up the crates that had arrived earlier and transporting them inside the slaughterhouse.

Ellie watched, gauging the right moment to sneak inside the building. She knew she shouldn't have been there. Visitor parking was at the front of the slaughterhouse, near the main entrance. The white vans of the county council environmental health department were parked in that area, but the health officers had a valid reason for being given access to the plant. Ellie didn't. If she'd followed the rules, gone inside and identified herself, she knew she would never have got beyond Reception. And she wanted to see a lot more than a couple of soft chairs and a few pot plants.

The two forklifts disappeared into the loading bay, the other one was out of sight behind the lorry. No one was around to observe her, so Ellie took the opportunity to push open the door beside the loading bay and slip through. There was a tiny office just inside, where the lorry drivers had to report on arrival, but the desk was temporarily unmanned. Ellie nipped quickly across the room and out of the door on the far side.

She was in the slaugherhouse proper now. It was a long, cavernous building with exposed steel rafters in the roof and silver air conditioning ducts snaking over the walls. It had the appearance and sound of a factory – machinery rattling, cogs whirring – but it smelt like a farm. It smelt of chickens, which was hardly surprising considering the number of birds that were processed there every day. Processed? Ellie thought. Why conceal the nature of the place with a euphemism? Killed, plucked and chopped up, that was what happened to the chickens.

Their deaths, like their lives, were on an industrial scale.

Ellie could see the forklift trucks lowering their mesh crates on to the ground at the beginning of the slaughter line. A team of men wearing gloves snapped open the lids of the crates and reached in, pulling out two chickens each by their feet. The birds were swung into the air and hung upside down on a moving belt that carried them away, squirming and clucking, and dipped them into a long, narrow bath that, from the warning signs on the wall, Ellie realised had an electric current running through the water to stun the chickens. From there, the conveyor belt took the unconscious birds through a hole in a partition wall that blocked Ellie's view of what happened next. She followed the route of the belt and eased open a door in the wall. She peered through the gap, and wished she hadn't. In the white-tiled room beyond, a couple of men in overalls were systematically cutting the throats of the broilers as they went past, the blood dripping down into a trough on the floor. Ellie watched for a moment, then closed the door, wondering what kind of a job that was: standing in a room like a large public lavatory, killing a chicken every few seconds. What did the men talk about in the evenings when they went home to their families with blood on their boots?

The partition wall didn't run the full width of the factory. There was a passageway at one side through which Ellie walked, emerging into another part of the production line where the broilers were dunked into a vat of hot water to scald them and loosen their feathers for plucking. The water in the vat was a disgusting brew of excrement, blood and feathers. Chicken shit soup, Ellie thought, her stomach turning as she looked at the steaming liquid. She'd thought that nothing could match the foul, fecal reek of the chicken shed at Gosling Hall Farm, but this room could. It could match it and more. Averting her eyes, she hurried past the vat and through a door into another self-contained chamber where a series of rotating rubber fingers stripped the feathers from the chickens, leaving their carcasses pale and naked.

A man in white overalls was monitoring the plucking machines, watched by a second man with a clipboard who looked to Ellie like a foreman. This second man saw her come into the chamber and gave a start. He stared at her, his brow furrowing, then he walked across to intercept her.

'Just a minute, what are you doing here?' he said.

Act confident, bluff your way out of it, Ellie told herself. She gave the foreman one of her most winning smiles.

'I'm so sorry, I seem to have got lost. Do you know where I might find the environmental health team? From the council.'

'The council people? They're through in the cutting room,' the foreman said.

'Thank you, I've been looking everywhere. That's over here, is it?'

Ellie started to walk away, but the foreman stepped in front of her. He studied her suspiciously.

'How did you get in here?'

'Through that door,' Ellie replied innocently. 'It's not easy finding your way about this place, is it? Thank you for your help. I'll just go and see how the environmental health officers are getting on.'

'You're from the council?'

'I'm keeping an eye on their typhoid investigation,' Ellie said, knowing she'd got as far as she was going to. The foreman wasn't that gullible.

'Do you have some kind of identification on you?' he asked.

'Identification?'

'Yes. Who are you?'

'My name's Ellie Mason.'

'And you're what exactly? A council officer?'

'No, I'm a journalist.'

'A *journalist*?'

The foreman took a pace back, his eyes opening wide with surprise. Then his mouth contracted into an angry pucker.

'I think you'd better come with me.'

He escorted her out of the plucking room and through a large, draughty hall where the broilers were cut up and their sections – breasts, legs, thighs, wings – arranged on polystyrene trays to be sealed in plastic and sent out to the supermarkets. Ellie took her time crossing the hall, studying what went on there – fascinated by the continuous stream of broilers coming in on four conveyor belts, the teams of men with knives who cut the breasts off the birds, the machines that then chopped up the remainders of the carcasses and the lines of women in white coats and caps and rubber gloves who did the packaging. She was surprised by how labour intensive this part of the production process was. She'd never given much thought to how the packs of two chicken breasts she'd frequently bought from her local SupaMar were made up. If pressed, she'd probably have speculated that it was all done by machine, not manually. But then that was the thing about the modern food business – the consumers *didn't* know exactly how their food was produced, and the manufacturers wanted to keep it that way.

The foreman didn't like her lingering. He kept turning towards her impatiently, urging her to hurry up.

'I've never been in a poultry processing factory before,' Ellie said, trying to engage him in conversation. 'How many birds do you kill each day?'

'I'm afraid I can't answer any questions,' the foreman replied stiffly.

'Do all these chickens go to SupaMar stores, or do you supply other supermarkets too?'

Ellie wanted to know, but she was also enjoying provoking the foreman, seeing how far she could push him. He was clearly irritated by her probing.

343

'You shouldn't be in here. Please get a move on,' he snapped.

'How many workers do you employ? Are they all being tested for typhoid? The bits of the chicken you don't use. You know, the skin, the giblets, the heads and necks and rib cages, do you sell those on to some other manufacturers to be turned into those delicious chicken nuggets our children are given in their school dinners?'

The foreman pulled open a door and almost pushed Ellie through it.

'I'm taking you to the manager. I'll let him deal with you.'

The manager's office was up a flight of steps to a gantry overlooking the factory floor. The foreman left Ellie outside for half a minute while he went in and spoke to the manager alone. When he came back out, he held the door open and waved Ellie in.

'Mr Morton will see you now.'

He made it sound as if they had a pre-arranged appointment. Ellie took the cue, deciding on the spur of the moment that that was the way to play it – take control of the situation and undermine the manager's authority on his own turf. She walked purposefully through the door and over to Morton's desk, holding out her hand.

'I'm Ellie Mason, from *The News*,' she said brightly. 'How do you do?'

The manager looked nonplussed. He gazed at Ellie's outstretched hand as if he'd never seen one before, then he reached out hesitantly and shook it. His grip was weak, slightly sticky. Ellie gave him one of her iron squeezes and sat down in the chair in front of the desk.

'It's good of you to see me,' she said, pulling out her notebook and pen. 'I hope I'm not going to take up too much of your time.'

Morton glanced uncertainly at her notebook. He was a small man, with rimless spectacles and dandruff on the shoulders of his suit jacket.

'This isn't an interview,' he said.

Ellie did her best to look startled.

'It isn't? I'm sorry, I thought that was why your foreman – he *is* your foreman, isn't he? – brought me here.'

'He brought you here because you were found wandering around the premises without authorisation.'

'Yes, that was unfortunate,' Ellie said. 'I'm afraid I somehow came in the wrong way. Still, now I'm here, perhaps I could ask you a few questions. This *is* the factory where chickens for SupaMar are processed, isn't it? I want to make sure of that.'

The manager was recovering his composure, reminding himself of his position. This was *his* factory, after all. *He* made the rules, and enforced them.

'I don't believe you came in the wrong way by accident, Miss Mason,' he said coldly. 'I think you deliberately sneaked in through the back, then tried to pass yourself off as an environmental health officer.'

'I never said I was an environmental health officer. I said I was looking for them. I didn't see them, by the way. Have they finished their work here?'

'Don't play games, Miss Mason. We both know what you're doing here.'

'Do we? Then maybe you could answer my questions.'

'I will answer no questions. I know who you are. I was warned about you.'

'Really? Warned by whom?'

'You were caught snooping around Gosling Hall Farm yesterday. Now you're caught snooping around here. This is private property. You've come here without permission. I've half a mind to call the police and have you arrested.

Ellie sighed. Was she going to have to explain the law of trespass to this man too?

'Mr Morton,' she said. 'A pack of chicken infected with typhoid bacteria has been traced back to your factory. Does that not worry you?'

'This factory has an excellent health and safety record,' Morton replied. 'You won't find a cleaner poultry process-ing plant anywhere in Europe. '

'Nevertheless, the contaminated chicken came from here.'

'There's no proof that the typhoid bacteria were picked up here,' Morton said. 'I think it's highly unlikely that they were. Our machines are checked and cleaned regularly, there is a Meat Hygiene Service inspector on duty every day, monitoring our activities. We have never had any bacterial or other infections detected on our premises, or in any of our poultry products.'

'Until now,' Ellie said.

'I've just told you, there is no conclusive proof that the typhoid bacteria came from here.'

Ellie found his complacency annoying, and disturbing.

'You seem to be in a state of denial about this,' she said. 'One person is dead, two more are in hospital because they caught typhoid from somewhere. There's no conclusive proof – as you say – that the bacteria came from your factory, but it's pretty likely they did. That's why the environmental health team are here investigating. Even if there were only a minute chance that the contamination occurred here, don't you think you should be taking the problem more seriously?'

'I am taking it seriously. We are cooperating fully with the environmental health officers. We have given them access to every part of the plant, we are allowing them to interview and test all our employees.'

'But the plant is still operating. Shouldn't you close it down until the source of the typhoid is identified?'

'I don't have to justify my actions to you, Miss Mason.'

The manager picked up the phone on the desk, punched in a number and spoke briefly to someone at the other end. Two minutes later, a uniformed security guard came into the office.

'This lady is just going,' Morton said. 'Will you escort her to her car and make sure she leaves the premises? And I mean, *make sure*.'

Ellie didn't go far. All she did, in fact, was change carparks – from the one at Elliston-Jones Ltd to the one at the Dog and Partridge pub which was a quarter of a mile away from the industrial park, on the fringes of a housing estate.

It was late afternoon. The day shift at the slaughterhouse would be ending soon, and Ellie thought it was likely that some of the workforce would call in at the nearest pub for a drink on their way home. It was certainly worth waiting around for a while on the off-chance. What did she have to lose?

She'd parked facing the entrance to the carpark so she could get a clear view of everyone who arrived. The first two cars she ruled out immediately. They came in the wrong way – from the opposite direction to the poultry plant. The next couple of cars contained lone men in suits who looked like salesmen or reps. Ellie ignored them. The following car was more promising: two men in jeans and casual shirts and work boots – not dirty boots like builders or other outdoor workers, but clean boots. These men were definitely blue collar, but they worked indoors somewhere – and Elliston-Jones was probably the biggest factory nearby. The men went inside the pub, but Ellie didn't go after them. She was waiting for a woman – or a group of women – some of the workers who packed the processed chicken parts. She had a feeling she'd get more out of them than the men.

Ten minutes later, a rusty old Honda Civic with a patched front wing pulled into the carpark. Four women got out. Two of them looked like mother and daughter, the other two were in their thirties, one of them a bleached blonde, the other a redhead in a low-cut top that revealed her freckly chest. Ellie would have placed a small bet on their being Elliston-Jones employees. She waited for ten minutes – giving the women time to get comfortable in the pub, to loosen up after their day at work. Then she went inside.

The women were sitting in the bay window of the lounge bar, talking animatedly. A peal of raucous female laughter rang out across the room as Ellie walked over to their table.

'I'm sorry to bother you,' Ellie said. 'But could I ask if you work at the chicken processing plant down the road? Elliston-Jones.'

'Yes, love, we do,' the bleached blonde replied. 'You looking for a job?'

'You don't want one there,' the redhead said. 'Believe me. Not unless you like squeezing bloody chicken tits all day.'

The other three women laughed. Ellie explained who she was, what she was doing there.

'Can I get you all another drink?'

The women exchanged glances. Then the blonde shrugged.

'Well, if you're buying.' She looked around at her friends. 'The same again, eh?'

Ellie went to the bar and came back with three rum and cokes, a half of lager and an apple juice for herself. The women shuffled their chairs along to make room for her. They were friendly, quite willing to talk to her. As Ellie sat down with them, she glanced towards the door and saw two men come into the bar. One of them was the Elliston-Jones security guard who'd accompanied her to her car and watched her drive away from the slaughterhouse. He was off duty, out of uniform, obviously coming in for a drink after work. He paused and stared at Ellie, unsure what to do. Ellie thought he might come over and confront her, but he kept walking to the bar and, while his companion ordered, pulled out his mobile phone and punched in a number.

'Thanks,' the blonde said to Ellie and took a sip of her rum and coke.

The security guard was talking to someone on his phone. Ellie knew she probably didn't have much time.

'What's it been like today?' she said. 'At the plant. You know, the typhoid business.'

'They're talking about closing the place down,' the red-head said. 'Just for a few days, until they've done all the tests.'

'Does that worry you?'

'Nah, I'll be glad of the time off.'

'We wouldn't,' the older woman said, nodding at the girl who looked like her daughter. 'Jackie and I need the money.'

'What about the health aspect of it?' Ellie asked. 'Are you frightened of catching the disease?'

'The council people have said there's not much risk, if we wash our hands thoroughly after handling the chicken,' the blonde replied. 'They've given us all these little plastic pots.'

'Yeah,' the redhead said. 'When they told me they were after a stool sample, I thought they wanted to look at my kitchen furniture.'

'How long have you all worked at the plant?' Ellie asked.

'Three years. And that's too long,' the redhead said. 'But there's not much else round here. You've been there the longest, haven't you, Trish?'

The older woman nodded.

'Seven years.'

'I've been there four,' Jackie said.

'Me too,' the blonde said.

'Have there ever been any health scares before?' Ellie asked.

'Not typhoid,' Trish replied.

'But other things?'

'Well, people sometimes get sick. You know, nothing serious. Vomiting, the runs, that kind of thing.'

'Caught from working at the plant?'

Trish shrugged.

'No one knows.'

'You seen inside?' the blonde said.

'I had an unauthorised look around. Before the foreman caught me and took me to the manager.'

The redhead grinned.

'You've met old Morton? Miserable git, isn't he? Living proof that you can survive for years with a pineapple stuck up your arse.'

'You see the scald tank?' the blonde said.

'Yes.'

'That's where it all comes from. They only clean it out once a day. It's full of germs. You work in there and sooner or later you're going to puke up.'

'What about the packing section? Does anyone get ill there?'

'Sometimes.'

'The smell used to make me want to throw up,' Jackie said. 'When I first started. But I've got used to it now.'

'No one's been abroad recently?' Ellie asked. 'To a place where typhoid's more common?'

'The council people asked us that,' Trish said. 'Interviewed us all one by one. I don't know anyone.'

'I went to Crete last summer,' the blonde said. 'They said that didn't count. It had to be recent. You know, the last month or so.'

'There are quite a few foreign workers at the plant, aren't there?'

'Yeah, we're in the minority, the English,' the redhead said. 'There's all sorts. Arabs, Lithuanians, Portuguese. Most of them only stay a few months. Lucky bastards.'

'Uh-oh, look what the cat's dragged in,' the blonde murmured softly.

Ellie turned her head. The slaughterhouse manager, Morton, had just come into the lounge. He glared at the group of women and marched purposefully over, his mouth thin as a razor blade.

'And just what is going on here?' he demanded.

'You what?' the redhead said insolently.

'Are you aware that this woman is a newspaper reporter? What's she been asking? Has she been asking questions about the factory?'

'We're just having a drink,' the blonde said. 'What's wrong with that?'

'You're in breach of your contracts,' Morton said.

'What, for having a drink?'

'For talking to a journalist. There's a confidentiality clause that prohibits you from revealing anything about the company to third parties.' Morton's gaze swung round on to Ellie. 'Elliston-Jones is a reputable company. I won't tolerate you trying to dig up dirt on it.'

'If there's no dirt to find, what are you worried about?' Ellie said.

'We've been trading for years. It's a good company, a good employer. As I told you before, our hygiene standards are second to none.'

'You want to tell that to the families of the woman who died and the ones who are in hospital?'

'What've you told her?' Morton asked the other four woman.

'Nothing,' Trish replied.

'You must have told her something. I'm warning you, if you carry on talking to her, you don't need to bother turning up for work tomorrow.'

'Hey,' Ellie said. 'There's no need to get heavy.' She stood up. 'I'll go. I don't want anyone losing their job.'

'You stay away from my factory and my workforce,' Morton said heatedly. 'I don't want to see you around here again.'

'Take it easy,' Ellie said. 'I'm going, OK?' She turned to the women. 'I'm sorry, I didn't mean to cause any problems.'

She picked up her shoulderbag and walked away from

the table. There was a door at the side of the room marked 'Toilets'. Ellie went through into the Ladies. She was at a basin, washing her hands, when the redhead came in.

'Has he gone?' Ellie said.

'No. He won't either, not until you leave. He's hanging around the bar, making sure you don't talk to us again.'

'What's he afraid of?'

'God knows. He's an old woman, a stickler for rules. He likes to be in charge.'

'He'll know you're talking to me.'

'I don't give a shit. Morton's a tosser. He can fire me if he wants. I'm sick of packing slimy chicken bits all day.'

The redhead took a pen and a scrap of paper out of her handbag and scribbled something on it. She passed the paper to Ellie.

'What's this?'

Ellie read the words on the paper: Ringmead Processing Ltd.

'It's over on the Hunstanton road, another meat packing firm,' the redhead said.

'What about it?'

'I've a friend who worked there for a few months. You might want to take a look at it.'

'Why?'

'Just check it out. It could be of interest to you.'

The redhead went into one of the toilet cubicles and locked the door.

The Ringmead Processing factory was much smaller than Elliston-Jones, but similar in construction and location – another breeze block and tin shed on a desolate industrial park, this one to the east of King's Lynn on the A149 that ran north up the Wash and along the Norfolk coast to Sheringham and Cromer.

There were two other units on the park, both with their own parking areas in front. Ellie pulled into a space outside one of the units – an agricultural chemicals depot that appeared to be closed for the night – and switched off her car engine. She was perfectly placed to observe the Ringmead Processing factory, but without arousing any suspicion. She wasn't in Ringmead Processing's carpark, so any security guards at the factory would have no cause to come out and ask her what she was doing, but she was near enough to get a clear view of the building and everyone who went in or out of it.

Take a look at it, that was what the redhead in the pub had said, declining to elaborate further. But take a look at what exactly? Certainly not the exterior of the factory. There was nothing interesting about four concrete walls and a metal roof. Whatever it was the redhead had been referring to, it had to be inside the building. It had to be something about the way the factory operated, or the meat products it packaged.

She could attempt to sneak in unnoticed, the way she had at Elliston-Jones, and before that at Gosling Hall Farm, but Ellie wasn't sure how viable an option that was. She'd got away with it twice, but three times might be pushing her luck too far and what she didn't want was to get caught in the act and thereby alert the factory management to the fact that a journalist was taking an interest in their activities. She had to be more discreet this time. But how?

A white transit van drove in off the main road and came to a halt outside the Ringmead Processing building. A group of people – ten or twelve of them, all foreign-looking – clambered out of the back of the van and went into the factory. Ten minutes later, a different group came out. More casual migrant workers, Ellie guessed. She saw three or four Chinese women, a couple of black men and five or six Asian men. They got into the back of the van and it drove off. Ellie checked her watch. It was just gone 8 p.m. Shift change.

She could try to talk to the workers, ask them about what

went on at the factory, but she didn't hold out much hope of getting very far. The four Englishwomen in the Dog and Partridge were one thing. They spoke English, had the classic British workers' contempt for management and authority. A group of migrant workers was different. They probably didn't have much English and they'd be too scared of losing their jobs to talk to a reporter.

Ellie thought hard, working through all the possible courses of action in her head. Slowly an idea began to take shape. Maybe there was another way. A way that meant she wouldn't have to talk to the workers, wouldn't have to get inside the factory. Someone else would do it for her. And she knew who. The more she thought about the idea, the more she liked it.

Too bad the transit van had gone. She needed to know where it was going, where the migrant workers lived. But she knew it would be back in the morning. She could deal with that then. She'd have to spend the night in a hotel. It didn't make sense to return to London tonight and then drive all the way back out at the crack of dawn. Ed Preston would have to give his approval, of course, but she couldn't see him objecting. She took out her mobile phone to call him.

Then she saw the lorry and put the phone down.

It was a yellow, open-backed lorry. It was turning into the industrial park and heading for the Ringmead Processing factory. Ellie could read the name on the side of the vehicle: J. Hollings Haulage. She recognised the name. She recognised something else too. On the back of the lorry were two large metal bins identical to the ones she'd seen at Gosling Hall Farm.

26

The men were all assembled in the kitchen of the house – fifteen of them crammed into the tiny space, some perched on the edge of the table, others squeezed into the corners, a few spilling out into the hall. Joe was there with Kwasi. Radu was there too, and the Croats, the Lithuanians, Kosovans and Serbs. Joe had never spoken to most of them. One or two he didn't even recognise by sight. They were the ones who were always working a night shift somewhere, the ones who needed the money badly enough to put up with the anti-social hours. They weren't working this evening though – at least, not yet. It was Friday – pay day. They would collect their wages before they went off in the van to the packhouse.

One of the residents – a Pole named Henryk – had stationed himself by the open front door, where he could watch the street. There was a muted undercurrent of excitement, of anticipation in the house. This was the most important moment of the week for all of them: the reason they endured the long hours in the fields and on the production lines and put up with the cramped, insalubrious accommodation. Money. Money to live on and, in most cases, to send back to families in their home countries.

Joe knew he was only going to be there for a short time, but he wondered what it was like for the men who had lived apart from their wives and children for years and would continue to do so for the foreseeable future. He couldn't imagine what pangs of loneliness and homesickness they felt, what memories they carried, what feelings of loss they suffered when they thought about their children growing up without them. There were few nomadic tribes left in the world. Most of the ancient wandering peoples had either chosen, or been forced, to settle permanently in one spot. But their place had been taken by a more modern, more diverse group of nomads spread all across western Europe – not tribes, but individuals following the opportunities for work the way their ancestors had followed the movement of their animals.

'They're here,' Henryk said, hurrying down the hall into the kitchen.

Eddie Tremain's dog, Skipper, was the first to arrive, trotting in and sniffing around the legs of the waiting men. Tremain himself came next. He was all dressed up – grey suit, pale blue shirt, jazzy tie – as if he were going out for the night. Barry was the last to come in. He too was more smartly dressed than usual – beige trousers with a casual open-necked shirt hanging down over them. His hair was combed up into short spikes, each one glistening with gel. Dangling from his right hand was a plastic carrier bag.

Tremain sat down on one of the two kitchen chairs that had been left unoccupied for him and Barry. The dog scuttled over to him and began yapping excitedly.

'You got Skipper's food? He's hungry.' the gangmaster asked Barry.

Barry took a tin of Pedigree Chum from his carrier bag and looked around the room, his gaze coming to rest on Kwasi.

'Hey, Sambo,' Barry said. 'Catch.'

He tossed the tin to Kwasi.

'Open it and put it in a bowl, will you?'

Kwasi weighed the tin in his hand, looking coolly at Barry as if he were contemplating throwing it back – maybe at his head.

'You hear me?' Barry said. 'You want your pay, put the fucking dog food in a bowl.'

Kwasi bit his lip and did as he was told, taking a cereal bowl from the cupboard next to the sink, opening the tin of Chum and tipping the contents into the bowl.

'Don't just stand there, Sambo,' Barry said. 'Put it on the fucking floor.'

Barry pulled out the other chair and sat down. Skipper scrambled over to the bowl, his paws skidding on the lino floor, and began to wolf down the dog food.

'Who's first?' Tremain said.

Barry rummaged in his bag and pulled out a handful of brown envelopes. He read out the name on the top envelope.

'Marko Klasnic.'

One of the Croats stepped forward and took the envelope from Barry.

'Stipe Simic. Henryk Lipinski. Kwasi Okanawhatever-yournameis.'

Barry read out the names in turn and the men collected their pay packets, tearing them open and checking carefully through the money inside before leaving the kitchen. Finally, only Radu and Joe were left.

'Radu,' Barry said.

Radu shuffled out from the corner where he'd been hunched over trying to avoid being noticed. He edged nervously around the dog. Tremain saw the movement and grinned.

'What's wrong? You don't like my dog? Say hello to Skipper, Radu. Go on, give him a stroke.'

Radu kept his eyes lowered, not looking at either Tremain or the dog. He held out his hand for his wages, but Barry kept the envelope back.

'He won't bite,' Tremain said. 'Well, he might, but not you. He doesn't like greasy foreign food.' The gangmaster gave a malicious laugh. 'Go on, stroke him.'

Radu didn't move. Tremain's tone got more aggressive.

'I said stroke him. What's the matter? Something wrong with him? Is there something wrong with my dog? You insult Skipper, you insult me.'

Radu started to tremble, his gaze still fixed on the floor. His breathing became laboured, triggering a sudden spasm of convulsive coughing.

'Get away from my dog,' Tremain yelled. 'I don't want him catching your filthy wop germs. Go on, get over there.'

Tremain lifted his foot and shoved Radu violently sideways. Radu stumbled, putting a hand on the sink to stop himself falling.

'Fucking greaseball,' Tremain said.

'He's a twat,' Barry said. 'Hey, Radu, you want your wages, say "I'm a fucking twat." Go on, "I'm a fucking twat," You can say that, can't you?'

Joe watched the scene – the gangmaster and Barry laughing now, Radu bent double coughing, his face flushed – and could bear it no longer. He knew he had to stay in character, but he couldn't stand by while a defenceless invalid like Radu was being abused in this way.

'You stop,' Joe said. 'Leave him alone. He not well.'

Tremain stopped laughing abruptly. His small polecat eyes swivelled round and locked on to Joe.

'And who the fuck are you?' the gangmaster said.

Joe avoided his gaze, assuming a subservient pose, hoping he could smooth things over, placate Tremain.

'I sorry,' he mumbled. 'But Radu sick man. Please leave alone.'

'Are you telling me what to do?' Tremain said.

'No, I no tell,' Joe said. 'I ask. Radu sick.'

Tremain got up from his chair. He was a big man, well over six feet tall with a belly to match.

'You're a lippy bastard, aren't you?' he said. 'Don't try to tell me what to do. I don't like it.'

'Excuse me,' Joe said meekly.

The gangmaster's dog had finished its meal. It padded away from the bowl, its pink tongue flicking around its hairy mouth, its tail wagging frantically.

'Let's teach him some respect,' Barry said.

He was on his feet now too. He grabbed hold of Joe's right arm and twisted it up behind his back. Joe submitted, resisting the urge to retaliate. Alban Cobani wouldn't fight back. He would take whatever was coming to him.

Barry increased the pressure on Joe's arm, forcing him to bend over.

'On your knees,' Barry said. 'You can lick out the dog's bowl. That's all you're fit for, you piece of shit. Go on, lick it!'

Barry rammed Joe's face down hard into the bowl that was still wet from the dog's saliva. Joe smelt the Chum and had to hold his breath to stop himself gagging. His nose and chin were grinding into the bowl as Barry pressed down from behind, his fingers entwined in Joe's hair, twisting and pulling it, his knuckles digging into the scalp.

'You watch your mouth, you fucking wop, OK?'

Barry gave one last push and released him suddenly. Joe lifted his head from the bowl, still on his hands and knees. The gangmaster stood over him, wanting his share of the fun. He lashed out with his foot, kicking Joe once in the ribs, then again, knocking him to the floor.

'Don't you ever fucking talk back to me again,' Tremain said.

Joe gasped and closed his eyes. He heard his pay packet fluttering down on to the lino next to him, then the patter of the dog's paws and the men's footsteps. But he didn't open his eyes until they'd gone.

'That's her,' Hasan said softly. 'Follow me at a distance.'

He slid out of the car and went after Yasmin. She was fifty metres ahead of him, walking away from her house towards the corner shop at the end of the street. She didn't look round, didn't have the slightest inkling that she was being tailed.

She went into the shop. Hasan waited outside for her. The car pulled in by the kerb, Farok in the driver's seat. He kept the engine running. It was almost dark. Hasan stepped back off the pavement into a gateway, hiding in the shadows. Yasmin, coming out of the shop and heading back home, didn't see him until it was too late. Hasan grabbed her around the waist and whisked her over to the car, whipping open the rear door and bundling her inside. By the time Yasmin thought about crying out, she was pinioned in Hasan's steely grasp, one of his hands clamped tight over her mouth.

The car moved off, speeding away around the corner and twisting through the streets, a mile, a mile and a half before it turned on to a patch of deserted wasteland behind a boarded-up pub. Yasmin saw the glint of a knife in Hasan's hand.

'You make a noise and I'll cut your throat,' Hasan said.

He took his hand away from her mouth, but kept hold of her body. The tip of the knife pricked the side of her neck.

'We don't want to harm you,' Hasan said. 'All we want is information. About the Kurdish girl who was in your house. You understand?'

'Yes, I understand.'

Yasmin's voice was a tremulous whisper. Her arms and legs were shaking. She was terrified.

'You know the girl I mean?' Hasan said.

'Yes.'

'What was she called?'

Yasmin swallowed.

'Sakar.'

'Sakar what?'

'She no give other name.'

'She wasn't called Irena Hourami?'

'No.'

360

'What did she look like? How old was she?'

'I'm not sure. Maybe twenty-five, twenty-six.'

'What about her clothes?' Hasan said.

'She have scarf on head, blue dress.'

'She was Kurdish?'

'I don't know. You say Kurdish. I don't know what she is.'

'You spoke to her?'

'A little. She no speak English.'

Farok looked round from the front seat and said in Turkish, 'It could be the wrong one.'

'No, it's her, I'm sure,' Hasan replied in the same language.

He went back to English.

'When did she arrive?' he asked Yasmin.

'I don't remember.'

Hasan jerked her head back roughly and pressed his knife to her windpipe.

'Then try harder,' he said. 'When?'

Yasmin struggled to speak. Her vocal cords seemed paralysed.

'Last week,' she mumbled.

'When last week? What day?'

'Thursday, maybe.'

'Who brought her?'

'Please, you hurting me.'

'I'll hurt you more if you don't answer my questions. Who brought her?'

'I don't know. I no see. She come to packhouse.'

'She came to a packhouse? Which one?'

'One near here. I don't remember name.'

'Wintertons?'

'Yes, that the one.'

'She just arrived? From where?'

'She no say,' Yasmin said. 'All she say, she come from place I never hear of. Diyar something.'

'Diyarbakir?'

'Yes, that it.'

'It's her,' Hasan said in Turkish. 'It has to be.'

'That all I know,' Yasmin said. 'Please, you let me go.'

'What happened to her?' Hasan said, speaking English again.

'She go. Lenny take her away,' Yasmin replied.

She didn't know who these two men were, but she knew they would kill her if she didn't cooperate. She would tell them whatever they wanted to know.

'Who's Lenny?' Hasan said.

'He drive van, work for gangmaster.'

'For Frank Parnell?'

'Yes, Mr Parnell.'

'Where did he take her?'

'I don't know. She go in van.'

'You don't know where?'

'No.'

'You're sure?'

Hasan's knife broke the skin on Yasmin's neck, drawing blood. Yasmin cried out in pain.

'I don't know. I swear,' she said urgently. 'If I know, I tell you. Please, I tell truth. Lenny take her.'

Hasan flipped the blade of his knife back into the handle and stowed the weapon away in his jacket pocket.

'You tell no one about this, you understand?' he said.

'Yes, I tell no one,' Yasmin replied.

'Get out.'

Yasmin didn't hesitate. She fumbled hurriedly for the catch and pushed open the door, scrambling out on to the wasteland. She watched the car drive off, turning out on to the road and disappearing into the night. Then her legs buckled beneath her and she collapsed to the ground.

27

Ellie yawned and checked her watch again. It was almost 8 a.m. The industrial park was quiet, deserted except for a couple of cars parked outside the Ringmead Processing factory. She had the car radio on, but was finding it difficult to stay awake. She'd spent the night in a hotel on the outskirts of King's Lynn, woken at six. Her room had been comfortable enough, but she hadn't slept well. She never did when she was away from home.

She was feeling the effects now. Her eyelids were starting to droop, her head lolled down on to her chest and her body gave a muscular spasm, jolting her suddenly back to consciousness. She wound down the window to let in some air and blinked a few times, trying to stop herself from dozing off again.

Maybe she'd got the time wrong. The nightshift workers had arrived at 8 p.m. Ellie had guessed that there were only two shifts a day, each lasting twelve hours, but perhaps she was wrong. Perhaps there were three eight-hour shifts and the nightshift had already ended. She'd have to go away and come back again later, catch the next change of shift. She grimaced at the thought. There were plenty of places in the country in which she could have enjoyed killing a few hours, but King's Lynn wasn't one of them.

The beeps for the eight o'clock news brought her attention back to the radio. She turned up the volume and listened to the headlines. The third story was the death overnight of Winifred Kirkpatrick, the typhoid victim from Swaffham. Ellie sat up and scrambled for her notebook and pen. Damn! How had she missed it? This was *her* story. She hated being upstaged by the BBC.

She scribbled down the details, but there weren't many. Mrs Kirkpatrick had passed away in the early hours of the morning, a brief statement from Queen Elizabeth Hospital giving the cause of death as organ failure brought on by the typhoid. Environmental health officers in Norfolk were still trying to trace the source of the disease, the report said. There had been no further cases of infection, but the Health Protection Agency was monitoring the situation.

Ellie put her notebook back in her bag. She'd call the hospital later, follow the story up, but right now she wanted to concentrate on the white transit van that was coming into the industrial park. It was the same one she'd seen the previous evening – she recognised the registration plate, the throaty roar of the vehicle's rusty exhaust pipe. It stopped outside the Ringmead Processing factory as before, and exchanged one group of workers for another. When the van pulled away with the nightshift employees on board, Ellie went after it.

They went along the bypass and into King's Lynn, Ellie's Mini a hundred metres behind the van. The female workers were dropped off first, at a house on a council estate, then the male workers were offloaded a few minutes later. Ellie made a note of the address and followed the empty van into the town centre where it pulled into the kerb outside an office. Ellie found a parking space further up the street and walked back. She wrote down the name on the plaque beside the office door – R. J. Cooper, Employment Agency – then went off in search of breakfast.

At about the time that Ellie was following the transit van in King's Lynn, Hasan and Farok were tailing an almost identical van thirty miles away in Thetford. Lenny Biddle was driving the van, taking migrant workers out to two farms near the town, then returning to one of Frank Parnell's houses and picking up more workers to be delivered to Winterton's packhouse. The Turks were right behind him on each of the trips, and when Lenny finally went back to Parnell's office shortly after 9 a.m, Hasan and Farok stayed close, parking their car on a sidestreet where they had a good view of the yard at the back of the gang-master's premises.

'Are we going to go in?' Farok said, lighting up a Turkish cigarette and blowing smoke out through the open window of the car.

'No, we watch for a while,' Hasan said.

'Why not snatch him, make him talk, the way we did the woman?'

'He's not going to be as easy as she was.'

'You think not?'

Farok took a flick knife from his pocket and flipped out the stiletto-thin blade. He'd lost his favourite knife in the skirmish with that son of a whore – the one who'd attacked them by throwing dinner plates, the bruise on Farok's nose still a livid, painful reminder of that encounter – but he'd acquired this new weapon immediately afterwards from a contact in Stoke Newington. Farok didn't like to be unarmed for even a single day. He was getting used to the knife. The action was smooth and well lubricated, the edge finely honed, the tip sharp as a needle.

'We show him this, he'll tell us anything we want.'

'Put that away,' Hasan said tersely. 'We have to be care-ful. It's broad daylight, there are people around.'

'We do it in the office. You go in the front way, I go in the back. Who's going to be there? A secretary? What's she going to do?'

Farok still had his knife out. He was twisting it round in his fingers, admiring the burnished gleam of the blade.

'I said, put it away,' Hasan snapped. 'This guy isn't some

stupid migrant worker. He's English, he looks tough. He won't be easily frightened. We have to bide our time, find out where he lives, find out where he's vulnerable. Then, and only then, do we make our move.'

Farok shrugged and slid the flick knife away into his pocket. Hasan was in charge. Farok was content to do as he was told. He inhaled on his cigarette and slouched lower in his seat, gazing lazily out through the windscreen.

It was lunchtime, and Farok had smoked his way through a whole packet of cigarettes, before Lenny emerged from the office. He turned out of the yard, heading somewhere on foot.

'See where he goes,' Hasan ordered.

Farok carried out the task willingly, glad of the chance to escape from the car and stretch his legs. Lenny didn't go far. He went into a sandwich shop and queued up at the counter. Farok went in after him, watching while Lenny bought a tuna and sweetcorn roll, a packet of cheese and onion crisps and a can of Diet Coke. He didn't glance round once, wasn't even aware that Farok was behind him. When Lenny left the shop, Farok stayed on for a few minutes, buying a couple of cheese and tomato sandwiches and two cans of Fanta to take back to the car.

They watched the office for the rest of the afternoon, dozing, taking it in turns to slip out to the public toilets near the bus station. Nothing happened to relieve the tedium until a little after five-thirty when Lenny came out of the office and climbed into the transit van. Hasan started up the car engine and they followed the van to two of Parnell's houses where it collected a dozen migrant workers and took them out to Winterton's packhouse for the nightshift. The dayshift workers were picked up and brought back to Thetford, then Lenny spent the next hour and a half shuttling groups of workers in from the outlying farms. His final trip was to a small semi in the eastern suburbs of Thetford. A young girl – maybe seven or eight years old – was riding her bike up and down the pavement. She stopped as the van pulled in and waited for Lenny to get out. He lifted her up in his arms and gave her a hug and a kiss, then put her down. They went up the drive of the house together, the little girl pushing her bike.

'Good,' Hasan said, watching from their parking place back up the street. 'He has a daughter.'

'Let's do it now,' Farok said impatiently.

Hasan held up a cautionary hand.

'Not yet. We wait a while longer.'

'For what?'

'You'll see.'

It was a Saturday, but Ellie knew that Joe would be out working during the day. If you were a migrant labourer, the word weekend had no real meaning. You worked seven days a week, sometimes two shifts a day, particularly in an intensive, seasonal sector like agriculture.

She'd arrived in Downham Market mid-afternoon, having spent the morning following up the death of Winifred Kirkpatrick. She parked on the street close to Joe's house, the address given to her by Ed Preston, and waited for him to come home. She had the radio on to pass the time, a Radio 4 play that was so dull and soporific that she dropped off in the middle, coming round only when the theme music of the following programme jolted her awake.

It was early evening, the sun low in the sky, when a white transit van came speeding down the road and swerved into a parking space outside Joe's house. Six men – including Joe – clambered out of the rear of the van. Ellie opened her door and got out, lifting her arms as if she were stretching, trying to draw attention to herself. Joe saw the movement and glanced in her direction as he crossed the pavement. He gave a start, pausing for a second. Then he nodded, a nod so slight that even the three men alongside him wouldn't have noticed it, and went into the house.

Ellie climbed back into her Mini and waited. Ten minutes later, Joe came out of the house and walked away up the street. Ellie gave him a few minutes start, then drove after him. Around the first corner, she accelerated and drew level with him, pulling into the kerb and stopping. Joe climbed into the passenger seat.

'Hi,' Ellie said.

'Hi. Keep going. You can drive me to the shops.'

Ellie drove off.

'Which shops?' she said.

'There's a mini-market just up here. Next right, I think.'

Ellie turned her head and gave him a cursory inspection.

'You look tired, and dirty,' she said.

'I *am* tired and dirty.'

'And you smell of sweat.'

'I've been picking cucumbers all day. Seven o'clock start, three fifteen-minute breaks, no shade anywhere, it's hard to stay fragrant.'

'Sounds tough.'

'I'm getting used to it. Pull in past the shops. I don't want anyone seeing me talking to you.'

'This far enough?'

'Yes, that's fine.'

Ellie stopped the car.

'You OK?' she said.

Joe nodded.

'I phoned the office earlier,' Ellie went on. 'Preston wanted to know when you were coming back.'

'Give it a few more days,' Joe said.

'He thinks you're having a holiday in the country at the newspaper's expense.'

Joe gave a hollow laugh.

'He should come and try it. It would do him good. It would do everyone good actually, to see how the farming industry really works.'

'You OK for money?'

'I'm all right. I got paid yesterday. If "paid" is the right word. Four days hard graft, ten to twelve hours a day. What do you reckon a fair wage for that would be?'

'Forty-eight hours?' Ellie said. 'What's the minimum wage these days?'

'Five thirty-five an hour.'

'That works out at – what, about £250? How much did you get?'

'Forty-five.'

'Forty-five pounds? That's all?'

'There was a hundred pound deduction for my work permit – which I haven't got yet, and probably never will. Fifty quid for my rent in Tremain's house, an "administrative charge" of £10, £55 tax and £10 national insurance. I'm an illegal migrant with no national insurance number. The tax and insurance are going straight into Tremain's pocket. No wonder he drives a Mercedes.'

'This happens to all his workers?'

'The guy is minting it. There are fifteen people in my house. At fifty quid a time, that's £750 a week Tremain is making. For a shitty little terrace in Downham Market. And he's got a lot more than one house he rents out.'

'We're in the wrong business.'

'Too right we are.'

'You want me to lend you some money?'

'I should be all right for the time being,' Joe said. 'I've got a pretty good picture of a migrant worker's life. You can tell Preston I'll be back in the office by the end of the week.'

'Any sign of Irena Hourami?' Ellie asked casually.

Joe gave her a look.

'Pardon?'

'Come on, Joe,' Ellie said. 'I know you're looking for her. Henry was asking me questions in the office. About the police investigation.'

'How's it going?'

'Not much progress. I spoke to Louise Crawford. She asked about you, by the way.'

'Did she?'

'Wanted to know why you weren't on the story.'

'What did you tell her?'

'That you were away for a couple of weeks. They're getting nowhere. You got a TV in your house?'

'A TV? You kidding?'

'So you won't have seen the appeals, asking if anyone's seen Irena. They've been on the radio too, but no one's come forward. It's not helped by the fact that the Met still haven't got a photograph of her from Turkey, so they don't really know what they're looking for.'

'And the Turks? You know, the killers?'

'Still at large.'

Joe rubbed a hand over his face. The stubble was getting longer, becoming a full beard. With the sweat and dirt from a day in the fields his skin was starting to itch. He scratched his jaw line with a fingernail that was chipped and black with grime, thinking fleetingly of that morning in Boulogne when he'd artificially dirtied his hands with soil from the flower bed. He didn't need to do that now, he had the real thing ingrained in his skin.

'Can I borrow your mobile?' he asked Ellie. 'To call Henry.'

Ellie took the phone from her bag and passed it across. Henry was curt when he came on the line.

'Yes? Who is this?'

'It's me, Joe.'

'Oh, sorry. I thought it was one of those infernal call centres. Saturday night, that's just when they like to harass you.'

'How've you got on?'

'Hang on a minute . . .' Henry said.

There was a pause, the sound of a door opening, then Henry came back on.

'Sorry about that. Only we've got these people here for dinner. Old friends of Ginnie's.'

'You want me to ring back later?'

'No, I can talk. I'm quite glad to get away actually. They're a ghastly bunch of bores. But I mustn't be too long. Ginnie will come looking for me. Yes, I've made a few enquiries, got that list of registered gangmasters you mentioned.'

'Is it long?'

'There are hundreds of them. Far too many to ring round.'

'Oh.' Joe was disappointed. 'Can you narrow it down in any way?'

'Well, I might have hit on something interesting. When I was checking up on Parnell and his assistant, Lenny – it's Lenny Biddle, by the way – I discovered that Parnell's wife has kept her maiden name at work. She's Marge Gomersall, not Parnell. Now that's not a very common name, is it? Gomersall. And on the list of gangmasters there's also a Gomersall. A Jimmy Gomersall, in Spalding.'

'You think they're related?' Joe said.

'I don't know. I've rung his contact number, but just got a recorded message saying the office is closed for the weekend. I'll try again on Monday . . .'

Henry broke off. Joe heard a woman's voice faintly in the distance, Henry calling out, 'Coming.' Then, 'Have to go, sorry. Ginnie's getting cross.'

'I'll call you again after the weekend,' Joe said.

He rang off and handed the phone back to Ellie.

'Thanks.' He looked at her. 'That's not the only reason you came, is it? To find out when I'm coming back.'

Ellie smiled.

'There's a story I'm working on. I wondered whether you might be able to help me with it.'

'Sure, how?'

'I've an idea. I want to run it past you, see what you think.'

371

'How much longer are we going to sit here?' Farok said wearily. 'I've had enough.'

Hasan looked at his watch.

'I want them settled for the evening, the daughter in bed, the neighbours all indoors. We have to catch them off guard.'

Farok shrugged but didn't argue. He gazed through the car windscreen at the house up the street.   A light came on in one of the upstairs front bedrooms. Farok caught a glimpse of the little girl in a pair of pink and white pyjamas, a woman coming into the room behind her.

'She's going to bed,' he said. 'Let's make our move.'

'Ten more minutes,' Hasan said. 'Then we go in.'

He surveyed the street, waiting for the right moment. Night was falling. The neighbourhood children had all been called inside, the front gardens and pavements were deserted. Lights glowed dimly in curtained windows. Overhead a flock of birds was circling, swirling around in a grey mass before flying away to their roosts.

Hasan reached out to open his door.

'Just a minute,' Farok said.

The front door of the house was opening. Lenny came out, still in the same jeans and shirt he'd been wearing earlier. He walked down the drive and got into the transit van.

'Perfect,' Hasan said.

'We follow him?' Farok said.

'No. Get down.'

They slid low in their seats, hiding their faces, as the van went past. Then they got out and ran up to the house. The front door was unlocked. Hasan opened it noiselessly and the two of them slipped inside.

'Get the daughter,' Hasan whispered, pointing upstairs.

Hasan crept along the hall. The unexpected creaking of a loose floorboard betrayed his presence and a woman's voice called out from the kitchen, 'Is that you, Lenny? Did you forget your wallet?'

Hasan stepped through the doorway. The woman was at the sink. She started to turn, but Hasan was too quick for her. He was across the room in three strides, one arm looping around the woman's body, the other darting to her face, cupping her mouth with a hand. She tried to scream, but the hand was sealing her lips tighter than a gag. Hasan pulled her towards him, his arm compressing her chest, squeezing the breath out of her. He half dragged, half carried her through into the sitting room just as Farok was coming downstairs with the little girl in his arms. He'd tied the cord of her dressing gown around her mouth to stop her crying out. The girl was petrified, her eyes bulging in terror.

Hasan sat down on the settee, still holding the mother. Farok took an armchair, the girl on his lap.

'You make a noise,' Hasan said. 'And we hurt your daughter. You understand?'

To emphasise the point, Farok produced his knife and flicked out the blade, holding it close to the girl's face.

'Not a sound,' Hasan said.

He took his hand away from the woman's face and released his grip on her body.

'Your husband,' he said. 'Where's he gone?'

'To get ... to get a Chinese takeaway,' the woman replied, her voice cracking. 'Who are you? What do you want?'

'You do as I say and we won't harm you,' Hasan said.

He could see the woman trembling. The little girl was sobbing silently, her shoulders heaving, the tears running down her face and into her gag.

'Let my daughter go,' the woman said. 'Let her come to me.'

Hasan shook his head. The woman gazed at her daughter, her own eyes welling with tears.

'Please, let me hold her,' she pleaded. 'She's frightened. It's all right, Chloe. I'm here. You're safe.'

'You have nothing to fear. We just want to talk to your husband,' Hasan said.

'Lenny? What's he done? What are you going to do to him?'

'If he cooperates, nothing.'

'Look, if it's money you're after . . .'

'We don't want money.'

'Then what . . .'

'Shut up. No more talking.'

They waited in silence, Hasan watching the door, listening for the sound of the van returning, the woman staring in anguish at her daughter who was rigid on Farok's knees, her streaming eyes flickering from her mother to the knife in her captor's hand.

Hasan heard the noise of an engine on the street, a van door slamming.

'Remember, not a sound,' he said.

The front door opened. Lenny came along the hall towards the kitchen. As he passed the open sitting room door, he glanced in and stopped dead.

'Stay where you are,' Hasan ordered.

He didn't want any instinctive reactions, any paternal heroics. Lenny took in the scene, expressions of surprise, puzzlement, anger then anxiety fleeting across his face.

'Who the hell are you?' he said.

'Sit down. Over there,' Hasan said.

Lenny hesitated.

'Now look, what the . . .'

'*Sit down!*'

Lenny stepped uncertainly into the room and lowered himself into the second armchair. The bag containing the Chinese takeaway fell from his hand.

'What've you done to my daughter,' he said. 'Let her go. Let her go, you bastards.'

Farok lifted his knife and very deliberately held the tip of the blade to Chloe's cheek.

'Calm down,' Hasan said. 'All we want is some information.'

'Information? What information?' Lenny said.

'There was a Kurdish woman in one of Parnell's houses – 33, Melrose Street. You took her somewhere. Where?'

'Kurdish woman?'

'Don't waste our time. You know who I mean. Where is she now?'

'I took her to Spalding,' Lenny said.

He didn't hesitate to tell them what they wanted to know. The Kurdish woman meant nothing to him. Protecting his wife and daughter was the only thing that concerned him.

'Spalding?'

'In Lincolnshire.'

'Why?'

'There was a journalist snooping around. He said the police were interested in the woman. She sounded like trouble so Frank told me to get rid of her.'

'Where in Spalding is she? Her address.'

'I don't know.'

Hasan looked at Farok who lifted the little girl's chin and held the knife to her throat. Lenny leaned forward in alarm.

'For God's sake, that's the truth. I *don't* know. I took her to a gangmaster, Jimmy Gomersall. He was going to give her a place to stay. That's all I know.'

'This gangmaster, where do we find him?'

'He has an office. Water Street. Number seventeen.'

'And his home?'

'I don't know where he lives. I've only ever been to his office. Look, I can't tell you any more. Let my daughter go now. Can't you see she's terrified?'

'The Kurdish woman, what was her name?' Hasan asked.

'Sakar something. I told Jimmy she was called Ligia Moreira. I said she was Portuguese. That makes the paperwork easier.'

'Ligia Moreira?'

'Yes.'

Hasan stood up and nodded at Farok. Farok got to his feet, still holding Chloe. The two men retreated to the doorway.

'You don't say a word about this to anyone,' Hasan said, looking at Lenny and his wife. 'If you do, we'll be back. Or our friends will be back. Not for you, but for your daughter. Remember that.'

Farok put Chloe down on the floor and let her go. The little girl ran across the room and threw herself into her mother's arms. Hasan and Farok walked to the front door and let themselves out.

28

It was a hot, cloudless day. Joe gazed up at the hazy blue sky and suppressed a sigh, wondering how he was going to get through another gruelling day in the fields. They were back at Coppice Wood Farm. The rows of cucumber plants stretched as far as the eye could see, starting just behind the farmhouse and spreading out across the gently-sloping land to the fringes of the wood on the rise, the beech and oak and sycamore trees standing out on the horizon. There was no shade anywhere. Even now, at 8 a.m., the heat of the sun was starting to feel oppressive. By noon, Joe knew from the previous day's work, it would be insufferable.

He walked across to the tractor, Marina beside him. Her dark hair was tied back with a rubber band, as always. Her skin was golden in the sun. There was something fresh, healthy about her. When they bent down to take a knife each from the bucket, their hands touched briefly. Joe felt the warmth of her fingers, a slight, unsettling tremor pulse up his arm. Marina straightened up. Her T-shirt was tight over her small breasts. She caught Joe's eye and smiled.

'Nice day,' she said.

'Is going to be hot,' Joe replied.

'I like hot day. The air here, is good. You know, clean. In Kiev, the air dirty. I live in apartment. Tower block. No countryside, no fields. Smoke everywhere. Working in factory is horrible. Is better to be outside like here.'

They took up their positions behind the tractor. The

picking system for cucumbers was pretty much the same as for courgettes – conveyor belts sticking out to right and left on the trailer, the workers following the tractor as it crossed the field, slicing off ripe cucumbers as they went.

'My grandmother, she grow cucumbers when I was a child,' Marina said.

'In Kiev?' Joe asked.

'Near Odessa. She had place in country. Piece of land for vegetable. I go there in summer holiday. I help her pick. A few cabbage, a few cucumber. It not work like this, it fun. We pick for short time, then sit down and eat cucumber.'

'She grow vegetable still?' Joe said.

'No, land gone. Taken away by government. They give to builder. He build apartments on it. My grandmother dead now. But she sad if she saw it. All concrete, no fields any more.'

Joe flexed his back and shoulder muscles, loosening them up for the repetitive grind of bending and picking. The sun was getting brighter. He had to screw up his eyes against the glare and wished he had some sunglasses, but migrant labourers didn't wear sunglasses.

The tractor pulled off. Marina raised her eyebrows wearily.

'Rest time over,' she said. 'Shit time begin.'

Joe grinned at her, then stooped down to pick a cucumber.

The routine of work had numbed Irena's emotions. The long, hard toil of twelve-hour days in the fields, or night-shifts in a packhouse left her too physically drained to dwell on her feelings. She thought about Ismail – sometimes that was all she did think about during those monotonous hours on the production line – but she was too tired to really grieve much. She worked, and when she'd finished working, she slept. There was little time for anything else.

She'd been working nights for three days now – sorting and wrapping cut flowers in a packhouse outside Spalding. One of Jimmy Gomersall's drivers had dropped her off outside her house at 8 a.m. There were two other migrant workers with her – a Chinese girl named Mae, and an older, pale-skinned woman called Rula. Their names were all Irena knew about them – or indeed about any of the other six women who shared the house. None of them talked to her, none of them made any effort to befriend her the way Yasmin had in Thetford. English was the lingua franca of the household and Irena's command of the language was too poor for her to join in their conversations. They weren't overtly hostile towards her, just indifferent.

Irena was on her own, and she felt her isolation deeply. Everything about England was alien to her: the countryside, the houses, the weather, the people – though she'd encountered very few native English. There were some in the fields and packhouses, but they kept themselves to themselves, not mixing much with the foreign workers. She missed her home in Turkey, missed her family, her own language, all those things that made up her identity, that gave her roots. Above all, of course, she missed Ismail. She wept for him still, crying silently on her mattress while the two other women who shared her bedroom slept. And when she thought about Ismail, she couldn't help but think also of that terrible night in London – the two were inextricably joined together in her memory – and the Turks who'd chased her through the streets. Were they still looking for her? she wondered. How much longer would she have to remain in hiding in this remote part of England? For days she had pondered those questions, but it was only now that she felt strong enough to seek some answers.

She still had the piece of paper that Anwar had given her, the paper with his phone number on. Ring us and let us know where you are, he'd told her before she left in Rafiq Khan's van. Maybe now was the time to do just that.

She washed herself in the bathroom basin, then left the house and walked into the centre of Spalding. There was a payphone near the supermarket where she bought her food. She went into the booth and studied the panel of information above the telephone. The written instructions on how to make a call were only in English, but accompanying the words were little pictures illustrating the steps that needed to be taken. Irena followed the pictures, picking up the receiver, inserting her money, dialling Anwar's number.

Anwar's voice came on the line. Irena felt the tears prick her eyes as she heard the familiar, friendly sound. But he was speaking English.

'We're not in at the moment . . .'

'It's me, Irena, ' Irena interrupted in Kurdish. 'Anwar?'

'. . . but please leave a message after the tone.'

'Anwar?'

The message came again, this time in Kurdish so Irena understood it. She didn't know what to do. She didn't want to speak to a machine, she wanted to speak to Anwar or Sara. Where were they?

The tone beeped. Irena had to make up her mind quickly.

'It's me,' she blurted out again. 'I'm OK. I'm in a place called Spalding. I don't know where that is. I'm sharing a house – number 24, Rodney Road. I have a different name now. I'm Ligia Moreira. Write to me, please. Let me know what's happening, when I can come back to London.'

She hung up, feeling frustrated. She'd prepared herself for a conversation with a person and ended up speaking to a cassette tape. The experience left her depressed, unsatisfied. But it had achieved one thing: she knew now that she could do it, she could make a phone call in England. She would come back later, maybe tomorrow or the day after, and try again.

The sun was hot on Joe's face. He could feel the rays prickling his skin, the beads of sweat on his forehead. He paused for a moment to wipe the moisture away with the back of his hand. Marina stopped picking too and arched her back, her hands on her hips. Their eyes met for a second. There was a mutual attraction there, Joe could sense it. Neither of them said anything. They didn't need to. They just looked at each other, then resumed their picking.

Joe thought about her as they followed the tractor across the field. It was a long time since he'd felt that frisson of sexual interest in a woman. He didn't know why it had been so long. Maybe he hadn't been looking, maybe he simply hadn't met anyone he wanted. He'd had these periods before, these spells when his sex life had lapsed into a sort of suspended animation. The first had been after his split with his wife. Some men bounced back after a divorce, returned straight to the fray and found a new partner within weeks. But Joe had been so bruised by the separation from Chiara, so emotionally drained by the guilt and acrimony, that it had taken him a couple of years to feel up to the rigours of the dating game again. There'd been only a few since Chiara: Rebecca, Alison, Caroline, briefly Ellie . . . their names a roll call of infatuation followed by disintegration, sometimes swift, sometimes prolonged. The method didn't really matter, the result was always the same. Disappointment, puzzlement, loneliness. As he got older, Joe found his nerve increasingly failing him, his mind reluctant to risk his heart on yet another venture into the unknown. And yet . . . he looked across at Marina, taking in the soft lines of her face, the curves of her body as she bent down to pick another cucumber . . . and yet, what was the point of life if you didn't occasionally take the plunge and damn the consequences?

She was turning her head now, smiling at him, the sweat gleaming on her brow. She held his gaze for a time, then her eyes strayed, looking past him at something in the distance. Joe glanced round. A dark blue minibus with tinted windows was speeding along the track from the farm-house. It came to a stop at the edge of the field and a group of men jumped out of the back. They were all identically dressed, in navy blue overalls and boots. They didn't look as if they belonged on a farm. There was something official, almost military about their bearing, their uniforms. They fanned out into a line and came jogging across the field towards the migrant workers.

It was Kwasi who realised first who they were. He'd been around long enough to recognise 'authority' when he saw it.

'Immigration!' he shouted. 'Run!'

Joe was rooted to the spot.

'What?' he said, watching the line of men drawing nearer.

Marina grabbed his arm.

'Bloody immigration. We run,' she said, dragging Joe with her as she turned and sprinted away through the cucumber plants.

The other migrant workers scattered and fled, legging it across the field with the immigration officers in hot pursuit.

'Where we go?' Joe said, pulling alongside Marina who was fast and nimble, light on her feet like a dancer.

'Woods,' she said. 'We hide in woods.'

They ran up the slight incline towards the trees on the top of the rise. Joe looked back. The immigration officers were outnumbered by the migrants. The officers knew they couldn't catch every worker, so they'd targeted particular individuals and were chasing them doggedly over the fields. The migrants, with more to lose than the officers, weren't going to give up and come quietly. They were running with all the gritty determination of people whose livelihoods were at stake. Capture meant detention and deportation. None of them was going to submit to that without a fight.

Kwasi was two fields away, racing through a crop of kos lettuces with an immigration officer close behind him. Two of the Chinese migrants were heading for the packhouse: a mistake for there was a second IND – Immigration and Nationality Directorate – van parked out of sight by the farm buildings, the officers lying in wait to pick off stray workers fleeing that way. Radu and the Croats, Marko and Stipe, had doubled back cunningly while the IND officers were focusing on the female workers, who were slower and easier to catch. The three men were dashing across a radish field towards the main road.

Up on the hill, Marina and Joe were nearly at the wood. They'd chosen the right direction. No one was coming after them. They paused at the edge of the field, glancing back for a moment. Kwasi was a speck in the distance, still running hard though the immigration officer on his tail had given up the chase. The Croats seemed to have escaped too, but Radu, too ill to run for long, had been caught. He was being escorted towards the IND van, an immigration officer on either side of him holding his arms.

'Shit,' Marina said. 'They got Radu. I don't know much about him. He legal? He got work permit?'

'I don't know,' Joe said.

'Maybe they leave rest of us, don't bother to catch now. But maybe not. We still hide. Come on.'

Marina plunged into the trees. Joe went after her. It was a dense patch of woodland that had been left unmanaged and neglected for years. The undergrowth was a thick jungle of brambles, nettles and long grass interspersed with clumps of rhododendron and holly. They forced a path through the vegetation and dropped to their knees, crawling under some low branches into the small space in the middle of a rhododendron bush. There was no room to sit up so they lay on the ground next to each other, their bodies touching. They were both panting, tired from the run up the hill. Joe took a few deep breaths. He wasn't wheezing, there was no tightness in his chest. That was a relief – his asthma inhaler was back at the house.

'You OK?' he said.

'Yes,' Marina replied. 'Immigration, they bastards. Why they try to catch us? We work hard. We do stuff the English no want to do. What the problem?'

'This happen to you before?'

'Yes. In packhouse.'

'The one here? On this farm?'

'No, different packhouse. Immigration people come. Foreman run in and tell us. We go out back way, hide in fields. It night so immigration no find us.'

'Why you do this?' Joe said. 'Is really better here than in Ukraine?'

'Is better than in Albania?' Marina riposted. 'That your answer. Yes, is better here. That why I come. That why you come, why everybody come. In Ukraine things harder than here. Much harder.'

'You want to go home? You miss home?'

'Yes, I miss sometimes.'

'You have family?'

'Some.'

'What about husband, children?'

Marina hesitated.

'No. No husband, no children,' she said. 'You have wife?'

'No,' Joe said. 'No wife, no children. How long you . . .'

Marina suddenly put a finger over his lips. She turned her head and whispered in his ear.

'Sssh, someone come.'

They lay still, listening. Marina was right. Someone had entered the wood. Joe could hear the rustle of the under-growth as feet and legs brushed through it. He lifted his head a little and saw them, caught glimpses of them, rather. The rhododendron bush was too dense to allow a clear view. But he saw flashes of blue overalls about twenty metres away, two IND officers pausing to look around.

'They came this way,' one of the officers said. 'I saw them.'

'We'll never find them in here,' the second officer replied. 'Shit!'

'What is it?'

'Bloody nettle. Stung me.'

'You look over there.'

'What for? It's all brambles and holly. It'll cut us to bits. They're probably not in here anyway. I bet they kept running, went out the other side. That's what I'd have done.'

'Maybe.'

'Look, what's the point? How many have we picked up already?'

'Six, I think. That's out here in the fields. There may be more in the packhouse.'

'That's a good haul. Who's going to complain at that?'

'Yeah, I suppose so.'

'Let's go. I'm knackered.'

The two men's voices faded as they walked back out of the wood. Joe waited a few minutes, listening hard, before he dared move. He turned his head. Marina's face was only a few inches away. He could feel her breath on his cheek. Her lips were parted, waiting. Joe kissed her, tasting the salt of sweat on her lips, smelling the dust of the field on her clothes and in her hair. Marina's arm curled around his neck, pulling him closer. Joe's hand slid up under her T-shirt. Her skin was warm, clammy. His fingers unclipped her bra. Her tongue was in his mouth. She pulled apart his shirt and slipped her hand inside. She exuded a fierce, animal heat. Her fingers moved lower, stroking him. Joe wanted her. He knew she wanted him. But it didn't feel right. He was deceiving her, he wasn't what she thought. He broke away.

'Marina . . .'

'What?' she said.

'Maybe we stop.'

'Stop? Why?'

'You don't know me.'

'What knowing got to do with it?'

'Is difficult. Not right.'

For a moment he longed for the complexities of fully-developed language, to be able to explain to her properly what he meant. He was weary of the simplistic, Albanian-immigrant English he'd been speaking for the past week, but he had to keep up the pretence.

'What difficult?' Marina said. 'Is easy. We do it.'

'Is not safe,' Joe said. 'We have no . . .' He reminded himself he was supposed to be Albanian. Would he know the word 'condom', or anything cruder.

'No thing,' he said, gesturing at his crotch. 'To make safe.'

'I don't care,' Marina said.

'I care.'

'No, we do it. We do it now.'

'No, is not safe.'

'Is safe,' Marina said. 'Is right time. You understand? Nothing happen, OK?'

She kissed him hard. There was something uncontrolled, almost desperate about her passion. Joe kissed her back. Just go with it, he thought. Stop thinking, for once. Take the plunge. His fingers found the button of her jeans, unfastened it, pulled open the zip. Then he was tugging at the denim, sliding the jeans down over her thighs.

The door leading up to Jimmy Gomersall's office was closed. Hasan pressed the bell a couple of times and waited. There was no response.

'What do we do now?' Farok said.

Hasan went into the adjacent burger bar and spoke to the teenager behind the counter, asking him if he knew Jimmy, if he knew whether the office ever opened on a Sunday or where Jimmy might be found. The kid didn't know who Jimmy Gomersall was. Nor did the burger bar manager, another teenager maybe a year or so older than the first kid.

Hasan went back outside. They'd driven around Spalding when they'd first arrived, looking for Water Street. Hasan wasn't impressed with the place. It was too small, too provincial for his liking. It had some attractive historical buildings, he could see that, but Hasan wasn't interested in architecture or history.

'Why don't we break in, look through his files like we did in Thetford?' Farok suggested.

'Don't be stupid,' Hasan said.

'What's stupid about it? We find out where she's living and go and get her.'

'Just force the door and walk in, you mean?'

'Why not?'

'That's why not,' Hasan said.

He jerked his head up at the adjoining building. Fastened to the wall, where it had a good view of the whole street, was a CCTV camera.

'They're probably all over the town centre,' Hasan said. 'linked to a control room somewhere.'

'So what're you saying? We come back when the office is open?'

'Tomorrow morning,' Hasan said.

Farok looked at him in dismay.

'Shit, what're we going to do here all day?'

It was early afternoon when Joe and Marina finally came out of Coppice Wood. They'd crept to the edge of the trees a few times during the course of the morning and lain flat on their stomachs, looking out over the farmland below to check whether it was safe to emerge. But the IND vans had always been there, the immigration officers presumably questioning the workers they'd chased and caught earlier. Joe and Marina had retreated to their hiding place under the rhododendron bush and idled away the hours – having sex again, talking and dozing intermittently.

Only when they were certain that the immigration people had gone did they risk leaving the cover of the wood and walking across the fields to the farmhouse. The farmer came out when he saw them in the yard.

'Where've you been?' Richard asked angrily.

He wasn't in the best of moods. An IND officer had spent two hours interrogating him – and interrogating was the right word – about his employment practices. It had been a long and unpleasant grilling during which the officer had gone through Richard's records, implying – no, openly accusing him of employing illegal foreign workers. Richard's defence had been simple. All his labour requirements, apart from a few full-time employees, were contracted out to a gangmaster. Eddie Tremain provided the workforce, and he had always assured Richard that his workers were legal. Richard was being a little disingenuous by relying on this to absolve himself of all blame. He knew – or at the very least, suspected – that many of the workers Tremain supplied were in the country illegally, but he didn't care about their status so long as they were good workers, and most of them were. He had enough on his plate without worrying about residence or work permits. Let Tremain deal with all that kind of paperwork. That was what Richard paid him for.

All in all, it had been a very bad morning. Almost no work had been done so far. The pickers in the fields had all either dispersed, fled God knows where, or been carted off by the IND officers. The packhouse had also been affected. Of the workforce on the production line, a good half had been found to be working without papers. They too had been driven away in the IND vans. And now this scruffy pair had turned up on his doorstep. What the hell was he supposed to do with them?

'Where are the others?' Richard demanded.

'We don't know,' Joe said. 'Immigration men, they go?'

'Yes, they've gone,' Richard said.

'How many they take?'

Richard shrugged.

'I'm not sure. Eleven, twelve maybe. What about you two, do you have work permits?'

'Yes, we have work permit,' Joe said glibly.

'You have them on you?'

'No, at house. What we do now?'

'Well, there's no point in getting the tractor out for two pickers. You can go in the packhouse and help out on the salad line. You've done that before?'

'Yes, we do before,' Joe said.

Richard took them into the packhouse and the foreman split them up, assigning Marina to the chlorine wash area and Joe to the end of the line where the bagged-up salads were packed into cardboard boxes.

'These pallets need taking over to the loading bay,' the foreman said. 'Can you drive a forklift truck?'

'I never try,' Joe said.

'It's not hard.'

The foreman showed him the controls, how to operate the truck, and left him to it. It was the easiest job Joe had had since arriving in Norfolk.

Half an hour after he'd started, Joe saw Kwasi enter the packhouse and walk over to him. They slapped hands.

'You escape too,' Joe said delightedly. 'That good.'

'Only just,' Kwasi said.

'I see man chasing you.'

'I thought I'd never shake him off. I must've run a couple of miles before he gave up. What happened to the others?'

'They get Radu.'

Kwasi winced.

'Yeah? Poor guy.'

'I don't know who else.'

'What about Grace?'

'I no see her. I think they take woman from her house. Chinese girl. I don't know name.'

'Lucy, you mean? And Marina?'

'Marina OK. We hide in woods. She over there now.'

For the remainder of the afternoon they worked in the packhouse. Everyone seemed subdued, on edge. The immigration raid had shaken them, reminded them of their precarious existence, of the wafer thin line between survival and deportation.

Barry too was more reflective than usual when he arrived to pick them up in the van. The IND officers had been to Tremain's office as well, asking questions, checking through the documentation on the workers he kept on his books. Tremain was devious, an experienced dissembler who had an answer for everything, but it had nevertheless been an uncomfortable few hours.

'How many we got?' Barry said as he counted them on board the van.

The Croats, Marko and Stipe, had shown up a few hours after Kwasi, having spent several hours hiding in a ditch. Two more men and Grace had followed, but that still only made eight out of the twenty or so workers Barry had brought to the farm that morning.

'Is that all? Fuck!' Barry said.

He caught hold of Marina's arm as she tried to climb into the back of the van.

'Why don't you come up front with me?' he said. 'It's more comfortable.'

'No, thanks,' Marina said. 'I stay with others.'

She shrugged off his hand and sat down next to Joe on the floor of the van. Barry shot her a look of intense hatred and slammed the doors shut.

It was a twenty minute journey back into Downham Market. Joe was acutely aware of Marina next to him all the way, their bodies touching, her leg rubbing against his as the van swayed to and fro.

Marina and Grace were dropped off first. Getting up to

leave the van, Marina bent down and whispered in Joe's ear, 'I see you.'

He watched her turn, smiling at him as she jumped down on to the road, then the doors closed and the van moved off.

Ellie was waiting for him outside his house, parked a little way up the street in her Mini. Joe didn't go to her straight away. There were others watching – Kwasi, the Croats. Instead, he went into the house and had a quick wash and a drink of water. When the others were safely out of the way, upstairs in their bedrooms, preparing food in the kitchen, Joe slipped quietly out of the front door.

'Sorry for the delay,' he said as he slid into the passenger seat next to Ellie. 'I didn't want anyone to see me.'

'No problem,' Ellie replied. 'We've enough time.'

They headed north out of Downham Market and up the A10 to King's Lynn. Ellie turned into a street of terraced houses, pulled into the kerb and turned off the car engine.

'That's the house,' she said. 'Four doors up. The tatty-looking one.'

'How far away is the processing plant? What's it called again?'

'Ringmead Processing. Ten minutes, maybe less at this time of day.'

'And the nightshift begins at eight?' Joe checked the dashboard clock. 'The van should be here any moment.'

'I'll follow you. I'm assuming it will go to Ringmead Processing, as last night, but if it goes somewhere else, I'll pick you up and take you straight back to Downham Market.'

'And if it doesn't, I'll be groping dead chickens all night,' Joe said. 'I can't wait.'

Ellie grinned at him.

'You know how it is. I'd do it myself, only I don't look the part. I'm too clean, too well groomed.'

'Careful,' Joe growled. 'I've had a stressful day.'

A transit van came past and double parked further up the street. The driver honked his horn.

'See you later,' Joe said, getting out of the car.

A group of men – four dark-skinned men, North African or Asian – was emerging from the house. Joe timed his approach so that he arrived at the rear of the van almost simultaneously with the group. The van driver hadn't got out of the cab, he was leaving it up to the men to let themselves into the back. Joe took hold of the door handle, confident, brazen. If he looked as if he belonged there, why should they question him?

He depressed the handle and swung open the door. A couple of the men glanced at him, but without any real curiosity. They were used to seeing new people, that was the nature of casual migrant work.

There were four women already inside the van. The four men and Joe joined them. No one said anything, no one gave Joe more than the most superficial of inspections.

The tricky bit would come at the Ringmead Processing factory. But Joe knew from his previous week's experience in packhouses that these places were generally fairly chaotic. There were always people coming and going, never the same workers on the shifts. The foremen were usually hassled and under pressure, short-staffed most of the time. They never knew exactly who the gangmasters were sending, never had an up-to-date list of names. One more worker would probably be a blessing to them.

Joe felt the van turn, then slow and come to a stop. As he climbed out through the doors, he saw the processing plant to his right, the name Ringmead Processing over the entrance. He looked left. Ellie's Mini was a hundred metres away, waiting in the carpark of another industrial unit. Joe followed the other workers into the factory, insinuating himself into the middle of the group where he would be less conspicuous. The nightshift foreman, as Joe had predicted, was running behind schedule, anxious to get everyone assigned to a place on the production line. He read out the list of names on his clipboard, but showed no surprise when it didn't tally with the number of people present.

'Mr Cooper send me,' Joe said, using the name of the gangmaster that Ellie had given him. 'He say I work here tonight.'

'No matter, let's get going,' the foreman replied, ushering them through on to the factory floor.

The other processing plants Joe had worked in had all been for vegetables. They had a musty, earthy smell. This one was different. It had an animal smell, a strong, unpleasant odour of poultry.

He was put in the packing section to begin with, standing by a conveyor belt that brought chicken pieces through from the cutting room. His job was to arrange the pieces – sometimes whole legs, sometimes breasts or drumsticks – on polystyrene trays and dispatch them to the machine that wrapped the trays in plastic film. It was boring, repetitive work, but he was used to that by now. The cold was the worst thing. The chicken had all been chilled and handling the pieces, even through rubber gloves, froze the tips of Joe's fingers.

After two hours, the workers were swapped around. Joe was moved to the other side of the wrapping machine where he had to pack the finished trays of chicken pieces into large plastic containers which were then taken by forklift truck to a cold store to await the refrigerated lorries that would transport them to the shops. The labels on the packages bore the SupaMar name, logo and barcode and read, 'British Farm Chicken'.

Joe worked steadily through the evening. He was tired, but not nearly as tired as he would have been if he'd done a full day's work at Coppice Wood Farm. The morning had mostly been spent dozing with Marina. Those idle few hours were standing him in good stead now.

At midnight, they had a twenty minute break. Most of the workers sat down to rest and eat the sandwiches and snacks they'd brought with them, but Joe wandered off to explore the plant. Like all the packhouses he'd been in, the building was basically a big shed with conveyor belts down the middle and occasional partition walls dividing off individual sections. One corner was occupied by offices for the Ringmead Processing management, but there was no one there at the moment. The offices were closed for the night. Closed, but not locked as Joe discovered when he opened the access door and went through into a corridor with offices along one side. He tried one of the doors, out of curiosity, and it swung open, revealing a desk and a wall of metal filing cabinets.

'What're you doing in here?' a voice behind him demanded.

Joe turned and saw the foreman watching him.

'Excuse me,' Joe said. 'I new here. I look for toilet.'

'The toilet? The workers' toilets are down the other end, near the entrance.'

'Oh, I no see them. Thank you.'

Joe squeezed past the foreman and back out on to the factory floor. He hadn't managed to check out every part of the building, but it seemed wise to keep a low profile for a while. If the foreman caught him out of bounds a second time, he might not be quite so understanding.

The next few hours were a hard, frustrating slog of packing chicken portions – frustrating because Joe knew he was at the wrong end of the production line. Ellie had explained to him her suspicions about the plant, but Joe couldn't investigate them further without somehow getting round to the other end of the line, where the chicken carcasses began their journey through the factory.

It was only after their next break, at 4 a.m., that he got the opportunity he'd been waiting for. The workers were changed around once again and Joe was transferred to the start of the production line.

Ringmead Processing wasn't a slaughterhouse. No live birds were brought into the plant. They arrived ready-killed in refrigerated containers or large vacuum-packed plastic bags. Or at least most of them did. After Joe had been working for half an hour, unpacking the chilled carcasses and putting them on the conveyor belt, he noticed that there were chickens coming on to the line from a different source – from a room at one side of the loading bay. During a temporary lull in the supply of chickens from the factory cold store, Joe sauntered across to this room and looked through the open door. There were four Chinese men inside, standing around a metal-topped table on which a pile of chickens had been dumped. These birds weren't plucked and decapitated like the other broilers, they still had their feathers and their heads, necks and feet. The Chinese men were plucking the chickens by hand, ripping off the feathers and throwing them on the floor. The necks and feet were then chopped off with a cleaver and the carcasses tossed into a plastic bin to be brought out on to the production line. The Chinese workers were all wearing white cotton face masks. Even from the door, several yards away from the plucking table, Joe could detect why. The room reeked of decomposing poultry, meat that wasn't yet rotten but was certainly on the turn.

Joe wondered why he hadn't noticed such a strong, putrid smell when he'd been working further down the conveyor belt. Then he realised that the newly-plucked chickens didn't come straight out from the side room. They were taken first into an adjoining room where another Chinese man in a mask was spraying the carcasses with liquid from a hose attached to a plastic cylinder. Joe caught a whiff of something chemical. The chicken carcasses were being sprayed with some kind of bleaching agent – to make them smell fresher.

A forklift truck was bringing more broilers out from the cold store. Joe went quickly back to his post to receive them. There were four large vacuum-sealed packs of chicken portions – not whole carcasses this time, but ready-cut breasts and legs. Joe sliced open one of the packs with a knife and tipped the contents on to the conveyor belt. The printed label on the plastic wrapping said, 'Iliescu Hiros S.A. Romania'. Stamped in English at the bottom of the label were the words, 'Use by July 8'. Joe stared for a moment at the date. July 8th was nearly two weeks ago, yet the chicken was only now being processed for distribution to SupaMar's British stores. He could remember clearly the date on the cling-wrapped chicken portions he'd been packing earlier. Every one had been marked, 'Sell by July 26.'

29

'You owe me breakfast,' Joe said when Ellie picked him up outside the migrant workers' house in King's Lynn the following morning.

He'd been brought back in the van and dropped off with the other men who'd been at the Ringmead Processing plant with him. He was tired and cold after twelve hours in the chilled interior of the factory. He was also ravenous, not having eaten a proper meal in thirty-six hours.

'Sounds fair enough,' Ellie said. 'Where do you want to go?'

'Anywhere. I don't care.'

'It's a bit early for the cafes in the town. Let's try outside.'

They found a truckers' café on the by-pass, a dilapidated wooden shack with three or four lorries parked on the dirt forecourt outside. Joe looked at the menu and went for the full breakfast of bacon, egg, sausage, fried bread, baked beans and chips.

'You think they do croissants?' Ellie said.

'Don't even think about asking,' Joe replied.

'What about a skinny latte?'

Joe gave her a look.

'I'll have the tea and toast,' Ellie said.

Joe went to the counter and placed their order. When he got back to their table he noticed that Ellie had moved the ketchup, brown sauce and vinegar bottles to the adjoining table.

'The smell was making me feel sick,' she explained.

'You should try a night at Ringmead Processing. The scent of raw poultry, you can't beat it.'

'You find anything?'

'A couple of things. You were right about the diseased chickens. Most of the poultry they process comes in already plucked and chilled. It just has to be cut up and packaged. But they also handle a small number of birds that haven't come from a slaughterhouse.'

'How many?'

'Hard to say. If last night's anything to go by, maybe a hundred a shift. They have to be plucked by hand, have their giblets removed, their heads and feet chopped off. There was a team of Chinese guys doing it all. They were slick, fast, very efficient.'

'You're sure they were diseased birds?' Ellie said.

'They didn't smell too healthy. They were spraying them with chemicals to clean them up, make the meat look fresher, smell better. They might have been diseased, or they might just have been old.'

'And they were being processed like all the other chickens?'

Joe nodded.

'Put on the conveyor belt and sent down the line to be cut up and packaged.'

'For human consumption?'

'Looked that way to me,' Joe said.

'Jesus. You're sure there wasn't some bit of the plant that took those carcasses and used them for something else? You know, like pet food. For cats or dogs.'

'I had a stint at the packing end of the line. Every chicken piece that came through was wrapped and given a SupaMar label and barcode.'

'So SupaMar are selling chicken from diseased birds. Or birds that died prematurely. Like the ones I saw in the bins at Gosling Hall Farm. Do you think SupaMar knows the origins of the meat?'

'That's the question, isn't it?' Joe said. 'But that's not the only question. When I was at the start of the production line, I opened some bags of vacuum-packed chicken pieces from Romania.'

'Romania?' Ellie said.

'A company called Iliescu Hiros S.A. The bags had a use-by date on them that was a fortnight old. The chicken pieces were repackaged as "British Farm Chicken" and given a new sell-by date.'

Ellie pulled a face.

'Ugh, this gets worse. Two-week-old chicken? What were the dates on it?'

She took her notebook and pen from her bag and wrote down what Joe told her, breaking off for a moment when the woman from behind the counter brought out their breakfasts. Ellie watched Joe cut up a sausage and dip a slice into the runny yolk of his egg.

'Thanks for checking this out for me,' she said.

'It was nothing,' Joe said. 'It was your idea. All I did was firm up your suspicions.'

Ellie drank some of her tea. It was dark and treacly, as if it had been stewing in a pot for a couple of months.

'What we've got is good,' she said. 'But I need more.'

Joe lifted his head from his plate and gazed at her dryly.

'I thought you might,' he said.

Ellie smiled.

'You'd do the same, you know you would. We have to find out whether SupaMar knows what they're selling, or whether it's all being done behind their back.'

Joe knew what was coming, but he let Ellie spell it out anyway.

'There has to be some documentation. Letters, correspondence between Ringmead Processing and SupaMar. If there's something in writing, we need to get our hands on it.'

'*We?* Me, you mean,' Joe said.

'Can you sneak into the Ringmead Processing offices, have a snoop around?'

'I can try.'

'It will mean going back there tonight, working another shift.'

'I can hardly wait,' Joe said.

There were two desks in Jimmy Gomersall's cramped little office, but only one was occupied – by a trim woman in her late fifties with permed hair and spectacles on a silver chain around her neck. She looked up from her work as Hasan and Farok walked in and smiled – a neutral smile that was neither warm nor cool, but simply a facial tic.

'We're looking for Jimmy,' Hasan said.

He glanced around the room, taking in the cheap chipboard furniture, the lino on the floor that was pockmarked by cigarette burns. If there was money in being a gangmaster, you wouldn't have known it from this office.

'Jimmy's not in today,' Janet said. 'Can I help you, I'm his secretary.'

She appraised the two men. She knew they weren't English. She was used to dealing with foreigners, the workers Jimmy contracted out to his clients, but these two puzzled her. They were smartly-dressed in light grey suits and were wearing a lot of expensive, flashy jewellery – gold rings, chains around their necks. Pimp-wear was how Janet thought of it.

'Are you looking for work?' she asked.

'No, for Jimmy,' Hasan replied. 'Will he be in later?'

'Not till tomorrow. He's gone fishing for a few days.'

'Ah.'

'Do you want to leave a message for him?'

Hasan smiled. The silver fillings in his teeth glinted.

'We're looking for someone,' he said. 'A Portuguese woman, Ligia Moreira. We believe she's working for Jimmy. Perhaps you know her?'

'What was her name again?'

'Ligia Moreira.'

'No, I'm sorry, I don't recognise the name. Jimmy has a lot of people on his books. You'll have to come back tomorrow and speak to him.'

'It's important we find her,' Hasan said. 'Could you check your records, give us a contact address?'

'I'm afraid I can't give out addresses,' Janet replied. Something about the two men – their appearance, their manner – made her ill at ease.

'Can you confirm that she's one of Jimmy's workers?' Hasan said. 'We know she came here. Lenny, Frank Parnell's assistant, brought her from Thetford. He told us that.'

'Lenny Biddle?'

'You know him?'

'Well, yes, I know Lenny.'

'You weren't here when she arrived, were you? She's in her mid-twenties, probably wearing a headscarf.'

'I'm not in every day. I only work part-time.'

'We really need to get in touch with her urgently. It's her mother, in Portugal, she's been taken ill. Ligia needs to go home.'

'Oh.'

Janet hesitated. The mention of Lenny Biddle's name had reassured her a little. Maybe the men were legitimate. And if this girl's mother was ill, it would only be right to let her know. Yet Janet still had her doubts about the two men, about what they were telling her. She felt uncomfortable with them in the office, wanted to get rid of them and let Jimmy deal with the problem when he returned.

'I'll have a look in the files,' she said. 'See what we've got.'

She opened a drawer in one of the metal cabinets, her back towards the men, shielding her actions, and leafed through the folders inside. It was the second time that morning she'd checked Jimmy's records. The first had been only half an hour earlier – in response to a phone call from London, a journalist asking about Irena Hourami, the Kurdish woman the police were trying to locate. Janet had seen the appeals on the television news, but there was no Irena Hourami on Jimmy's books – no Kurdish workers at all, in fact – and she'd told the journalist so.

It was strange that these two men had now come asking for information about one of Jimmy's workers. Was there a connection? Janet didn't think there could be. The names were different, so were the nationalities. This woman, Ligia Moreira, was Portuguese. There she was. Janet glanced at her file. Jimmy had put her in one of the houses he sub-let – number 24, Rodney Road. Janet flicked through a few more folders, just for show, then closed the drawer and turned back to the men.

'I'm sorry, there's nothing,' she said. 'The best thing would be for you to come back in the morning and talk to Jimmy.'

'We'll do that,' Hasan said.

He followed Farok down the stairs and through the door on to the street.

'Tomorrow?' Farok said. 'We have to spend another day in this dump?'

'Maybe not,' Hasan said.

'What do you mean?'

'I mean we find this Jimmy Gomersall before tomorrow.'

'And how do we do that, we don't know where he lives?'

'There was a photograph on the wall of his office. A pub darts team – the Red Lion at Deeping St John.'

'You think Gomersall's in the team?'

'Let's go there and ask,' Hasan said.

* * *

402

The car pulled in outside Alexandra Court. There was a woman driving, a 45-year-old Hackney social worker named Wendy Moore. Next to her, in the front passenger seat, was Khaled Hourami. He glanced out of the window at the block of flats. This was the first time he'd been back since . . . since that evening. That was how he thought of it – just a time and place. All the other details of what had happened there, what he'd seen, he'd shut away in a corner of his brain – memories that would torment him in nightmares, as they had for the previous week, but which in his waking hours he tried ruthlessly to suppress, if not obliterate.

'Are you sure you're up to this,' Wendy asked gently. 'You don't need to go in, you know. If you tell me where your things are, I can bring them out for you.'

Khaled shook his head. He had to do this. Only by confronting your demons could you expunge them.

'No, I'll do it myself,' he said.

'I'll come with you.'

Khaled didn't argue. Having Wendy there might help him through the ordeal. He'd liked her since she'd first come to see him in hospital. She'd been back several times, usually on her own, but once with a police officer, a female detective who'd asked him questions about his parents' deaths. Having Wendy there to protect him during the traumatic interview had meant a lot to him. She was a warm, sympathetic woman with children of her own. Khaled knew he could trust her. She would look after him now too, when they went into the flat.

Wendy touched him on the arm.

'Come on, let's get it over with.'

They left the car and went up the path to the entrance to the block of flats. Khaled paused outside the door to number six. He had his key in his hand, but he was trembling so much he couldn't insert it into the lock. Wendy did it for him, then stood back, sensing that Khaled should go in first. The flat would, in due course, be assigned to another family on the council waiting list, but until that happened, it was still Khaled's home.

He stepped over the threshold and stopped. The flat smelt stale and airless. The odours of cooking, of the spices and garlic his mother used, had gone and with them another of the links between himself and his dead parents seemed to have been severed. It didn't smell like his home any longer, it didn't sound or feel like it. It was just a deserted flat, a shell devoid of the people that had brought it to life. Khaled felt a tear well up in the corner of his eye and made himself move. Do what needed to be done and then get out and never go back.

He walked quickly down the hall to his bedroom and gathered up his belongings – removing clothes from the chest of drawers and wardrobe, shoes from under the bed, a few books from the shelf next to the door. There wasn't much. They'd left Turkey with nothing, never had the money to acquire many possessions since their arrival in England. Wendy came in with a suitcase she'd found in his parents' room. She helped him pack, then placed a couple of framed photographs face down on the top of his clothes.

'I got them from the mantelpiece in the sitting room,' she said. 'You'll want them with you.'

Khaled didn't turn the photographs over. It would have been too harrowing. He knew what they were – a photograph of his parents on their wedding day and another of the three of them, Khaled 12 years old, standing smiling in front of the penguin enclosure at London Zoo where his parents had taken him as a birthday treat.

'Thank you,' Khaled said.

'We can collect anything you've forgotten another time.'

'I've got all the things I need.'

'We'll go to the Rashid's then.'

Khaled had no relatives in England. He'd spent the nights since he'd been discharged from hospital in a social services hostel, but now he was going to stay with another Kurdish family in Stoke Newington. They would look after him until the family court decided his future.

He picked up the suitcase. Wendy went ahead of him along the hall. As he reached the front door, Khaled paused to take a last look around.

'I'll give you a couple of minutes,' Wendy said. 'I'll be in the car.'

This flat was the first and only home Khaled had known in England. It was small and basic, but he'd been happy here. Happy, that is, until ... until it happened. The memories started to flood back, the images of his mother and father making the tears flow down his face. Khaled rubbed his eyes savagely with his sleeve, trying to erase the vivid, painful pictures. He turned to go ... and saw the red light flashing on the answerphone on the hall table.

He stared at the light for a few seconds. Then he pressed the button to play back the message.

Joe slept for most of the day. The long hours in the fields and packhouse, followed by the 12-hour nightshift at Ringmead Processing were taking their toll on him. He was shattered, his body an exhausted wreck. He'd told Ellie he'd be back in the office by the end of the week, but the way he was feeling now, he couldn't see himself surviving that many more days as a migrant worker. He'd had enough of dirt and sweat and aching limbs. He longed to kill off Alban Cobani and return to being Joe Verdi.

He had the bedroom to himself. Kwasi wasn't there – he'd have gone off to work long before Joe got back from King's Lynn with Ellie – and Radu, of course, had been detained by the immigration officers. He'd be in custody somewhere, having his background and status investigated. Joe hoped that someone would take notice of Radu's blood-flecked coughing and get him the medical assistance he so obviously needed.

In the late afternoon, still not fully recovered from his nightshift, Joe washed and changed his shirt, then made a simple meal of pasta and tomato sauce. Ellie was picking him up again at seven to take him to Ringmead for another shift.

He was sitting at the kitchen table, finishing his pasta, when Kwasi and the others came back in the van.

'How're you doing?' Kwasi said.

He was glistening with sweat, his shirt stuck to his body. He went to the sink and drank three mugs of water in quick succession.

'Barry wanted to know where you were. Boy, he was in a foul mood today. Must've been the raid yesterday.'

'What you tell him?' Joe said.

'That you were sick.'

Kwasi filled his mug with water again and drank it more slowly.

'There pasta in pan for you,' Joe said. 'If you want.'

'That's good of you, man, I'm starving.'

'My turn to make food.'

Kwasi tipped the pasta out on to a plate and sat down at the table.

'You weren't here last night,' he said.

'I work nightshift,' Joe replied. 'Friend get me job.'

'Yeah?' Kwasi grinned. 'I thought you must have a woman somewhere.'

'No, no woman. Where you go today?'

'A packhouse. Arranging baking potatoes on trays. Four of them wrapped in plastic. Man, what a waste of time.'

'Was Marina there?'

'No. I don't know where she went today. You getting it on with her?'

'What you mean?'

'You know.' Kwasi thrust his hips forward lewdly. 'Jiggety-jig.'

'Why you ask?'

'You think I haven't noticed the way you look at her?' Kwasi gave a coarse laugh. 'Hey, you don't have to say, man. I understand. These things happen. Me and Grace, we have an arrangement.'

'But you have wife.'

'In Ghana. A wife I haven't seen for three years. You think a man can go for three years without it? Come *on*.'

Kwasi ate a forkful of pasta.

'This is good,' he said. 'What you put in the sauce?'

'Just tomato, garlic and onion,' Joe said.

'You can cook, you know.'

'I work in Italy for time. I learn there.'

'What work?'

'Pick olives, and tomatoes.'

'That pay?'

'Not good.'

'Like here then,' Kwasi said. 'I'm getting fed up of fields and packhouses. Maybe it's time to go back to London. Find work there again.'

The back door flew open suddenly. Kwasi and Joe spun round and saw a woman stumbling into the kitchen. It was Grace. She was breathing heavily, as if she'd been running. Kwasi leapt up and went to her.

'Grace, you OK? What's happened?'

'Immigration . . . they come to house,' Grace gasped. 'I think Lucy give them address. Four men . . . in van.'

Kwasi helped her over to the table and made her sit down.

'Just now?' he said.

Grace nodded.

'They come in front. I was in kitchen. I run out back, hide under caravan.'

'They take people away?'

'All, I think.'

'*All?*' Joe was on his feet. 'Was Marina there?'

'Yes, she there.'

407

'They take her?'

'I don't see. She was in house so . . .'

Joe didn't hear the rest of the sentence. He was already running out of the back door, sprinting along the side passage and out on to the street.

It took him ten minutes to reach Marina's house. He slowed and came to a stop a short distance away. He knew he was too late. There was no van parked by the kerb, no IND officers hauling migrant workers across the pavement. They'd come and gone.

Joe approached the house. He was out of breath, panting noisily. The front door was still open – they hadn't even bothered to close it behind them. Joe walked in. The house was silent. He knew there was no one there, but he checked anyway, going through all the rooms one by one. There were two plates of half-eaten food on the kitchen table, a pan of luke-warm water on the hob. In the front room, clothes were strewn across the mattresses, a discarded shoe left in a corner. Upstairs, he found a towel on the bathroom floor, hastily abandoned beneath the washbasin. The two bedrooms showed more evidence of a sudden, enforced departure – clothes dumped on the floor, an unfinished sandwich and a half-full mug of tea sitting on the bare floorboards next to one of the mattresses. It was a ghost house, the residents – including Marina – spirited away, almost certainly never to return.

Joe went back downstairs, feeling more tired than ever. He walked slowly out of the front door and away up the street.

Henry poured himself a second glass of Chateau Caronne Ste Gemme, the 'rather interesting blackcurrant with a hint of autumn mushroom', claret that his wine merchant had recommended to him, and retreated to his study to 'work' – a euphemism for drink, read and escape from his family. Henry had two teenage daughters whom he loved dearly.

They were sweet, gifted, vivacious girls, but Henry found them a little wearing. He was an old-fashioned father who pined somewhat for the life of a Victorian man of letters, when a gentleman could absent himself from the bosom of his family and not be bothered by trivial distractions like the washing up.

His peace, though, lasted only a few minutes before his wife, Ginnie, came into the study clutching her car keys and a hardback book.

'I'm off now,' she said. 'I'm taking the BMW. I'll leave you to look after the girls.'

'*What?*' Henry said, aghast. 'Where are you going?'

'It's my book group this evening. I *told* you.'

'Did you?'

Ginnie went out to a book group every few weeks, ostensibly to discuss a book – generally the latest offering of some highly-regarded novelist Henry had never heard of. Henry had his doubts about exactly how much literary discussion went on at these meetings. There seemed to be an awful lot of wine drinking and gossiping. Ginnie never came back with any fascinating insights into the human condition or the novelist's art, but she always had up-to-the-minute information on where everyone was going for their holidays and what new clothes she should be acquiring to add to her already – in Henry's view – more than adequate wardrobe.

Henry caught a glimpse of the name on the front of the hardback his wife was holding.

'Don't you find that stuff boring?' he said. 'Why don't you read something more interesting, like Jilly Cooper?'

'Jilly Cooper?' Ginnie said disdainfully. 'She's nothing but humping in Herefordshire.'

'That sounds pretty interesting to me,' Henry said. 'I met her once, you know, at a reception. Charming woman. And it's Gloucestershire. All the humping is in Gloucestershire.'

'I prefer Herefordshire, it's more alliterative.'

'Oh, ho,' Henry said. 'I'm glad to see you're getting something out of this book group besides a hangover.'

'Emily needs to do her piano practice,' Ginnie said. 'Can you supervise her? She's got her exam next Friday.'

'Supervise?' Henry said warily. 'What do you mean?'

'I mean drag her away from that bloody television and stand over her while she goes through her pieces. There's a little blue book in which Mrs Lucas has written the things that need work. OK? Don't wait up, I'll probably be late.'

Ginnie went out of the room. Henry heard the front door close, a car engine start up, and relaxed. He settled back in his armchair, took a sip of wine and opened *The News* to the crossword. Half an hour later, his glass long empty and the crossword virtually complete – bar a couple of tricky clues that had annoyingly frustrated him – Henry felt a prick of conscience about Emily and her piano practice. Well, not so much a prick of conscience as a prick of calculated self-interest. Ginnie would undoubtedly ask him if he'd done what she'd asked and he was a very unconvincing liar. Better to carry out her instructions and avoid the possibility of a row.

Henry went in search of his daughter. She was curled up in the corner of the sofa watching some appalling digital pop music channel, and Henry knew that nothing short of a nuclear explosion would dislodge her. He attempted some civilised, adult negotiation with her without any noticeable effect, then resorted to the childish tactic of capturing the remote control, switching off the television and stuffing the remote safely out of reach in his pocket.

'You can have it back when you've done your practice,' he said.

Emily capitulated with magnificent ill-grace, stomping through into the music room, banging open the lid of the piano and hammering out a couple of fortissimo scales with enough force to make even a Steinway shudder.

'Right, what's your first piece?' Henry said, leafing

through the little blue book in which Emily's teacher had written her practice notes. 'Kabalevsky, March, let's try that. Kabalevsky? Didn't he used to play midfield for Spartak Moscow?'

Emily ignored the joke – as she did most of her father's remarks – and opened the book of Grade 4 pieces on the music rest.

'Mrs Lucas says you need to work on your staccatos.' Henry peered at the music. 'Which ones are the staccatos?'

'The notes with dots over them. Everyone knows what staccato means,' Emily replied with scathing contempt.

'I know what it means,' Henry said, his pride wounded. 'It's the past participle of the Italian verb staccare, meaning "to separate". I had a classical education, you know. I'm not as stupid as I appear.'

'That would be difficult,' Emily said dryly.

'Bloody cheek. You want your pocket money, I expect a bit more respect. Now come on, for God's sake, let's get this out of the way.'

Emily started to play. She wasn't a bad pianist, when she could be bothered to concentrate. But she was lazy, needed to be constantly pushed to do anything. Like me, Henry thought. It was dispiriting to see your own faults reflected in your children. You always thought – hoped – that somehow they might transcend the flaws in their genes.

In the brief silence that followed the end of the piece, Henry heard the distant ringing of a telephone. Not the fixed line in the house, but the ringtone of a mobile.

'Is that your phone?' he asked Emily.

'No.'

'Well, it's not mine. It surely can't be Gemma's, can it?'

Gemma was Henry's elder daughter. She was currently out at a friend's house and Henry found it difficult to believe that she might have left her mobile phone behind. She never went anywhere without the damn thing. It was always fixed so firmly to her ear that it seemed as if the manufacturer had included a tube of superglue as an accessory.

'It's not Gemma's,' Emily said. 'It's the wrong tone.'

Henry went out of the music room. The noise was coming from his study. From his desk, to be precise. There was a mobile phone on the surface, partially hidden by a dictionary that had fallen over on top of it. Henry extricated the phone and remembered suddenly whose it was – Joe Verdi's. Henry had brought it back from France with Joe's passport and other belongings. The weight of the dictionary must have switched the phone on. Henry punched the 'yes' key.

'Hello?'

'Is that Joe Verdi?'

It was a boy's voice. He sounded hesitant, unsure of himself. Maybe a little anxious.

'This is Joe's phone,' Henry said. 'Do you want to leave a message for him?'

'He's not there?'

'Not at the moment.'

'Oh.' The boy was clearly disappointed. 'When will he be back?'

'I'm not sure.'

'OK. I'll call back . . .'

'Hang on a minute,' Henry said quickly. He'd guessed who the boy was. 'That's not Khaled, is it?'

'Yes.'

'My name's Henry Weaver. I'm a colleague of Joe's. Is there something you want to tell him? I can probably get a message to him.'

'Well, I don't know . . . I think I'd . . .'

'I work with Joe, on *The News*. Where are you calling from, Khaled?'

'I'm with this family, in Stoke Newington. They're looking after me now.'

412

'What did you want to talk to Joe about? I'm sure I can help you.'

There was a silence on the line.

'Khaled?' Henry said. 'Is it important? If it is, you must tell me.'

'I've heard from my aunt,' Khaled said. 'She left a message on the answerphone . . . at the flat . . .'

'What was the message?'

'She gave her address.'

'You know where she is?' Henry grabbed a pen and scrabbled around for something to write on. 'Where?'

'Spalding.'

'In Lincolnshire?'

'I don't know. She just said Spalding. Number twenty-four, Rodney Road. She's using a different name – Ligia Moreira.'

Henry scribbled down the details.

'I'll get the message to Joe, don't worry, Khaled. Was there anything else?'

'No. Just that.'

'I'll get Joe to call you as soon as he can. OK?'

Henry hung up. Then he checked his address book and moved across to the landline, phoning Ellie on her mobile.

'You've been in contact with Joe, haven't you?' he said when she answered. 'Where is he?'

'Right now?' Ellie said. 'Inside a King's Lynn chicken processing plant – looking for incriminating documents, I hope.'

'And you?'

'I'm waiting outside in the carpark for him.'

'Can you get him out?'

'Not very easily. Why?'

Henry told her.

'Shit,' Ellie said. 'Irena Hourami? Have you informed the police?'

'No, this is our story,' Henry said. 'We can handle it.'

'We?'

'You'll need help. Give me your location, I'm coming up.'

'Henry, you don't need to bother. Joe and I can take care of it.'

'Why should you two have all the fun?' Henry said.

30

Joe pushed open the door to the office section and slipped through, glancing back to make sure that no one was watching him. The offices seemed deserted, as they had the night before, the lights switched off, the doors closed – but again not locked, as Joe verified when he walked down the corridor trying the handles. It was gone eleven o'clock. It had taken him a long time to find an opportunity to sneak away from the production line – three hours of arranging chicken pieces on polystyrene trays, three hours of tedium during which he'd wondered continually about Marina, where she was, what was going to happen to her.

He had to put her out of his mind now though, concentrate solely on the job he'd come here to do. Which office should he check first? There were plastic signs on some of the doors – Sales Manager, Production Manager, Human Resources. The door at the far end of the corridor was marked, 'General Manager'. That seemed a good place to start. If there were documents relating to transactions between Ringmead Processing and its customers, they would probably be here, in the boss's office. Joe depressed the handle. The door didn't open. This one was locked. That, in itself, was interesting. Why lock only one office? Joe crouched down and examined the door. There was no way to pick the lock. He had no tools and didn't know how, in any case. He could force it, kick the door in, but he baulked at that. Looking for documents was one thing –

that he could justify as a legitimate extension of his work as a reporter – but actually committing criminal damage seemed a step too far. It took him out of the territory of investigative journalism and into the realms of burglary.

He went back to the sales manager's office. Maybe the contracts and correspondence with customers would be kept there. The filing cabinets were all locked. Joe looked around the office. The keys had to be somewhere. No one took filing cabinet keys home with them. They'd be kept in the office so the files could be easily accessed even if the sales manager wasn't there.

They were in a tray on top of the desk – four keys for the four cabinets. Joe unlocked the first and went through each of the drawers in turn. He didn't know exactly what he was looking for. He was simply hoping that something would strike him as important, that something would stand out from all the routine office dross and catch his attention.

Nothing did. He went through all four filing cabinets, flicking through the documents they contained. It was a hurried, cursory examination, but he didn't have time for anything more thorough. He'd been gone from his post for – he checked his watch – more than twenty minutes now. How long would it be before the foreman noticed his absence and came looking for him?

He closed the last of the drawers. He'd found no mention of SupaMar in any of the folders. That struck him as peculiar. SupaMar was clearly a Ringmead Processing customer – he'd personally packed several hundred trays of chicken pieces with the supermarket's label on them. So why didn't there appear to be any correspondence between Ringmead Processing and SupaMar? No contracts, no invoices, no order forms. He had to be looking in the wrong place.

He went out into the corridor and back to the general manager's office. He'd remembered something from his earlier inspection: not every door had a sign on it, some were blank. He tried the unmarked door just before the general manager's office. It was unlocked. Joe went in. It was obviously a secretary's office, a connecting door in one wall leading through into the general manager's office. Unfortunately, the connecting door was also locked. Joe swore under his breath and paused to consider what to do next. He was running out of time. Maybe the foreman was already searching the factory for him.

Then he noticed the furniture in the office. A desk, a swivel chair, a bookcase, a couple of other chairs for visitors and . . . two grey metal filing cabinets. Of course. The boss didn't do his own filing. He didn't clutter up his own office with cabinets, they would all be in his secretary's office. The keys were less evident this time, but after a couple of minutes searching Joe eventually found them in the bottom drawer of the desk. He unlocked the filing cabinets and went through the contents, looking for any mention of SupaMar. There was none.

Joe sat down in the secretary's chair and thought about it. It didn't make sense. Ringmead Processing processed chicken for SupaMar, there was no doubt about that. Supermarkets and their suppliers didn't communicate solely by phone and email. There had to be something in writing too, commercial documents setting out their terms of business. So where were those documents? Certainly not in the general manager's secretary's office, nor in the sales manager's office. Where else could they be then? Maybe they *were* in the general manager's office. Maybe he did have filing cabinets of his own. That could have been why his office was locked. All the sensitive, confidential material was kept in there.

Joe would have to break the door down after all. That wasn't something he really wanted to contemplate doing. But if that was what it took to find the information . . .

He froze.

A door down the corridor had clicked open. There were footsteps on the lino tiles.

Joe slid rapidly off the chair and crawled into the knee-hole aperture of the desk, curling up into a ball in the confined space. The office door opened. Joe heard someone come in. He held his breath, imagining the person – it had to be the foreman – looking around the office. Eyes checking the corners, behind the door, just a perfunctory inspection, Joe hoped. If the foreman came further into the room, checked behind the desk . . .

The footsteps receded into the corridor. The office door snapped shut. Joe started breathing again. He waited a few minutes, then crawled out from under the desk. He stepped over to the connecting door with the general manager's office and examined it. It was a typical modern office door – a couple of sheets of thin plywood over an egg box framework, a flimsy-looking lock. One good kick and he could break it down.

But first make sure the foreman had gone. Joe crept over to the other door and peered cautiously out into the corridor, listening for any sounds in the adjoining offices. He heard nothing, saw nothing. Joe turned to go back to the connecting door. It was then that it came to him – a sudden realisation that seemed so obvious that he wondered why he hadn't thought of it before. No wonder he hadn't found anything incriminating. He'd been looking for the wrong thing.

Finding out where Jimmy Gomersall lived hadn't been difficult. Hasan and Farok had driven out of Spalding to the village of Deeping St John at lunchtime and, while Farok waited in the car, Hasan had gone into the Red Lion pub. Farok had wanted to accompany him, but Hasan had insisted on going alone. He was aware that neither of them looked English. Farok, in particular, with his beard and truculent manner, was likely to be viewed with a certain wariness, if not hostility. He fitted too well the stereotyped image of a Muslim extremist and this was a very rural, very white part of the country. The only foreigners in the area were migrant agricultural labourers and they, almost certainly, would never have ventured into a pub like the Red Lion. One Turk at the bar, especially one as smartly dressed as Hasan, would cause no problems. Two might well arouse the prejudices of the locals, make them suspicious, and that was the last thing Hasan wanted.

The pub was an old Victorian coaching inn to which various unsightly extensions had been added over the years. There was a carpark at the front, the ugly expanse of grey tarmac tempered by tubs of flowers around the perimeter, and a beer garden at the rear – a patch of yellowing grass on which picnic tables and umbrellas had been placed. A small children's play area containing a slide and see-saw completed the picture of a pub that was family friendly.

Hasan went to the lounge bar and sat on a stool. It was a quiet Monday lunchtime. There weren't many other customers. The landlord looked bored. He served Hasan with the orange juice and soda water he'd ordered, then drifted away to the other end of the bar and started rinsing a few dirty glasses. Hasan looked around the lounge. An elderly couple was seated at a table in one of the alcoves, eating lunch, but every other table was empty. Through the bay window at the back of the room, Hasan saw two women at one of the picnic tables outside, a couple of young children with them drinking blackcurrant squash through straws. There were framed paintings and prints on the walls of the lounge and, next to the bar, a collection of photographs of the pub darts team like the one Jimmy Gomersall had in his office.

'You ever win anything?' Hasan said to the landlord.

'Uh?'

'Your darts team.'

The landlord – a tall, heavily-built man whose head almost brushed the underside of the fake wooden beams behind the bar – came over and looked at the display of photos.

'Not recently,' he said. 'A few years back – eight, nine, maybe more – we won the local pub league, but we haven't done much since.'

'You play yourself?'

'Nah. No time. I'm always behind the bar, pulling pints.'

'Jimmy Gomersall plays, doesn't he?'

'Jimmy, yes. He's probably our best player, not that that's saying much. You know him?'

'I'm supposed to be meeting him here. Half twelve, we said.'

'Jimmy's always late.'

'I know he's been away fishing for a few days,' Hasan said.

The landlord grinned.

'Fishing? I know Jimmy's fishing trips. He'll have been up late last night, having a few. More than a few. He's probably still in his tent, sleeping it off.'

'I'll hang on anyway,' Hasan said. 'Give him a bit more time.'

He ordered another orange juice and soda water and sipped it slowly. He never drank alcohol. He couldn't understand the British penchant for getting drunk. He'd seen it many times in Memet Dil's pubs in London. Young men and women too pissed to stand up, vomiting on the street, even passing out sometimes. Jimmy Gomersall sounded like one of those. An idiot. That was good. He'd be weak, easy to deal with.

Hasan waited half an hour, then got up from his stool.

'Had enough?' the landlord said.

'It doesn't look as if he's going to show up,' Hasan replied. 'Does he live in the village? He only gave me his office address.'

'Just outside,' the landlord said.

'I'll put a message through his door. Is it easy to find?'

'Turn left out of the pub and take the first right. The house is about half a mile up the road. A bungalow on the left. It's the only house out there, you can't miss it.'

'Thanks.'

Hasan went back to Farok and the car and they drove out of the village. The bungalow was set back a little from the road, surrounded on three sides by fields. The nearest other house was a quarter of a mile away. Farok reversed the car off the road a short distance up a farm track and stopped. They had a clear view of the bungalow, but wouldn't be too obvious to anyone approaching the house. The windows open to allow a cooling breeze to blow through the car, they settled down to wait for Jimmy Gomersall to come home.

Ellie saw the shadowy figure slinking around the side of the Ringmead Processing factory and running across the carpark towards her. The figure flitted through a puddle of light from one of the high flood lamps illuminating the area. Ellie caught a glimpse of his face, though she knew already who it was.

'Successful?' she said, as Joe slid into the car beside her. He was holding a thin sheaf of papers in his right hand.

'Up to a point,' Joe replied.

'Meaning?'

'It's not what you thought, not what you wanted.'

'Let me see.'

Ellie almost snatched the papers away from him. She clicked on the overhead light and peered at the typewritten text.

'What are these?' she said.

'Letters. Copies of letters, rather. I didn't take the originals – seemed too much like theft. I copied them on the machine in the sales manager's office.'

'They're addressed to Elliston-Jones.'

'That's right. Ringmead Processing's biggest customer.'

'What about SupaMar?' Ellie said. 'You were looking for documents relating to them.'

'There weren't any.'

Ellie turned and stared at him.

'None?'

'Not one. And you know why? Because Ringmead Processing don't sell their chicken products to SupaMar.'

'What about the SupaMar labels and barcodes you saw being put on the packages?'

'Oh, the chicken ends up in a SupaMar store all right,' Joe said. 'I've got the proof here.'

He felt in his pocket and took out a wad of labels ready-printed with the SupaMar name and logo.

'I nicked these from the packing section before I went off to look around the offices. But SupaMar didn't give them to Ringmead Processing. If you check the labels, and the barcodes on them, I think you'll find they were allocated to Elliston-Jones.'

'You're saying that Elliston-Jones are sub-contracting work to Ringmead Processing without SupaMar's knowledge?'

'Spoils the story a bit, I know. It would be nice if SupaMar were the villain of the piece, knowingly selling dodgy chicken in their stores, but I don't think they are. They don't need to do something like that.'

'You're sure that's not being unduly fair to them?' Ellie said, unable to conceal her disappointment.

'Think about it,' Joe said. 'OK, they're a supermarket, so they're a nasty, rapacious, ruthless bunch of retail thugs, but they're also very smart. They know what they're doing. They have a reputation to maintain. They can't afford to have customers complaining about the food they sell, or worse, getting ill from eating it. Not because they care all that much about their customers' welfare – we know they don't because of all the crap they put in their products – but because health scandals affect their profits. Selling diseased chickens, repacking Romanian chicken as British and changing the sell-by dates, that's not something SupaMar would ever risk doing. It's simply not worth their while.'

'But Elliston-Jones know the source of the chicken?' Ellie said.

'Yes. Those documents confirm that, I've checked. Elliston-Jones know full well that Ringmead Processing are importing cheap chicken from Romania and using dead and diseased birds from poultry farms – not just Gosling Hall, but other farms as well.'

'There's supposed to be a Meat Hygiene Service inspector on duty every day at Ringmead Processing, just as there is at Elliston-Jones,' Ellie said. 'How come this scam hasn't been noticed?'

'Because the inspector goes home at five o'clock,' Joe said. 'All the abuses occur at night. That's when the dodgy chicken comes in, and when it goes out to Elliston-Jones, all ready to be added to Elliston-Jones' legitimate shipments for SupaMar.'

Ellie was silent for a time, reading through the documents. Finally she tossed the papers aside in disgust.

'So SupaMar is in the clear,' she said, an edge of bitterness in her voice.

'Not at all,' Joe replied. 'I have no doubt that it's their practices that prompted something like this to happen in the first place. I would guess that the price they're paying Elliston-Jones for the chicken is so low that to make any profit Elliston-Jones have to resort to this kind of scam. You get what you pay for, after all. You could say that it's only the supermarket's obsession with cost-cutting and screwing suppliers that has caused this to occur. They're not a party to the racket, but they're partly responsible for the conditions that have brought it about. And don't forget, at the end of the day, they *have* been selling this chicken in their stores.'

Joe touched Ellie on the arm.

'Hey, it's still a great story. An important story. You should be proud of yourself.'

'Maybe,' Ellie admitted reluctantly. 'It's just not as good as I'd hoped.'

'They never are,' Joe said. 'You know that.'

He turned his head as the beam of headlights swept across the front of Ellie's car. A familiar black Mitsubishi 4x4 was pulling in next to them. Joe saw Henry at the wheel.

'What's going on?'

'I was going to tell you,' Ellie said. 'We've found Irena Hourami.'

It was nearly midnight when Jimmy Gomersall finally showed up. He and his two mates had stopped fishing hours earlier, when the light by the river had begun to fade, but they'd spent the time since in the pub having a couple of pints. Well, maybe not a couple. It might have been four or five, who was counting?

Jimmy could take his drink – he'd had plenty of experience at it – but he knew nevertheless that he was over the limit. That didn't stop him driving. It just made him drive more slowly. You had to be careful on Lincolnshire's roads. The straight carriageways, running for miles without a bend, encouraged speeding, reckless overtaking. Crashes were common, the sorry shrines of withering flowers by the roadside a reminder of the dangers.

He turned into the drive outside his bungalow and got out of his van, steadying himself on the door before he went round to the back to unload his fishing tackle. He stumbled across the paving slabs in the darkness and unlocked the front door of the house. That was when Hasan and Farok took him.

Jimmy didn't see or hear them coming. His senses, his brain were too dulled by alcohol to respond quickly to external stimuli. All he knew was that someone – he wasn't sure if there was more than one person – suddenly grabbed hold of him, propelled him roughly through into the sitting room of the bungalow and hurled him to the floor, his wicker fishing basket and rod still dangling from his shoulders. A light snapped on. Jimmy blinked, dazzled by the sudden brightness, and rolled over groaning. He'd injured his arm in the fall, caught it on the edge of his fishing basket. He saw one man standing over him, another pulling the curtains across the front window.

'Uh? Who the . . . whass going on?' Jimmy said groggily.

A foot thudded hard into his ribs. Jimmy grunted, curling his knees up instinctively to protect himself. His head felt fuzzy. He couldn't think straight.

'We want some information,' Hasan said.

'Wha'?' Jimmy squinted up at him. 'Who are you? What're you . . .'

The foot smashed into his body again. Jimmy gasped, clutching at himself.

'Lenny Biddle brought a girl to you last week,' Hasan said. 'He said she was Portuguese, that her name was Ligia Moreira. You remember?'

Jimmy pushed himself up on to one elbow, gazing blearily at Hasan. His ribs and chest ached, his arm too.

'Who?'

Hasan whipped out his knife and crouched down beside Jimmy, holding the blade to the gangmaster's throat.

'Ligia Moreira. Where is she?'

'Ligia?'

'The girl. Where've you put her?'

Hasan leaned closer. The gangmaster stank of beer. Hasan slapped him across the face, trying to sober him up.

'She's in one of your houses, isn't she? Which one? What's the address?'

'He's drunk,' Farok said.

'Pull down his trousers,' Hasan said. 'We'll cut his balls off.'

425

'No!'

Jimmy seemed to come to his senses.

'No, I remember,' he said. 'Let me think.'

Hasan pulled his knife away and drew back. Jimmy was frowning, closing and opening his eyes as if he were unable to see properly.

'The address,' Hasan said impatiently.

'Give me time . . . Rodney Road. She's in Rodney Road.'

'Spalding?'

'Yes.'

'What number?'

'Twenty-four. Number twenty-four.'

Hasan stood up, turning.

'What if he rings the police when we've gone?' Farok said.

Hasan pirouetted, his foot swinging round and slamming into the side of Jimmy's head, knocking him unconscious.

'He'll be phoning no one.'

The Mitsubishi was doing a steady seventy up the A17. There wasn't much traffic around at this time of night and the road ahead was mostly clear. Occasionally, they caught up with a slower-moving vehicle and Henry pulled out to overtake, pushing the Shogun Sport to eighty and above. It was 26.7 miles from Ringmead Processing, King's Lynn, to Rodney Road, Spalding, the distance calculated to the nearest tenth of a mile by the Mitsubishi's integrated GPS system. Henry reckoned they could be there in under twenty minutes, if he put his foot down.

They talked as they drove, Henry telling Joe about Khaled's phone call, Joe describing his week as a migrant agricultural labourer. Ellie sat in the back, reading through the documents Joe had taken from the Ringmead Processing offices, working out in her head how she was going to write the story, who she was going to call next morning – after they'd picked up Irena Hourami.

On the dashboard, the table-mat-sized screen of the GPS system glowed softly in the darkness, a flashing dot pin-pointing their exact position on the illuminated road map. Every so often, the system's slightly bossy female voice would break in, giving Henry directions on where to go next.

'Doesn't that voice get on your nerves?' Joe said.

'Jennifer? No, I quite like it actually.'

'*Jennifer?* You've given your GPS system a name?'

'She needs a name, don't you think? She's my friend.'

'Henry, she's not a person, she's a computer-generated voice.'

'I know, but she sounds human. I think she has a nice voice – confident, reassuring. She reminds me of the matron at my prep school. Even when I know where I'm going, I like to hear her voice telling me where to turn. Sometimes I think I could fall in love with her. Is that some kind of weird sexual perversion?'

'Undoubtedly.'

'Maybe I should seek psychiatric help. Or perhaps there's a support group for people like me. You know, like Alcoholics Anonymous.'

'Support groups need more than one person to treat,' Joe said. 'You seriously think there's anyone else in the world who's got the hots for their satellite navigation system?'

'Take the next left,' Jennifer said.

Henry glanced at the GPS screen. They were entering the outskirts of Spalding.

'Five minutes and we'll be there,' he said.

The front door of the house was locked, but it presented only a minor obstacle to the Turks. Farok smashed the sole of his shoe into the wood panel next to the handle and the door crashed open. They burst into the downstairs front room first, flicking on the light and dragging the three women who'd been asleep there from their mattresses. One of the women, terrified by this sudden intrusion, began to scream. Hasan slapped her violently across the cheek and brandished his knife in the faces of the other women.

'No noise, understand?'

The women, clad only in their underwear, reached for sheets to cover themselves up. Hasan's piercing eyes took in their features, remembering the night in Memet Dil's garage when the girl had escaped. None of these women was Irena Hourami.

'In the kitchen, all of you,' Hasan ordered.

They herded the women down the hall to the kitchen, then Farok went upstairs and brought down three more trembling, petrified women. Irena wasn't among them.

'Ligia Moreira,' Hasan said. 'Where is she?'

The women were huddled together, staring in terror at the two men. One – a Chinese woman in a pink T-shirt – was sobbing uncontrollably. Hasan hit her so hard she fell to the floor.

'*Where is she?*'

The Chinese woman curled up into a ball, her hands clutching her head. One of the other women – a pale-skinned Eastern European – took half a pace forward.

'She not here. She work nightshift,' she said.

'Where?'

'Packhouse. Gibson Brothers.'

'Where's that?'

'I don't know.'

Hasan raised his fist. The woman retreated, cowering, her hands in front of her face.

'I don't know,' she screamed. 'We go there in van. No see way.'

'How far away is it?'

'Ten, fifteen minute in van. That all I know.'

Hasan spun on his heel and walked away, past the shattered front door and out to the car.

428

* * *

Joe saw the open door as they pulled in to the kerb and sensed immediately that something was wrong. He looked around. He could see the tail-lights of a car in the distance ahead of them, too far away to identify, but there were no other vehicles in sight, and no people.

'I think we'd better hurry,' he said urgently, scrambling out of the Mitsubishi and running into the house.

The six women were still in the kitchen. They were clustered in a group around the table. Two of them were crying, the others trying to comfort them. They all looked up in alarm as Joe burst into the room. One of the women screamed.

Joe held out his hands, palms pressing the air, trying to calm the woman down.

'Easy now, I'm a friend. Friend, OK?'

The women shuffled away from him, backing into the corner of the kitchen. Frightened eyes stared at him.

'I'm a friend. There's nothing to be scared about,' Joe said.

Ellie came into the room behind him. The migrant women looked at her, then back at Joe. Ellie's presence seemed to reassure them, take the edge off their terror.

'What's happened here?' Joe said. 'Why are you all out of bed? Why are you so distressed?'

The women glanced uneasily at one another, but no one replied.

'We're here to help you,' Ellie said. 'Is Ligia Moreira here?'

'Please,' Joe said. 'This is important. Do you understand what we're saying? Where is Ligia?'

Finally, one of the women plucked up the courage to speak.

'Men come,' she said, her voice quavering. 'Two men.'

'What men?' Joe said.

'I don't know. One have beard, one have this . . .' She gestured to her upper lip. '. . . hair on mouth.'

429

'A moustache?'

'Yes.'

'The Turks,' Joe said to Ellie. He turned back to the migrant woman. 'Did they take Ligia away?'

The woman shook her head.

'Ligia not here. She work.'

'A nightshift? Where?'

'Gibson Brothers. Is packhouse. We don't know where is. But is near here.'

'You told the men this?'

'Yes.'

Ellie whipped out her mobile phone and punched in a number for directory enquiries. She asked for Gibson Brothers, Spalding.

'Can you confirm their address for me.' She glanced at Joe. 'Fenny Lane, Little Walpole, near Spalding?'

Joe nodded rapidly.

'Sounds right.'

He ran back down the hall. Ellie came after him, her thumb jabbing at the keypad of her phone.

'Fenny Lane, Little Walpole,' Joe said to Henry as he jumped into the Mitsubishi. 'Can your GPS gadget find that?'

'Relax,' Henry said calmly. 'Jennifer can find anything.'

The farmland flashed by outside the car, a blur of shadowy fields and crops tinted a burnished grey in the moonlight. The speedometer was touching seventy miles an hour, a dangerously high speed for the narrow country road.

'There's no answer from the packhouse,' Ellie said, giving up and putting her phone away in her pocket. 'The offices must be closed.'

'Shit!'

Joe stared anxiously ahead through the windscreen.

'The Turks are going to get there before us.'

'How much of a head start have they got?' Henry asked.

'Five minutes, maybe more.'

'That's not long.'

'It's all they need to kill Irena.'

'Turn right, two hundred metres,' the voice of the GPS system instructed, and Henry eased his foot down on to the brake pedal.

Joe studied the glowing GPS screen. The Gibson Brothers packhouse was highlighted in green, the position of the Mitsubishi by the flashing red light. An illuminated yellow line showed the route the computer had chosen to get them to their destination.

'Did you programme in the quickest, or the most direct route?' he asked Henry.

'The quickest, of course. Isn't that what we want?'

'It's taking us in a wide dogleg to the east. But there's another road here, you see? A short cut.'

Henry took his eyes momentarily off the carriageway to glance at the GPS screen.

'That's not a road, it's a farm track. It could be impassable.'

'We can't afford to let the Turks get to her first,' Joe said.

'What the hell, let's give it a shot. Hang on.'

Henry braked heavily and spun the steering wheel. The Mitsubishi careered off the road on to the dirt track. Henry switched to 4-wheel drive and accelerated. The track was rutted, pitted with potholes, but the Shogun Sport's suspension and thick tyres glided easily over the uneven surface. Occasionally, they encountered a deeper hole and the vehicle jolted violently, bouncing them out of their seats. Joe and Ellie clung to the handles in the roof as Henry maintained a reckless sixty miles an hour, driving almost blind along the track. There were deep drainage channels on either side. One tiny miscalculation and they'd crash nose first into a ditch. At that speed their chances of survival were negligible.

The Mitsubishi hit another crevasse and slewed

suddenly sideways. Henry hammered down on the brake and hauled the wheel to the right, fighting desperately to control the skid. The tyres slid across the loose dirt, then bit in, regaining their grip. The car straightened up and sped on along the track. Joe opened his eyes and took a deep breath.

They could see the packhouse now, about a quarter of a mile away, the front of the building illuminated by security lights. Then they saw headlights away to their left, another car heading for the packhouse.

'It's them,' Joe said. 'It has to be. Can we beat them to it?'

'You just watch,' Henry said.

He floored the accelerator, hunched tensely over the steering wheel. The Mitsubishi surged forward, the engine roaring. The other car – a Mercedes saloon – was getting nearer. It had left the main road and was on the lane leading to the packhouse. Joe watched it. He could see two figures in the front, but couldn't make out their faces. The farm track joined the lane almost directly opposite the entrance to the packhouse carpark. Joe could see the junction ahead of them. Fifty metres. Forty. The other car was closing. It was going to get there first. No, at the same time. They were on a collision course. Henry didn't flinch, didn't slow one iota. Joe and Ellie braced themselves for the inevitable crash.

But the Mercedes suddenly slowed, the driver braking abruptly, the tyres burning, screaming across the tarmac. The Mitsubishi erupted in front of it, speeding into the carpark and heading in a straight line for the packhouse.

'You get the girl,' Henry shouted. 'I'll take care of the Turks.'

He jammed on the brakes outside the front door of the packhouse. Joe and Ellie leaped out and ran into the building. Henry hit the accelerator pedal and put the Mitsubishi into a tight turn, trying to cut the Mercedes off as it crossed the carpark. But he was seconds too late. The Mercedes screeched to a halt. Before Henry could do anything to stop them, Hasan and Farok were out of the car and running into the packhouse.

The uniformed security guard stepped out in front of Joe, waving his arms, a warning shout forming on his lips.

'Hey, you . . .'

Joe hit him with his shoulder, barging him out of the way, choking off the rest of the sentence. The guard stumbled backwards and overbalanced, falling heavily to the floor of the foyer.

Joe and Ellie threw open a door and sprinted through on to the factory floor. Conveyor belts were moving down the centre of the vast shed, workers in gloves and white coats and caps standing alongside it sorting cut flowers into bundles.

Joe stared around. Which one was Irena? There must have been two dozen women on the production line, some of them with their backs to him. What did she look like? Young, mid-twenties, headscarf, that was the only description he had. He ran over to the conveyor belts. The women all looked the same in their white uniforms.

'Irena?' Joe yelled. 'Irena Hourami?'

A face jolted up further down the line. A young woman, Middle Eastern complexion and . . . *yes*, she was wearing a headscarf beneath her regulation cap.

'Irena?'

Joe ran towards her. Irena stared at him fearfully, her mouth twisting into a grimace as if she were about to scream. Then she backed away, turning to run.

'No!' Joe shouted. 'I'm a friend, Irena. Khaled told me where you were. Khaled.'

Irena stopped dead at the mention of her nephew's name. She swung round, letting Joe approach her.

'Khaled?'

'That's right, ' Joe said. 'I know Khaled.'

'You friend?'

'Yes. We have to get you out of here.'

'*Joe!*'

It was Ellie's voice. Sharp, urgent, demanding his attention. Joe looked over his shoulder. The two Turks were coming out on to the factory floor, pausing, looking his way. Irena saw them too and let out a gasp of terror. Joe grasped her arm and started running. Ellie came with them. They raced down the length of the shed. When Joe glanced back, he saw the Turks pursuing them. Both men had knives in their hands.

Joe and Irena reached the end of the conveyor belt, where the flowers were packed into cardboard boxes and stacked on wooden pallets. A forklift truck was being manoeuvred into position to remove one of the pallets.

'Take Irena,' Joe called to Ellie. 'Get out the back way. Go!'

Joe leaped on to the forklift truck and pushed the operator off his seat. Then he took hold of the steering wheel and spun the vehicle round, his foot depressing the throttle. The Turks were five metres away. Joe went straight for them, the metal prongs on the front of the truck at knee height. Hasan threw himself to one side in an athletic dive. Farok tried the same, but left it a fraction too late. One of the prongs caught him on the leg, ripping through his trousers and into the muscle underneath. He screamed and collapsed to the floor, writhing in agony. Joe whipped the truck back round, looking for Hasan, but Hasan had scrambled to his feet and was darting away through a door into the loading bay. Joe abandoned the forklift and went after the Turk on foot. He saw him on the far side of the loading bay, heading out through the high vehicle exit into the yard at the rear of the factory. There was no sign of Ellie and Irena. They must already have got out.

Joe hared through the exit and stopped, looking around. He was wheezing from the exertion. Ellie and Irena were fifty metres to his left. They'd gone the wrong way, searching for the access road round to the front of the factory. Instead of a clear run to the carpark and the safety of Henry's car, they'd found their path blocked by a two-metre high wire mesh fence. Hasan was running purposefully towards them, the steel blade glinting in his right hand. Ellie took the only escape route open to her. She grabbed Irena's hand, ran down the low earth perimeter embankment and out on to the open fields next to the packhouse. Hasan went after them.

The ground was dry and firm under foot. The crop of flowers had been harvested so there was no vegetation to slow them down, just low rows of stubble. Ellie ran flat out, dragging Irena along beside her. But Hasan was faster. Slowly, he began to narrow the gap between them. Ellie glanced over her shoulder, saw the Turk getting nearer. Joe was thirty metres behind Hasan. He was tiring, feeling the effects of the chase, but he forced himself to keep going. He had to get to Hasan, somehow stop him before the Turk could reach Ellie and Irena.

Irena was slowing down. Ellie too was losing strength. She thought about stopping and trying to fight the Turk off, but that would have been a suicidal move against a man with a knife. They had to keep running. There was no alternative. But they *couldn't* keep running. They simply didn't have the energy. Their legs were heavy, their lungs starved of oxygen. Irena was stumbling, close to exhaustion. Ellie couldn't pull her along for much longer.

Then Ellie saw her own shadow appear suddenly on the earth in front of her, Irena's too. She twisted her head round. There were headlights behind them, a vehicle racing towards them at speed. Ellie recognised the outline of Henry's Mitsubishi. The car sped past Joe, then went after Hasan. The Turk looked round in a panic, trying to dodge out of the way. But the Mitsubishi was already alongside him. An arm shot out of the window. Something caught

Hasan on the back of the head and he went down like a skittle.

Joe slowed to a jog and stopped beside Hasan's unconscious body, panting hard, his chest heaving, his legs aching. The knife had fallen from the Turk's hand and lay on the ground a few feet away. Ellie and Irena were climbing into the Mitsubishi. Henry circled round and drove slowly back to Joe.

'What did you hit him with?' Joe said breathlessly.

'A *Wine Collector* magazine,' Henry replied. 'It happened to be in the car. There was nothing else to hand.'

'A *Wine Collector* magazine?'

'Going at fifty miles an hour, it's quite a weapon. How is he?'

'Out cold. Probably for some time,' Joe said.

Ellie was on her mobile, phoning the police. Irena was next to her, leaning back in her seat, gasping for air.

'Thanks,' Joe said to Henry. 'That was a hell of a drive.'

Henry gave a modest shrug.

'These gas guzzlers have their uses.'

31

'You've had a busy night,' Louise Crawford said dryly.

It was four o'clock in the morning. She'd been summoned from her bed at one and driven all the way from London to Spalding, but still managed somehow to look fresh and composed, her jacket and trousers neatly pressed, her eyes as clear and shrewd as ever.

'Yeah,' Joe said. 'It has been somewhat eventful. You know the details?'

Crawford nodded.

'I read the statements you and your two colleagues gave. You're quite a team.'

Joe sipped the cup of coffee the duty sergeant had given him. They were in an interview room at Spalding police station, facing each other over a bare wooden table. There was a tape recorder at one end of the table, but it wasn't switched on. Crawford had asked for a moment alone with him, an informal chat off the record.

'How's Irena?' Joe said.

'A bit shaken, but basically OK.'

'You get much out of her? Her English isn't very good.'

'I brought a Kurdish interpreter with me.'

'Of course. I should've known you'd be prepared. You're taking her back to London?'

'Yes.'

'And the Turks?'

'They're in hospital, both under police guard. Hasan

Mustafa has concussion, Farok Gurcan a broken leg. I didn't know you could drive a forklift truck.'

'It's amazing what you learn when you're a migrant Albanian labourer.'

'You could've been killed, you know. You should've called the police, let us handle it.'

'I wondered when you'd get round to that,' Joe said. 'Is that why you're here, to give me the official Met bollocking?'

'What you did was utterly stupid. And irresponsible. If you'd called us immediately, we could have had Irena picked up long before the Turks got near her.'

'Does it matter now? She's safe. You've got your witness. The Turks are in custody.'

'You put Irena's life in danger because you wanted the glory of finding her. Isn't that right?'

Joe ran his hand over his face. His beard was itching. He couldn't wait to shave it off, to have a shower, change his clothes. To get back to his real life. He was tired of being Alban Cobani, tired of picking vegetables and living in squalor.

'Isn't that right?' Crawford repeated.

'It's the middle of the night. I'm exhausted,' Joe said. 'Can we have this discussion some other time?'

'You baffle me, you know. You put your own life at risk too. For a story. For an article that will be read and forgotten the next day. Why? What makes you do it?'

'It's my job. Is that a good enough answer?' Joe said.

Crawford glanced at her watch and stood up.

'You're a pain in the arse,' she said.

'You told me that already,' Joe said.

'You got lucky this time. Irena's all right. So are you. Stick to reporting in future. Next time, things might not work out so well.'

She went to the door of the interview room.

'I'll see you around, chief inspector,' Joe said.

Crawford turned.

'I know. That's what depresses me.'

Ellie came across the office and sat down at the empty desk opposite Joe's work station. He pushed his chair away from his terminal and gave her his full attention. She looked drained. So did Joe. Neither of them had been to bed. They'd driven back to London from Spalding and come straight into the office.

'How's it going?' Joe said.

Ellie yawned.

'I've been making a few enquiries. That vacuum-packed chicken from Romania you saw being processed at Ringmead. I checked out the company that exported it, Iliescu Hiros S.A. They're a meat packing firm in Galati in the east of the country. And six weeks ago in Galati there was an outbreak of typhoid. Three people died, two of whom worked at the meat plant. It never got any news coverage over here. The Romanian authorities don't seem to have done anything about it.'

'That was the source of the contamination?'

'Seems pretty certain to me. I called the Food Standards Agency. They're going to look into it.'

'And the victims here?'

'Joseph Goodwin's out of danger, making a good recovery. There've been no other cases.'

'What about Ringmead Processing?'

'I spoke to my contact at Norfolk environmental health, told him what we'd found at the plant. They're going to go in there tonight unannounced with a team from the Meat Hygiene Service. I reckon they'll find enough to warrant prosecuting both Ringmead and Elliston-Jones. How about you? I gather we're sharing the front page tomorrow.'

'I'm just finishing the Hourami story. I had a word with the Met earlier. They picked Memet Dil up from his home before dawn. He's being held in custody. He'll be appearing before the magistrates tomorrow morning.'

'And Irena?'

'She's identified Dil, made a full statement.'

'What's going to happen to her?'

Joe shrugged.

'It's too early to say. The best outcome would be she's given permission to stay and Khaled goes to live with her. I don't think she can go back to Turkey. It's too dangerous. Memet Dil has too many friends there.'

'And your features on life as an illegal migrant worker?'

'Give me time, I've got to write the bloody things first. Preston wants to run them next week.'

'Henry suggested we all went for a drink later.'

'Sounds good. Where is he?'

'When he rang, he'd just got out of bed and was making himself a bacon sandwich.'

'All right for some.'

'You realise we're never going to hear the end of this. Henry will be dining out on it for years. How I floored a homicidal maniac with a *Wine Collector* magazine.'

Ellie got to her feet.

'By the way, I thought you might be interested in this. Preston gave it to me earlier.'

She held out a sheet of paper.

'It's a press release from SupaMar. Their timing is perfect.'

'What's it about, the typhoid?'

'They've announced record annual profits and plans to open another 78 new stores over the next year. That's more than one a week.' Ellie smiled wryly. 'It's good to know that irony's not dead yet.'

The warder unlocked the door from the detention wing and escorted Marina out into the visiting area. She saw Joe sitting at the table and gave a start. She frowned, her expression puzzled, confused. He looked different. He'd shaved off his beard, his clothes were smarter, cleaner. Marina sat down opposite him and waited for the warder to move away before she spoke.

'What you doing here, Alban?' she said. 'How you get here? I don't understand.'

She looked paler than Joe remembered, her face more drawn. But maybe it was the cheerless surroundings of the detention centre. Maybe he was seeing the grim institutional environment reflected in her appearance.

'How are you, Marina?'

'OK.'

'Are they treating you well?'

Marina glanced around, making sure the warder was out of ear-shot.

'What going on? Why you come? What if they catch you too? Lock you up like me.'

'I'm not who you think I am,' Joe said.

'What you mean?'

He told her. She listened wide-eyed with astonishment, then kept staring at him when he'd finished.

'You not from Albania? You work for newspaper? Everything you do was just for newspaper story?'

'Not everything,' Joe said gently.

Her eyes were bewildered, turning angry as she absorbed what he'd said.

'You lie to me. You pretend to be Albanian worker. It all made up. Why you come now? What you want from me?'

'To see how you are.'

'Why? For what? You not Alban now, you someone else.'

'And you?' Joe said. 'Maybe you're not who you seem either. The duty officer who brought me in. He called you *Mrs* Savitska. You're married, aren't you?'

Marina licked her lips. She shrugged.

'Yes, I married.'

'You have children?'

'One. A boy.'

'How old?'

'Three.'

'You left him in Kiev to come here to work?'

'My mother look after him. That why I come to England. For him. There no work in Kiev. Pay is better here too. I can send money home for my son.'

'And your husband?'

'He no work. He drink.'

She looked at him. Her eyes seemed sadder now, tinged with a bleak melancholy.

'What happen to me?' she said.

'I spoke to the assistant governor on the phone before I came,' Joe said. 'You're not an asylum seeker, or a political refugee. You're what they call an economic migrant. They'll deport you – put you on a plane back to Kiev.'

'When?'

'Soon. Will you cope in the Ukraine?'

'Cope?'

'Find a job, be able to support your son.'

'I don't know. I try.'

They fell silent. Joe wondered why he'd come. He was concerned for her welfare, her future. They were genuine enough feelings, but underlying them was a sense of guilt, a sense that he'd used her. For one brief moment in the woods they'd been close, yet now there was the distance of strangers between them.

'I'm sorry,' he said. 'I lied about who I was. But . . . what happened . . . that was the real me. I meant it.'

'I mean it too.' She gave a wan smile. 'Thank you for coming. But you go now . . . what your name again?'

'Joe.'

'You go now, Joe. You have life here in England. I have life in Ukraine. They different.'

She held out her hand. Joe shook it. It was cold, formal, but anything more intimate seemed inappropriate. She stood up from the table. Joe stayed where he was, watching as the warder led Marina away through the door to the detention wing and locked it behind them.

Joe pulled into the kerb outside the house and turned off the engine. For a couple of minutes he didn't move. He studied the house through the car window. It was only a few days since he'd been living there, but already the memory seemed to have faded. It was part of a different life, the details he recalled belonged to a different person. Not to Joe Verdi, but to Alban Cobani. And Alban Cobani was no more.

Joe climbed out and went round to the back door of the house. Kwasi was alone in the kitchen, chopping courgettes at the table. He stopped as Joe walked in. They looked at each other, Kwasi frowning, his expression uncertain.

'Where've you been, man?' he said. 'You've got new clothes, you've shaved. What's going on?'

'I've got a lot of explaining to do,' Joe said. 'I'll tell you on the way.'

'The way where?'

'To London.'

'*London?*'

'I'm taking you out for the night. Maybe a few nights. You can stay with me in my flat. Look for a job, if you feel like it.'

Joe scraped the courgettes off the table and dumped them in the bin.

'You won't be needing those. You remember that roast chicken you mentioned? That roast chicken and fried potatoes you sometimes dream about?'

'We're having roast chicken?'

'You can have anything you like,' Joe said.

'Where we going?'

'I know this nice little Italian restaurant.'